I0663160

# Friends, though divided

## A Tale of the Civil War

## G. A. Henty

**Friends, though divided: A Tale of the Civil War**

Copyright © 2019 Indo-European Publishing

All rights reserved

The present edition is a reproduction of previous publication of this classic work. Minor typographical errors may have been corrected without note, however, for an authentic reading experience the spelling, punctuation, and capitalization have been retained from the original text.

ISBN: 978-1-64439-279-9

# PREFACE

My dear lads: Although so long a time has elapsed since the great civil war in England, men are still almost as much divided as they were then as to the merits of the quarrel, almost as warm partisans of the one side or the other. Most of you will probably have formed an opinion as to the rights of the case, either from your own reading, or from hearing the views of your elders.

For my part, I have endeavored to hold the scales equally, to relate historical facts with absolute accuracy, and to show how much of right and how much of wrong there was upon either side. Upon the one hand, the king by his instability, bad faith, and duplicity alienated his best friends, and drove the Commons to far greater lengths than they had at first dreamed of. Upon the other hand, the struggle, begun only to win constitutional rights, ended—owing to the ambition, fanaticism, and determination to override all rights and all opinions save their own, of a numerically insignificant minority of the Commons, backed by the strength of the army—in the establishment of the most complete despotism England has ever seen.

It may no doubt be considered a failing on my part that one of my heroes has a very undue preponderance of adventure over the other. This I regret; but after the scale of victory turned, those on the winning side had little to do or to suffer, and one's interest is certainly with the hunted fugitive, or the slave in the Bermudas, rather than with the prosperous and well-to-do citizen.

Yours very sincerely,
G.A. HENTY

# CONTENTS

# CHAPTER I

## THE EVE OF THE WAR

It was a pleasant afternoon in the month of July, 1642, when three young people sat together on a shady bank at the edge of a wood some three miles from Oxford. The country was undulating and picturesque, and a little more than a mile in front of them rose the lofty spire of St. Helen's, Abingdon. The party consisted of two lads, who were about fifteen years of age, and a girl of ten. The lads, although of about the same height and build, were singularly unlike. Herbert Rippinghall was dark and grave, his dress somber in hue, but good in material and well made. Harry Furness was a fair and merry-looking boy; good humor was the distinguishing characteristic of his face; his somewhat bright and fashionably cut clothes were carelessly put on, and it was clear that no thought of his own appearance or good looks entered his mind. He wore his hair in ringlets, and had on his head a broad hat of felt with a white feather, while his companion wore a plain cap, and his hair was cut closely to his head.

"It is a bad business, Harry," the latter said, "but, there is one satisfaction that, come what may, nothing can disturb our friendship. We have never had a quarrel since we first met at the old school down there, six years ago. We have been dear friends always, and my only regret has been that your laziness has prevented our being rivals, for neither would have grudged the other victory."

"No, indeed, Herbert. But there was never a chance of that. You have always been Mr. Gregory's prize boy, and are now head of the school; while I have always been in his bad books. But, as you say, Herbert, we have been dear friends, and, come what will, we'll continue so. We cannot agree on the state of the kingdom, and shall never do so. We have both taken our views from our parents; and indeed it seems to me that the question is far too difficult a one for boys like us to form any opinion of it. When we see some of the best and wisest in the land ranging themselves on either side, it is clear that even such a wise noddle as yours—to say nothing of a feather brain like mine—cannot form any opinion on a subject which perplexes our elders and betters."

"That is true, Harry; but still—"

"No, no, Herbert, we will have no argument. You have the best of it there, and I fall back upon authority. My father, the colonel, is

1

for the king; yours for the Parliament. He says that there are faults on both sides, and indeed, for years he favored the Commons. The king's acts were unconstitutional and tyrannical, and my father approved of the bold stand which Sir George Elliot made against him. Now, however, all this has been changed, he tells me, and the Commons seek to rule without either king or peers. They have sought to impose conditions which would render them the lords absolute of England, and reduce the king to a mere puppet. They have, too, attacked the Church, would abolish bishops, and interfere in all matters spiritual. Therefore, my father, while acknowledging the faults which the king has committed, and grieving over the acts which have driven the Parliament to taking up a hostile attitude to him, yet holds it his duty to support him against the violent men who have now assumed power, and who are aiming at the subversion of the constitution and the loss of the country."

"I fear, also," Herbert said, "that the Commons have gone grievously beyond their rights, although, did my father hear me say so, I should fall under his gravest displeasure. But he holds that it is necessary that there should be an ecclesiastical sweep, that the prelates should have no more power in the land, that popery should be put down with an iron hand, and that, since kings cannot be trusted to govern well, all power should be placed in the hands of the people. My own thoughts do incline toward his; but, as you say, when one sees men like my Lord Falkland, who have hitherto stood among the foremost in the ranks of those who demand that the king shall govern according to law, now siding with him against them, one cannot but feel how grave are the difficulties, and how much is to be said on either side. How is one to choose? The king is overbearing, haughty, and untrue to his word. The Parliament is stiff-necked and bent upon acquiring power beyond what is fair and right. There are, indeed, grievous faults on both sides. But it seems to me that should the king now have his way and conquer the Commons, he and his descendants will henceforth govern as absolute monarchs, and the liberty of the people will be endangered; while on the other hand, should the Parliament gain the upper hand, they will place on a firm basis the liberties of Englishmen, and any excesses which they may commit will be controlled and modified by a future parliament, for the people of England will no more suffer tyranny on the part of the Commons than of the king; but while they cannot change the one, it is in their power to elect whom they will, and to send up men who will govern things moderately and wisely."

"At any rate," Harry said, "my father thinks that there is

neither moderation nor wisdom among the zealots at Westminster; and as I hear that many nobles and country gentlemen throughout England are of the same opinion, methinks that though at present the Parliament have the best of it, and have seized Portsmouth, and the Tower, and all the depots of arms, yet that in the end the king will prevail against them."

"I trust," Herbert continued earnestly, "that there will be no fighting. England has known no civil wars since the days of the Roses, and when we see how France and Germany are torn by internal dissensions, we should be happy indeed that England has so long escaped such a scourge. It is indeed sad to think that friends should be arrayed against each other in a quarrel in which both sides are in the wrong."

"I hope," Harry said, "that if they needs must fight, it will soon be over, whichever way fortune may turn."

"I think not," Herbert answered. "It is a war of religion as much as a war for power. The king and the Commons may strive who shall govern the realm; but the people who will take up arms will do it more for the triumph of Protestantism than for that of Pym and Hampden."

"How tiresome you both are," Lucy Rippinghall interrupted, pouting. "You brought me out to gather flowers, and you do nothing but talk of kings and Parliament, as if I cared for them. I call it very rude. Herbert is often forgetful, and thinks of his books more than of me; but you, Master Harry, are always polite and gentle, and I marvel much that you should be so changed to-day."

"Forgive me," Harry said, smiling. "We have been very remiss, Miss Lucy; but we will have no more of high politics, and will, even if never again," he said sadly, "devote all our energies to getting such a basket of flowers for you as may fill your rooms with beaupots. Now, if your majesty is ready to begin, we are your most obedient servants."

And so, with a laugh, the little party rose to their feet, and started in quest of wild flowers.

The condition of affairs was at the outbreak of the civil war such as might well puzzle older heads than those of Harry Furness or Herbert Rippinghall, to choose between the two powers who were gathering arms.

The foundations of the difficulty had been laid in the reign of King James. That monarch, who in figure, manners, and mind was in the strongest contrast to all the English kings who had preceded him, was infinitely more mischievous than a more foolish monarch could have been. Coarse in manner—a buffoon in demeanor—so

3

weak, that in many matters he suffered himself to be a puppet in the hands of the profligates who surrounded him, he had yet a certain amount of cleverness, and an obstinacy which nothing could overcome. He brought with him from Scotland an overweening opinion of the power and dignity of his position as a king. The words—absolute monarchy—had hitherto meant only a monarch free from foreign interference; to James they meant a monarchy free from interference on the part of Lords or Commons. He believed implicitly in the divine right of kings to do just as they chose, and in all things, secular and ecclesiastical, to impose their will upon their subjects.

At that time, upon the Continent, the struggle of Protestantism and Catholicism was being fought out everywhere. In France the Huguenots were gradually losing ground, and were soon to be extirpated. In Germany the Protestant princes had lost ground. Austria, at one time halting between two opinions, had now espoused vehemently the side of the pope, and save in Holland and Switzerland, Catholicism was triumphing all along the line. While the sympathies of the people of England were strongly in favor of their co-religionists upon the Continent, those of James inclined toward Catholicism, and in all matters ecclesiastical he was at variance with his subjects. What caused, if possible, an even deeper feeling of anger than his interference in church matters, was his claim to influence the decisions of the law courts. The pusillanimity of the great mass of the judges hindered them from opposing his outrageous claims, and the people saw with indignation and amazement the royal power becoming infinitely greater and more extended than anything to which Henry VIII. or even Elizabeth had laid claim. The negotiations of the king for a marriage between his son and the Infanta of Spain raised the fears of the people to the highest point. The remembrance of the Spanish armada was still fresh in their minds, and they looked upon an alliance with Spain as the most unholy of contracts, and as threatening alike the religion and liberties of Englishmen.

Thus when at King James' death King Charles ascended the throne, he inherited a legacy of trouble. Unhappily, his disposition was even more obstinate than that of his father. His training had been wholly bad, and he had inherited the pernicious ideas of his father in reference to the rights of kings. Even more unfortunately, he had inherited his father's counselors. The Duke of Buckingham, a haughty, avaricious, and ambitious noble, raised by King James from obscurity, urged him to follow the path of his father, and other evil counselors were not wanting. King Charles, indeed, had an

4

advantage over his father, inasmuch as his person was stately and commanding, his manner grave and dignified, and his private life irreproachable. The conflicts which had continued throughout the reign of his father between king and Parliament speedily broke out afresh. The Commons refused to grant supplies, unless the king granted rights and privileges which he deemed alike derogatory and dangerous. The shifty foreign policy of England was continued, and soon the breach was as wide as it had been during the previous reign.

After several Parliaments had been called and dissolved, some gaining advantage from the necessities of the king, others meeting only to separate after discussions which imbittered the already existing relations, for ten years the king dispensed with a Parliament. The murder of the Duke of Buckingham by Felton brought no alleviation to the situation. In Ireland, Wentworth, Earl of Strafford, ruled with tyrannical power. He was a man of clear mind and of great talent, and his whole efforts were devoted to increasing the power of the king, and so, as he considered, the benefit of the country. In Ireland he had a submissive Parliament, and by the aid of this he raised moneys, and ruled in a manner which, tyrannical as it was, was yet for the benefit of that country. The king had absolute confidence in him, and his advice was ever on the side of resistance to popular demands. In England the chief power was given to Archbishop Land, a high church prelate, bent upon restoring many of the forms of Catholic worship, and bitterly opposed to the Puritan spirit which pervaded the great mass of the English people.

So far the errors had been entirely upon the side of the king. The demands of the Commons had been justified by precedent and constitutional rule. The doings of the king were in equal opposition to these. When at last the necessity of the situation compelled Charles to summon a Parliament, he was met by them in a spirit of absolute defiance. Before any vote of supply would he taken, the Commons insisted upon the impeachment of Strafford, and Charles weakly consented to this. The trial was illegally carried on, and the evidence weak and doubtful. But the king's favorite was marked out for destruction, and to the joy of the whole kingdom was condemned and executed. A similar fate befell Laud, and encouraged by these successes, the demands of the Commons became higher and higher.

The ultimatum which at last the Puritan party in Parliament delivered to the king, was that no man should remain in the royal council who was not agreeable to Parliament; that no deed of the

5

king should have validity unless it passed the council, and was attested under their hands; that all the officers of the state and principal judges should be chosen with consent of Parliament, and enjoy their offices for life; that none of the royal family should marry without consent of Parliament or the council; that the penal laws should be executed against Catholics; that the votes of popish lords should not be received in the Peers, and that bishops should be excluded from the House; that the reformation of the liturgy and church government should be carried out according to the advice of Parliament; that the ordinances which they had made with regard to the militia should be submitted to; that the justice of Parliament should pass upon all delinquents, that is, upon all officials of the state and country who had assisted in carrying out the king's ordinances for the raising of taxes; that a general pardon should he granted, with such exceptions as should he advised by Parliament; that the fort and castles should be disposed of by consent of Parliament; and that no peers should be made but with the consent of both Houses. They demanded also that they should have the power of appointing and dismissing the royal ministers, of naming guardians for the royal children, and of virtually controlling military, civil, and religious affairs.

As it was clear that these demands went altogether beyond the rights of the Commons, and that if the king submitted to them the power of the country would be solely in their hands, while he himself would become a cipher, he had no course open to him but to refuse assent, and to appeal to the loyal nobility and gentry of the country.

It is true that many of these rights have since been obtained by the Houses of Parliament; but it must be remembered that they were altogether alien at the time to the position which the kings of England had hitherto held, and that the body into whose hands they would be intrusted would be composed solely of one party in the state, and that this party would be controlled by the fanatical leaders and the ministers of the sects opposed to the Established Church, which were at that time bitter, narrow, and violent to an extent of which we have now no conception.

The attitude thus assumed by Parliament drove from their ranks a great many of the most intelligent and enlightened of those who had formerly sided with them in their contest against the king. These gentlemen felt that intolerable as was the despotic power of a king, still more intolerable would it be to be governed by the despotic power of a group of fanatics. The liberty of Englishmen was now as much threatened by the Commons as it had been threatened by the king, and to loyal gentlemen the latter alternative was preferable. Thus there were on both sides earnest and conscientious men who grieved deeply at being forced to draw swords in such a quarrel, and who felt that their choice of sides was difficult in the extreme. Falkland was the typical soldier on the royal side, Hampden on that of the Commons.

It is probable that were England divided to-morrow under the same conditions, men would be equally troubled upon which side to range themselves. At this period of the struggle, with the exception of a few hot-headed followers of the king and a few zealots on the side of the Commons, there was a general hope that matters would shortly be arranged, and that one conflict would settle the struggle.

The first warlike demonstration was made before the town of York, before whose walls the king, arriving with an armed force, was refused admittance by Sir John Hotham, who held the place for the Parliament. This was the signal for the outbreak of the war, and each party henceforth strained every nerve to arm themselves and to place their forces in the field.

The above is but a brief sketch of the circumstances which led the Cavaliers and Puritans of England to arm themselves for civil war. Many details have been omitted, the object being not to teach the history of the time, but to show the general course of events which had led to so broad and strange a division between the people of England. Even now, after an interval of two hundred years, men still discuss the subject with something like passion, and are as strong in their sympathies toward one side or the other as in the days when their ancestors took up arms for king or Commons.

It is with the story of the war which followed the conversation of Harry Furness and Herbert Rippinghall that we have to do, not with that of the political occurrences which preceded it. As to these, at least, no doubts or differences of opinion can arise. The incidents of the war, its victories and defeats, its changing fortunes, and its final triumph are matters beyond the domain of politics, or of opinion; and indeed when once the war began politics ceased to have much further sway. The original questions were lost sight of, and men fought for king or Parliament just as soldiers nowadays fight for England or France, without in any concerning themselves with the original grounds of quarrel.

# CHAPTER II

## FOR THE KING

It was late that evening when Sir Henry Furness returned from Oxford; but Harry, anxious to hear the all-absorbing news of the day, had waited up for him.

"What news, father?" he said, as Sir Henry alighted at the door.

"Stirring news, Harry; but as dark as may be. War appears to be now certain. The king has made every concession, but the more he is ready to grant, the more those Puritan knaves at Westminster would force from him. King, peers, bishops, Church, all is to go down before this knot of preachers; and it is well that the king has his nobles and gentry still at his back. I have seen Lord Falkland, and he has given me a commission in the king's name to raise a troop of horse. The royal banner will be hoisted at Nottingham, and there he will appeal to all his loyal subjects for aid against those who seek to govern the nation."

"And you think, sir, that it will really be war now?" Harry asked.

"Ay, that will it, unless the Commons go down on their knees and ask his majesty's pardon, of which there is, methinks, no likelihood. As was to be expected, the burghers and rabble of the large towns are everywhere with them, and are sending up petitions to the Commons to stand fast and abolish everything. However, the country is of another way of thinking, and though the bad advisers of the king have in times past taken measures which have sorely tried our loyalty, that is all forgotten now. His majesty has promised redress to all grievances, and to rule constitutionally in future, and I hear that the nobles are calling out their retainers in all parts. England has always been governed by her kings since she was a country, and we are going to try now whether we are to be governed in future by our kings or by every tinker, tailor, preacher, or thief sent up to Westminster. I know which is my choice, and to-morrow I shall set about raising a troop of lads of the same mind."

"You mean to take me, sir, I hope," Harry said.

"Take you?" his lather repeated, laughing. "To do what?"

"To fight, certainly," Harry replied. "I am sure that among the tenants there is not one who could use the small sword as I can, for you have taught me yourself, and I do not think that I should be more afraid of the London pikemen than the best of them."

"No, no, Harry," his father said, putting his hand on the boy's shoulder; "I do not doubt your bravery. You come of a fighting stock indeed, and good blood cannot lie. But you are too young, my boy."

"But if the war goes on for a couple of years, father."

"Ay, ay, my boy; but I hope that it will be ended in a couple of months. If it should last—which God forbid!--you shall have your chance, never fear. Or, Harry, should you hear that aught has happened to me, mount your horse at once, my boy; ride to the army, and take your place at the head of my tenants. They will of course put an older hand in command; but so long as a Furness is alive, whatever be his age, he must ride at the head of the Furness tenants to strike for the king. I hear, by the way, Harry, that that Puritan knave, Rippinghall, the wool-stapler, is talking treason among his hands, and says that he will add a brave contingent to the bands of the Commons when they march hither. Hast heard aught about it?"

"Nothing, father, but I hope it is not true. I know, however, that Master Rippinghall's thoughts and opinions lie in that direction, for I have heard from Herbert—"

"Ah, the son of the wool-stapler. Hark you, Harry, this is a time when we must all take sides for or against the king. Hitherto I have permitted your acquaintance with the wool-stapler's son, though, in truth, he be by birth no fit companion for you. But times have changed now. The sword is going to be drawn, and friends of the king can no longer be grip hands with friends of the Commons. Did my own brother draw sword for Parliament, we would never speak again. Dost hear?"

"Yes, sir; and will of course obey your order, should you determine that I must speak no more to Herbert. But, as you say, I am a boy yet, too young to ride to the wars, and Herbert is no older. It will be time for us to quarrel when it is time for us to draw the sword."

"That is so, Harry, and I do not altogether forbid you speaking with him. Still the less you are seen together, the better. I like the lad, and have made him welcome here for your sake. He is a thoughtful lad, and a clever one; but it is your thoughtful men who plot treason, and until the storm be overpast, it is best that you see as little of him as may be. And now I have eaten my supper, and it is long past the time that you should have been in bed. Send down word by Thomas Hardway to Master Drake, my steward, to bid him send early in the morning notices that all my tenants shall assemble here to-morrow at four in the afternoon, and bid the cook come to me. We shall have a busy day to-morrow, for the Furness tenantry never gather at the hall and go out empty. And short though be the notice, they shall not do so this time, which to some of us may, perchance, be the last."

The next day there was bustle and hurry at Furness Hall. The ponds were dragged for fish; the poultry yard was scoured for its finest birds; the keepers were early afield, and when they returned with piles of hares and rabbits, these were seized by the cook and converted into huge pies and pasties. Two sheep were slaughtered, and the scullions were hard at work making confections of currants, gooseberries, plums, and other fruits from the garden. In the great hall the tables were laid, and when this was done, and all was in readiness, the serving men were called up to the armory, and there, throughout the day, the cleaning of swords and iron caps, the burnishing of breast and back pieces, the cleaning of firelocks, and other military work went on with all haste.

The Furness estates covered many a square mile of Berkshire, and fifty sturdy yeomen dismounted before Furness Hall at the hour named by Sir Henry. A number of grooms and serving men were in attendance, and took the horses as they rode up, while the major-domo conducted them to the great picture gallery. Here they were received by Sir Henry with a stately cordiality, and the maids handed round a great silver goblet filled with spiced wine.

At four exactly the major-domo entered and announced that the quota was complete, and that every one of those summoned was present.

"Serve the tables then," Sir Henry said, as he led the Way to the great dining-hall.

Sir Henry took the head of the broad table, and bade Harry sit on his right hand, while the oldest of the tenants faced him at the opposite end. Then a troop of servants entered bearing smoking joints, cold boars' heads, fish, turkeys, geese, and larded capons. These were placed upon the table, with an abundance of French wine, and of strong ale for those who preferred it, to wash down the viands. The first courses were followed by dishes of meats and confections, and when all was finished and cleared away Sir Henry Furness rose to his feet.

"Fill your glasses all," he said; "and bumpers. The toast which I give you to-day is 'The king, God bless him.' Never should Englishmen drink his health more earnestly and solemnly than to-day, when rebels have driven him from his capital, and pestilent traitors threatened him with armed force. Perhaps, my friends, you, like me, may from time to time have grumbled when the tax-collectors have come round, and you have seen no one warrant for their demands. But if the king has been forced so to exceed his powers, it was in no slight degree because those at Westminster refused to grant him the sums which were needful. He has, too, been surrounded by bad advisers. I myself loved not greatly either Stratford or Laud. But I would rather bear their high-handed ways, which were at least aimed to strengthen the kingdom and for the honor of the king, than be ground by these petty tyrants at Westminster, who would shut up our churches, forbid us to smile on a Sunday, or to pray, except through our noses; who would turn merry England into a canting conventicle, and would rule us with a rod to which that of the king were as a willow wand. Therefore it is the duty of all true men and good to drink the health of his majesty the king, and confusion to his enemies."

Upstanding, and with enthusiastic shouts, the whole of the tenants drank the toast. Sir Henry was pleased with the spirit which was manifested, and when the cheering had subsided and quiet was again restored, he went on:

"My friends, I have summoned you here to tell you what many of you no doubt know already—that the king, driven from London by the traitors of Parliament, who would take from him all power, would override the peers, and abolish the Church, has appealed to his faithful subjects to stand by him, and to maintain his cause. He will, ere a fortnight be past, raise his banner at Nottingham. Already Sir John Hotham, the rebel Governor of York, has closed the gates of that city to him, and it is time that all loyal men were on foot to aid his cause. Lord Falkland has been pleased to grant me a commission to raise a troop of horse in his service, and I naturally come to you first, to ask you to follow me."

He paused a moment, and a shout of assent rang through the hall.

"There are," he said, "some among you whom years may prevent from yourselves undertaking the hardships of the field, but these can send substitutes in their sons. You will understand that none are compelled to go; but I trust that from the long-standing friendship between us, and from the duty which you each owe to the king, none will hold back. Do I understand that all here are willing to join, or to furnish substitutes?"

A general shout of "All" broke from the tenants.

"Thank you, my friends, I expected nothing else. This will give me fifty good men, and true, and I hope that each will be able to bring with him one, two, or more men, in proportion to the size of his holding. I shall myself bear the expense of the arms and outfit of all these; but we must not strip the land of hands. Farming must still go on, for people must feed, even if there be war. As to the rents, we must waive our agreements while the war lasts. Each man will pay me what proportion of his rent he is able, and no more. The king will need money as well as men, and as all I receive will be at his service, I know that each of you will pay as much as he can to aid the common cause. I have here a list of your names. My son will take it round to each, and will write down how many men each of you may think to bring with him to the war. No man must be taken unwillingly. I want only those whose hearts are in the cause. My son is grieving that he is not old enough to ride with us; but should aught befall me in the strife, I have bade him ride and take his place among you."

Another cheer arose, and Harry went round the table taking down the names and numbers of the men, and when his total was added up, it was found that those present believed that they could bring a hundred men with them into the field.

"This is beyond my hopes," Sir Harry said, as amid great cheering he announced the result. "I myself will raise another fifty from my grooms, gardeners, and keepers, and from brave lads I can gather in the village, and I shall be proud indeed when I present to his majesty two hundred men of Furness, ready to die in his defense."

After this there was great arrangement of details. Each tenant gave a list of the arms which he possessed and the number of horses fit for work, and as in those days, by the law of the land each man, of whatsoever his degree, was bound to keep arms in order to join the militia, should his services be required for the defense of the kingdom, the stock of arms was, with the contents of Sir Henry's armory, found to be sufficient for the number of men who were to be raised. It was eight o'clock in the evening before all was arranged, and the party broke up and separated to their homes.

For the next week there was bustle and preparation on the Furness estates, as, indeed, through all England. As yet, however, the Parliament were gathering men far more rapidly than the king. The Royalists of England were slow to perceive how far the Commons intended to press their demands, and could scarcely believe that civil war was really to break out. The friends of the Commons, however, were everywhere in earnest. The preachers in the conventicles throughout the land denounced the king in terms of the greatest violence, and in almost every town the citizens were arming and drilling. Lord Essex, who commanded the Parliamentary forces, was drawing toward Northampton with ten thousand men, consisting mainly of the train-bands of London; while the king, with only a few hundred followers, was approaching Nottingham, where he proposed to unfurl his standard and appeal to his subjects.

In a week from the day of the appeal of Sir Henry two troops, each of a hundred men strong, drew up in front of Furness Hall. To the eye of a soldier accustomed to the armies of the Continent, with their bands trained by long and constant warfare, the aspect of this troop might not have appeared formidable. Each man was dressed according to his fancy. Almost all wore jack-boots coming nigh to the hip, iron breast and back pieces, and steel caps. Sir Henry Furness and four gentlemen, his friends, who had seen service in the Low Countries, and had now gladly joined his band, took their places, Sir Henry himself at the head of the body, and two officers with each troop. They, too, were clad in high boots, with steel breast and back pieces, thick buff leather gloves, and the wide felt hats with feathers which were worn in peace time. During the war some of the Royalist officers wore iron caps as did their foes. But the majority, in a spirit of defiance and contempt of their enemies, wore the wide hat of the times, which, picturesque and graceful as it was, afforded but a poor defense for the head. Almost all wore their hair long and in ringlets, and across their shoulders were the white scarfs typical of their loyalty to the king. Harry bestrode a fine horse which his father had given him, and had received permission to ride for half the day's march by his side at the head of the troop. The trumpeter sounded the call, Sir Henry stood up in his stirrups, drew his sword and waved it over his head, and shouted "For God and King." Two hundred swords flashed in the air, and the answering shout came out deep and full. Then the swords were sheathed, the horses' heads turned, and with a jingle of sabers and accouterments the troop rode gayly out through the gates of the park.

Upon their way north they were joined by more than one band of Cavaliers marching in the same direction, and passed, too, several bodies of footmen, headed by men with closely-cropped heads, and somber figures, beside whom generally marched others whom their attire proclaimed to be Puritan preachers, on their way to join the army of Essex. The parties scowled at each other as they passed; but as yet no sword had been drawn on either side, and without adventure they arrived at Nottingham.

Having distributed his men among the houses of the town, Sir Henry Furness rode to the castle, where his majesty had arrived the day before. He had already the honor of the personal acquaintance of the king, for he had in one of the early parliaments sat for Oxford. Disgusted, however, with the spirit that prevailed among the opponents of the king, and also by the obstinacy and unconstitutional course pursued by his majesty, he had at the dissolution of Parliament retired to his estate, and when the next House was summoned, declined to stand again for his seat.

"Welcome, Sir Henry," his majesty said graciously to him, "you are among the many who withstood me somewhat in the early days of my reign, and perchance you were right to do so; but who have now, in my need, rallied round me, seeing whither the purpose of these traitorous subjects of mine leads them. You are the more welcome that you have, as I hear, brought two hundred horsemen with you, a number larger than any which has yet joined me. These," he said, pointing to two young noblemen near him, "are my nephews, Rupert and Maurice, who have come to join me."

Upon making inquiries, Sir Henry found that the prospects of the king were far from bright. So far, the Royalists had been sadly behindhand with their preparations. The king had arrived with scarce four hundred men. He had left his artillery behind at York for want of carriage, and his need in arms was even greater than in men, as the arsenals of the kingdom had all been seized by the Parliament. Essex lay at Northampton with ten thousand men, and had he at this time advanced, even the most sanguine of the Royalists saw that the struggle would be a hopeless one.

The next day, at the hour appointed, the royal standard was raised on the Castle of Nottingham, in the midst of a great storm of wind and rain, which before many hours had passed blew the royal standard to the ground—an omen which those superstitiously inclined deemed of evil augury indeed. The young noblemen and gentlemen, however, who had gathered at Northampton, were not of a kind to be daunted by omens and auguries, and finding that Essex did not advance and hearing news from all parts of the country that the loyal gentlemen were gathering their tenants fast, their hopes rose rapidly. There was, indeed, some discontent when it was known that, by the advice of his immediate councilors, King Charles had dispatched the Earl of Southampton with Sir John Collpeper and Sir William Uvedale to London, with orders to treat with the Commons. The Parliament, however, refused to enter into any negotiations whatever until the king lowered his standard and recalled the proclamation which he had issued. This, which would have been a token of absolute surrender to the Parliament, the king refused to do. He attempted a further negotiation; but this also failed.

The troops at Nottingham now amounted to eleven hundred men, of which three hundred were infantry raised by Sir John Digby, the sheriff of the county. The other eight hundred were horse. Upon the breaking off of negotiations, and the advance of Essex, the king, sensible that he was unable to resist the advance of Essex, who had now fifteen thousand men collected under him, fell back to Derby, and thence to Shrewsbury, being joined on his way by many nobles and gentlemen with their armed followers. At Wellington, a town a day's march from Shrewsbury, the king had his little army formed up, and made a solemn declaration before them in which he promised to maintain the Protestant religion, to observe the laws, and to uphold the just privileges and freedom of Parliament.

The Furness band were not present on that occasion, as they had been dispatched to Worcester with some other soldiers, the whole under the command of Prince Rupert, in order to watch the movements of Essex, who was advancing in that direction. While scouring the ground around the city, they came upon a body of Parliamentary cavalry, the advance of the army of Essex. The bands drew up at a little distance from each other, and then Prince Rupert gave the command to charge. With the cheer of "For God and the king!" the troop rushed upon the cavalry of the Parliament with such force and fury that they broke them utterly, and killing many, drove them in confusion from the field, but small loss to themselves.

This was the first action of the civil war, the first blood drawn by Englishmen from Englishmen since the troubles in the commencement of the reign of Mary.

# CHAPTER III

# A BRAWL AT OXFORD

News in those days traveled but slowly, and England was full of conflicting rumors as to the doings of the two armies. Every one was unsettled. Bodies of men moving to join one or other of the parties kept the country in an uproar, and the Cavaliers, or rather the toughs of the towns calling themselves Cavaliers, brought much odium upon the royal cause by the ill-treatment of harmless citizens, and by raids on inoffensive country people. Later on this conduct was to be reversed and the Royalists were to suffer tenfold the outrages now put upon the Puritans. But there can be no doubt that the conduct of irresponsible ruffians at that time did much to turn the flood of public opinion in many places, where it would otherwise have remained neutral, against the crown.

To Harry the time passed but slowly. He spent his days in Abingdon hearing the latest news, and occasionally rode over to Oxford. This city was throughout the civil war the heart of the Royalist party, and its loss was one of the heaviest blows which befell the crown. Here Harry found none but favorable reports current. Enthusiasm was at its height. The university was even more loyal than the town, and bands of lads smashed the windows of those persons who were supposed to favor the Parliament. More than once Harry saw men pursued through the streets, pelted with stones and mud, and in some cases escaping barely with their lives. Upon one occasion, seeing a person in black garments and of respectable appearance so treated, the boy's indignation was aroused, for he himself, both from his conversations with his friend Herbert, and the talk with his father, was, although enthusiastically Royalist, yet inclined to view with respect those who held opposite opinions.

"Run down that alley!" he exclaimed, pushing his horse between the fugitive and his pursuers.

The man darted down the lane, and Harry placed himself at the entrance, and shouted to the rabble to abstain.

A yell of rage and indignation replied, and a volley of stones was thrown. Harry fearlessly drew his sword, and cut at some of those who were in the foreground. These retaliated with sticks, and Harry was forced backward into the lane. This was too narrow to enable him to turn, his horse, and his position was a critical one. Finding that he was a mark for stones, he leaped from the saddle, thereby disappearing from the sight of those in the ranks behind, and sword in hand, barred the way to the foremost of his assailants. The contest, however, would have been brief had not a party of young students come up the lane, and seeing from Harry's attire that he was a gentleman, and likely to be of Cavalier opinions, they at once, without inquiring the cause of the fray, threw themselves into it, shouting "Gown! gown!" They speedily drove the assailants back out of the lane; but these, reinforced by the great body beyond, were then too strong for them. The shouts of the young men, however, brought up others to their assistance, and a general melee took place, townsmen and gownsmen throwing themselves into the fray without any inquiry as to the circumstances from which it arose. The young students carried swords, which, although contrary to the statutes of the university, were for the time generally adopted. The townspeople were armed with bludgeons, and in some cases with hangers, and the fray was becoming a serious one, when it was abruptly terminated by the arrival of a troop of horse, which happened to be coming into the town to join the royal forces. The officer in command, seeing so desperate a tumult raging, ordered his men to charge into the crowd, and their interference speedily put an end to the fight.

Harry returned to their rooms with some of his protectors and their wounds were bound up, and the circumstances of the fight were talked over. Harry was much blamed by the college men when he said that he had been drawn into the fray by protecting a Puritan. But when his new friends learned that he was as thoroughly Royalist as themselves, and that his father had gone with a troop to Nottingham, they took a more favorable view of his action, but still assured him that it was the height of folly to interfere to protect a rebel from the anger of the townspeople.

"But, methinks," Harry said, "that it were unwise in the extreme to push matters so far here. In Oxford the Royalists have it all their own way, and can, of course, at will assault their Puritan neighbors. But it is different in most other towns. There the Roundheads have the upper hand and might retort by doing ill to the Cavaliers there. Surely it were better to keep these unhappy differences out of private life, and to trust the arbitration of our cause to the arms of our soldiers in the field."

There was a general agreement that this would indeed be the wisest course; but the young fellows were of opinion that hot heads on either side would have their way, and that if the war went on attacks of this kind by the one party on the other must be looked for.

Harry remained for some time with his friends in Christ church, drinking the beer for which the college was famous. Then, mounting his horse, he rode back to Abingdon.

Two days later, as he was proceeding toward the town, he met a man dressed as a preacher.

"Young sir," the latter said, "may I ask if you are Master Furness?"

"I am," the lad replied.

"Then it is to you I am indebted for my rescue from those who assaulted me in the streets of Oxford last week. In the confusion I could not see your face, but I inquired afterward, and was told that my preserver was Master Furness, and have come over to thank you for your courtesy and bravery in thus intervening on behalf of one whom I think you regard as an enemy, for I understand that Sir Henry, your father, has declared for the crown."

"I acted," Harry said, "simply on the impulse of humanity, and hold it mean and cowardly for a number of men to fall upon one."

"We are," the preacher continued, "at the beginning only of our troubles, and the time may come when I, Zachariah Stubbs, may be able to return to you the good service which you have done me. Believe me, young sir, the feeling throughout England is strong for the Commons, and that it will not be crushed out, as some men suppose, even should the king's men gain a great victory over Essex—which, methinks, is not likely. There are tens of thousands throughout the country who are now content to remain quiet at home, who would assuredly draw the sword and go forth to battle, should they consider their cause in danger. The good work has begun, and the sword will not be sheathed until the oppressor is laid low."

"We should differ who the oppressor is," Harry replied coldly. "I myself am young to discuss these matters, but my father and those who think with him consider that the oppression is at present on the side of the Commons, and of those whose religious views you share. While pretending to wish to be free, you endeavor to bind others beneath your tyranny. While wishing to worship in your way unmolested, you molest those who wish to worship in theirs. However, I thank you for your offer, that should the time come your good services will be at my disposal. As you say, the issue of the conflict is dark, and it may be, though I trust it will not, that some day you may, if you will, return the light service which I rendered you."

"You will not forget my name?" the preacher said—"Zachariah Stubbs, a humble instrument of the Lord, and a preacher in the Independent chapel at Oxford. Thither I cannot return, and am on my way to London, where I have many friends, and where I doubt not a charge will be found for me. I myself belong to the east countries, where the people are strong for the Lord, and I doubt not that some of those I know will come to the front of affairs, in which case my influence may perhaps be of more service than you can suppose at present. Farewell, young sir, and whatever be the issues of this struggle, I trust that you may safely emerge from them."

The man lifted his broad black hat, and went on his way, and Harry rode forward, smiling a little to himself at the promise given him.

The time passed slowly, and all kinds of rumors filled the land. At length beacon fires were seen to blaze upon the hills, and, as it was known that the Puritans had arranged with Essex that the news of a victory was so to be conveyed to London, the hearts of the Royalists sank, for they feared that disaster had befallen their cause. The next day, however, horsemen of the Parliament galloping through the country proclaimed that they had been defeated; but it was not till next day that the true state of affairs became known. Then the news came that the battle had indeed been a drawn one.

On the 26th of October Charles marched with his army into Oxford. So complete was the ignorance of the inhabitants as to the movements of the armies that at Abingdon the news of his coming was unknown, and Harry was astonished on the morning of the 27th at hearing a great trampling of horsemen. Looking out, he beheld his father at the head of the troop, approaching the house. With a shout of joy the lad rushed downstairs and met his father at the entrance.

"I did not look to be back so soon, Harry," Sir Henry said, as he alighted from his horse. "We arrived at Oxford last night, and I am sent on with my troop to see that no Parliament bands are lurking in the neighborhood."

Before entering the house the colonel dismissed his troop, telling them that until the afternoon they could return to their homes, but must then re-assemble and hold themselves in readiness to advance, should he receive further orders. Then, accompanied by his officers, he entered the house. Breakfast was speedily prepared, and when this was done justice to Sir Henry proceeded to relate to Harry, who was burning with impatience to hear his news, the story of the battle of Edgehill.

"We reached Shrewsbury, as I wrote you," he said, "and stayed there twenty days, and during that time the army swelled and many nobles and gentlemen joined us. We were, however, it must be owned, but a motley throng. The foot soldiers, indeed, were mostly armed with muskets; but many had only sticks and cudgels. On the 12th we moved to Wolverhampton, and so on through Birmingham and Kenilworth. We saw nothing of the rebels till we met at Edgecot, a little hamlet near Banbury, where we took post on a hill, the rebels being opposite to us. It must be owned," Sir Henry went on, "that things here did not promise well. There were dissensions between Prince Rupert, who commanded the cavalry, and Lord Lindsey, the general in chief, who is able and of great courage, but hot-headed and fiery. In the morning it was determined to engage, as Essex's forces had not all come up, and the king's troops were at least as numerous as those of the enemy. We saw little of the fighting, for at the commencement of the battle we got word to charge upon the enemy's left. We made but short work of them, and drove them headlong from the field, chasing them in great disorder for three miles, and taking much plunder in Kineton among the Parliament baggage-wagons. Thinking that the fight was over, we then prepared to ride back. When we came to the field we found that all was changed. The main body of the Roundheads had pressed hotly upon ours and had driven them back. Lord Lindsey himself, who had gone into the battle at the head of the pikemen carrying a pike himself like a common soldier, had been mortally wounded and taken prisoner, and grievous slaughter had been inflicted. The king's standard itself had been taken, but this had been happily recovered, for two Royalist officers, putting on orange scarfs, rode into the middle of the Roundheads, and pretending that they were sent by Essex, demanded the flag from his secretary, to whom it had been intrusted. The scrivener gave it up, and the officers, seizing it, rode through the enemy and recovered their ranks. There was much confusion and no little angry discussion in the camp that night, the footmen accusing the horsemen of having deserted them, and the horsemen grumbling at the foot, because they had not done their work as well as themselves. In the morning the two armies still faced each other, neither being willing to budge a foot, although neither cared to renew the battle. The rest of the Parliamentary forces had arrived, and they might have struck us a heavy blow had they been minded, for there was much discouragement in our ranks. Lord Essex, however, after waiting a day and burying his dead, drew off from the field, and we,

20

remaining there, were able to claim the victory, which, however, my son, was one of a kind which was scarce worth winning. It was a sad sight to see so many men stretched stark and dead, and these killed, not in fighting with a foreign foe, but with other Englishmen. It made us all mightily sad, and if at that moment Lord Essex had had full power from the Parliament to treat, methinks that the quarrel could have been settled, all being mightily sick of such kind of fighting."

"What is going to be done now, father?" Harry asked.

"We are going to move forward toward London. Essex is moving parallel with us, and will try to get there first. From what we hear from our friends in the city, there are great numbers of moderate men will be glad to see the king back, and to agree to make an end of this direful business. The zealots and preachers will of course oppose them. But when we arrive, we trust that our countenance will enable our friends to make a good front, and to overcome the opposition of the Puritans. We expect that in a few days we shall meet with offers to treat. But whether or no, I hope that the king will soon be lodged again in his palace at Whitehall."

"And do you think that there will be any fighting, sir?"

"I think not. I sincerely hope not," the colonel said.

"Then if you think that there will only be a peaceable entry, will you not let me ride with you? It will be a brave sight to see the king enter London again; one to tell of all one's life."

The colonel made no reply for a minute or two.

"Well, Harry, I will not say you nay," he said at length. "Scenes of broils and civil war are not for lads of your age. But, as you say, it would be a thing to talk of to old age how you rode after the king when he entered London in state. But mind, if there be fighting, you must rein back and keep out of it."

Harry was overjoyed with the permission, for in truth time had hung heavily on his hands since the colonel had ridden away. His companionship with Herbert had ceased, for although the lads pressed hands warmly when they met in Abingdon, both felt that while any day might bring news of the triumph of one party or the other, it was impossible that they could hold any warm intercourse with each other. The school was closed, for the boys of course took sides, and so much ill-will was caused that it was felt best to put a stop to it by closing the doors. Harry therefore had been left entirely upon his own resources, and although he had ridden about among the tenants and, so far as he could, supplied his father's place, the time often hung heavy on his hands, especially during the long hours of the evening. After thanking his father for his kindness, he rushed wildly off to order his horse to be prepared for him to accompany the troop, to re-burnish the arms which he had already chosen as fitting him from the armory, and to make what few preparations were necessary for the journey.

It was some days, however, before any move was made. The king was occupied in raising money, being sorely crippled by want of funds, as well as of arms and munitions of war. At the beginning of November the advance was made, Sir Henry with his troop joining Prince Rupert, and advancing through Reading without opposition as far as Maidenhead, where he fixed his quarters. Two days later he learned that Essex had arrived with his army in London. On the 11th King Charles was at Colnbrook. Here he received a deputation from the Houses of Parliament, who proposed that the king should pause in his advance until committees of both Houses should attend him with propositions "for the removal of these bloody distempers and distractions." The king received the deputation favorably, and said that he would stop at Windsor, and there receive the propositions which might be sent him.

Unfortunately, however, the hopes which were now entertained that peace would be restored, were dashed to the ground by an action which was ascribed by the Royalists to the hotheadedness of Prince Rupert, but which the king's enemies affirmed was due to the duplicity of his majesty himself. On this point there is no evidence. But it is certain that the advance made after this deputation had been received rendered all further negotiation impossible, as it inspired the Commons with the greatest distrust, and enabled the violent portion always to feign a doubt of the king's word, and great fears as to the keeping of any terms which might be made, and so to act upon the timid and wavering. The very day after the deputation had left, bearing the news to London of the king's readiness to treat, and inspiring all there with hope of peace, Prince Rupert, taking advantage of a very thick mist, marched his cavalry to within half a mile of the town of Brentford before his advance was discovered, designing to surprise the train of artillery at Hammersmith and to push on and seize the Commons and the city.

The design might have been successful, for the exploits of Rupert's horse at the battle of Edgehill had struck terror into the minds of the enemy. In the town of Brentford, however, were lodged a regiment of foot, under Hollis, and these prepared manfully to resist. Very valiantly the prince, followed by his horse, charged into

22

the streets of Brentford, where the houses were barricaded by the foot soldiers, who shot boldly against them. Many were killed, and for three hours the contest was resolutely maintained. The streets had been barricaded, and Prince Rupert's men fought at great disadvantage. At length, as evening approached, and the main body of the Cavaliers came up, the Parliament men gave way, and were driven from the town. Many were taken prisoners, and others driven into the river, the greater portion, however, making their way in boats safely down the stream. The delay which their sturdy resistance had made saved the city. Hampden was bringing his men across from Acton. Essex had marched from Chelsea Fields to Turnham Green, and the road was now blocked. After it was dark the Train-Bands advanced, and the Parliament regiments, reinforced by them, pushed on to Brentford again; the Royalists, finding that the place could not be held, fell back to the king's quarters at Hounslow.

The chroniclers describe how wild a scene of confusion reigned in London that evening. Proclamations were issued ordering all men to take up arms; shops were closed, the apprentice boys mustered in the ranks, and citizens poured out like one man to defend the town. They encamped upon the road, and the next day great trains of provisions sent by the wives of the merchants and traders reached them, and as many came out to see the forces, the scene along the road resembled a great fair.

In this fight at Brentford Harry Furness was engaged. The Royalists had anticipated no resistance here, not knowing that Hollis held the place, and Sir Henry did not think of ordering Harry to remain behind. At the moment when it was found that Hollis was in force and the trumpets sounded the charge, the lad was riding in the rear of the troop, talking to one of the officers, and his father could take no step to prevent his joining. Therefore, when the trumpets sounded and the troops started off at full gallop toward the town, Harry, greatly exulting in his good luck, fell in with them and rode down the streets of Brentford. The musketry fire was brisk, and many of the troop rolled from their horses. Presently they were dismounted and ordered to take the houses by storm. With the hilts of their swords they broke in the doors, and there was fierce lighting within.

Harry, who was rather bewildered with the din and turmoil of the fight, did as the rest, and followed two or three of the men into one of the houses, whose door had been broken open. They were assailed as they entered by a fire of musketry from the Parliament men within. Those in front fell, and Harry was knocked down by the butt of a pike.

When he recovered he found himself in a boat drifting down the stream, a prisoner of the Roundheads.

For a long time Harry could hear the sounds of the guns and cannon at Brentford, and looking round at the quiet villages which they passed on the banks, could scarce believe that he had been engaged in a battle and was now a prisoner. But little was said to him. The men were smarting under their defeat and indulged in the bitterest language at the treachery with which, after negotiations had been agreed upon, the advance of the Royalists had been made. They speedily discovered the youth of their captive, and, after telling him brutally that he would probably be hung when he got to London, they paid no further attention to him. The boat was heavily laden, and rowed by two oars, and the journey down was a long one, for the tide met them when at the village of Hammersmith, and they were forced to remain tied up to a tree by the bank until it turned again. This it did not do until far in the night, and the morning was just breaking when they reached London.

It was perhaps well for Harry that they arrived in the dark, for in the excited state of the temper of the citizens, and their anger at the treachery which had been practiced, it might have fared but badly with him. He was marched along the Strand to the city, and was consigned to a lock-up in Finsbury, until it could be settled what should be done to him. In fact, the next day his career was nearly being terminated, for John Lilburn, a captain of the Train Bands, who had been an apprentice and imprisoned for contumacy, had been captured at Brentford, and after being tried for his life, was sentenced to death as a rebel. Essex, however, sent in word to the Royalist camp that for every one of the Parliament officers put to death, he would hang three Royalist prisoners. This threat had its effect, and Harry remained in ignorance of the danger which had threatened him.

The greatest inconvenience which befell him was that he was obliged to listen to all sorts of long harangues upon the part of the Puritan soldiers who were his jailers. These treated him as a misguided lad, and did their best to convert him from the evil of his ways. At last Harry lost his temper, and said that if they wanted to hang him, they might; but that he would rather put up with that than the long sermons which they were in the habit of delivering to him. Indignant at this rejection of their good offices, they left him to himself, and days passed without his receiving any visit save that of the soldier who brought his meals.

# CHAPTER IV

## BREAKING PRISON

Harry's place of confinement was a cell leading off a guardroom of the Train Bands. Occasionally the door was left open, as some five or six men were always there, and Harry could see through the open door the citizens of London training at arms. Several preachers were in the habit of coming each day to discourse to those on guard, and so while away the time, and upon these occasions the door was generally left open, in order that the prisoner might be edified by the sermons. Upon one occasion the preacher, a small, sallow-visaged man, looked into the cell at the termination of his discourse, and seeing Harry asleep on his truckle bed, awoke him, and lectured him severely on the wickedness of allowing such precious opportunities to pass. After this he made a point of coming in each day when he had addressed the guard, and of offering up a long and very tedious prayer on behalf of the young reprobate. These preachings and prayings nearly drove Harry out of his mind. Confinement was bad enough; but confinement tempered by a course of continual sermons, delivered mostly through the nose, was a terrible infliction. At last the thought presented itself to him that he might manage to effect his escape in the garb of the preacher. He thought the details over and over in his mind, and at last determined at any rate to attempt to carry them into execution.

One day he noticed, when the door opened for the entry of the preacher, that a parade of unusual magnitude was being held in the drill yard, some officer of importance having come down to inspect the Train Band. There were but four men left in the guardroom and these were occupied in gazing out of the window. The preacher came direct into the cell, as his audience in the guardroom for once were not disposed to listen to him, and shutting the door behind him, he addressed a few words of exhortation to Harry, and then, closing his eyes, began a long prayer. When he was fairly under way, Harry sprang upon him, grasping him by the throat with both hands, and forced him back upon the bed. The little preacher was too much surprised to offer the smallest resistance, and Harry, who had drawn out the cords used in supporting the sacking of the bed, bound him hand and foot, keeping, while he did so, the pillow across his face, and his weight on the top of the pillow, thereby nearly putting a stop to the preacher's prayers and exhortations for all time. Having safely bound him, and finding that he did not struggle in the least, Harry removed the pillow, and was horrified to see his prisoner black in the face. He had, however, no time for regret or inquiry how far the man had gone, and stuffing a handkerchief into his mouth, to prevent his giving any alarm should he recover breath enough to do so, Harry placed his high steeple hat upon his head, his Geneva bands round his throat, and his long black mantle over his shoulders. He then opened the door and walked quietly forth. The guards were too much occupied with the proceedings in the parade ground to do more than glance round, as the apparent preacher departed. Harry strode with a long and very stiff step, and with his figure bolt upright, to the gate of the parade ground, and then passing through the crowd who were standing there gaping at the proceedings within, he issued forth a free man.

For awhile he walked at a brisk pace, and then, feeling secure from pursuit, slackened his speed; keeping westward through the city, he passed along the Strand and out into the country beyond. He wore his beaver well down over his eyes, and walked with his head down as if meditating deeply, in order to prevent any passers-by from observing the youthfulness of his face. When he arrived at the village of Chelsea, he saw, in front of a gentleman's house, a horse hitched up to a hook placed there for that purpose. Conceiving that for a long journey four legs are much more useful than two, and that when he got beyond the confines of London he should attract less suspicion upon a horse than if striding alone along the road, he took the liberty of mounting it and riding off. When he had gone a short distance he heard loud shouts; but thinking these in no way to concern him, he rode on the faster, and was soon beyond the sound of the voices. He now took a northerly direction, traveled through Kensington, and then keeping east of Acton, where he knew that some Parliament troops were quartered, he rode for the village of Harrow. He was aware that the Royalists had fallen back to Oxford, and that the Parliament troops were at Reading. He therefore made to the northwest, intending to circuit round and so reach Oxford. He did not venture to go to an inn, for although, as a rule, the keepers of these places were, being jovial men, in no way affected toward the Commons, yet he feared meeting there persons who might question and detain him. He obtained some provision at a small village shop, in which he saw a buxom woman standing behind her counter. She appeared vastly surprised when he entered and asked for a manchet of bread, for the contrast between his ruddy countenance and his Puritan hat and bands was so striking that they could not fail to be noticed. The good woman looked indeed too astonished to be able to attend to Harry's request, and he was obliged to say, "Mother, time presses, and I care not to be caught loitering here."

Divining at once that he was acting a part, and probably endeavoring to escape the pursuit of the Commons, the good woman at once served him with bread and some slices of ham, and putting these in the wallets of the saddle, he rode on.

The next morning, in riding through the village of Wickham, his career was nearly arrested. Just as he passed a sergeant followed by three or four Parliament soldiers came out from an inn, and seeing Harry riding past, addressed him:

"Sir, will it please you to alight, and to offer up a few words of exhortation and prayer?"

Harry muttered something about pressing business. But in his sudden surprise he had not time to think of assuming either the nasal drone or the scriptural words peculiar to these black-coated gentry. Struck by his tone, the sergeant sprang forward and seized his bridle.

"Whom have we here?" he said; "a lad masquerading in the dress of a preacher. This must be explained, young sir."

"Sergeant," Harry said, "I doubt not that thou art a good fellow, and not one to get a lad in a scrape. I am the son of a London citizen; but he and my mother are at present greatly more occupied with the state of their souls than with the carrying on of their carnal business. Being young, the constant offering up of prayers and exhortations has vexed me almost to desperation, and yesterday, while the good preacher who attends then was in the midst of the third hour of his discourse I stole downstairs, and borrowing his hat and cloak, together with his horse, determined to set out to join my uncle, who is a farmer down in Gloucestershire, and where in sooth the companionship of his daughters—girls of my own age—suits my disposition greatly better than that of the excellent men with whom my father consorts."

The soldiers laughed, and the sergeant, who was not at heart a bad fellow, said:

"I fear, my young sir, that your disposition is a godless one, and that it would have been far better for you to have remained under the ministration of the good man whose hat you are wearing than to have sought the society of your pretty cousins. However, I do not know but that in the unregenerate days of my own youth I might not have attempted an escapade like yours. I trust," he

27

continued, "you are not tainted with the evil doctrines of the adherents of King Charles."

"In truth," Harry said, "I worry not my head with politics. I hear so much of them that I am fairly sick of the subject, and have not yet decided whether the Commons is composed of an assembly of men directly inspired with power for the regeneration of mankind, or whether King Charles be a demon in human shape. Methinks that when I grow old enough to bear arms it will be time enough for me to make up my mind against whom to use them. At present, a clothyard is the stick to which I am most accustomed, and as plows and harrows are greatly more in accord with my disposition, I hope that for a long time I shall not see the interior of a shop again; and I trust that the quarrels which have brought such trouble into this realm, and have well-nigh made my father and mother distraught, will at least favor my sojourn in the country, for I am sure that my father will not venture to traverse England for the sake of bringing me back again."

"I am not sure," the sergeant said, "that my duty would not be to arrest you and to send you back to London. But as, in truth, I have no instructions to hinder travelers, I must even let you go."

With a merry farewell to the group, and a laugh far more in accordance with his years than with the costume which he wore, Harry set spurs to his horse and again rode forward.

He met with no further adventure on the road. When he found by inquiries that he had passed the outposts of the Parliament forces, he joyfully threw the hat, the bands, and cloak into a ditch, for experience had taught him that, however useful as a passport they might be while still within the lines of the troops of the Commons, they would be likely to procure him but scant welcome when he entered those of the Royalists. Round Oxford the royal army were encamped, and Harry speedily discovered that his father was with his troop at his own place. Turning his head again eastward, he rode to Abingdon, and quickly afterward was at the hall.

The shout of welcome which the servitor who opened the door uttered when he saw him speedily brought his father to the entrance, and Sir Henry was overjoyed at seeing the son whom he believed to be in confinement in London. Harry's tale was soon told, and the colonel roared with laughter at the thought of his boy masquerading as a Puritan preacher.

"King Charles himself," he said, "might smile over your story, Harry; and in faith it takes a great deal to call up a smile into his majesty's face, which is, methinks a pity, for he would be more loved, and not less respected, did he, by his appearance and manner, do something to raise the spirits of those around him."

When once seated in the hall Harry inquired of his father what progress had been made since he was taken prisoner, for he had heard nothing from his guards.

"Things are as they were," his father said. "After our unfortunate advance we fell back hither, and for six weeks nothing was done. A fortnight since, on the 2d of January, a petition was brought by deputies from the Common Council of London, asking the king to return to the capital when all disturbance should be suppressed. King Charles, however, knew not that these gentlemen had the power to carry out their promises seeing that the seditious have the upper hand in the capital, and answered them to that effect. His answer was, however, methinks, far less conciliatory and prudent than it might have been, for it boots not to stir up men's minds unnecessarily, and with a few affectionate words the king might have strengthened his party in London. The result, however, was to lead to a fierce debate, in which Pym and Lord Manchester addressed the multitude, and stirred them up to indignation, and I fear that prospects of peace are further away than ever. In other respects there is good and bad news. Yorkshire and Cheshire, Devon and Cornwall, have all declared for the crown; but upon the other hand, in the east the prospects are most gloomy. There, the seven counties, Norfolk, Suffolk, Essex, Cambridge, Herts, Lincoln, and Huntingdon, have joined themselves into an association, and the king's followers dare not lift their heads. At Lichfield, Lord Brook, a fierce opponent of bishops and cathedrals, while besieging a party of Cavaliers who had taken possession of the close, was shot in the eye and killed. These are the only incidents that have taken place."

For some weeks no event of importance occurred. On the 22d of February the queen, who had been absent on the Continent selling her jewels and endeavoring to raise a force, landed at Burlington, with four ships, having succeeded in evading the ships of war which the Commons had dispatched to cut her off, under the command of Admiral Batten. That night, however, the Parliament fleet arrived off the place, and opened fire upon the ships and village. The queen was in a house near the shore, and the balls struck in all directions round. She was forced to get up, throw on a few clothes, and retire on foot to some distance from the village to the shelter of a ditch, where she sat for two hours, the balls sometimes striking dust over them, and singing round in all

29

directions. It was a question whether the small force which the queen brought with her was not rather a hindrance than an assistance to the royal cause, for the Earl of Newcastle, who had been sent to escort her to York, was authorized by the king to raise men for the service, without examining their consciences, that is to say, to receive Catholics as well as Protestants. The Parliament took advantage of this to style his army the Catholic Army, and this, and some tamperings with the Papists in Ireland, increased the popular belief that the king leaned toward Roman Catholicism, and thus heightened the feelings against him, and embittered the religious as well as the political quarrel.

Toward the end of March commissioners from the Parliament, under the Earl of Northumberland, came to Oxford with propositions to treat. It is questionable whether the offers of the Commons were sincere. But Charles, by his vacillation and hesitation, by yielding one day and retracting the next, gave them the opportunity of asserting, with some show of reason, that he was wholly insincere, and could not be trusted; and so the commission was recalled, and the war went on again.

On the 15th of April Parliament formally declared the negotiations to be at an end, and on that day Essex marched with his army to the siege of Reading. The place was fortified, and had a resolute garrison; but by some gross oversight no provisions or stores had been collected, and after an unsuccessful attempt to relieve the town, when the Royalist forces failed to carry the bridge at Caversham, they fell back upon Wallingford, and Reading surrendered. Meanwhile skirmishes were going on all over the country. Sir William Waller was successful against the Royalists in the south and west. In the north Lord Newcastle was opposed to Fairfax, and the result was doubtful; while in Cornwall the Royalists had gained a battle over the Parliament men under Lord Stamford.

Meanwhile, the king was endeavoring to create a party in the Parliament, and Lady Aubigny was intrusted with the negotiations. The plot was, however, discovered. Several members of Parliament were arrested, and two executed by orders of the Parliament.

Early in June Colonel Furness and his troop were called into Oxford, as it was considered probable that some expeditions would be undertaken, and on the 17th of that month Prince Rupert formed up his horse and sallied out against the outlying pickets and small troops of the Parliament. Several of these he surprised and cut up, and on the morning of the 19th reached Chalgrove Field, near Thame. Hampden was in command of a detachment of

Parliamentary troops in this neighborhood, and sending word to Essex, who lay near, to come up to his assistance, attacked Prince Rupert's force. His men, however, could not stand against the charge of the Royalists. They were completely defeated, and Hampden, one of the noblest characters of his age, was shot through the shoulder. He managed to keep his horse, and ride across country to Thame, where he hoped to obtain medical assistance. After six days of pain he died there, and thus England lost the only man who could, in the days that were to come, have moderated, and perhaps defeated, the ambition of Cromwell.

Essex arrived upon the scene of battle a few minutes after the defeat of Hampden's force, and Prince Rupert fell back, and crossing the Thames returned to Oxford, having inflicted much damage upon the enemy.

Shortly after this event, one of the serving men rushed in to Harry with the news that a strong band of Parliament horse were within three or four miles of the place, and were approaching. Harry at once sent for the steward, and a dozen men were summoned in all haste. On their arrival they set to work to strip the hall of its most valued furniture. The pictures were taken down from the walls, the silver and plate tumbled into chests, the arms and armor worn by generations of the Furnesses removed from the armory, the choicest articles of furniture of a portable character put into carts, together with some twenty casks of the choicest wine in the cellars, and in four hours only the heavier furniture, the chairs and tables, buffets and heavy sideboards remained in their places.

Just as the carts were filled news came that the enemy had ridden into Abingdon. Night was now coming on, and the carts at once started with their contents for distant farms, where the plate and wine were to be buried in holes dug in copses, and other places little likely to be searched by the Puritans. The pictures and furniture were stowed away in lofts and covered deeply with hay.

Having seen the furniture sent off, Harry awaited the arrival of the Parliament bands, which he doubted not would be dispatched by the Puritans among the townspeople to the hall. The stables were already empty except for Rollo, Harry's own horse. This he had at once, the alarm being given, sent off to a farm a mile distant from the hall, and with it its saddle, bridle, and his arms, a brace of rare pistols, breast and back pieces, a steel cap with plumes, and his sword. It cost him an effort to part with the last, for he now carried it habitually. But he thought that it might be taken from him, and, moreover, he feared that he might be driven into drawing it, when the consequences might be serious, not only for himself, but for the mansion of which his father had left him in charge.

At nine a servitor came in to say that a party of men were riding up the drive. Harry seated himself in the colonel's armchair, and repeated to himself the determination at which he had arrived of being perfectly calm and collected, and of bearing himself with patience and dignity. Presently he heard the clatter of horses' hoofs in the courtyard, and two minutes later, the tramp of feet in the passage. The door opened, and an officer entered, followed by five or six soldiers.

This man was one of the worst types of Roundhead officers. He was a London draper, whose violent harangues had brought him into notice, and secured for him a commission in the raw levies when they were first raised. Harry rose as he entered.

"You are the son of the man who is master of this house?" the officer said roughly.

"I am his son and representative," Harry said calmly.

"I hear that he is a malignant fighting in the ranks of King Charles."

"My father is a colonel in the army of his gracious majesty the king," Harry said.

"You are an insolent young dog!" the captain exclaimed. "We will teach you manners," and rising from the seat into which he had thrown himself on entering the hall, he struck Harry heavily in the face.

The boy staggered back against the wall; then with a bound he snatched a sword from the hand of one of the troopers, and before the officer had time to recoil or throw up his hands, he smote him with all his force across the face. With a terrible cry the officer fell back, and Harry, throwing down the sword, leaped through the open window into the garden and dashed into the shrubberies, as half a dozen balls from the pistols of the astonished troopers whizzed about his head.

For a few minutes he ran at the top of his speed, as he heard shouts and pistol shots behind him. But he knew that in the darkness strangers would have no chance whatever of overtaking him, and he slackened his pace into a trot. As he ran he took himself to task for not having acted up to his resolution. But the reflection that his father would not disapprove of his having cut down the man who had struck him consoled him, and he kept on his way to the farm where he had left his horse. In other respects, he felt a wild delight at what had happened. There was nothing for him now but to join the Royal army, and his father could hardly object to his taking his place with the regiment.

"I wish I had fifty of them here," he thought to himself; "we would surround the hall, and pay these traitors dearly. As for their captain, I would hang him over the door with my own hands. The cowardly ruffian, to strike an unarmed boy! At any rate I have spoiled his beauty for him, for I pretty nearly cut his face in two, I shall know him by the scar if I ever meet him in battle, and then we will finish the quarrel.

"I shall not be able to see out of my right eye in the morning," he grumbled; "and shall be a nice figure when I ride into Oxford."

As he approached the farm he slackened his speed to a walk; and neared the house very carefully, for he thought it possible that one of the parties of the enemy might already have taken up his quarters there. The silence that reigned, broken by the loud barking of dogs as he came close, proved that no stranger had yet arrived, and he knocked loudly at the door. Presently an upper window was opened, and a woman's voice inquired who he was, and what he wanted.

"I am Harry Furness, Dame Arden," he said. "The Roundheads are at the hall, and I have sliced their captain's face; so I must be away with all speed. Please get the men up, and lose not a moment; I want my arms and horse."

The farmer's wife lost no time in arousing the house, and in a very few minutes all was ready. One man saddled the horse, while another buckled on Harry's breast and back pieces; and with a hearty good-by, and amid many prayers for his safety and speedy return with the king's troops, Harry rode off into the darkness. For awhile he rode cautiously, listening intently lest he might fall into the hands of some of the Roundhead bands. But all was quiet, and after placing another mile or two between himself and Abingdon, he concluded that he was safe, drew Rollo's reins tighter, pressed him with his knees, and started at full gallop for Oxford.

# CHAPTER V

# A MISSION OF STATE

When Harry rode into Oxford with the news that the Roundheads had made a raid as far as Abingdon, no time was lost in sounding to boot and saddle, and in half an hour the Cavalier horse were trotting briskly in that direction. They entered Abingdon unopposed, and found to their disgust that the Roundheads had departed an hour after their arrival. A party went up to Furness Hall, and found it also deserted. The Roundheads, in fact, had made but a flying raid, had carried off one or two of the leading Royalists in the town, and had, on their retirement, been accompanied by several of the party favorable to the Commons, among others, Master Rippinghall and the greater portion of his men, who had, it was suspected, been already enrolled for the service of the Parliament. Some of the Royalists would fain have sacked the house of the wool-stapler; but Colonel Furness, who had accompanied the force with his troop, opposed this vehemently.

"As long as we can," he said, "let private houses be respected. If the Puritans commence, it will be time for us to retort. There are gentlemen's mansions all over the country, many of them in the heart of Roundhead neighborhoods, and if they had once an excuse in our proceedings not one of these would be safe for a minute."

Leaving a strong force of horse in Abingdon, Prince Rupert returned to Oxford, and Colonel Furness again settled down in his residence, his troop dispersing to their farms until required, a small body only remaining at Furness Hall as a guard, and in readiness to call the others to arms if necessary. The colonel warmly approved of the steps that Harry had taken to save the valuables, and determined that until the war was at an end these should remain hidden, as it was probable enough that the chances of the strife might again lead the Roundheads thither.

"I hope, father," Harry Furness said the following day, "that you will now permit me to join the troop. I am getting on for sixteen, and could surely bear myself as a man in the fray."

"If the time should come, Harry, when the fortune of war may compel the king to retire from Oxford—which I trust may never be—I would then grant your request, for after your encounter with the officer who commanded the Roundheads here, it would not be safe

34

for you to remain behind. But although you are too young to take part in the war, I may find you employment. After a council that was held yesterday at Oxford, I learned, from one in the king's secrets, that it was designed to send a messenger to London with papers of importance, and to keep up the communication with the king's friends in that city. There was some debate as to who should be chosen. In London, at the present time, all strangers are closely scrutinized. Every man is suspicious of his neighbor, and it is difficult to find one of sufficient trust whose person is unknown. Then I have thought that maybe you could well fulfill this important mission. A boy would be unsuspected, where a man's every movement would be watched. There is, of course, some danger attending the mission, and sharpness and readiness will be needed. You have shown that you possess these, by the manner in which you made your escape from London, and methinks that, did you offer, your services would be accepted. You would have, of course, to go in disguise, and to accept any situation which might appear conformable to your character and add to your safety."

Harry at once gladly assented to the proposal. He was at the age when lads are most eager for adventure, and he thought that it would be great fun to be living in London, watching the doings of the Commons, and, so far as was in his power, endeavoring to thwart them. Accordingly in the afternoon he rode over with Sir Henry to Oxford. They dismounted in the courtyard of the building which served as the king's court, and entering, Sir Henry left Harry in an antechamber, and, craving an audience with his majesty, was at once ushered into the king's cabinet. A few minutes later he returned, and motioned to Harry to follow him. The latter did so, and the next moment found himself in the presence of the king. The latter held out his hand for the boy to kiss, and Harry, falling on one knee, and greatly abashed at the presence in which he found himself, pressed his lips to King Charles' hand.

"I hear from your father, my trusty Sir Henry Furness, that you are willing to adventure your life in our cause, and to go as our messenger to London, and act there as our intermediary with our friends. You seem young for so delicate a work; but your father has told me somewhat of the manner in which you escaped from the hands of the traitors at Westminster, and also how you bore yourself in the affair with the rebels at his residence. It seems to me, then, that we must not judge your wisdom by your years, and that we can safely confide our interests in your hands. Your looks are frank and boyish, and will, therefore, excite far less suspicion than that which would attend upon an older and graver-looking personage. The letters will be prepared for you to-morrow, and, believe me, should success finally crown our efforts against these enemies of the crown, your loyalty and devotion will not be forgotten by your king."

He again held out his hand to Harry, and the boy left the cabinet with his heart burning with loyalty toward his monarch, and resolved that life itself should be held cheap if it could be spent in the service of so gracious and majestic a king.

The next morning a royal messenger brought out a packet of letters to Furness Hall, and Harry, mounting with his father and the little body of horse at the hall, rode toward London. His attire was that of a country peasant boy. The letters were concealed in the hollow of a stout ashen stick which he carried, and which had been slightly weighted with lead, so that, should it be taken up by any but its owner, its lightness would not attract attention. Sir Henry rode with him as far as it was prudent to do toward the outposts of the Parliament troops. Then, bidding him a tender farewell, and impressing upon him the necessity for the utmost caution, both for his own sake and for that of the king, he left him.

It was not upon the highroad that they parted, but near a village some little distance therefrom. In his pocket Harry had two or three pieces of silver, and between the soles of his boots were sewn several gold coins. These he did not anticipate having to use; but the necessity might arise when such a deposit would prove of use. Harry walked quietly through the village, where his appearance was unnoticed, and then along the road toward Reading. He soon met a troop of Parliament horsemen; but as he was sauntering along quietly, as if merely going from one village to another, no attention whatever was paid to him, and he reached Reading without the slightest difficulty. There he took up his abode for the night at a small hostelry, mentioning to the host that his master had wanted him to join the king's forces, but that he had no stomach for fighting, and intended to get work in the town. The following morning he again started, and proceeded as far as Windsor, where he slept. The next day, walking through Hounslow and Brentford, he stopped for the night at the village of Kensington, and the following morning entered the city. Harry had never before been in the streets of London, for in his flight from his prison he had at once issued into the country, and the bustle and confusion which prevailed excited great surprise in his mind. Even Oxford, busy as it was at the time, and full of the troops of the king and of the

36

noblemen and gentlemen who had rallied to his cause, was yet quiet when compared with London. The booths along the main streets were filled with goods, and at these the apprentices shouted loudly to all passer-by, "What d'ye lack? What d'ye lack?" Here was a mercer exhibiting dark cloths to a grave-looking citizen; there an armorer was showing the temper of his wares to an officer. Citizens' wives were shopping and gossiping; groups of men, in high steeple hats and dark cloak, were moving along the streets. Pack horses carried goods from the ships at the wharves below the bridge to the merchants, and Harry was jostled hither and thither by the moving crowd. Ascending the hill of Ludgate to the great cathedral of St. Paul's, he saw a crowd gathered round a person on an elevated stand in the yard, and approaching to see what was going on, found that a preacher was pouring forth anathemas against the king and the Royal party, and inciting the citizens to throw themselves heart and soul into the cause. Especially severe was he upon waverers, who, he said, were worse than downright enemies, as, while the one withstood the Parliament openly in fair fight, the others were shifted to and fro with each breeze, and none could say whether they were friends or enemies. Passing through the cathedral, where regular services were no longer held, but where, in different corners, preachers were holding forth against the king, and where groups of men strolled up and down, talking of the troubles of the times, he issued at the eastern door, and entering Cheapside, saw the sign of the merchant to whom he had been directed.

This was Nicholas Fleming, a man of Dutch descent, and well spoken of among his fellows. He dealt in silks and velvets from Genoa. His shop presented less outward appearance than did those of his neighbors, the goods being too rich and rare to be exposed to the weather, and he himself dealing rather with smaller traders than with the general public. The merchant—a grave-looking man—was sitting at his desk when Harry entered. A clerk was in the shop, engaged in writing, and an apprentice was rolling up a piece of silk. Harry removed his hat, and went up to the merchant's table, and laying a letter upon it, said:

"I have come, sir, from Dame Marjory, my aunt, who was your honor's nurse, with a letter from her, praying you to take me as an apprentice."

The merchant glanced for a moment at the boy. He was expecting a message from the Royalist camp, and his keen wit at once led him to suspect that the bearer stood before him, although his appearance in nowise justified such a thought, for Harry had assumed with his peasant clothes a look of stolid stupidity which certainly gave no warrant for the thought that a keen spirit lay behind it. Without a word the merchant opened the letter, which, in truth, contained nearly the same words which Harry had spoken, but whose signature was sufficient to the merchant to indicate that his suspicions were correct.

"Sit down," he said to the lad. "I am busy now; but will talk with you anon."

Harry took his seat on a low stool, while the merchant continued his writing as before, as if the incident were too unimportant to arrest his attention for a moment. Harry amused himself by looking round the shop, and was specially attracted by the movements of the apprentice, a sharp-looking lad, rather younger than himself, and who, having heard what had passed, seized every opportunity, when he was so placed that neither the merchant nor his clerk could observe his face to make grimaces at Harry, indicative of contempt and derision. Harry was sorely tempted to laugh; but, with an effort, he kept his countenance, assuming only a grim of wonder which greatly gratified Jacob, who thought that he had obtained as companion a butt who would afford him infinite amusement.

After the merchant had continued his writing for an hour, he laid down his pen, and saying to Harry "Follow me; I will speak to Dame Alice, my wife, concerning thee," left the shop and entered the inner portion of the house, followed by Harry. The merchant led him into a sitting-room on the floor above, where his wife, a comely dame, was occupied with her needle.

"Dame," he said, "this is a new apprentice whom my nurse, Marjory, has sent me. A promising-looking youth, is he not?"

His wife looked at him in surprise.

"I have never heard thee speak of thy nurse, Nicholas, and surely the lad looks not apt to learning the mysteries of a trade like thine."

The merchant smiled gravely.

"He must be more apt than he looks, dame, or he would never have been chosen for the service upon which he is engaged. Men do not send fools to risk their lives; and I have been watching him for the last hour, and have observed how he bore himself under the tricks of that jackanapes, Jacob, and verily the wonder which I at first felt when he presented himself to me has passed away, and what appeared to me at first sight a strange imprudence, seems now to be a piece of wisdom. But enough of riddles," he said, seeing that his wife's astonishment increased as he went on. "This lad is a messenger from Oxford, and bears, I doubt not, important documents. What is thy true name, boy?"

"I am Harry Furness, the son of Sir Henry Furness, one of the king's officers," Harry said; "and my papers are concealed within this staff."

Thereupon he lifted his stick and showed that at the bottom a piece of wood had been artfully fitted into a hollow, and then, by being rubbed upon the ground, so worn as to appear part of a solid whole. Taking his knife from his pocket, he cut off an inch from the lower end of the stick, and then shook out on to the table a number of slips of paper tightly rolled together.

"I will examine these at my leisure," the merchant said; "and now as to thyself. What instructions have you?"

"I am told, sir, to take up my abode with you, if it so pleases you; to assume the garb and habits of an apprentice; and, moreover, to do such messages as you may give me, and which, perhaps, I may perform with less risk of observation, and with more fidelity than any ordinary messenger."

"The proposal is a good one," the trader said. "I am often puzzled how to send notes to those of my neighbors with whom I am in correspondence, for the lad Jacob is sharp—too sharp, indeed, for my purpose, and might suspect the purport of his goings and comings. I believe him to be faithful, though overapt to mischief. But in these days one cares not to risk one's neck unless on a surety. The first thing will be, then, to procure for thee a suit of clothes, suitable to thy new position. Under the plea that at present work is but slack—for indeed the troubles of the times have well-nigh ruined the trade in such goods as mine, throwing it all into the hands of the smiths—I shall be able to grant thee some license, and to allow thee to go about and see the city and acquaint thyself with its ways. Master Jacob may feel, perhaps, a little jealous; but this matters not. I somewhat misdoubt the boy, though perhaps unjustly. But I know not how his opinions may go toward matters politic. He believes me, I think, as do other men, to be attached to the present state of things; but even did his thoughts jump otherwise, he would not have opened his lips before me. It would be well, therefore, for you to be cautious in the extreme with him, and to find out of a verity what be his nature and disposition. Doubtless, in time, he will unbosom to you and you may see whether he has any suspicions, and how far he is to be trusted. He was recommended to me by a friend at Poole, and I know not the opinions of his people. I will come forth with you now and order the clothes without delay, and we will return in time for dinner, which will be at twelve, of which time it now lacks half an hour."

Putting on his high hat, the merchant sallied out with Harry into the Cheap, and going to a clothier's was able to purchase ready-made garments suitable to his new position as a 'prentice boy. Returning with these, he bade the lad mount to the room which he was to share Jacob, to change with all speed, and to come down to dinner, which was now nearly ready.

The meal was to Harry a curious one. The merchant sat at one end of the table, his wife at the other. The scrivener occupied a place on one side, and his fellow-apprentice and himself on the other. The merchant spoke to his wife on the troubles of the times in a grave, oracular voice, which appeared to be intended chiefly for the edification of his three assistants, who ate their dinner in silence, only saying a word or two in answer to any question addressed to them. Harry, who was accustomed to dine with his father, was somewhat nice in his ways of eating. But, observing a sudden look of interest and suspicion upon the face of the sharp boy beside him at his manner of eating, he, without making so sudden a change as to be perceptible, gradually fell into the way of eating of his companion, mentally blaming himself severely for having for a moment forgotten his assumed part.

"I shall not need you this afternoon, Roger," the merchant said; "and you can go out and view the sights of the city. Avoid getting into any quarrels or broils, and especially observe the names writ up on the corner of the houses, in order that you may learn the streets and so be able to find your way about should I send you with messages or goods."

Harry spent the afternoon as directed, and was mightily amused and entertained by the sights which he witnessed. Especially was he interested in London Bridge, which, covered closely with houses, stretched across the river, and at the great fleet of vessels which lay moored to the wharves below. Here Harry spent the greater portion of the afternoon, watching the numerous boats as they shot the bridge, and the barges receiving merchandise from the vessels.

At five o'clock the shop was shut, and at six supper was served in the same order as dinner had been. At eight they retired to bed.

"Well, Master Roger," said Jacob, when they were done, "and what is thy father?"

"He farms a piece of land of his own," Harry said. "Sometimes

40

I live with him; but more often with my uncle, who is a trader in Bristol—a man of some wealth, and much respected by the citizens."

"Ah! it is there that thou hast learnt thy tricks of eating," Jacob said. "I wondered to see thee handle thy knife and fork so daintily, and in a manner which assuredly smacked of the city rather than of the farm."

"My uncle," Harry said, "is a particular man as to his habits, and as many leading citizens of the town often take their meals at his house, he was ever worrying me to behave, as he said, more like a Christian than a hog. What a town is this London! What heaps of people, and what wonderful sights!"

"Yes," the apprentice said carelessly. "But you have as yet seen nothing. You should see the giant with eight heads, at the Guildhall."

"A giant with eight heads?" Henry exclaimed wonderingly. "Why, he have five more than the giant whom my mother told me of when I was little, that was killed by Jack, the Giant Killer. I must go and see him of a surety.'"

"You must mind," the apprentice said; "for a boy is served up for him every morning for breakfast."

"Now you are trying to fool me," Harry said. "My mother warned me that the boys of London were wickedly disposed, and given to mock at strangers. But I tell thee, Master Jacob, that I have a heavy fist, and was considered a fighter in the village. Therefore, mind how thou triest to fool me. Mother always said I was not such a fool as I looked."

"You may well be that," Jacob said, "and yet a very big fool. But at present I do not know whether your folly is more than skin deep, and methinks that the respectable trader, your uncle, has taught you more than how to eat like a Christian."

Harry felt at once that in this sharp boy he had a critic far more dangerous than any he was likely to meet elsewhere. Others would pass him unnoticed; but his fellow-apprentice would criticise every act and word, and he felt somewhat disquieted to find that he had fallen under such supervision. It was now, he felt, all-important for him to discover what were the real sentiments of the boy, and whether he was trustworthy to his master, and to be relied upon to keep the secret which had fallen into his possession.

"I have been," he said, "in the big church at the end of this street. What a pother the preachers do surely keep up there. I should be sorely worried to hear them long, and would rather thrash out a load of corn than listen long to the clacking of their tongues."

"Thou wilt be sicker still of them before thou hast done with them. It is one of the duties of us apprentices to listen to the teachers, and if I had my way, we would have an apprentices' riot, and demand to be kept to the terms of our indentures, which say nothing about preachers. What is the way of thinking of this uncle of yours?"

"He is a prudent man," Roger said, "and says but little. For myself, I care nothing either way, and cannot understand what they are making this pother about. So far as I can see, folks only want to be quiet, and do their work. But even in our village at home there is no quiet now. Some are one way, some t'other. There are the Church folk, and the meeting-house folk, and it is as much as they can do to keep themselves from going at each other's throats. I hear so much about it that my brain gets stupid with it all, and I hate Parliament and king worse than the schoolmaster who used to whack me for never knowing the difference between one letter and another."

"But you can read and write, I suppose?" Jacob said; "or you would be of little use as an apprentice."

"Yes, I can read and write," Roger said; "but I cannot say that I love these things. I doubt me that I am not fitter for the plow than for a trade. But my Aunt Marjory was forever going on about my coming to London, and entering the shop of Master Nicholas Fleming, and as it seemed an easy thing to sell yards of silks and velvets, I did not stand against her wishes, especially as she promised that if in a year's time I did not like the life, she would ask Master Nicholas to cancel my indentures, and let me go back again to the farm."

"Ah, well," Jacob said, "it is useful to have an aunt who has been nurse to a city merchant. The life is not a bad one, though our master is strict with all. But Dame Alice is a good housewife, and has a light hand at confections, and when there are good things on the table she does not, as do most of the wives of the traders, keep them for herself and her husband, but lets us have a share also."

"I am fond of confections,", Harry said; "and my Aunt Marjory is famous at them; and now, as I am very sleepy, I will go off. But methinks, Jacob, that you take up hugely more than your share of the bed."

After a little grumbling on both sides the boys disposed themselves to sleep, each wondering somewhat over the character of the other, and determining to make a better acquaintance shortly.

42

# CHAPTER VI

## A NARROW ESCAPE

During the next few days Harry was kept hard at work delivering the various minute documents which he had brought in the hollow of his stick. Sometimes of an evening he attended his master to the houses where he had taken such messages, and once or twice was called in to be present at discussions, and asked to explain various matters connected with the position of the king. During this time he saw but little of the apprentice Jacob, except at his meals, and as the boy did not touch upon his frequent absence, or make any allusion to political matters, when in their bedroom alone at night, Harry hoped that his suspicions had been allayed.

One morning, however, on waking up, he saw the boy sitting upright in bed, staring fixedly at him.

"What is the matter; Jacob, and what are you doing?"

"I am wondering who and what you are!" the boy said.

"I am Roger, your fellow apprentice," Harry replied, laughing.

"I am not sure that you are Roger; I am not sure that you are an apprentice," the boy said. "But if you were, that would not tell me who you are. If you were merely Roger the apprentice, Dame Alice would not pick out all the tit-bits at dinner, and put them on your plate, while I and Master Hardwood have to put up with any scraps which may come. Nor do I think that, even for the purpose of carrying his cloak, our master would take you with him constantly of an evening. He seems mighty anxious too, for you to learn your way about London. I do not remember that he showed any such care as to my geographical knowledge. But, of course, there is a mystery, and I want to get to the bottom of it, and mean to do so if I can."

"Even supposing that there was a mystery," Harry said, "what good would it do to you to learn it, and what use would you make of your knowledge?"

"I do not know," the boy said carelessly. "But knowledge is power."

"You see," Harry said, "that supposing there were, as you say, a mystery, the secret would not be mine to tell, and even were it so before I told it, I should want to know whether you desired to know it for the sake of aiding your master, if possible, or of doing him an injury.

"I would do him no injury, assuredly," Jacob said. "Master Fleming is as good a master as there is in London. I want to find

43

out, because it is my nature to find out. The mere fact that there is a mystery excites my curiosity, and compels me to do all in my power to get to the bottom of it. Methinks that if you have aught that you do not want known, it would be better to take Jacob Plummer into your confidence. Many a man's head has been lost before now because he did not know whom to trust."

"There is no question of losing heads in the matter," Harry said, smiling.

"Well, you know best," Jacob replied, shrugging his shoulders; "but heads do not seem very firmly on at present."

When he went out with Master Fleming that evening Harry related to him the conversation which he had had with Jacob.

"What think you, Master Furness? Is this malapert boy to be trusted, or not?"

"It were difficult to say, sir," Harry answered. "His suspicions are surely roused, and as it seemed to me that his professions of affection and duty toward yourself were earnest, methinks that you might enlist him in your cause, and would find him serviceable hereafter, did you allow me frankly to speak to him. He has friends among the apprentice boys, and might, should he be mischievously inclined, set one to follow us of a night, and learn whither you go; he might even now do much mischief. I think that it is his nature to love plotting for its own sake. He would rather plot on your side than against it; but if you will not have him, he may go against you."

"I have a good mind to send him home to his friends," the merchant said. "He can know nothing as yet."

"He might denounce me as a Royalist," Harry said; "and you for harboring me. I will sound him again to-night, and see further into his intentions. But methinks it would be best to trust him."

That night the conversation was again renewed.

"You see, Jacob," Harry said, "that it would be a serious matter, supposing what you think to be true, to intrust you with the secret. I know not whether you are disposed toward king or Parliament, and to put the lives of many honorable gentlemen into the hands of one of whose real disposition I know little would be but a fool's trick."

"You speak fairly, Roger," the boy said. "Indeed, What I said to you was true. I trouble my head in no way as to the politics and squabbles of the present day; but I mean to rise some day, and there is no better way to rise than to be mixed up in a plot. It is true that the rise may be to the gallows; but if one plays for high stakes, one must risk one's purse. I love excitement, and believe that I am no fool. I can at least be true to the side that I engage upon, and of the two, would rather take that of the king than of the Parliament, because it seems to me that there are more fools on his side than on the other, and therefore more chance for a wise head to prosper."

Harry laughed.

"You have no small opinion of yourself, Master Jacob."

"No," the boy said; "I always found myself able to hold my own. My father, who is a scrivener, predicted me that I should either come to wealth or be hanged, and I am of the same opinion myself."

After further conversation next day with the merchant, Harry frankly confided to Jacob that evening that he was the bearer of letters from the king. Of their contents he said that he knew nothing; but had reason to believe that another movement was on foot for bringing about the overthrow of the party of Puritans who were in possession of the government of London.

"I deemed that such was your errand," the boy said. "You played your part well; but not well enough. You might have deceived grown-up people; but you would hardly take in a boy of your own age. Now that you have told me frankly, I will, if I can, do anything to aid. I care nothing for the opinions of one side or the other; but as I have to go to the cathedral three times on Sunday, and to sit each time for two hours listening to the harangues of Master Ezekiel Proudfoot, I would gladly join in anything which would be likely to end by silencing that fellow and his gang. It is monstrous that, upon the only day in the week we have to ourselves, we should be compelled to undergo the punishment of listening to these long-winded divines."

When Harry was not engaged in taking notes, backward and forward, between the merchant and those with whom he was negotiating, he was occupied in the shop. There the merchant kept up appearances before the scrivener and any customers who might come in, by instructing him in the mysteries of his trade; by showing him the value of the different velvets and silks; and by teaching him his private marks, by which, in case of the absence of the merchant or his apprentice, he could state the price of any article to a trader who might come in. Harry judged, by the conversations which he had with his host, that the latter was not sanguine as to the success of the negotiations which he was carrying on.

"If," he said, "the king could obtain one single victory, his friends would raise their heads, and would assuredly be supported by the great majority of the population, who wish only for peace; but so long as the armies stood facing each other, and the Puritans are all powerful in the Parliament and Council of the city, men are afraid to be the first to move, not being sure how popular support would be given."

One evening after work was over Harry and Jacob walked together up the Cheap, and took their place among a crowd listening to a preacher at Paul's Cross. He was evidently a popular character, and a large number of grave men, of the straitest Puritan appearance, were gathered round him.

"I wish we could play some trick with these somber-looking knaves," Jacob whispered.

"Yes," Harry said; "I would give much to be able to do so; but at the present moment I scarcely wish to draw attention upon myself."

"Let us get out of this, then," Jacob said, "if there is no fun to be had. I am sick of these long-winded orations."

They turned to go, and as they made their way through the crowd, Harry trod upon the toe of a small man in a high steeple hat and black coat.

"I beg your pardon," Harry said, as there burst from the lips of the little man an exclamation which was somewhat less decorous than would have been expected from a personage so gravely clad. The little man stared Harry in the face, and uttered another exclamation, this time of surprise. Harry, to his dismay, saw that the man with whom he had come in contact was the preacher whom he had left gagged on the guardroom bed at Westminster.

"A traitor! A spy!" shouted the preacher, at the top of his voice, seizing Harry by the doublet. The latter shook himself free just as Jacob, jumping in the air, brought his hand down with all his force on the top of the steeple hat, wedging it over the eyes of the little man. Before any further effort could be made to seize them, the two lads dived through the crowd, and dashed down a lane leading toward the river.

This sudden interruption to the service caused considerable excitement, and the little preacher, on being extricated from his hat, furiously proclaimed that the lad he had seized, dressed as an apprentice, was a malignant, who had been taken prisoner at Brentford, and who had foully ill-treated him in a cell in the guardroom at Finsbury. Instantly a number of men set off in pursuit.

"What had we best do, Jacob?" Harry said, as he heard the clattering of feet behind them.

"We had best jump into a boat," Jacob said, "and row for it. It is dark now, and we shall soon be out of their sight."

At the bottom of the lane were some stairs, and at these a number of boats. As it was late in the evening, and the night a foul one, the watermen, not anticipating fares, had left, and the boys, leaping into a boat, put out the sculls, and rowed into the stream, just as their pursuers were heard coming down the lane.

"Which way shall we go?" Harry said.

"We had better shoot the bridge," Jacob replied. "Canst row well?"

"Yes," Harry said; "I have practiced at Abingdon with an oar."

"Then take the sculls," Jacob said, "and I will steer. It is a risky matter going through the bridge, I tell you, at half tide. Sit steady, whatever you do. Here they come in pursuit, Roger. Bend to the sculls," and in a couple of minutes they reached the bridge.

"Steady, steady," shouted Jacob, as the boat shot a fall, some eight feet in depth, with the rapidity of an arrow. For a moment it was tossed and whirled about in the seething waves below, and then, thanks to Jacob's presence of mind and Harry's obedience to his orders, it emerged safely into the smooth water below the bridge. Harry now gave up one of the sculls to Jacob, and the two boys rowed hard down the stream.

"Will they follow, think you?" Harry said.

"I don't think," Jacob laughed, "that any of those black-coated gentry will care for shooting the bridge. They will run down below, and take boat there; and as there are sure to be hands waiting to carry fares out to the ships in the pool, they will gain fast upon us when once they are under way."

The wind was blowing briskly with them, and the tide running strong, and at a great pace they passed the ships lying at anchor.

"There is the Tower," Jacob said; "with whose inside we may chance to make acquaintance, if we are caught. Look," he said, "there is a boat behind us, rowed by four oars! I fear that it is our pursuers."

"Had we not better land, and take our chance?" Harry said.

"We might have done so at first," Jacob said; "it is too late now. We must row for it. Look," he continued, "there is a bark coming along after the boat. She has got her sails up already, and the wind is bringing her along grandly. She sails faster than they row, and if she comes up to us before they overtake us, it may be that the captain will take us in tow. These sea-dogs are always kindly."

The boat that the boys had seized was, fortunately, a very light and fast one, while that in pursuit was large and heavy, and the four watermen had to carry six sitters. Consequently, they gained but very slowly upon the fugitives. Presently a shot from a pistol whizzed over the boys' heads.

"I did not bargain for this, friend Roger," Jacob said. "My

head is made rather for plots and conspiracies than for withstanding the contact of lead."

"Row away!" Harry said. "Here is the ship just alongside now."

As the vessel, which was a coaster, came along, the crew looked over the side, their attention, being called by the sound of the pistol and the shouts of those in chase.

"Throw us a rope, sir," Jacob shouted. "We are not malefactors, but have been up to a boyish freak, and shall be heavily punished if we are caught."

Again the pistol rang out behind, and one of the Sailors threw a rope to the boys. It was caught, and in a minute the boat was gliding rapidly along in the wake of the ship. She was then pulled up alongside, the boys clambered on board, and the boat was sent adrift, The pursuers continued the chase for a few minutes longer, but seeing the ship gradually drawing away from them, they desisted, and turned in toward shore.

"And who are you?" the captain of the brig said.

"We are apprentices, as you see," Jacob said. "We were listening to some preaching at Paul's Cross. In trying to get out from the throng—being at length weary of the long-winded talk of the preacher—we trod upon the feet of a worthy divine. He, refusing to receive our apologies, took the matter roughly, and seeing that the crowd of Puritans around were going to treat us as malignant roisterers, we took the liberty of driving the hat of our assailant over his eyes, and bolting. Assuredly, had we been caught, we should have been put in the stocks and whipped, even if worse pains and penalties had not befallen us, for ill-treatment of one of those who are now the masters of London."

"It was a foolish freak," the captain said, "and in these days such freaks are treated as crimes. It is well that I came along. What do you purpose to do now?"

"We would fain be put ashore, sir, somewhere in Kent, so that we may make our way back again. Our figures could not have been observed beyond that we were apprentices, and we can enter the city quietly, without fear of detection."

The wind dropped in the evening, and, the tide turning, the captain brought to anchor. In the morning he sailed forward again. When he neared Gravesend he saw a vessel lying in the stream.

"That is a Parliament ship," he said.

At that moment another vessel of about the same size as that in which they were was passing her. She fired a gun, and the ship at once dropped her sails and brought up.

48

"What can she be doing now, arresting the passage of ships on their way down? If your crime had been a serious one, I should have thought that a message must have been brought down in the night for her to search vessels coming down stream for the persons of fugitives. What say you, lads? Have you told me the truth?"

"We have told you the truth, sir," Harry said; "but not the whole truth. The circumstances are exactly as my friend related them. But he omitted to say that the preacher recognized in me one of a Cavalier family, and that they may suspect that I was in London on business of the king's."

"Is that so?" the captain said. "In that case, your position is a perilous one. It is clear that they do not know the name of the ship in which you are embarked, or they would not have stopped the one which we see far ahead. If they search the ship, they are sure to find you."

"Can you swim, Jacob?" Harry asked the other.

He nodded.

"There is a point," Harry said, "between this and the vessel of war, and if you sail close to that you will for a minute or two be hidden from the view of those on her deck. If you will take your ship close to that corner we will jump overboard and swim on shore. If then your vessel is stopped you can well say that you have no fugitives on board, and let them search."

The captain thought the plan a good one, and at once the vessel's head was steered over toward the side to which Harry had pointed. As they neared the corner they for a minute lost sight of the hull of the man-of-war, and the boys, with a word of thanks and farewell to the captain, plunged over and swam to the bank, which was but some thirty yards away. Climbing it, they lay down among the grass, and watched the progress of the vessel. She, like the one before, was brought up by a gun from the man-of-war, and a boat from the latter put out and remained by her side for half an hour. Then they saw the boat return, the vessel hoist her sails again, and go on her way.

"This is a nice position into which you have brought me, Master Roger," Jacob said. "My first step in taking part in plots and conspiracies does not appear to me to lead to the end which I looked for. However, I am sick of the shop, and shall be glad of a turn of freedom. Now let us make our way across the marshes to the high land. It is but twenty miles to walk to London, if that be really your intent."

"I shall not return to London myself," Harry said; "but shall make my way back to Oxford. It would be dangerous now for me to

49

appear, and I doubt not that a sharp hue and cry will be kept up. In your case it is different, for as you have been long an apprentice, and as your face will be entirely unknown to any of them, there will be little chance of your being detected."

"I would much rather go with you to Oxford," the lad said. "I am weary of velvets and silks, and though I do not know that wars and battles will be more to my taste, I would fain try them also. You are a gentleman, and high in the trust of the king and those around him. If you will take me with you as your servant I will be a faithful knave to you, and doubt not that as you profit by your advantages, some of the good will fall to my share also."

"In faith," Harry said, "I should hardly like you to be my servant, Jacob, although I have no other office to bestow at present. But if you come with me you shall be rather in the light of a major-domo, though I have no establishment of which you can be the head. In these days, however, the distinctions of master and servant are less broad than before, and in the field we shall be companions rather than master and follower. So, if you like to cast in your fortunes with mine, here is my hand on it. You have already proved your friendship to me as well as your quickness and courage, and believe me, you will not find me or my father ungrateful. But for you, I should now be in the cells, and your old master in no slight danger of finding himself in prison, to say nothing of the upset of the negotiations for which I came to London. Therefore, you have deserved well, not only of me, but of the king, and the adventure may not turn out so badly as it has begun. We had best strike south, and go round by Tunbridge, and thence keeping west, into Berkshire, and so to Oxford. In this way we shall miss the Parliament men lying round London, and those facing the Royalists between Reading and Oxford."

This order was carried out. The lads met with but few questioners, and replying always that they were London apprentices upon their way home to visit their friends for a short time, passed unsuspected. At first the want of funds had troubled them, for Harry had forgotten the money sewn up in his shoe. But presently, remembering this, and taking two gold pieces out of their hiding-place, they went merrily along the road and in five days from starting arrived at Oxford.

# CHAPTER VII

## IN A HOT PLACE

Making inquiries, Harry found that his father was living at a house in the college of Brazenose, and thither he made his way. Not a little surprised was the trooper, who was on guard before the door, to recognize his master's son in one of the two lads who, in the clothes of apprentices shrunk with water and stained with mud and travel, presented themselves before him. Harry ascended at once to Sir Henry's room, and the latter was delighted to see him again, for he had often feared that be had acted rashly in sending him to London. Harry briefly told his adventures, and introduced his friend Jacob to his father.

Sir Henry immediately sent for a clothier, and Harry was again made presentable; while a suit of serviceable clothes adapted to the position of a young gentleman of moderate means was obtained for Jacob. Then, accompanied by his son, Sir Henry went to the king's chambers, and informed his majesty of all that had happened. As, from the reports which had reached the king of the temper of the people of London, he had but small hope that anything would come of the attempt that was being made, he felt but little disappointed at hearing of the sudden return of his emissary. Harry was again asked in, and his majesty in a few words expressed to him his satisfaction at the zeal and prudence which he had shown, and at his safe return to court.

On leaving the king Harry awaited anxiously what his father would determine concerning his future, and was delighted when Sir Henry said, "It is now a year once these troubles began, Harry, and you have so far embarked upon them, that I fear you would find it difficult to return to your studies. You have proved yourself possessed of qualities which will enable you to make your way in the world, and I therefore think the time has come when you can take your place in the ranks. I shall ask of the king a commission for you as captain in my regiment, and as one of my officers has been killed you will take his place, and will have the command of a troop."

Harry was delighted at this intimation; and the following day received the king's commission.

A few days afterward he had again to ride over to Furness Hall, which was now shut up, to collect some rents, and as he returned through Abingdon he saw Lucy Rippinghall walking in the streets. Rather proud of his attire as a young cavalier in full arms, Harry dismounted and courteously saluted her.

"I should hardly have known you, Master Furness," she said. "You look so fierce in your iron harness, and so gay with your plumes and ribands. My brother would be glad to see you. My father as you know, is away. Will you not come in for a few minutes?"

Harry, after a few moments' hesitation, assented. He longed to see his old friend, and as the latter was still residing at Abingdon, while he himself had already made his mark in the royal cause, he did not fear that any misconstruction could be placed upon his visit to the Puritan's abode. Herbert received him with a glad smile of welcome.

"Ah, Harry," he said, "so you have fairly taken to man's estate. Of course, I think you have done wrong; but we need not argue on that now. I am glad indeed to see you. Lucy," he said, "let supper be served at once."

It was a pleasant meal, and the old friends chatted of their schooldays and boyish pastimes, no allusion being made to the events of the day, save that Herbert said, "I suppose that you know that my father is now a captain in the force of the Commons, and that I am doing my best to keep his business going during his absence."

"I had heard as much," Harry answered. "It is a heavy weight to be placed on your shoulders, Herbert."

"Yes," he said, "I am growing learned in wools, and happily the business is not falling off in my hands."

It was characteristic of the civil war in England that during the whole time of its existence the affairs of the country went on as usual. Business was conducted, life and property were safe, and the laws were enforced just as before. The judges went their circuits undisturbed by the turmoil of the times, acting under the authority alike of the Great Seals of the King and Parliament. Thus evildoers were repressed, crime put down, and the laws of the land administered just as usual, and as if no hostile armies were marching and fighting on the fair fields of England. In most countries during such troubled times, all laws have been at an end, bands of robbers and disbanded soldiers have pillaged and ruined the country, person and property alike have been unsafe, private broils and enmities have broken forth, and each man has carried his life in his hand. Thus, even in Abingdon, standing as it did halfway between the stronghold of the crown at Oxford, and the Parliament army at Reading, things remained quiet and tranquil. Its fairs and markets were held as usual, and the course of business went on unchecked.

On his return to Oxford Harry learned that the king, with a portion of the army, was to set out at once for Gloucester, to compel that city, which had declared for the Commons, to open its gates. With a force of thirteen thousand men the king moved upon Gloucester. When he arrived outside its walls, on the 10th of August, he sent a summons to the town to surrender, offering pardon to the inhabitants, and demanding an answer within two hours. Clarendon has described how the answer was returned. "Within less than the time described, together with a trumpeter, returned two citizens from the town with lean, pale, sharp, and bad visages, indeed, faces so strange and unusual, and in such a garb and posture, that at once made the most severe countenances merry, and the most cheerful heart sad, for it was impossible such ambassadors could bring less than a defiance. The men, without any circumstance of duty or good manners, in a pert, shrill, undismayed accent, said that they brought an answer from the godly city of Gloucester to the king, and were so ready to give insolent and seditious answers to any questions, as if their business were chiefly to provoke the king to violate his own safe-conduct." The answers which these strange messengers brought was that the inhabitants and soldiers kept the city for the use of his majesty, but conceived themselves "only bound to obey the commands of his majesty signified by both houses of Parliament." Setting fire to the houses outside their walls, the men of Gloucester prepared for a resolute resistance. The walls were strong and well defended, and the king did not possess artillery sufficient to make breaches therein, and dreading the great loss which an assault upon the walls would inflict upon his army, he determined to starve the city into submission. The inhabitants, although reduced to sore straits, yet relying upon assistance coming to them, held out, and their hopes were not disappointed, as Essex, at the head of a great army, was sent from London to relieve the place. Upon his approach, the king and his councilors, deciding that a battle could not be fought with advantage, drew off from the town, and gave up the siege.

Both armies now moved in the direction of London; but Prince Rupert, hearing that a small body of Parliament horse were besieging the house of Sir James Strangford, an adherent of the crown, took with him fifty horse, and rode away to raise the siege, being ever fond of dashing exploits in the fashion of the knights of old. The body which he chose to accompany him was the troop commanded by Harry Furness, whose gayety of manner and lightness of heart had rendered him a favorite with the prince. The besieged house was situated near Hereford; and at the end of a long day's march Prince Rupert, coming in sight of the Roundheads, charged them with such fury that they were overthrown with scarce any resistance, and fled in all directions. Having effected his object, the prince now rode to Worcester, where he slept, and thence by a long day's march to a village where he again halted for the night.

An hour after his arrival, a messenger came in from Lady Sidmouth, the wife of Sir Henry Sidmouth, asking him to ride over and take up his abode for the night at her house. Bidding Harry accompany him, the prince rode off, leaving the troop under the charge of Harry's lieutenant, Jacob, who had proved himself an active soldier, and had been appointed to that rank at Gloucester. The house was a massive structure of the reign of Henry VIII.; but being built at a time when the castellated abodes were going out of fashion, was not capable of standing a siege, and had not indeed been put in any posture of defense. Sir Henry was with the king, and only a few retainers remained in the house. Prince Rupert was received at the entrance by Lady Sidmouth, who had at her side her daughter, a girl of fourteen, whom Harry thought the most beautiful creature he had ever seen. The prince alighted, and doffing his broad plumed hat, kissed the lady's hand, and conducted her into the house again, Harry doing the same to her daughter.

"You must pardon a rough reception," the lady said to the prince. "Had I had notice of your coming, I would have endeavored to receive you in a manner more befitting; but hearing from one of my retainers, who happened to be in the village when you arrived, of your coming, I thought that the accommodation—poor as it is— would be better than that which you could obtain there."

Prince Rupert replied gayly, and in a few minutes they were seated at supper. The conversation was lightly kept up, when suddenly a tremendous crash was heard, shouts of alarm were raised, and a retainer rushed into the hall, saying that the place was attacked by a force of Roundheads.

"Defense is hopeless," the lady said, as Prince Rupert and Harry drew their swords. "There are but five or six old men here, and the door appears to be already yielding. There is a secret chamber here where you can defy their search."

Prince Rupert, dreading above all things to be taken prisoner, and seeing that resistance would be, as their hostess said, vain, followed her into an adjoining room hung with arras. Lifting this, she showed a large stone. Beneath it, on the floor was a tile, in no way differing from the others. She pressed it, and the stone, which was but slight, turned on a hinge, and disclosed an iron door. This she opened with a spring, showing a small room within, with a ladder leading to another above.

"Mount that," she said. "You will find in the chamber above a large stone. Pull the ladder up with you and lower the stone, which exactly fits into the opening. Even should they discover this chamber, they will not suspect that another lies above it."

Prince Rupert, taking a light from her hands, hastily mounted, followed by Harry, and pulled the steps after him, just as they heard the iron door close. It needed the united strength of the prince and Harry to lift the stone, which was a large one, with an iron ring in the center, and to place it in the cavity. Having done this, they looked round. The room was about eight feet long by six wide, and lighted by a long narrow loophole extending from the ground to the roof. They deemed from its appearance that it was built in one of the turrets of the building.

"That was a narrow escape, Master Harry," the prince said. "It would have been right bad news for my royal uncle if I had been caught here like a rat in a trap. I wonder we heard nothing of a Roundhead force in this neighborhood. I suppose that they must have been stationed at some place further north, and that the news of our passing reached them. I trust that they have no suspicion that we are in the house; but I fear, from this sudden attack upon an undefended building, that some spy from the village must have taken word to them."

Lady Sidmouth had just time to return to the hall when the doors gave way, and a body of Roundheads burst into the room. They had drawn swords in their hands, and evidently expected an attack. They looked round with surprise at seeing only Lady Sidmouth and her daughter.

"Where is the malignant Rupert?" the leader exclaimed. "We have sure news that he rode, attended by an officer only, hither, and that he was seen to enter your house."

"If you want Prince Rupert, you must find him," the lady said calmly. "I say not that he has not been here; but I tell you that he is now beyond your reach."

"He has not escaped," the officer said, "for the house is surrounded. Now, madam, I insist upon your telling me where you have hidden him."

"I have already told you, sir, that he is beyond your reach, and

55

nothing that you can do will wring any further explanation from me."

The officer hesitated. For a moment he advanced a step toward her, with a menacing gesture. But, heated as the passions of men were, no violence was done to women, and with a fierce exclamation he ordered his troopers to search the house. For a quarter of an hour they ransacked it high and low, overturned every article of furniture, pulling down the arras, and tapping the walls with the hilts of their swords.

"Take these two ladies away," he said to his lieutenant, "and ride with them at once to Storton. They will have to answer for having harbored the prince."

The ladies were immediately taken off, placed on pillions behind two troopers, and carried away to Storton. In the meantime the search went on, and presently the hollow sound given by the slab in the wall was noticed. The spring could not be discovered, but crowbars and hammers being brought, the slab of stone was presently shivered. The discovery of the iron door behind it further heightened their suspicion that the place of concealment was found. The door, after a prolonged resistance, was battered in. But the Roundheads were filled with fury, on entering, to discover only a small, bare cell, with no signs of occupation whatever. The search was now prolonged in other directions; but, becoming convinced that it was useless, and that the place of concealment was too cunningly devised to admit of discovery, the captain ordered the furniture to be piled together, and setting light to it and the arras in several places, withdrew his men from the house, saying that if a rat would not come out of his hole, he must be smoked in it.

The prince and Harry from their place of concealment had heard the sound of blows against the doors below.

"They have found the way we have gone," the prince said, "but I think not that their scent is keen enough to trace us up here. If they do so, we will sell our lives dearly, for I will not be taken prisoner, and sooner or later our troop will hear of the Roundheads' attack, and will come to our rescue."

They heard the fall of the iron door, and the exclamations and cries with which the Roundheads broke into the room below. Then faintly they heard the sound of voices, and muffled knocks, as they tried the walls. Then all was silent again.

"The hounds are thrown off the scent," the prince said. "It will need a clever huntsman to put them on it. What will they do next, I wonder?"

Some time passed, and then Harry exclaimed:

"I perceive a smell of something burning, your royal highness."

"Peste! methinks I do also," the prince said. "I had not thought of that. If these rascals have set fire to the place we shall be roasted alive here."

A slight wreath of smoke was seen curling up through the crevice of the tightly-fitting stone.

"We will leap out, and die sword in hand," the prince said; and seizing the ring, he and Harry pulled at it. Ere they raised the stone an inch, a volume of dense smoke poured up, and they at once dropped it into its place again, feeling that their retreat was cut off. The prince put his sword in its scabbard.

"We must die, my lad," he said. "A strange death, too, to be roasted in a trap. But after all, whether by that or the thrust of a Roundhead sword makes little difference in the end. I would fain have fallen in the field, though."

"Perhaps," Harry suggested, "the fire may not reach us here. The walls are very thick, and the chamber below is empty."

The prince shook his head.

"The heat of the fire in a house like this will crack stone walls," he said.

He then took off his cloak and threw it over the stone, dressing it down tightly to prevent the smoke from curling in. Through the loophole they could now hear a roar, and crackling sounds, and a sudden glow lit up the country.

"The flames are bursting through the windows," Harry said. "They will bring our troop down ere long."

"The troop will do us no good," Prince Rupert replied. "All the king's army could not rescue us. But at least it would be a satisfaction before we die to see these crop-eared knaves defeated."

Minute after minute passed, and a broad glare of light illumined the whole country round. Through the slit they could see the Roundheads keeping guard round the house in readiness to cut off any one who might seek to make his escape, while at a short distance off they had drawn up the main body of the force. Presently, coming along the road at a rapid trot, they saw a body of horse.

"There are our men," the prince exclaimed.

The Roundheads had seen them too. A trumpet was sounded, and the men on guard round the house leaped to their horses, and joined the main body, just as the Cavaliers charged upon them. The

Roundheads fought stoutly; but the charge of the Cavaliers was irresistible. Furious at the sight of the house in flames, and ignorant of the fate which had befallen their prince and their master's son, they burst upon the Roundheads with a force which the latter were unable to withstand. For four or five minutes the fight continued, and then such of the Roundheads as were able clapped spurs to their horses and galloped off, hotly pursued by the Cavaliers. The pursuit was a short one. Several of the Cavaliers were gathered at the spot where the conflict had taken place, and were, apparently, questioning a wounded man. Then the trumpeter who was with them sounded the recall, and in a few minutes the Royalist troops came riding back. They could see Jacob pointing to the burning building and gesticulating with his arms. Then a party dashed up to the house, and were lost to sight.

The prince and Harry both shouted at the top of their voices, but the roar of the flames and the crash of falling beams deadened the sound. The heat had by this time become intense. They had gradually divested themselves of their clothing, and were bathed in perspiration.

"This heat is terrific," Prince Rupert said. "I did not think the human frame could stand so great a heat. Methinks that water would boil were it placed here."

This was indeed the case—the human frame, as is now well known, being capable of sustaining a heat considerably above that of boiling water. The walls were now so hot that the hand could not be borne upon them for an instant.

"My feet are burning!" the prince exclaimed, "Reach down that ladder from the wall."

They laid the ladder on the ground and stood upon it, thus avoiding any contact with the hot stone.

"If this goes on," Prince Rupert said, with a laugh; "there will be nothing but our swords left. We are melting away fast, like candles before a fire. Truly I do not think that there was so much water in a man as has floated down from me during the last half-hour."

Harry was so placed that he could command a sight through the loophole, and he exclaimed, "They are riding away!"

This was indeed the case. The whole building was now one vast furnace, and having from the first no hope that their friends, if there, could have survived, they had, hearing that Lady Sidmouth and her daughter had been taken to Storton, determined to ride thither to take them from the hands of the Roundheads, and to learn from them the fate of their leaders.

Another two hours passed. The heat was still tremendous, but they could not feel that it was increasing. Once or twice they heard terrific crashes, as portions of the wall fell. They would long since have been roasted, were it not for the cool air which flowed in through the long loophole, and keeping up a circulation in the chamber, lowered the temperature of the air within it. At the end of the two hours Harry gave a shout.

"They are coming back."

The light had now sunk to a quiet red glow, so that beyond the fact that a party was approaching, nothing could be seen. They rode, however, directly toward the turret, and then, when they halted, Harry saw the figures of two ladies who were pointing toward the loophole. Harry now stepped from the ladder on to the door and shouted at the top of his voice through the loophole. The reply came back in a joyous shout.

"We are being roasted alive," Harry cried. "Get ladders as quickly as possible, with crowbars, and break down the wall."

Men were seen to ride off in several directions instantly, and for the first time a ray of hope illumined, the minds of the prince and Harry that they might be saved. Half an hour later long ladders tied together were placed against the wall, and Jacob speedily made his appearance at the loophole.

"All access is impossible from the other side," he said, "for the place where the house stood is a red-hot furnace, Most of the walls have fallen. We had no hope of finding you alive."

"We are roasting slowly," Harry cried. "In Heaven's name bring us some water."

Soon a bottle of water was passed in through the loophole, and then three or four ladders being placed in position, the men outside began with crowbars and pickaxes to enlarge the loophole sufficiently for the prisoners to escape. It took three hours' hard work, at the end of which time the aperture was sufficiently wide to allow them to emerge, and utterly exhausted and feeling, as the prince said, "baked to a turn," they made their way down the ladder, being helped on either side by the men, for they themselves were too exhausted to maintain their feet.

# CHAPTER VIII

## THE DEFENSE OF AN OUTPOST

The effect of the fresh air and of cordials poured down their throats soon restored the vigor to Prince Rupert and Harry Furness. They were still weak, for the great effort which nature had made to resist the force of the heat during those long hours had taxed their constitutions to the utmost.

Lady Sidmouth was rejoiced indeed to find them alive, for she had made sure that they were lost. It was not until she had been placed in a room strongly barred, and under a guard at Storton, that she perceived the light arising from her residence, and guessed that the men of the Commons, unable to find the hiding-place of Prince Rupert, had set it on fire. Then she had knocked loudly at the door; but the sentry had given no answer either to that or to her entreaties for a hearing. She soon, indeed, desisted from her efforts, for the fire which blazed up speedily convinced her that all hope was gone. When Jacob and the Royalists arrived, driving out the small remnant of the Roundheads who remained in the village, he had found Lady Sidmouth and her daughter bathed in tears, under the belief that their guests had perished in the old house that they loved so well. It was with no hope that they had mounted on the instant, and ridden at full gallop to the castle, and it was not until they saw that that wall was still standing that even the slightest hope entered their minds. Even then it appeared incredible that any one could be alive, and the shout from the loophole had surprised almost as much as it had delighted them.

In the course of three or four hours, refreshed and strengthened by a hearty breakfast and draughts of burgundy, the prince and Harry mounted their horses. Lady Sidmouth determined to remain for a few days at one of her tenant's houses, and then to go quietly on to Oxford—for by this time the main army of Essex was rapidly moving east, and the country would soon be secure for her passage. The prince and Harry rode at full speed to rejoin the army. That night, by riding late, they reached it. They found that Essex had, in his retreat, surprised Cirencester and had passed Farringdon.

The prince, with five thousand horse, started, and marching with great rapidity, got between Reading and the enemy, and, near Newbury, fell upon the Parliament horse. For several hours sharp skirmishing went on, and Essex was forced to halt his army at

Hungerford. This gave time for the king, who was marching at the head of his infantry, to come up. The royal army occupied Newbury, and by the position they had taken up, were now between the Roundheads and London.

On the morning of the 20th of September the outpost of each force became engaged, and the battle soon raged along the whole line. It was to some extent a repetition of the battle of Edgehill. Prince Rupert, with his Cavaliers, swept away the horse of the enemy; but the pikemen of London, who now first were tried in combat, forced back the infantry of the king. Prince Rupert, returning from the pursuit, charged them with all his cavalry; but so sharply did they shoot, and so steadily did the line of pikes hold together, that the horse could make no impression upon them.

The night fell upon an undecided battle, and the next morning the Roundheads, as at Edgehill, drew off from the field, leaving to the Royalists the honor of a nominal success, a success, however, which was in both cases tantamount to a repulse.

Three leading men upon the king's side fell—Lords Falkland, Carnarvon, and Sunderland. The former, one of the finest characters of the times, may be said to have thrown away his life. He was utterly weary of the terrible dissensions and war in which England was plunged. He saw the bitterness increasing on both sides daily—the hopes of peace growing less and less; and as he had left the Parliamentary party, because he saw that their ambition was boundless, and that they purposed to set up a despotic tyranny, so he must have bitterly grieved at seeing upon the side of the king a duplicity beyond all bounds, and want of faith which seemed to forbid all hope of a satisfactory issue. Thus, then, when the day of Newbury came, Falkland, whose duties in nowise led him into the fight, charged recklessly and found the death which there can be little doubt he sought.

Although the Cavaliers claimed Newbury as a great victory, instead of advancing upon London they fell back as usual to Oxford.

During the skirmishes Harry had an opportunity of doing a service to an old friend. The Parliament horse, although valiant and better trained than that of the Royalists, were yet unable to withstand the impetuosity with which the latter always attacked, the men seeming, indeed, to be seized with a veritable panic at the sight of the gay plumes of Rupert's gentlemen. In a fierce skirmish between Harry's troop and a party of Parliament horse of about equal strength, the latter were defeated, and Harry, returning with the main body, found a Puritan officer dismounted, with his back against a tree, defending himself from the attacks of three of his men. Harry rode hastily up and demanded his surrender. The officer looked up, and to his surprise Harry saw his friend Herbert.

"I am your prisoner, Harry," Herbert said, as he lowered the point of his sword.

"Not at all!" Harry exclaimed. "It would indeed be a strange thing, Herbert, were I to make you a prisoner. I thought you settled at Abingdon?"

Ordering one of his troopers to catch a riderless horse which was galloping near, he spoke for a moment or two with his friend, and then, as the horse was brought up, he told him to mount and ride.

"But you may get into trouble for releasing me," Herbert said.

"I care not if I do," Harry replied. "But you need not be uneasy about me, for Prince Rupert will stand my friend, and hold me clear of any complaint that may be made. I will ride forward with you a little, till you can join your friends."

As Harry rode on by the side of Herbert a Royalist officer, one Sir Ralph Willoughby, dashed up.

"What means this?" he exclaimed. "Do I see an officer of his majesty riding with one of the Roundheads? This is treason and treachery!"

"I will answer to the king, if need be," Harry said, "for my conduct. I am not under your orders, Sir Ralph, and shall use my discretion in this matter. This gentleman is as a brother to me."

"And I would cut down my brother," Sir Ralph said furiously, "if I found him in the ranks of the enemy!"

"Then, sir, we differ," Harry replied, "for that would not I. There are your friends," he said to Herbert, pointing to a body of Roundheads at a short distance, "Give me your word, however, that you will not draw sword again to-day."

Herbert readily gave the required promise, and riding off, was soon with his friends. Sir Ralph and Harry came to high words after he had left; and the matter might then and there have been decided by the sword, had not a party of Roundheads, seeing two cavalry officers so near to them, charged down, and compelled them to ride for their lives.

The following day Sir Ralph reported the circumstance to the general, and he to Prince Rupert. The prince laughed at the charge.

"Harry Furness," he said, "is as loyal a gentleman as draws sword in our ranks, and as he and I have been well-nigh roasted together, it were vain indeed that any complaint were made to me touching his honor. I will speak to him, however, and doubt not that his explanation will be satisfactory."

The prince accordingly spoke to Harry, who explained the circumstances of his relations with the young Roundhead.

"Had he been a great captain, sir," Harry said, "I might have deemed it my duty to hold him in durance, however near his relationship to myself. But as a few weeks since he was but a schoolboy, methought that the addition of his sword to the Roundhead cause would make no great difference in our chances of victory that afternoon. Moreover, I had received his pledge that he would not draw sword again in the battle."

As even yet, although the bitterness was quickly increasing, it was far from having reached that point which it subsequently attained, and prisoners on both sides were treated with respect, no more was said regarding Harry's conduct in allowing his friend to escape. But from that moment, between himself and Sir Ralph Willoughby there grew up a strong feeling of animosity, which only needed some fitting pretext to break out.

It was, indeed, an unfortunate point in the royal cause, that there was very far from being unity among those who fought side by side. There were intrigues and jealousies. There were the king's men, who would have supported his majesty in all lengths to which he might have gone, and who were ever advising him to resist all attempts at pacification, and to be content with nothing less than a complete defeat of his enemies. Upon the other hand, there were the grave, serious men, who had drawn the sword with intense reluctance, and who desired nothing so much as peace—a peace which would secure alike the rights of the crown and the rights of the people.

They were shocked, too, by the riotous and profligate ways of some of the wilder spirits, and deemed that their cause was sullied by the reckless conduct and wild ways of many of their party. Sir Henry Furness belonged to this section of the king's adherents, and Harry, who had naturally imbibed his father's opinions, held himself a good deal aloof from the wild young spirits of the king's party.

Skirmishes took place daily between the cavalry outposts of the two armies. Sir Henry was asked by the prince to send some of his troops across the river to watch the enemy, and he chose that commanded by Harry, rather for the sake of getting the lad away from the temptations and dissipation of Oxford than to give him an opportunity of distinguishing himself. The troop commanded by Sir Ralph Willoughby was also on outpost duty, and lay at no great distance from the village in which Harry quartered his men after crossing the river. The Roundhead cavalry were known to be but three or four miles away, and the utmost vigilance was necessary.

Harry gave orders that the troops should be distributed through the village—five men to a house. Straw was to be brought in at night, and laid on the floor of the kitchens, and the men were there to sleep, with their arms by their sides, ready for instant service. One of each party was to stand sentry over the five horses which were to be picketed to the palings in front of the house. At the first alarm he was at once to awake his comrades, who were to mount instantly, and form in column in the street. Two pickets were placed three hundred yards from the village, and two others a quarter of a mile further in advance. Harry and Jacob took up their residence in the village inn, and arranged alternately to visit the pickets and sentries every two hours.

"They shall not catch us napping, Jacob. This is my first command on detached duty. You and I have often remarked upon the reckless ways of our leaders. We have an opportunity now of carrying our own ideas into effect."

At three o'clock Jacob visited the outposts. All was still, and nothing had occurred to give rise to any suspicion of the vicinity of an enemy. Half an hour later one of the advanced pickets galloped in. They heard, he said, a noise as of a large body of horse, away to the right, and it seemed as if it was proceeding toward Chalcombe, the village where Sir Ralph Willoughby's troop was quartered. Two minutes later, thanks to Harry's arrangements, the troop were mounted and in readiness for action.

The first faint dawn of day had begun. Suddenly the stillness was broken by the sound of pistol shots and shouts from the direction of Chalcombe, which lay a mile away.

"It is likely," Harry said, "that Sir Ralph has been caught napping. He is brave, but he is reckless, and the discipline of his troop is of the slackest. Let us ride to his rescue."

The troop filed out from the village, and turned down the side road leading to Chalcombe. Harry set spurs to his horse and led the column at a gallop. The sound of shots continued without intermission, and presently a bright light shot up.

"Methinks," Harry said to Jacob, "the Roundheads have caught our men asleep, and it is an attack upon the houses rather than a cavalry fight."

It was scarcely five minutes from the time they started when they approached the village. By the light of a house which had been set on fire, Harry saw that his conjecture was well founded. The Roundheads were dismounted, and were attacking the houses.

Halting just outside the village, Harry formed his men with a front across the whole road, and directed the lines to advance, twenty yards apart. Then, placing himself at their head, he gave the word, and charged down the street upon the Roundheads. The latter, occupied by their attack upon the houses, were unconscious of the presence of their foe until he was close upon them, and were taken utterly by surprise. The force of the charge was irresistible, and the Roundheads, dispersed and on foot, were cut down in all directions. Groups of twos and threes stood together and attempted resistance, but the main body thought only of regaining their horses. In three minutes after the Royalists entered the village the surviving Roundheads were in full flight, hotly pursued by the victorious Cavaliers. These, being for the most part better mounted, overtook and slew many of the Roundheads, and not more than half the force which had set out returned to their quarters at Didcot. The pursuit continued to within half a mile of that place, and then Harry, knowing that there was a force of Roundhead infantry there, drew off from the pursuit, and returned to Chalcombe. He found that more than half of Sir Ralph Willoughy's men had been killed, many having been cut down before they could betake themselves to their arms, those quartered in the inn, and at two or three of the larger houses, having alone maintained a successful resistance until the arrival of succor.

Sir Ralph Willoughby was furious. The disaster was due to his own carelessness in having contented himself with placing two pickets in advance of the village, and permitting the whole remainder of his force to retire to bed. Consequently the picket, on riding in upon the approach of the enemy, were unable to awake and call them to arms before the Roundheads were upon them. In his anger he turned upon Harry, and fiercely demanded why he had not sent him news of the approach of the enemy.

"You must have known it," he said. "Your men were all mounted and in readiness, or they could not have arrived here so soon. You must have been close at hand, and only holding off in order that you might boast of having come to my relief."

Harry, indignant at these words, turned on heel without deigning to give an answer to the angry man, and at once rode back to his own quarters. Two hours later Prince Rupert rode up. The firing had been reported, and Prince Rupert had ridden with a body of horse to Chalcombe. Here he had heard Sir Ralph Willoughby's version of the story, and had requested that officer to ride with him to Harry's quarters. The prince, with several of his principal officers, alighted at the inn, outside which Harry received him. Prince Rupert led the way into the house.

"Master Furness," he said, "Sir Ralph Willoughby accuses you of having played him false, and left his party to be destroyed on account of the quarrel existing between you, touching that affair at

Newbury. What have you to say to this? He alleges that you must have been close at hand, and moved not a finger to save him until half his troop was destroyed."

"It is wholly false, sir," Harry said. "Seeing that the enemy were so close, I had placed my pickets well in advance, and ordered my men to lie down in their clothes, with their arms beside them, on straw in the kitchens, ready to mount at a moment's warning. I quartered five in each house, having their horses fastened in front, and one of each party stationed at the door, where he could observe the horses and wake the men on the instant. Thus, when my pickets came in with the news that troops were heard moving toward Chalcombe, my troop was in less than two minutes in the saddle. As we rode out of the village we heard the first shot, and five minutes later charged the Roundheads in the streets of the village. Had we not hastened, methinks that neither Sir Ralph Willoughby nor any of his troops would have been alive now to tell the tale. You can question, sir, my lieutenant, or any of my troopers, and you will hear that matters went precisely as I have told you."

"You have done well indeed, Master Furness," Prince Rupert said warmly, "and I would that many of my other officers showed the same circumspection and care as you have done. Now, Sir Ralph, let me hear what arrangements you made against surprise."

"I set pickets in front of the village," Sir Ralph said sulkily.

"And what besides?" the prince asked. "Having done that, did you and your officers and men go quietly to sleep, as if the enemy were a hundred miles away?"

Sir Ralph was silent.

"Fie, for shame, sir!" the prince said sternly. "Your own carelessness has brought disaster upon you, and instead of frankly owning your fault, and thanking Master Furness for having redeemed your error, saved the remnant of your troop, and defeated the Roundheads heavily, your jealousy and envy of the lad have wrought you to bring false accusations against him. Enough, sir," he said peremptorily, seeing the glance of hatred which Sir Ralph cast toward Harry. "Sufficient harm has been done already by your carelessness—see that no more arises from your bad temper. I forbid this quarrel to go further; until the king's enemies are wholly defeated there must be no quarrels between his friends. And should I hear of any further dispute on your part with Master Furness, I shall bring it before the king, and obtain his warrant for your dismissal from this army."

The following day Harry and his troop moved further down the river, the enemy having fallen back from Didcot. He was placed at a village where there was a ford across the river. The post was of importance, as its position prevented the enemy from making raids into the country, where stores of provisions and cattle had been collected for the use of the army at Oxford. Harry's force was a small one for the defense of such a post; but there appeared little danger of an attack, as Prince Rupert, with a large force of cavalry, lay but a mile or two distant. A few days after their arrival, however, Prince Rupert started with his horse to drive back a party of the enemy whom he heard were lying some miles north of Reading.

"Prince Rupert never seems to have room for two ideas in his head at the same time," Jacob said. "The moment he hears of an enemy off he rides at full gallop, forgetting that he has left us alone here. It is well if the Roundheads at Reading do not sally out and attack us, seeing how useful this ford would be to them."

"I agree with you, Jacob, and we will forthwith set to work to render the place as defensible as we may."

"We had best defend the other side of the ford, if they advance," Jacob said. "We could make a far better stand there."

"That is true, Jacob; but though we could there bar them from entering our country, they, if they obtained the village, would shut the door to our entering theirs. No, it is clear that it our duty to defend the village as long as we can, if we should be attacked."

Harry now set his men to work to make loopholes in the cottages and inclosure walls, and to connect the latter by banks of earth, having thorn branches set on the top. Just at the ford itself stood a large water-mill, worked by a stream which here ran into the river. Harry placed sacks before all the windows, leaving only loopholes through which to fire. Some of the troop carried pistols only; others had carbines; and some, short, wide-mouthed guns, which carried large charges of buckshot. Pickets were sent forward a mile toward Reading.

Early in the afternoon these galloped in with the news that a heavy column of infantry and cavalry, with two pieces of artillery, were approaching along the road. Harry at once dispatched a messenger, with orders to ride until he found Prince Rupert, to tell him of the state he was in, and ask him to hurry to his assistance, giving assurance that he would hold the village as long as possible. All now labored vigorously at the works of defense. Half an hour after the alarm had been given the enemy were seen approaching.

"There must be over five hundred men, horse and foot," Jacob said, as from the upper story of the mill he watched with Harry the approach of the enemy. "With fifty men we shall never be able to defend the circuit of the village."

"Not if they attack all round at once," Harry agreed. "But probably they will fall upon us in column, and behind stone walls we can do much. We must keep them out as long as we can; then fall back here, and surround ourselves with a ring of fire."

As soon as it was known that the enemy were approaching Harry had given orders that all the inhabitants should evacuate their houses and cross the river, taking with them such valuables as they could carry. There were several horses and carts in the village, and these were at once put in requisition, and the people crossing and recrossing the river rapidly carried most of their linen and other valuables over in safety, the men continuing to labor for the preservation of their goods, even after the fight commenced.

The Roundheads halted about four hundred yards from the village. Just as they did so there was a trampling of horses, and Sir Ralph Willoughby, with his troop, now reduced to thirty strong, rode into the village. He drew up his horse before Harry.

"Master Furness," he said, "Prince Rupert has forbidden me to test your courage in the way gentlemen usually do so. But there is now a means open. Let us see which will ride furthest—you or I— into the ranks of yonder horsemen."

Harry hesitated a moment; then he said gravely:

"My life is not my own to throw away, Sir Ralph. My orders are to hold this place. That I can best do on foot, for even if our troops united were to rout the enemy's cavalry, their footmen would still remain, and would carry the village. No, sir, my duty is to fight here."

"I always thought you a coward!" Sir Ralph exclaimed; "now I know it," and, with a taunting laugh, he ordered his men to follow him, issued from the village, and prepared, with his little band, to charge the Roundhead horse, about a hundred and fifty strong.

Just as they formed line, however, the enemy's' guns opened, and a shot struck Sir Ralph full in the chest, hurling him, a shattered corpse, to the ground.

His men, dismayed at the fall of their leader, drew rein.

"Fall back, men," Harry shouted from behind, "fall back, and make a stand here. You must be cut to pieces if you advance."

The troop, who had no other officer with them, at once obeyed Harry's orders. They had heard the conversation between him and their leader, and although prepared to follow Sir Ralph, who was the landlord of most of them, they saw that Harry was right, and that to attack so numerous a body of horse and foot was but to invite destruction.

# CHAPTER IX

## A STUBBORN DEFENSE

A half-dozen or so of Sir Ralph Willoughby's troopers declared that now their lord was dead they would fight no further, and straightway rode off through the village and across the ford. The rest, however, seeing that a brave fight against odds was about to commence, declared their willingness to put themselves under Harry's orders. They were at once dismounted and scattered along the line of defenses. After the Roundhead cannon had fired a few shots their cavalry charged, thinking to ride into the village. But the moment Sir Ralph's troopers had re-entered it Harry had heaped up across the road a quantity of young trees and bushes which he had cut in readiness. Not a shot was fired until the horsemen reached this obstacle, and then so heavy a fire was poured upon them, as they dismounted and tried to pull it asunder, that, with a loss of many men, they were forced to retreat.

The infantry now advanced, and a severe fight began. Harry's eighty men, sheltered behind their walls, inflicted heavy damage upon the enemy, who, however, pressed on stoutly, one column reaching the obstruction across the road, and laboring to destroy it. All the horses, with the exception of twenty, had been sent across the ford, and when Harry saw that in spite of the efforts of his men the enemy were destroying the abattis, he mounted twenty men upon these horses, placing Jacob at their head. Then he drew off as many defenders from other points as he could, and bade these charge their pistols and blunderbusses to the mouth with balls. As the enemy effected a breach in the abattis and streamed in, Jacob with his horse galloped down upon them at full speed. The reserve poured the fire of their heavily loaded pieces upon the mass still outside, and then aided Jacob's horse by falling suddenly on those within. So great was the effect that the enemy were driven back, and the column retired, the breach in the abattis being hastily filled up, before the cavalry, who were waiting the opportunity, could charge down upon it.

In the meantime, however, the enemy were forcing their way in at other points, and Harry gave word for the outside line of houses to be fired. The thatched roofs speedily were in flames, and as the wind was blowing from the river dense clouds of smoke rolled down upon the assailants. It was now only the intervals between the houses which had to be defended, and for an hour the stubborn resistance continued, the Royalist troops defending each house with its inclosure to the last, and firing them as they retreated, their own loss being trifling in comparison with that which they inflicted upon their assailants.

At last the whole of the defenders were gathered in and round the mill. This was defended from attack by the mill stream, which separated it from the village, and which was crossed only by the road leading down to the ford. The bridge was a wooden one, and this had been already partly sawn away. As soon as the last of the defenders crossed the remainder of the bridge was chopped down. Along the line of the stream Harry had erected a defense, breast high, of sacks of wheat from the mill. The enemy, as they straggled out through the burning village, paused, on seeing the strong position which yet remained to be carried. The mill stream was rapid and deep, and the approaches swept by the fire from the mill. There was a pause, and then the cannon were brought up and fire opened upon the mill, the musketry keeping up an incessant rattle from every wall and clump of bushes.

The mill was built of wood, and the cannon shot went through and through it. But Harry directed his men to place rows of sacks along each floor facing the enemy, and lying down behind these to fire through holes pierced in the planks. For half an hour the cannonade continued, and then the enemy were seen advancing, carrying beams and the trunks of small trees, to make a bridge across the stream. Had Harry's men been armed with muskets it would have been next to impossible for the enemy to succeed in doing this in the face of their fire. But the fire of their short weapons was wild and uncertain, except at short distances. Very many of the Roundheads fell, but others pressed forward bravely, and succeeded in throwing their beams across the stream. By this time Harry had led out all his force from the mill, and a desperate fight took place at the bridge. The enemy lined the opposite bank in such force that none of the defenders could show their heads above the barricade of sacks, and Harry came to the conclusion that further resistance was vain. He ordered Jacob to take all the men with the exception of ten and to retire at once across the ford. He himself with the remainder would defend the bridge till they were fairly across, and would then rush over and join them as he might.

With a heavy heart Jacob was preparing to obey this order, when he heard a loud cheer, and saw Prince Rupert, heading a large body of horse, dash into the river on the other side. The enemy saw him too. There was an instant cessation of their fire, and before Prince Rupert had gained the bank the Roundheads were already in full retreat for Reading. The bridge was hastily repaired, and the prince pursued for some distance, chasing their cavalry well-nigh into Reading. Their infantry, however, held together, and regained that town in safety.

Upon his return Prince Rupert expressed his warm admiration at the prolonged and gallant defense which Harry had made, and said that the oldest soldier in the army could not have done better. At Harry's request he promised the villagers that the next day money should be sent out from the king's treasury to make good the losses which they had sustained. Then he left a strong body of horse to hold the village, and directed Harry to ride with him with his troop to Oxford.

"I have a mission for you, Master Furness," he said, as they rode along. "I have already told his majesty how coolly and courageously you conducted yourself in that sore strait in which we were placed together. The king has need of a messenger to Scotland. The mission is a difficult one, and full of danger. It demands coolness and judgment as well as courage. I have told his majesty that, in spite of your youth, you possess these qualities, but the king was inclined to doubt whether you were old enough to be intrusted with such a commission. After to-day's doings he need have no further hesitation. I spoke to your father but yesterday, and he has given consent that you shall go, the more readily, methinks, because the good Cavalier thinks that the morals and ways of many of our young officers to be in no wise edifying for you, and I cannot but say that he is right. What sayest thou?"

Harry expressed his willingness to undertake any mission with which he might be charged. He thought it probable that no great movements would be undertaken in the south for some time, and with a lad's natural love of adventure, was pleased at the thought of change and variety.

The Scots were at this time arranging for a close alliance with the Parliament, which had sent emissaries to Edinburgh to negotiate a Solemn League and Covenant. Sir Henry Vane, who was an Independent, had been forced to accede to the demand of the Scotch Parliament, that the Presbyterian religious system of Scotland should be adopted as that of England, and after much chaffering for terms on both sides, the document was signed, and was to bind those who subscribed it to endeavor, without respect of persons, to extirpate popery and prelacy.

On the 25th of September, nearly a week after the battle of Newbury, all the members of Parliament still remaining in London assembled in St. Margaret's Church, and signed the Solemn League and Covenant; but even at this moment of enthusiasm the parties were not true to each other. The Scotch expected that

71

Presbyterianism would be introduced into England, and that Episcopacy would be entirely abolished. The English members, however, signed the declaration with the full intent of preserving their own religion, that of a form of Episcopacy, altered much indeed from that of the Church of England, but still differing widely from the Scotch system.

The king had many adherents in Scotland, chief of whom was the Earl of Montrose, a most gallant and loyal nobleman.

Upon the day after the fight in the village the king, on Prince Rupert's recommendation, appointed Harry Furness to bear dispatches to the earl, and as he was going north, Prince Rupert placed Lady Sidmouth and her daughter under his charge to convey to the army of the Earl of Newcastle, under whom her husband was at this time engaged.

Upon asking what force he should take with him the prince said that he had better proceed with his own troop, as an escort to the ladies, as far as the camp of Newcastle, filling up the places of those who had fallen in the skirmishes and fight of Newbury with other men, so as to preserve his full tale of fifty troopers. When he had fulfilled the first part of his mission he was to place his troop at the earl's service until his return, and to proceed in such manner and disguise as might seem best to him.

Harry started for the north in high spirits, feeling very proud of the charge confided to him. Lady Sidmouth and her daughter were placed in a light litter between two horses. Harry took his place beside it. Half the troop, under the command of the lieutenant, rode in front; the other half followed. So they started for the north. It was a long journey, as they were forced to avoid many towns occupied by Roundheads. Upon the fourth day of their journey they suddenly heard the explosion of pistols, and the shouts of men in conflict. Harry ordered his lieutenant to ride forward with half the troop to some rising ground just in front, and there they saw a combat going on between a party of Cavaliers and a force of Roundheads, much superior to them in numbers. Harry joined the lieutenant, and sending back a man with orders to the remaining half of the troop to form a guard round the litter, he headed the advance party, and the twenty-five men rode headlong down into the scene of conflict. It was a sharp fight for a few minutes, and then the accession of strength which the Cavaliers had gained gave them the superiority, and the Roundheads fell back, but in good order.

"You arrived just in time, sir," the leader of the party engaged said. "I am Master John Chillingworth, and am marching to Hardley House, which the Puritans are about to besiege. There is no time to delay, for see you not on yonder hill the gleam of pikes? That is the

72

enemy's footmen. It is only an advanced party of their horse with which we have had this affair. You cannot go forward in this direction. There is a strong body of Roundheads lying a few miles to the north."

Harry rode back to Lady Sidmouth, and after a consultation with her and with Master Chillingworth, they decided to throw themselves into Hardley House, where the addition of strength which they brought might enable them to beat off the Roundheads, and then to proceed on their way. They learned indeed from a peasant that several bodies of Roundheads were advancing from various directions, and that Hardley House was strong and well defended. Of the choice of evils, therefore, they thought this to be the lightest, and, after an hour's hard riding, they arrived before its walls. It was an old castellated building, with bastions and walls capable of standing a siege. The party were gladly received by the master, Sir Francis Burdett, who had placed his castle in a posture of defense, but was short of men. Upon the news of the approach of the enemy he had hastily driven a number of cattle into the yard, and had stores of provisions sufficient to stand a siege for some time.

In a short time the Parliament force, consisting of five hundred footmen and two hundred horse, appeared before the castle, and summoned it to surrender. Sir Francis refused to do so, and fired a gun in token of defiance. Soon a train was seen approaching in the distance, and four guns were dragged by the enemy to a point of high ground near the castle. Here the Roundheads began to throw up a battery, but were mightily inconvenienced while doing so by the guns of the castle, which shot briskly against them. Working at night, however, in two days they completed the battery, which, on the third morning, opened fire upon the castle. The guns were much heavier than those upon the walls, and the shot, directed at a curtain between two towers, battered the stone sorely. The Parliament footmen were drawn back a space from the walls so as to avoid the fire of muskets from the defenders. There were in all in the castle about two hundred men, one hundred having been collected before the arrival of the troops of horse. These determined upon making a desperate resistance when the wall should give way, which would, they doubted not, be upon the following day. Everything that could be done was tried to hinder the destruction made by the enemy's shot. Numbers of sacks were filled with earth, and lowered from the walls above so as to hang in regular order before it, and so break the force of the shot. This had some effect, but gradually the wall crumbled beneath the blows of the missiles from the Roundhead guns.

73

"We are useless here, save as footmen," Harry said that night to his host. "There is a postern gate, is there not, behind the castle? Methinks that if we could get out in the dark unobserved, and form close to the walls, so that their pickets lying around might not suspect us of purposing to issue forth, we might, when daylight dawned, make an attack upon their guns, and if we could spike these the assault would probably cease."

The attempt was determined upon. The Roundhead infantry were disposed behind as well as in front of the castle, so as to prevent the escape of the besieged; but the camp was at a distance of some four hundred yards. The chains of the drawbridge across the moat were oiled, as were the bolts of the doors, and at three in the morning the gate was opened, and the drawbridge lowered across the moat. A thick layer of sacks was then placed upon the drawbridge. The horses' hoofs were also muffled with sacking, and then, one by one, the horses were led out, the drawbridge was drawn up again, and all was quiet. No sound or motion in the Puritan camp betrayed that their exit was observed, and they could hear the challenges of the circuit of sentries passed from man to man.

When the first streak of dawn was seen in the east the troop mounted their horses, and remained quiet until the light should be sufficient to enable them to see the nature of the ground over which they would have to pass. This they would be able to do before they themselves were observed, standing as they were close under the shadow of the walls of the castle. As soon as it was sufficiently light the trumpets sounded, and with a burst they dashed across the country. Heeding not the bugle calls in the camp of the Puritan infantry, they rode straight at the guns. These were six hundred yards distant, and before the artillerymen could awake to their danger, the Royalists were upon them. Those that stood were cut down, and in a minute the guns were spiked. Then the cavalry swept round, and as the Puritan horse hastily formed up, they charged them. Although but half their numbers, they had the superiority in the surprise at which they took their foes, and in the fact of the latter being but half armed, not having had time to put on their breastplates. The combat was a short one, and in a few minutes the Puritans were flying in all directions. The pikemen were now approaching on either side in compact bodies, and against these Harry knew that his horsemen could do nothing. He therefore drew them off from the castle, and during the day circled round and round the place, seizing several carts of provisions destined for the wants of the infantry, and holding them in a sort of leaguer.

That night, finding that their guns were disabled, their horse defeated, and themselves cut off, the rebel infantry drew off, and gave up the siege of the place. The next morning the cavalry re-entered the castle in triumph, and having received the hearty thanks of Sir Francis Burdett, and leaving with him the troop of Master Chillingworth, who intended to remain there, Harry proceeded on his way north, and reached York without further adventure.

During the ten days that they had journeyed together Lady Sidmouth had been greatly pleased with the attention and character of Harry Furness. He was always cheerful and courteous, without any of that light tone of flippancy which distinguished the young Cavaliers of the period, and her little daughter was charmed with her companion. Harry received the hearty thanks of Sir Henry Sidmouth for the care with which he had conducted his wife through the dangers of the journey, and then, having so far discharged his duty, he left his troop at York, and started for Scotland.

On the way he had discussed with Jacob the measures which he intended to take for his journey north. Jacob had begged earnestly to accompany him, and as Harry deemed that his shrewdness might be of great use, he determined to take him with him, as well as another of his troop. The latter was a merry fellow, named William Long. He was of grave and sober demeanor, and never smiled, even while causing his hearers to be convulsed with laughter. He had a keen sense of humor, was a ready-witted and courageous fellow, and had frequently distinguished himself in the various skirmishes. He was the son of a small tenant of Sir Henry Furness.

His farm was near the hall, and, although three or four years older than Harry, he had as a boy frequently accompanied him when out hawking, and in other amusements. Harry felt that, with two attached and faithful comrades like these, he should he able to make his way through many dangers. At York he had procured for himself and his followers suits of clothes of a grave and sober cut, such as would be worn by yeomen; and here they laid aside their Cavalier garments, and proceeded northward. They traveled quietly forward as far as Durham, and then went west, as Berwick was held for the Parliament. They carried weapons, for at that time none traveled unarmed, and the country through which they had to pass was greatly disturbed, the moss troopers having taken advantage of the disorders of the times to renew the habits of their forefathers, and to make raids upon their southern neighbors, and carry off cattle and horses. They carried with them but little money, a small quantity in their valises, and a few gold pieces concealed about their persons, each choosing a different receptacle, so that in case of pillage some at least might retain sufficient to carry them on their way. Avoiding the large towns, where alone they would be likely to be questioned, they crossed the border, and rode into Scotland.

Upon the day after their crossing the frontier they saw a body of horsemen approaching them. These drew up when they reached them, Harry having previously warned his comrades to offer no resistance, as the party were too strong for them, and his mission was too important to allow the king's cause to be hazarded by any foolish acts of pugnacity.

"Are you for the king or the kirk?" the leader asked.

"Neither for one nor the other," Harry said. "We are peaceable yeomen traveling north to buy cattle, and we meddle not in the disputes of the time."

"Have you any news from the south?"

"Nothing," Harry replied. "We come from Durham, and since the news of the battle of Newbury, no tidings have come of importance."

The man looked inquisitively at the horses and valises; but Harry had chosen three stout ponies sufficiently good to carry them, but offering no temptations to pillagers, and the size of the valises promised but little from their contents.

"Since you are riding north to buy cattle," the leader said, "you must have money with you, and money is short with us in these bad times."

"We have not," Harry said; "judging it possible that we might meet with gentlemen who felt the pressure of the times, we have provided ourselves with sufficient only to take us up to Kelso, where dwells our correspondent, who will, we trust, have purchased and collected sufficient cattle for us to take south when we shall learn that a convoy of troops is traveling in this direction, for we would not place temptation in the way of those whom we might meet."

"You are a fellow of some humor," the leader said grimly. "But it is evil jesting on this side of the border."

"I jest not," Harry said. "There is a proverb in Latin, with which doubtless your worship is acquainted, to the effect that an empty traveler may sing before robbers, and, although far from including you and your worshipful following in that category, yet we may be pardoned for feeling somewhat light-hearted, because we are not overburdened with money."

The leader looked savagely at the young man; but seeing that his demeanor and that of his followers was resolute, that they carried pistols at their holsters and heavy swords, and deeming that nothing but hard knocks would come of an attack upon them, he surlily bade his company follow him, and rode on his way again.

# CHAPTER X

# THE COMMISSIONER OF THE CONVENTION

At Kelso Harry procured changes of garments, attiring himself as a Lowland farmer, and his companions as two drovers. They were, as before, mounted; but the costume of English farmers could no longer have been supported by any plausible story. They learned that upon the direct road north they should find many bodies of Scotch troops, and therefore made for the coast. Two days' riding brought them to the little port of Ayton.

After taking their supper in the common room of the hostelry, there was a stir outside, and three men, attired as Puritan preachers, entered the room. Mine host received them with courtesy, but with none of the eager welcome usually displayed to guests; for these gentry, although feared—for their power was very great at the time—were by no means loved, and their orders at a hostelry were not likely to swell the purse of the host. Stalking to an unoccupied table next to that at which Harry and his party were sitting, they took their seats and called for supper.

Harry made a sign to his companions to continue talking together, while he listened attentively to the conversation of the men behind him. He gathered from their talk that they were commissioners proceeding from the Presbyterian Convention in London to discuss with that at Edinburgh upon the points upon which they could come to an agreement for a common basis of terms. Their talk turned principally upon doctrinal questions, upon which Harry's ignorance was entire and absolute; but he saw at once that it would do good service to the king if he could in some way prevent these men continuing upon their journey, and so for a time arrest the progress of the negotiations between the king's enemies in England and Scotland, for at this time the preachers were the paramount authorities in England. It was they who insisted upon terms, they who swayed the councils of the nation, and it was not until Cromwell, after overthrowing the king, overthrew the Parliament, which was for the main part composed of their creatures, that the power of the preachers came to an end. It would, of course, have been easy for Harry and his friends to attack these men during their next day's journey, but this would have involved the necessity of killing them—from which he shrank—for an assault upon three godly men traveling on the high business of the Convention to the Scottish capital would have caused such an outcry that Harry could not hope to continue on his way without the certainty of discovery and arrest.

Signing to his comrades to remain in their seats, he strolled off toward the port, and there entered a public house, which, by its aspect, was frequented by seafaring men. It was a small room that he entered, and contained three or four fishermen, and one whom a certain superiority in dress betokened to be the captain of a vessel. They were talking of the war, and of the probability of the Scottish army taking part in it. The fishermen were all of the popular party; but the captain, who seemed a jovial fellow, shrugged his shoulders over the religious squabbles, and said that, for his part, he wanted nothing but peace.

"Not," he said, "that the present times do not suit are rarely in purse. Men are too busy now to look after the doings of every lugger that passes along the coast, and never were French goods so plentiful or so cheap. Moreover," he said, "I find that not unfrequently passengers want to be carried to France or Holland. I ask no questions; I care not whether they go on missions from the Royalists or from the Convention; I take their money; I land them at their destination; no questions are asked. So the times suit me bravely; but for all that I do not like to think of Englishmen and Scotchmen arrayed against their fellows. I cannot see that it matters one jot whether we are predestinate or not predestinate, or whether it is a bishop who governs a certain church or a presbyter. I say let each worship in his own way, and not concern himself about his fellows. If men would but mind their own affairs in religion as they do in business it would be better for us all."

Harry, as he drank the glass of beer he had ordered, had joined occasionally in the conversation, not taking any part, but agreeing chiefly with the sea-captain in his desire for peace.

"I too," he said, "have nothing to grumble at. My beasts fetch good prices for the army, and save that there is a want of hands, I was never doing better. Still I would gladly see peace established."

Presently the fishermen, having finished their liquor, retired, and the captain, looking keenly at Harry, said, "Methinks, young sir, that you are not precisely what you seem!"

"That is so," Harry replied; "I am on business here, It matters not on which side, and it may be that we may strike a bargain together."

"Do you want to cross the channel?" the captain asked, laughing. "You seem young to have put your head in a noose already."

"No," Harry said, "I do not want to cross myself; but I want to send some others across. I suppose that if a passenger or two were

78

placed on board your ship, to be landed in Holland, you would not deem it necessary to question them closely, or to ascertain whether they also were anxious to arrive at that destination?"

"By no means," the captain replied. "Goods consigned to me will be delivered at the port to which they are addressed, and I should consider that with passengers as with goods, I must carry them to the port for which their passage is taken."

"Good," Harry said; "if that is the case, methinks that when you sail—and," he asked, breaking off, "when do you sail?"

"To-morrow morning, if the wind is fair," the captain answered. "But if it would pay me better to stop for a few hours, I might do so."

"To-morrow night, if you will wait till then," Harry said, "I will place three passengers on board, and will pay you your own sum to land them at Flushing, or any other place across the water to which you may be bound. I will take care that they will make no complaints whatever, or address any remonstrance to you, until after you have fairly put to sea. And then, naturally, you will feel yourself unable to alter the course of your ship."

"But," the captain observed, "I must be assured that these passengers who are so anxious to cross the water are not men whose absence might cause any great bother. I am a simple man, earning my living as honestly as the times will allow me to do, and I wish not to embroil myself with the great parties of the State."

"There may be an inquiry," Harry replied; "but methinks it will soon drop. They are three preachers of London, who are on their way to dispute concerning points of religion with the divines in Scotland. The result of their disputation may perchance be that an accord may be arrived at between the divines of London and Edinburgh; and in that case, I doubt not that the army now lying at Dundee would move south, and that the civil war would therefore become more extended and cruel than ever."

The captain laughed.

"I am not fond of blackbirds on board my ship," he said. "They are ever of ill omen on the sea. But I will risk it for so good a cause. It is their pestilent religious disputes which have stirred up the nations to war, and I doubt not that even should some time elapse before these gentlemen can again hold forth in England, there are plenty of others to supply their place."

An agreement was speedily arrived at as to the terms of passage, for Harry was well provided with money, having drawn at Kelso from an agent devoted to the Royal cause, upon whom he had letters of credit.

The next morning early Harry went to a carter in the town,

and hired a cart for the day, leaving a deposit for its safe return at night. Then, mounting their horses, the three Royalists rode off just as the preachers were going forth from the inn. The latter continued their course at the grave pace suitable to their calling and occupation, conversing vigorously upon the points of doctrine which they intended to urge upon their fellows at Edinburgh. Suddenly, just where the road emerged from a wood on to a common, three men dashed out, and fell upon them. The preachers roared lustily for mercy, and invoked the vengeance of the Parliament upon those who ventured to interfere with them.

"We are charged," one said, "with a mission to the Convention at Edinburgh, and it is as much as your heads are worth to interfere with us."

"Natheless," Harry said, "we must even risk our heads. You must follow us into the wood, or we shall be under the necessity of 'blowing out your brains.'"

Much crestfallen, the preachers followed their captors into the wood. There they were despoiled of their hats and doublets, tied securely by cords, gagged, and placed, in spite of their remonstrances and struggles, in three huge sacks.

At midnight the Annette was lying alongside the wharf at Ayton, when a cart drove up. Three men alighted from it, and one hailed the captain, who was standing on deck.

"I have brought the three parcels thou wottest of," he said. "They will need each two strong men to carry them on board."

The captain, with two sailors, ascended to the quay.

"What have we here?" said one of the sailors; "there is some live creature in this sack."

"It is a young calf," Harry said; "when you are well out to sea you can give it air."

The men laughed, for having frequently had passengers to cross to the Continent, they shrewdly guessed at the truth; and the captain had already told them that the delay of a day would put some money into each of their pockets. Having seen the three sacks deposited on the deck of the ship, when the sails were immediately hoisted, and the Annette glided away on her course seaward, the cart was driven round to the house where it had been hired. The stipulated price was paid, the deposit returned, and the hirer then departed.

Riding toward Edinburgh, Harry agreed with his comrades that as he, as the apparent leader of the party, would be the more likely to be suspected and arrested, it would be better for the documents of which they were the carriers, as well as the papers found upon the persons of the Puritans, to be intrusted to the

80

charge of Jacob and William Long. Harry charged them, in the event of anything happening to him, to pay no heed to him whatever, but to separate from him and mix with the crowd, and then to make their way, as best they might, to the Earl of Montrose.

"It matters nothing," he said, "my being arrested, They can prove nothing against me, as I shall have no papers on my body, while it is all-important that you should get off. The most that they can do to me is to send me to London, and a term of imprisonment as a malignant is the worst that will befall me."

The next day they entered the town by the Canongate, and were surprised and amused at the busy scene passing there. Riding to an inn, they put up their horses and dismounted. Harry purposed to remain there for three or four days to learn the temper of the people.

The next morning he strolled out into the streets, followed at some little distance by Jacob and William Long, He had not the least fear of being recognized, and for the time gave himself up thoroughly to the amusement of the moment. He had not proceeded far, however, when he ran full tilt against a man in a black garb, who, gazing at him, at once shouted out at the top of his voice, "Seize this man, he is a malignant and a spy," and to his horror Harry discovered the small preacher with whom he had twice already been at loggerheads, and who, it seems, had been dispatched as a member of a previous commission by his party in London.

In a moment a dozen sturdy hands seized him by his collar. Feeling the utter uselessness of resistance, and being afraid that should he attempt to struggle, his friends might be drawn into the matter, Harry quietly proceeded along the street until he reached the city guardhouse, in a cell of which he was thrust.

"One would think," he muttered to himself, "that little preacher is an emissary of Satan himself. Go where I will, this lantern-jawed knave is sure to crop up and I feel convinced that until I have split his skull I shall have no safety. I thought I had freed myself of him forever when I got out of London; and here, in the middle of the Scotch capital, he turns up as sharpsighted and as venomous as ever."

An hour or two later Harry was removed under a guard to the city prison, and in the evening the doors were opened and a guard appeared and briefly ordered him to follow. Under the escort of four men he was led through the streets to a large building, and then conducted to a room in which a number of persons, some of them evidently of high rank, were sitting. At the head of the table was a man of sinister aspect. He had red hair and eyebrows, and a foxy, cunning face, and Harry guessed at once that he was in the presence of the Earl of Argyll—a man who, even more than the rest of his treacherous race, was hated and despised by loyal Scotchmen. In all their history, a great portion of the Scottish nobles were ever found ready to take English gold, and to plot against their country. But the Argylls had borne a bad pre-eminence even among these. They had hunted Wallace, had hounded down Bruce, and had ever been prominent in fomenting dissensions in their country; the present earl was probably the coldest and most treacherous of his race.

"We are told," he said sternly to the prisoner, "that you are a follower of the man Charles; that you have been already engaged in plottings among the good citizens of London, and we shrewdly suspect that your presence here bodes no good to the state. What hast thou to say in thy defense?"

"I do not know that I am charged with any offence," Harry said quietly. "I am an English gentleman, who, wishing to avoid the disorders in his own country, has traveled north for peace and quietness. If you have aught to urge against me or any evidence to give, I shall be prepared to confute it. As for the preacher, whose evidence has caused my arrest, he hath simply a grudge against me for a boyish freak, from which he suffered at the time when I made my escape from a guardroom in London, and his accusation against me is solely the result of prejudice."

Harry had already, upon his arrival at the jail, been searched thoroughly, having been stripped, and even the folds and linings of his garments ripped open, to see that they contained no correspondence. Knowing that nothing whatever could have been found against him, unless, indeed, his followers had also fallen into the hands of the Roundheads, Harry was able to assume a position of injured innocence.

"Your tone comports not with your condition," the Earl of Argyll said harshly. "We have found means here to make men of sterner mold than thine speak the truth, and in the interests of the state we shall not hesitate to use them against you also. The torturer here hath instruments which would tear you limb from limb, and, young sir, these will not be spared unless that malapert tongue of thine gives us the information we desire to learn."

"I decline to answer any questions beyond what I have already said," Harry replied firmly. "I tell you that I am an English gentleman traveling here on my own private business, and it were foul wrong for me to be seized and punished upon the suspicion of such a one as that man there;" and he pointed contemptuously to the preacher.

"You will be brought up again in two days," the earl said, "and

82

if by that time you have not made up your mind to confess all, it will go hard with you. Think not that the life of a varlet like you will weigh for one moment in the scale with the safety of the nation, or that any regard for what you may consider in England the usages of war will prevail here."

He waved his hand, and Harry was conducted back to jail, feeling far more uneasy than he had done, for he knew that in Scotland very different manners prevailed to those which characterized the English. In England, throughout the war, no unnecessary bloodshed took place, and up to that time the only persons executed in cold blood had been the two gentlemen convicted of endeavoring to corrupt the Parliament in favor of the king. But in Scotland, where civil broils were constant, blood was ever shed recklessly on both sides; houses were given to the flames; men, women, and children slaughtered; lands laid waste; and all the atrocities which civil war, heightened by religious bigotry, could suggest, perpetrated.

Late that evening, the door of the prison opened, and a preacher was shown into the room.

"I have come," he said in a nasal tone, "misguided young man, to pray you to consider the wickedness of your ways. It is written that the ungodly shall perish, and I would fain lead you from the errors of your way before it is too late."

Harry had started as the speaker began; but he remained immovable until the jailer closed the door.

"Jacob," he exclaimed, "how mad, how imprudent of you! I ordered you specially, if I was arrested, to pay no heed, but to make your way north."

"I know that you did," Jacob said. "But you see you yourself talked of remaining for three days in Edinburgh. Therefore, I knew that there could be no pressing need of my journey north; and hearing some whispers of the intention of the lord president to extract from a certain prisoner the news of a plot with which he was supposed to be connected, I thought it even best to come and see you."

"But how have you obtained this garb?" Harry asked; "and how, above all, have you managed to penetrate hither?"

"Truly," Jacob said, "I have undertaken a difficult task in thy behalf, for I have to-night to enter into a disputation with many learned divines, and I dread that more than running the risk of meeting the Earl of Argyll, who, they say, has the face of a fox, and the heart of a devil."

"What mean you?" Harry asked.

"After we saw you dragged off by the townsmen, on being

denounced by that little preacher whose hat I spoiled in St. Paul's churchyard, we followed your orders, and made back to our hostelry. There William Long and myself talked the matter over. In the first place, we took all the papers and documents which were concealed about us, and lifting a board in the room, hid them beneath it, so that in case of our arrest they would be safe. As we took out the documents, the commission which we borrowed from the preachers met our eyes, and it struck me that, armed with this, we might be enabled to do you service. I therefore at once purchased cloaks and hats fitting for us as worthy divines from London, and then, riding a mile or two into the country, we changed our garments, and entered the good city of Edinburgh as English divines. We proceeded direct to the house of the chief presbyter, to whom the letters of commission were addressed, and were received by him with open arms. I trust that we played our part rarely, and, in truth, the unctuousness and godliness of William Long passeth belief, and he plays his part well. Looking as he does far older than I—although in these days of clean-shaven faces I can make up rarely for thirty—he assumed the leading part. The presbyter would fain have summoned a number of his divines for a discussion this evening. But we, pleading fatigue, begged him to allow us two days of rest. He has, however, invited a few of his fellows, and we are to wrestle with them this evening in argument. How we shall get out of it I know not, for my head is altogether in ignorance of the points in issue. However, there was, among the documents of the preachers, one setting forth the points in which the practice of the sect in England and Scotland differed, with the heads of the arguments to be used. We have looked through these, and, as well as we could understand the jumble of hard words, have endeavored to master the points at issue, so we shall to-night confine ourselves to a bare exposition of facts, and shall put off answering the arguments of the other side until the drawn battle, which will be fixed for the day after to-morrow. By the way, we accounted for the absence of our colleague by saying that he fell sick on the way."

"But what is the use of all this risk?" Harry asked, laughing at the thought of his two followers discussing theology with the learned divines of the Scotch Church.

"That, in truth," Jacob said, "I do not yet exactly see; but I trust that to-morrow we shall have contrived some plan of getting you out of this prison. I shall return at the same time to-morrow evening."

"How did you get in here?" he asked.

"I had an order from the chief presbyter for entry. Saying that I believed I knew you, and that my words might have some effect in turning you from the evil of your ways, I volunteered to exhort you, and shall give such an account of my mission as will lead them to give me a pass to see you again to-morrow night."

The following evening Jacob again called, this time accompanied by William. They brought with them another dress similar to their own. Their visit was an hour later than upon the preceding evening.

"I learned," Jacob said, "that the guard was changed at eight o'clock, and it is upon this that the success of our scheme depends. William will immediately leave, and as he has been seen to enter by the guards without, and by those at the prison gate, he will pass out without questioning. In half an hour a fresh guard will be placed at both these points, and you and I will march out together, armed with permission for two preachers to pass."

The scheme appeared a hopeful one, and William took his departure after a few minutes, saying to the guards without that he went to fetch a book of reference which he needed to convince the hard-hearted reprobate within. He left the door partly ajar, and the guards without were edified by catching snatches of a discourse of exceeding godliness and unction, delivered by the preacher to the prisoner.

Presently a trampling without informed Harry and Jacob that the guard was being changed, and half an hour later they opened the door, and Jacob, standing for a moment as they went out, addressed a few words of earnest exhortation to the prisoner supposed to be within, adjuring him to bethink himself whether it was better to sacrifice his life in the cause of a wicked king than to purchase his freedom by forsaking the error of his ways, and turning to the true belief. Then, closing the door after him, Jacob strode along, accompanied by Harry, to the guardroom. They passed through the yard of the prison to the gate. There Jacob produced his pass for the entrance and exit of two divines, and the guard, suspecting no evil, at once suffered them to go forth. William had already been to the inn where they stopped, and had told the host that he was charged to examine the chamber where the persons who abode there upon the previous day had stopped. There he had taken the various documents from their hiding-place, and had made his way from the city. Outside the gates he was joined by the others, and all, at a speedy but still dignified pace, made their way to the spot where the horses were concealed, in a little wood in a retired valley. Here they changed their dress, and, making a bonfire of the garments which they had taken off, mounted their horses, and rode for the north.

# CHAPTER XI

# MONTROSE

They stopped for the night at a village fifteen miles away from Edinburgh, and after they had had their supper Harry inquired of Jacob how his dispute with the divines had passed off the evening before.

Jacob burst into a fit of laughter.

"It was the funniest thing you ever saw," he said, "Imagine a large room, with the chief presbyter sitting at a table, and eight other men, with sour countenances and large turned-down collars and bands, sitting round it. William Long and I faced them at the other end, looking as grave and sanctimonious as the rest of them. The proceedings were, of course, opened with a lengthy prayer, and then the old gentleman in the center introduced us as the commissioners from London. William rose, and having got up by heart the instructions to the commissioners, he said that he would first briefly introduce to his fellow divines the points as to which differences appeared to exist between the Presbyterians of the north and those of the south, and concerning which he was instructed to come to an agreement with them. First, he gave a list of the points at variance; then he said that he understood that these, quoting from his document, were the views of his Scotch brethren; and he then proceeded to give briefly the arguments with which he had been furnished. He said that his reverend brother and himself were much wearied with long travel, and that they would fain defer the debate for another two days, but that in the meantime they would be glad to hear the views of their friends. Then did one after another of these eight worthy men rise, and for six mortal hours they poured forth their views. I do not know whether it was most difficult to avoid laughter or yawning; but, indeed, Master Harry, it was a weary time. I dared not look at William, for he put such grave attention and worshipful reverence on his face that you would have thought he had been born and bred to the work. When the last of the eight had sat dawn he rose again, and expressed a marvelous admiration of the learning and eloquence which his brethren had displayed. Many of their arguments he said, were new to him—and in this, indeed, I doubt not he spoke truth—and he perceived that it would be hard to answer all that they had so learnedly adduced. Upon the other hand, he had much to say; but he was willing to allow that upon some points he should have difficulty in combating their views. He prayed them, therefore, to defer the meeting for two days, when he would willingly give them his views upon the subject, and his learned brother would also address them. He proposed that the party should be as small a one as that he saw before him, and that, after hearing him, they should, if possible, come to some arrangement upon a few, at least, of the points in dispute, so as to leave as small a number as might be open to for the public disputation which would follow. The worshipful party appeared mightily taken with the idea, and, after an hour's prayer from the chairman, we separated. I hardly slept all night for laughing, and I would give much to see the faces of that honorable council when they hear that they have been fooled."

"You have both shown great wisdom, Jacob," Harry said, "and have behaved in a sore strait with much judgment and discretion. It was lucky for you that your reverend friend did not, among his eight champions, think of inviting our little friend from London, for I fear that he would at once have denounced you as not being the divines whose credentials you presented."

"I was afraid of that," Jacob said, "and therefore begged him specially, on this our first conference, to have only ministers of his own circle present. He mentioned that one or two godly ministers from London were present in the capital. I replied that I was well aware of that, but that, as these men were not favored with the instructions of the convention, and knew not the exact turn which affairs had taken up to the period of my leaving, their presence might be an embarrassment—which, indeed, was only the truth."

"We must make a circuit to-morrow," Harry said, "to avoid Stirling, and will go round by Doune, and thence make for the north. Once among the mountains we shall be safe from all pursuit, and from any interference by the Roundheads, for I believe that the clans of this part are all in favor of Montrose—Argyll's power lying far to the west."

"It will be a comfort," Jacob said, "not to be obliged to talk through one's nose, and to cast one's eyes upward. I imagine that these Highlanders are little better than savages."

"That is so," Harry said. "They are, I believe, but little changed since the days when the Romans struggled with them, and could make no head north of the Forth."

The next day, by a long circuit, they traveled round Stirling, and reached the bridge of Doune, there crossing the Teith unquestioned. They soon left the main road, and struck into the hills. They had not traveled far when three strange figures suddenly presented themselves. These men were clad in a garb which to the lads was strange and wild indeed. The kilt, as worn by Highlanders on show occasions in the present day is a garment wholly unlike that worn by their ancestors, being, indeed, little more than a masquerade dress. The kilt of the old time resembled indeed the short petticoat now worn by savage peoples. It consisted of a great length of cloth wound round and round the loins, and falling like a loose petticoat to the knees, a portion being brought over one shoulder, and then wrapped round and round the body. It was generally of dark material; the tartans now supposed to be peculiar to the various clans being then unknown, or at least not worn by the common people, although the heads of the clans may have worn scarfs of those patterns. A Highland gentleman or chief, however, dressed in the same garb as Englishmen—that is, in armor, with doublet and hose. His wild followers lived in huts of the most primitive description, understood no language but their own, obeyed the orders of their chiefs to the death, and knew nothing either of kings or of parliaments. For arms these men carried a broad target or shield made of bull's hide, and a broadsword of immense length hanging behind them, the hilt coming above the shoulder.

What they said the lads could not understand. But when Harry repeated the word "Montrose," the Highlanders nodded, and pointed to signify that the road they were pursuing was the right one, and two of them at once set out with them as escorts.

For several days they traveled north, stopping at little groups of cabins, where they were always received with rough hospitality, the assertion of their guides that they were going to the great earl being quite sufficient passport for them. Bannocks of oatmeal with collops, sometimes of venison, sometimes of mountain sheep, were always at their service, washed down by a drink new to the boys, and which at first brought the water into their eyes. This was called usquebaugh, and had a strange peaty flavor, which was at first very unpleasant to them, but to which before they left Scotland they became quite accustomed. The last two days they traveled upon broad roads again, and being now in a country devoted to the Earl of Montrose, were under no apprehension whatever of interference.

At last they reached the place where the earl was residing. His castle differed in no way from those of the nobility of England. It was surrounded by walls and towers, and had a moat and other means of defense. The gate was guarded by men similar in appearance to their guides, but dressed in better material, and with some attempt at uniformity. Large numbers of these were gathered in the courtyard, and among them were men-at-arms attired in southern fashion. The guides, having performed their duty of conducting these strangers from the borders of their country, now handed them over to an officer, and he, upon learning their errand, at once conducted them to the earl.

Montrose was a noble figure, dressed in the height of the fashion of the day. His face was oval, with a pointed mustache; long ringlets fell round his head; and his bearing was haughty and majestic. He rose from his chair and advanced a step toward them.

"Do I understand," he said, "that you are bearers of dispatches from his gracious majesty?"

"We are, sir," Harry said. "The king was pleased to commit to me various documents intended for your eye. We left him at Oxford, and have journeyed north with as little delay as might be in these times. The dispatches, I believe, will speak for themselves, I have no oral instructions committed to me."

So saying, Harry delivered the various documents with which they were charged. The earl instructed the officer to see that they were well lodged and cared for, and at once proceeded to his private cabinet to examine the instructions sent him by the king. These were in effect that, so soon as the army of the convention moved south from Dundee, he should endeavor to make a great raid with his followers upon the south, specially attacking the country of Argyll, so as to create a diversion, and, if possible, cause the recall of the Scotch army to defend their own capital.

For some weeks the lads stopped with Montrose. They had been furnished with garments suitable to their condition, and Harry was treated by the earl with the greatest kindness and courtesy. He often conversed with him as to the state of politics and of military affairs in England, and expressed himself as sanguine that he should be able to restore the authority of the king in Scotland.

"These sour men of the conventicles have ever been stiff-necked and rebellious," he said, "and have enforced their will upon our monarchs. I have not forgotten," he went on, striking the hilt of his sword angrily, "the insults which were put upon Queen Mary when she was preached to and lectured publicly by the sour fanatic Knox, and was treated, forsooth, as if she had been some trader's daughter who had ventured to laugh on a Sunday. Her son, too, was kept under the control of these men until he was summoned to England. It is time that Scotland were rid of the domination of these knaves, and if I live I will sweep them from the land. In courage my wild men are more than a match for the Lowlanders. It is true that in the old days the clans could never carry their forays southward, for, unaccustomed to discipline and unprovided with horses or even with firearms, they fared but badly when opposed to steel-clad men and knights in armor. But I trust it will be different this time. I cannot hope to infuse any great discipline among them. But they can at least be taught to charge in line, and their broad claymores may be trusted to hew a way for them through the lines of the Lowlanders. I trust, above all things, that the king will not be persuaded to negotiate with the traitors who are opposed to him. I know, Master Furness, that, from what you have said, your views run not there with mine, and that you think a compromise is desirable. But you do not know these fanatics as I do. While they clamor for toleration, they are the narrowest of bigots, and will themselves tolerate nothing. Already I have news that the convention between the Scotch conventicle and the English rebels is agreed to, and that an order has gone forth that the Presbyterian rites are to be observed in all the churches of England. They say that thousands of divines will be turned from their churches and their places filled with ignorant fanatics, and this they call religious liberty. Why, when Laud was in power his rule was as a silken thread compared to the hempen rope of these bigots, and should the king make terms with them, it will be only to rule henceforth at their bidding, and to be but an instrument in their hands for enforcing their will upon the people of these countries."

Much as Harry desired peace and leaned toward compromise, he saw that there was much in what the earl said. All the accounts that reached them from the youth told of the iron tyranny which was being exercised throughout England. Everywhere good and sincere men were being driven from their vicarages to live how best they might, for refusing to accept the terms of the convention. Everywhere their places were filled with men at once ignorant, bigoted, and intolerant; holy places were desecrated; the cavalry of the Commons was stabled in St. Paul's; the colored windows of the cathedrals and churches were everywhere destroyed; monuments were demolished; and fanaticism of the narrowest and most stringent kind was rampant.

During the time they spent at the castle the lads were greatly amused in watching the sports and exercises of the Highlanders. These consisted in throwing great stones and blocks of wood, in contests with blunted claymores, in foot races, and in dances executed to the wild and strange music of the bagpipes—music which Jacob declared was worse than the caterwauling upon the housetops in Cheapside.

The lads had deferred their journey south owing to the

90

troubled state of the country, and the fact that the whole of the south of Scotland was in the hands of the convention. They were therefore waiting an opportunity for taking ship and traveling by sea into Wales, where the followers of the king were in the ascendency. At length the earl told them that an occasion offered, and that although he would gladly keep them by him to accompany him when he moved south, if they considered that their duty compelled them to leave he would place them on board a ship bound for that destination. He did not furnish them with any documents, but bade Harry repeat to the king the sentiments which he had expressed, which, indeed, were but the repetition of loyal assurances which he had sent south by a trusty messenger immediately upon their arrival at the castle.

The boat in which they embarked was a small one, but was fast; which proved fortunate, for they were twice chased by ships of the Parliament. They landed, however, safely at Pembroke, and thence made their way through the mountains of Wales to Hereford, and joined the king, who was still at Oxford.

Events had traveled but slowly in England; the doings of the convention being at that time of greater importance than those of the armies. On the 19th of January the Scotch army had entered England, having marched from Edinburgh through the snow. The Marquis of Newcastle was in winter quarters at York. The town of Newcastle had held out successfully against the Scots. The English regiments in Ireland had been recalled; but had been defeated near Nantwich by Sir Thomas Fairfax. Negotiation after negotiation between the king and the Parliament had failed, and the king had issued writs for a Parliament to assemble at Oxford. This met on the 22d of January, and forty-three peers and a hundred and eighteen commoners had taken their place beside many absent with the army. Of the peers a large majority were with the Royalist Parliament at Oxford while at Westminster a majority of the members sent up by the towns assembled. The Royalist Parliament was sitting at Oxford when Harry arrived; but their proceedings had not upon the whole been satisfactory to the king. They had, indeed, passed votes for the raising of taxes and supplies; but had also insisted upon the king granting several reforms. Charles, untaught by adversity, was as obstinate as ever; and instead of using the opportunity for showing a fair disposition to redress the grievances which had led to the civil war, and to grant concessions which would have rallied all moderate persons to his cause, he betrayed much irritation at the opposition which he met with, and the convocation of Parliament, instead of bringing matters nearer to an issue, rather heightened the discontents of the times. The Parliament at Westminster, upon their side, formed a council, under the title of the committee of the two kingdoms, consisting of seven lords, fourteen members of the commons, and four Scottish commissioners, into whose hands the entire conduct of the war, the correspondence with foreign states, and indeed the whole executive power of the kingdom was given.

The king received Harry with great condescension and favor, and heard with satisfaction of the preparations which Montrose was making for an invasion of the Lowlands of Scotland, and promised Sir Henry to bestow the rank of knighthood upon his son as soon as he attained the age of twenty-one.

For some weeks Harry resided with his father at Furness Hall. He then fell back into Oxford upon the advance of an army from London destined to besiege that town. This force was far greater than any that the king could raise. It consisted of two separate forces, under the command of Essex and Waller. Presently the town was besieged, and although the walls were very strong, the attacking force was so numerous that resistance appeared to be hopeless. On the night of the 3d of June the king left the city secretly, attended only by two or three personal friends, and passed safely between the two armies. These, instead of acting in unison, in which case the besieging lines would have been complete, and the king unable to leave the place, were kept apart by the dissensions of their generals. A council of war took place, and Essex determined to march to the west. The committee in London ordered him to retrace his steps, and go in pursuit of the king, who had made for Worcester. But Essex replied to the committee that he could not carry on war in pursuance of directions from London, and that all military discipline would be subverted if they took upon themselves to direct his plans.

In the meantime, Waller, raising the siege of Oxford, had gone in pursuit of the king. Charles, seeing that his enemies were separated, returned to Oxford, where he was received with great enthusiasm, and the whole force there, marching out, fell upon Waller at Cropredy Bridge, near Banbury, and defeated him. Having scattered the rebels here, he turned his course west in pursuit of Essex, for his force was sufficient to cope with either of the armies separately, although he had been unable to meet them when united.

Harry and his father were not present at the battle of Cropredy Bridge, having with their troops left Oxford on the approach of the Roundheads, together with many other bodies of cavalry, as they could do no good in the case of a siege, and were wanted in the north, where Rupert was on his way to take the command. Joining his force, amounting in all to twenty thousand men, they advanced toward York. Leaving the greater portion of his army at a short distance away, Rupert entered York with two thousand men. Newcastle was in favor of prudent steps, knowing that dissensions existed in the Parliamentary army between the Scots and their English allies. Prince Rupert, however, insisted that he had the command of the king to fight at once, and so, with all the force he could collect, advanced against the Scots. Newcastle was much offended at the domineering manner and headstrong course of the prince and took no part in the forthcoming battle, in which his military genius and caution would have been of vast service to the royal cause.

On the 2d of July, having rested two days, the Royalist army marched out against the Roundheads. The contending parties met on Marston Moor, and it was late in the evening when the battle began. It was short but desperate, and when it ended four thousand one hundred and fifty men had been killed. Here, as in every other fight in which he was engaged, the impetuosity of Prince Rupert proved the ruin of the Royalists. With his cavaliers upon the right of the Royalist army, he charged the Scotch horse, scattered them in every direction and rode after them, chasing and slaying. The center of each army, composed of infantry, fought desperately, and without much advantage to either side. But upon the Royalist left the fate of the day was decided. There a new element was introduced into the struggle, for the right of the Roundhead force was commanded by Cromwell, who had raised and disciplined a body of cavalry called the Ironsides. These men were all fanatics in religion and fought with a sternness and vigor which carried all before them. In the eastern counties they had already done great service; but this was the first pitched battle at which they had been present. Their onslaught proved irresistible. The Royalist cavalry upon the left were completely broken, and the Roundhead horse then charged down upon the rear of the king's infantry. Had Rupert rallied his men and performed the same service upon the Parliament infantry, the battle might have been a drawn one; but, intoxicated with victory, he was chasing the Scottish horse far away, while Cromwell's Ironsides were deciding the fate of the battle. When he returned to the field all was over. Fifteen hundred prisoners, all the artillery, and more than a hundred banners had fallen into the hands of the cavalry; and with the remnants of his army Prince Rupert retired with all haste toward Chester, while Newcastle left York and embarked at Scarborough for the Continent.

Colonel Furness' troop had been with the wing under Prince Rupert, and deep indeed was their mortification when, upon returning to the field of battle, they found that all was lost.

"Unless a very different discipline is introduced upon our side," Colonel Furness said to his son that night in York, "it is clear that the king's cause is ruined. The Ironsides fight in a solid mass, and, after having given a charge, they are ready at order to wheel about and to deliver their attack wheresoever their general commands them. With us, no sooner do we defeat the enemy than we break into confusion, each man scatters in pursuit as if we were hunting a fox, and when at last we draw rein, miles away from the battle, we ever find that upon our return our footmen have been defeated. I fear much that Prince Rupert, with all his bravery, is a hindrance rather than an aid to the Royal cause. His counsels have always been on the side of resistance. He has supported the king in his too obstinate insistance upon what he deems his rights, while in the field his command is fatal to us. I fear, my boy, that the struggle will end badly, and I foresee bad times for England, and for all of us who have supported the cause of the king."

As the dispirited army marched back they received news which somewhat raised their hearts. The king had marched after Essex into Cornwall, and there had driven him into sore straits. He had endeavored to induce Essex to make a general treaty of peace; but the earl replied that he had no authority to treat, and that, even did he do so, the Parliament would not submit to be bound by it. With a considerable portion of his cavalry, he succeeded in passing through the Royal lines; but the whole of the infantry under General Skippon were forced to capitulate, the king giving them honorable terms, and requiring only the surrender of the artillery, arms, and ammunition. The whole of the army returned as scattered fugitives to London.

The king resolved again to march upon the capital. Montrose was now in arms in Scotland, and had gained two considerable victories over the Covenanters. The defeat at Marston had been outbalanced by the victories over Waller and Essex, and the Scotch, alarmed by the successes of Montrose, were ready to listen to terms, Steadily the king advanced eastward, and at Newbury the armies again met. As upon the previous occasion on that field, the battle led to no decisive results. Each side fought stoutly, and at nightfall separated without achieving substantial results. The king fell back upon Oxford, and the Parliament army upon Readings and negotiations were once again renewed between king and Parliament.

# CHAPTER XII

## AN ESCAPE FROM PRISON

There was no sadder or more gloomy face among the officers of the Parliament than that of Herbert Rippinghall—sad, not from the sour asceticism which distinguished the great portion of these officers, but from his regrets over the struggle in which he was taking a part. While Harry Furness saw much to find fault with in the conduct of many of his fellows, and in the obstinacy with which the king refused to grant concessions which might up to this time have restored peace to the land, Herbert, on his side, was shocked at the violence and excessive demands on the part of the Parliament, and at the rank hypocrisy which he saw everywhere around him. Both lads still considered that the balance of justice was on the side upon which they fought. But both, Herbert perhaps because more thoughtful, therefore more strongly, saw that the faults upon one side balanced those upon the other. Herbert had not taken up the sword willingly, as Harry had done. He was by disposition far less prone to adventure and more given to sober thought, and the violence of his father and the bigoted opinions which he held had repelled him from rather than attracted him toward the principles which he advocated. When, however, the summons came from his father to join him at Reading, with the rest of the hands employed in the business, he did not hesitate. He still hoped that the pacific party in Parliament would overcome the more violent, and that the tyranny of a small minority toward which the country appeared to be drifting would be nipped in the bud.

The divisions, indeed, in the Parliament were far greater than in the councils of the king. Between the Independents and the Presbyterians a wide gulf existed. The latter party, which was much the more numerous in Parliament, and which had moreover the countenance and alliance of the Scotch Presbyterians, viewed with the greatest jealousy the increasing arrogance of the Independents and of the military party. They became alarmed when they saw that they were rapidly drifting from the rule of the king to that of Cromwell, and that while they themselves would be satisfied with ample concessions and a certain amount of toleration, the Independents were working for much more than this. Upon the Presbyterian side, Lord Essex was regarded as their champion with the army, as against Cromwell, Fairfax, and Ireton. So strong did the feeling become that it was moved in the Commons "that no member of either House should, during the war, enjoy or execute any office or command, civil or military." A long and furious debate followed; but the ordinance was passed by the Lower House, and went up to the Lords, and was finally passed by them.

Now, however, occurred an episode which added greatly to the religious hatred prevailing between the two parties, and shocked many of the adherents of the Parliament by the wanton bigotry which it displayed. Archbishop Laud had now lain for four years in prison, and by an ordinance of Parliament, voted by only seven lords, he was condemned for high treason, and was beheaded on the 10th of January. This cruel and unnecessary murder showed only too plainly that the toleration which the Dissenters had clamored for meant only toleration for themselves, and intolerance toward all others; and a further example of this was given by the passing of an ordinance forbidding the use of the Liturgy of the Church of England in any place of worship in the country.

Rendered nervous by the increasing power of the Independents, the majority in Parliament now determined to open fresh negotiations with the king, and these offered a fairer prospect of peace than any which had hitherto preceded them. Commissioners were appointed by Parliament and by the king, and these met at Uxbridge, a truce being made for twenty days. Had the king been endowed with any sense of the danger of his position, or any desire to treat in a straightforward and honest manner with his opponents, peace might now have been secured. But the unfortunate monarch was seeking to cajole his foes rather than to treat with them, and his own papers, afterward discovered, show too plainly that the concessions which he offered were meant only to be kept so long as it might please him. The twenty precious days were frittered away in disputes. The king would grant one day concessions which he would revoke the next. The victories which Montrose was gaining in the north had roused his hopes, and the evil advice of his wife and Prince Rupert, and the earnest remonstrances which he received from Montrose against surrendering to the demands of Parliament, overpowered the advice of his wiser counselors. At the end of twenty days the negotiations ceased, and the commissioners of Parliament returned to London, convinced that there was no hope of obtaining a permanent peace with a man so vacillating and insincere as the king.

Herbert had been with his father at Uxbridge, as the regiment of foot to which he belonged was on guard here, and it was with a heavy heart that he returned to London, convinced that the war must go on, but forboding as great a disaster to the country in the despotism which he saw the Independents would finally establish as in the despotism of King Charles.

There was a general gloom in the city when the news of the unsuccessful termination of the negotiations became known. The vast majority of the people were eagerly desirous of peace. The two years which the war had already lasted had brought nothing save ruin to trade and general disaster, and the great body of the public who were not tinged with the intense fanaticism of the Independents, and who did not view all pleasure and enjoyment in life as sinful, longed for the merry old days when Englishmen might smile without being accused of sin, and when life was not passed solely in prayer and exhortation. Several small riots had broken out in London; but these were promptly suppressed. Among the 'prentice boys, especially, did the spirit of revolt against the gloomy asceticism of the time prevail, and there can be little doubt that if at this period, or for a long time subsequent, the king could have appeared suddenly in the city at the head of a few score troops, he would have been welcomed with acclamation, and the great body of the citizens would have rallied round him.

When the Parliament commissioners reached London Fairfax received his commission as sole general of the army. The military services of Cromwell were of such importance that Fairfax and his officers urged that an exception should be made to the ordinance in his case, and that he should be temporarily appointed lieutenant-general and chief commander of horse. The moderate party yielded to the demand of the Independents. The Earls of Essex, Manchester, and Denbigh gave in their resignations. Many of the more moderate advisers of Charles also retired to their estates, despairing of a conflict in which the king's obstinacy admitted of no hope of a favorable termination. They, too, had, as much perhaps as the members of the recalcitrant Parliament, hoped for reforms; but it was clear that the king would never consent to reign except as an absolute monarch, and for this they were unprepared. The violent party among the Cavaliers now ruled supreme in the councils of Charles. For a short time the royal cause seemed in the ascendant. Leicester had been taken by storm, Taunton was besieged, Fairfax was surrounding Oxford, but was doing nothing against the town. On the 5th of June he was ordered to raise the siege, and to go to the Midland counties after the royal army. On the 13th Fairfax and Cromwell joined their forces, and pursued the king, whom they overtook the next day near Naseby.

Herbert had accompanied the army of Fairfax, and seeing the number and resolution of the troops, he hoped that a victory might be gained which would terminate for good and all this disastrous conflict. The ground round Naseby is chiefly moorland. The king's army was drawn up a mile from Market Harborough. Prince Rupert commanded the left wing, Sir Marmaduke Langdale the right, Lord Ashley the main body. Fairfax commanded the center of the Roundheads, with General Skippon under him. Cromwell commanded the right and Ireton the left. Rupert had hurried on with his horse in advance, and coming upon the Roundheads, at once engaged them. So sudden was the attack that neither party had formed its lines for battle, and the artillery was in the rear. Between the armies lay a wide level known as Broadmoor. It was across this that Rupert had ridden, and charging up the hill on the other side, fell upon the left wing of Fairfax. Cromwell, upon the other hand, from the extreme right charged down the hill upon Langdale's squadrons. Prince Rupert, as usual, carried all before him. Shouting his battle cry, "Queen Mary," he fell upon Ireton's left wing, and drove them from the field, chasing them back to Naseby, where, as usual, he lost time in capturing the enemy's baggage. Cromwell, with his Ironsides, upon the other hand, had broken Langdale's horse and driven them from the field. In the center the fight was hot. The king's foot had come up the hill and poured volley after volley into the parliament ranks. Hand to hand the infantry were fighting, and gradually the Roundheads were giving way. But now, as at Marston, Cromwell, keeping his Ironsides well in hand, returned from the defeat of Langdale's horse, and fell upon the rear of the Royalists. Fairfax rallied his men as he saw the horse coming up to his assistance. Rupert's troopers were far from the field, and a panic seizing the king's reserve of horse, who had they charged might have won the day, the Earl of Carnewarth, taking hold of King Charles' horse, forced him from the field, and the battle ended, with the complete defeat of the royal troops, before Rupert returned to the field of battle.

The Royalists lost in killed and prisoners five thousand men, their twelve guns, and all their baggage train, and what was of even greater importance, the king's private cabinet, which contained documents which did more to precipitate his ruin even than the defeat of his army. Here were found letters proving that while he had professed his desire to treat, he had no intention of giving way in the slightest degree. Here were copies of letters to foreign princes asking for aid, and to the Papists in Ireland, promising all kinds of concessions if they would rise in his favor. Not only did the publication of this correspondence and of the private letters between the king and queen add to the indignation of the Commons and to their determination to fight to the bitterest end, but it disgusted and alienated a vast number of Royalists who had hitherto believed in the king and trusted to his royal word.

Among the prisoners taken at Naseby was Harry Furness, whose troop had been with Langdale's horse, and who, his charger having been shot, had fallen upon the field, his head being cut by the sweep of the sword of a Roundhead soldier, who struck at him as he was lying on the ground. Soon after the battle, when it became known what prisoners had been taken, he was visited by his friend Herbert.

"We are changing sides, Herbert," Harry said, with a faint smile. "The last time we met you were nigh falling into the hands of the Royalists, now I have altogether fallen into yours."

"Yes, and unfortunately," Herbert said, "I cannot repeat your act of generosity. However, Harry, I trust that with this great battle the war is nearly over, and that all prisoners now taken will speedily be released. At any rate, I need not assure you that you will have my aid and assistance in any matter."

The Parliamentary leaders did not allow the grass to grow under their feet after Naseby. Prince Rupert, with considerable force, had marched to Bristol, and Fairfax and Cromwell followed him there. A considerable portion of the prisoners were sent to London, but some were retained with the army. Among these was Harry Furness, whom it was intended to confine with many others in some sure place in the south. Under a guard they were conducted to Reading, where they were for awhile to be kept. Essex and Cromwell advanced to Bristol, which they surrounded; and Prince Rupert, after a brave defense, was forced to capitulate, upon terms similar to those which had been granted by the king to the army of Lord Essex the year before. In his conduct of the siege the prince had certainly not failed. But this misfortune aroused the king's anger more than the faults which had done such evil service on the fields of Naseby and Marston, and he wrote to the prince, ordering him to leave the kingdom at once.

It would have been well had King Charles here ceased the struggle, for the cause of the Royalists was now hopeless. Infatuated to the last, however, and deeming ever that the increasing contentions and ill-will between the two parties in Parliament would finally end by one of them bidding for the Royal support, and agreeing to his terms, the king continued the contest. Here and there isolated affrays took place; risings in Kent and other counties occurring, but being defeated summarily by the vigor of Fairfax and his generals.

The time passed but slowly with Harry at Reading. He and his fellow-prisoners were assigned quarters in a large building, under the guard of a regiment of Parliament troops. Their imprisonment was not rigorous. They were fairly fed and allowed exercise in a large courtyard which adjoined the house. The more reckless spirits sang, jested, wrote scurrilous songs on the Roundheads, and passed the time as cheerfully as might be. Harry, however, with the restlessness of his age, longed for liberty. He knew that Prince Charles was in command of the army in the west, and he longed to join him and try once more the fortunes of battle. The guard set round the building was close and vigilant, and the chances of escape appeared small. Still, Harry thought that if he could escape from an upper window on a dark night he could surely make his way through the line of sentries. He had observed on moonlight nights the exact position which each of these occupied. The intervals were short between them; but it would be quite possible on a dark night for a person to pass noiselessly without being perceived. The watch would have been even more strict than it was, had not the Puritans regarded the struggle as virtually at an end, and were, therefore, less careful as to their prisoners than they would otherwise have been. Harry prepared for escape by tearing up the blankets of his bed and knotting them into ropes. A portion he wrapped round his shoes, so as to walk noiselessly, and taking advantage of a dark, moonless night, when the fog hung thick upon the low land round Reading, he opened his window, threw out his rope, and slipped down to the ground.

So dark was the fog that it was difficult for him to see two paces in advance, and he soon found that the careful observations which he had taken of the place of the sentries would be altogether useless. Still, in the darkness and thickness of the night, he thought that the chance of detection was small. Creeping quietly and noiselessly along, he could hear the constant challenges of the sentries round him. These, excited by the unusual darkness of the night, were unusually vigilant. Harry approached until he was within a few yards of the line, and the voices of the men as they challenged enabled him to ascertain exactly the position of those on the right and left of him. Passing between these, he could see neither, although they were but a few paces on either hand, and he would have got off unobserved had he not suddenly fallen into a deep stream running across his way, and which in the darkness he did not see until he fell into it. At the sound there was an instant challenge, and then a piece was discharged. Harry struggled across the stream, and clambered out on the opposite side. As he did so a number of muskets were fired in his direction by the men who came rushing up to the point of alarm. One ball struck him in the shoulder. The rest whizzed harmlessly by, and at the top of his speed he ran forward.

He was now safe from pursuit, for in the darkness of the night it would have been absolutely impossible to follow him. In a few minutes he ceased running, for when all became quiet behind him, he could no longer tell in what direction he was advancing. So long as he could hear the shouts of the sentries he continued his way, and then, all guidance being lost, he lay down under a hedge and waited for morning. It was still thick and foggy; but wandering aimlessly about for some time, he succeeded at last in striking upon a road, and judging from the side upon which he had entered it in which direction Reading must lie, he took the western way and went forward. The ball had passed only through the fleshy part of his shoulder, missing the bone; and although it caused him much pain, he was able, by wrapping his arm tightly to his body, to proceed. More than once he had to withdraw from the road into the fields beyond, when he heard troops of horse galloping along.

After a long day's walk he arrived near Abingdon, and there made for the hall. Instead of going to the door he made for the windows, and, looking in, saw a number of Roundhead soldiers in the hall, and knew that there was no safety for him. As he glanced in one of the soldiers happened to cast his eyes up, and gave a shout on seeing a figure looking in at the window. Instantly the rest sprang to their feet, and started out to secure the intruder. Harry fled along the road, and soon reached Abingdon. He had at first thought of making for one of his father's farms; but he felt sure that here also Roundhead troops would be quartered. After a moment's hesitation he determined to make for Mr. Rippinghall's. He knew the premises accurately, and thought that he might easily take refuge in the warehouses, in which large quantities of wool were wont to be stored. The streets were deserted, for it was now late at night, and he found his way without interruption to the wool-stapler's. Here he climbed over a wall, made his way into the warehouse, and clambering over a large number of bales, laid himself down next to the wall, secure from any casual observation. Here he went off to sleep, and it was late next day before he opened his eyes. He was nearly uttering an exclamation at the pain which his movement on waking gave to his wounded arm. He, however, repressed it, and it was well he did so, as he heard voices in the warehouse. Men were removing bales of wool, and for some hours this process went on. Harry, being well back, had little fear that he should be disturbed.

The hours passed wearily. He was parched and feverish from the pain of his wound, and was unable to deliberate as to his best course. Sometimes he dozed off into snatches of sleep, and after one of these he found that the warehouse was again silent, and that darkness had set in. He determined to wait at least for another day, and also that he would early in the morning look out from the window before the men entered, in hopes that he might catch sight of his old playfellow, Lucy, who would, he felt sure, bring him some water and refreshment if she were able. Accordingly, in the morning, he took his place so as to command a view of the garden, and presently to his great surprise he saw Herbert, whom he had believed with the army, come out together with Lucy. They had not taken four paces in the garden when their attention was attracted by a tap at the window, and looking up, they were astonished at beholding Harry's pale face there. With an exclamation of surprise they hurried into the warehouse.

"My dear Harry," Herbert exclaimed, "how did you get here? The troops have been searching for you high and low. Your escape from Reading was bruited abroad a few hours after it took place, and the party at the hall having reported seeing some one looking in at the window, there was no doubt felt that you had gained this neighborhood, and a close watch has been kept. All your father's farms have been carefully examined, and their occupants questioned, and the general belief is that you are still hidden somewhere near."

"I got a ball through my shoulder," Harry said, "in making my way through the sentries, and have felt myself unable to travel until I could obtain some food. I thought that I should be safer from search here, and believing you were away in the army, thought that your sister would perhaps be moved by compassion to aid her old playfellow."

"Yes, indeed," the girl said; "I would have done anything for you, Harry. To think of your being hidden so close to us, while we were sleeping quietly. I will at once get you some food, and then you and Herbert can talk over what is best to be done."

So saying she ran into the house, and returned in a few minutes with a bowl of milk and some freshly made cakes, which Harry drank and ate ravenously. In the meantime, he was discussing with Herbert what was the best course to pursue.

"It would not be safe," Herbert said, "for you to try and journey further at present. The search for you is very keen, and it happens, unfortunately, that the officer in command here is the very man whose face you sliced when he came to Furness Hall some two years back. It would be a bad thing for you were you to fall into his hands."

Lucy at first proposed that Harry should be taken into the house, and go at once to bed. She and Herbert would then give out that a friend had arrived from a distance, who was ill, and, waiting upon him themselves, should prevent suspicion being attracted. This, however, Herbert did not think would be safe. It would be asked when the inmate had arrived, and who he was, and why the servants should not, as usual, attend upon him.

"I think," he said, "that if to-night I go forth, having said at dinner in the hearing of the servant that I am expecting a friend from London, you can then join me outside, and return with me. You must crop off those long ringlets of yours, and turn Roundhead for the nonce. I can let you have a sober suit which was made for me when I was in London, and which has not yet been seen by my servants. I can say that you are in bad health, and this will enable you to remain at home, sleeping upon a couch to nurse your shoulder."

"The shoulder is of no consequence," Harry said. "A mere flesh wound like that would not detain me away from the saddle. It is only the fatigue and loss of blood, together with want of food, which has weakened me."

As no other course presented itself this was followed. Harry remained during the day in his place of concealment in the warehouse, and at nightfall went out, and, being joined by Herbert, returned with him to the house. The door was opened by Lucy and he entered unperceived by the domestics. The first operation was to cut off the whole of his hair close to his head. He was then attired in Herbert's clothes, and looked, as Lucy told him, a quiet and decent young gentleman. Then he took his place on a couch in the sitting-room, and Herbert rung for supper, which he had ordered to be prepared for a guest as well as for Lucy and himself.

# CHAPTER XIII

# PUBLIC EVENTS

For some days Harry remained quietly with his friend. He did not stir beyond the door, although he had but little fear of any of his old friends recognizing him. The two years which had passed since he was at school had greatly changed his appearance, and his closely-cut hair, and the somber and Puritanical cut of his garments so completely altered him that it would have been a keen eye indeed which had recognized him when merely passing in the street. A portion of each day he spent out in the garden strolling with Lucy, or sitting quietly while she read to him. The stiffness in his arm was now abating, and as the search for him had to a great extent ceased, he intended in a short time to make for Oxford.

The news from the various points at which the conflict still continued was everywhere disastrous for the king. Montrose had been defeated. The king, endeavoring to make his way north to join him, had been smartly repulsed. The Royalists were everywhere disorganized and broken. Negotiations were once again proceeding, and as the Scottish army was marching south, and the affairs of the crown seemed desperate, there was every hope that the end of the long struggle was approaching. Harry's departure was hastened by a letter received by Herbert from his father, saying that he had obtained leave from his regiment, and should be down upon the following day.

"My father will not blame me," Herbert said, "for what I have done, when he comes to know it. But I am not sure that he would himself approve of your remaining here. His convictions are so earnest, and his sense of duty so strong, that I do not think he would harbor his nearest relative, did he believe him to be in favor of the king."

Harry next morning mounted a horse of Herbert's and started to ride from the town, after taking an affectionate farewell of his hosts. When two miles out of Abingdon he suddenly came upon a body of Parliament horse, in the leader of whom he recognized, by a great scar across his face, the officer with whom he had fallen out at Furness Hall. Relying upon his disguise, and upon the fact that it was only for a minute that the officer had seen him, he rode quietly on.

"Whom have we here?" the Roundhead said, reining in his horse.

"My name is Roger Copley, and I am making my way from London to my people, who reside in the west. There is no law, I believe, against my so doing."

"There is no law for much that is done or undone," the Roundhead said. "Malignants are going about the country in all sorts of disguises, stirring up men to ungodly enterprises, and we cannot be too particular whom we let pass. What hast thou been doing in London?"

"I have been serving my time as apprentice to Master Nicholas Fleming, the merchant in velvets and silks in the Chepe."

"Hast thou any papers to prove thy identity?"

"I have not," Harry said; "not knowing that such were needed. I have traveled thus far without interruption or question, and am surprised to find hindrance upon the part of an officer of the Commons."

"You must turn your horse, and ride back with me into Abingdon," the officer said. "I doubt me much that you are as you pretend to be. However, it is a matter which we can bring to the proof."

Harry wondered to himself of what proof the matter was capable. But without a word he turned his horse's head toward Abingdon. Scarcely a word was spoken on the way, and Harry was meditating whether he should say that he had been staying with his friend Herbert. But thinking that this might lead the latter into trouble, he determined to be silent on that head. They stopped at the door of the principal trader in the town and the captain roughly told his prisoner to alight and enter with him.

"Master Williamson," he said, "bring out some pieces of velvet. This man, whom I suspect to be a Cavalier in disguise, saith that he has been an apprentice to Master Nicholas Fleming, a velvet dealer of London. I would fain see how far his knowledge of these goods extends. Bring out five or six pieces of various qualities, and put them upon your table promiscuously, and not in order of value."

The mercer did as requested.

"These goods," he said, "were obtained from Master Fleming himself. I bought them last year, and have scarce sold a piece of such an article since."

Harry felt rather nervous at the thought of being obliged to distinguish between the velvets, for although he had received some hints and instructions from the merchant, he knew that the appearance of one kind of velvet differed but slightly from that of the inferior qualities. To his satisfaction, however, he saw at the end of the rolls the pieces of paper intact upon which Master Fleming's private marks were placed.

"I need not," he said, "look at the velvets, for I see my master's private marks upon them, and can of course tell you their value at once."

So saying, from the private marks he read off the value of each roll of velvet per yard, and as these tallied exactly with the amount which the mercer had paid for them, no further doubts remained upon the mind of the officer.

"These marks," he said to the mercer, "are, I suppose, private, and could not be read save by one in the merchant's confidence?"

"That is so," the mercer replied. "I myself am in ignorance of the meaning of these various symbols."

"You will forgive me," the Parliament officer said to Harry. "In these times one cannot be too suspicious, and even the best friends of the Commons need not grudge a little delay in their journeyings, in order that the doings of the malignants may be arrested."

Harry in a few words assured the officer that he bore him no malice for his arrest, and that, indeed, his zeal in the cause did him credit. Then again mounting his horse, he quietly rode out of Abingdon. This time he met with no difficulties, and an hour later entered Oxford.

Here he found his father and many of his acquaintances. A great change had come over the royal city. The tone of boastfulness and anticipated triumph which had pervaded it before the second battle of Newbury had now entirely disappeared. Gloom was written upon all faces, and few entertained any hopes of a favorable termination to their cause. Here a year passed slowly and heavily. The great proportion of Sir Henry Furness' troop were allowed to return to their farms, as at present there was no occasion for their services in the field.

All this time the king was negotiating and treating; the Parliament quarreling furiously among themselves. The war had languished everywhere. In the west a rising had been defeated by the Parliament troops. The Prince of Wales had retired to France; and there was now no force which could be called an army capable of taking the field.

The bitterness of the conflict had for a long time ceased; and in the general hope that peace was at hand, the rancor of Cavalier against Roundhead softened down, A great many of the adherents of Charles returned quietly to their homes, and here they were allowed to settle down without interruption.

The contrast between this state of things and that which

prevailed in Scotland was very strong, and has been noted by more than one historian. In England men struggled for principle, and, having fought the battle out, appeared to bear but little animosity to each other, and returned each to his own pursuits unmolested and unharmed. In Scotland, upon the other hand, after the defeat of Montrose, large numbers of prisoners were executed in cold blood, and sanguinary persecutions took place.

In Parliament the disputes between the Independents and Presbyterians grew more and more bitter, the latter being strengthened by the presence of the Scotch army in England. They were greatly in the majority in point of numbers; but the Independents made up for their numerical weakness by the violence of their opinions, and by the support of the army, which was entirely officered by men of extreme views.

The king, instead of frankly dealing with the Commons, now that his hopes in the field were gone, unhappily continued his intrigues, hoping that an open breach would take place between the parties. On the 5th of December he wrote to the speaker of the House of Lords, offering to send a deputation to Westminster with propositions for the foundation of a happy and well-grounded peace. This offer was declined, and he again wrote, offering himself to proceed to Westminster to treat in person. The leaders of Parliament, and indeed with reason, suspected the sincerity of the king. Papers had been found in the carriage of the Catholic Archbishop of Tuam, who was killed in a skirmish in October, proving that the king had concluded an alliance with the Irish rebels, and that he had agreed, if they would land ten thousand men in England, that popery should be re-established in Ireland, and the Protestants brought under subjection. Letters which have since been discovered prove that in January, 1646, while urging upon the Parliament to come to terms, he was writing to the queen, saying that he was only deceiving them. In his letter he said:

"Now, as to points which I expected by my treaty at London. Knowing assuredly the great animosity which is betwixt the Independents and Presbyterians, I had great reason to hope that one of the factions would so address themselves to me that I might, without great difficulty, obtain my so just ends, and, questionless, it would have given me the fittest opportunity. For considering the Scots' treaty that would be besides, I might have found means to put distractions among them, though I had found none."

Such being the spirit that animated the king, there is little reason for surprise that the negotiations came to nothing. The last hope of the crown was destroyed when, on the 22d of March, Lord

Astley, marching from Worcester to join the king at Oxford, was defeated at Stow, in the Wold, and the three thousand Cavaliers with him killed, captured, or dispersed. Again the king sent a message to Parliament, offering to come to Whitehall, and proposing terms similar to those which he had rejected when the negotiators met at Uxbridge. His real object, however, was to produce such an effect by his presence in London as would create a reaction in his favor. Three days after he had sent this message he wrote to Digby:

"I am endeavoring to get to London, so that the conditions may be such as a gentleman may own, and that the rebels may acknowledge me king, being not without hope that I shall be able so to draw either the Presbyterians or Independents to side with me for exterminating the one or the other, that I shall be really king again."

These offers were rejected by Parliament, and the army of Fairfax advanced toward Oxford. In the meanwhile, Montreuil, a special ambassador from France, h ad been negotiating with the Scottish commissioners in London to induce the Scots to take up the cause of the king. He then proceeded to Edinburgh, and afterward to the Scotch army. At first the Scotch were willing to receive him; but they perceived the danger which would be involved in a quarrel with the English Parliament. Already there were many causes of dispute. The army had not received the pay promised them when they marched south, and being without money had been obliged to live upon the country, creating great disorders and confusion, and rendering themselves bitterly hated by the people. Thus their answers continued to be ambiguous, making no absolute promise, but yet giving a sort of encouragement to the king to place himself in their hands.

Toward the end of April Fairfax was drawing so close around Oxford that the king felt that hesitation was no longer possible, and accompanied only by his chaplain, Dr. Michael Hudson, and by a groom of his bedchamber, named Jack Ashburnham, he left Oxford at night, and after many adventures arrived at the Scotch army, before Newark, where upon his arrival "many lords came instantly to wait on his majesty, with professions of joy to find that he had so far honored their army as to think it worthy his presence after so long an opposition." Lord Leven, however, who commanded the Scotch army, while receiving the king with professions of courtesy and honor, yet gave him to understand that he must in some way consider himself as a prisoner. The king, at the request of the

Scotch, signed an order to his governor of Newark, who had been for months bravely holding out, to surrender the place, and this having been done, the Scottish army with the king marched to Newcastle.

After the king's surrender to the Scotch the civil war virtually ceased, although many places still held out. Oxford, closely invested, maintained itself until the 22d of June, when it capitulated to Fairfax, upon the terms that the garrison "should march out of the city of Oxford with their horses and complete arms that properly belong under them proportionable to their present or past commands, flying colors, trumpets sounding, drums beating, matches alight at both ends, bullets in their mouths, and every soldier to have twelve charges of powder, match and bullet proportionable." Those who desired to go to their houses or friends were to lay down their arms within fifteen miles of Oxford, and then to have passes, with the right of free quarter, and those who wished to go across the sea to serve any foreign power were to be allowed to do so. This surrender was honorable to both parties, and upon the city being given up, the garrison marched out, and then scattered to their various houses and counties, without let or molestation from the troops of the Commons.

Harry Furness and his father had not far to go. They were soon installed in their old house, where although some confusion prevailed owing to its having been frequently in the occupation of bodies of Parliament troops, yet the damage done was not serious, and in a short time it was restored to its former condition. Several of the more valuable articles were allowed to remain in the hiding-places in which they had been concealed, as none could yet say how events might finally turn out. A portion of the Parliamentary troops were also disbanded, and allowed to return to their homes; among these were Master Rippinghall and his son, and for some months matters went on at Abingdon as if the civil war had never been. Harry often saw his friend Herbert; but so long as the king remained in a doubtful position in the army of the Scots, no close intercourse could take place between members of parties so opposed to each other.

The time went slowly with Harry, for after the past three years of excitement it was difficult to settle down to a quiet life at Furness Hall. He was of course too old now for schooling, and the times were yet too disturbed for men to engage in the field sports which occupy so large a portion of country life. Colonel Furness, indeed, had determined that in no case would he again take up arms. He was discontented with the whole course of events, and foresaw that, with the unhappy temper of the king, no favorable issue could possibly be looked for. He had done his best, he said, for the crown and would do no more. He told his son, however, that he should place no rein upon his inclinations should he choose to meddle further in the matter. Harry would fain have gone abroad, whither so many of the leading Cavaliers had already betaken themselves, and entered the service of some foreign court for a few years. But his father dissuaded him from this, at any rate for the present.

"These delays and negotiations," he said, "cannot last forever. I care not whether Presbyterians or Independents get the power over our unhappy country. The Independents are perhaps the more bigoted; the Presbyterians the more intolerant. But as the latter would certainly respect the royal authority more than the former, whose rage appears to me to pass the bounds of all moderation, I would gladly see the Presbyterians obtain the upper hand."

For months the negotiations dragged wearily on, the king, as usual, maintaining an indecisive attitude between the two parties. At length, however, the negotiations ended in a manner which brought an eternal disgrace upon the Scotch, for they agreed, upon the receipt of a large sum of money as the deferred pay of the army, to deliver the king into the hands of the English Parliament. A great convoy of money was sent down from London, and the day that the cash was in the hands of the Scots they handed over the king to the Parliamentary commissioners sent down to receive him. The king was conducted to Holmby House, a fine mansion within six miles of Northampton, and there was at first treated with great honor. A large household and domestic servants were chosen for him, an excellent stable kept, and the king was allowed a large amount of personal liberty. The nobles and gentlemen of his court were permitted to see him, and in fact he was apparently restored to his rank and estate. The Presbyterian party were in power; but while they treated the king with the respect due to his exalted station, they had no more regard to the rights of his conscience than to those of the consciences of the people at large. He desired to have chaplains of the Episcopal church; but the Parliament refused this, and sent him two Presbyterian ministers, whom the king refused to receive.

While King Charles remained at Holmby Parliament quarreled furiously. The spirit of the Independents obtained a stronger and stronger hold upon the army. Cromwell himself, with a host of others, preached daily among them, and this general, although Fairfax was the commander-in-chief, came gradually to be regarded as the leader of the army. There can be no doubt that Cromwell was thoroughly sincere in his convictions, and the charges of hypocrisy which have been brought against him, are at least proved to be untrue. He was a man of convictions as earnest as those of the king himself, and as firmly resolved to override the authority of the Parliament, when the Parliament withstood him.

Three days after the king arrived at Holmby House the Commons voted that the army should be disbanded, with the exception of troops required for the suppression of rebellion in Ireland, and for the service of the garrisons. It was also voted that there should be no officers, except Fairfax, of higher rank than colonel, and that every officer should take the covenant and conform to the Presbyterian Church. A loan was raised in the city to pay off a portion of the arrears of pay due to the army. The sum, however, was insufficient, and there were great murmurings among the men and officers. Fourteen of the latter petitioned Parliament on the subject of arrears, asking that auditors should be appointed to report on what was due to them, and laying down some conditions with regard to their employment in Ireland. Five days afterward the House, on receipt of this petition, declared that whoever had a hand in promoting it, or any other such petition, was an enemy to the State, and a disturber of the public peace. The army were furious at this declaration. Deputations from them went to the House, and from the House to the army. The Presbyterian members were highly indignant at their pretensions, and Cromwell saw that the time was at hand when the army would take the affair entirely into their hands. The soldiers organized a council of delegates, called "Adjutators," to look after their rights. The Parliament voted eight weeks' pay, and a committee went to the army to see it disbanded. The army declined to disband, and said that eight times eight weeks' pay was due. The feeling grew hotter and hotter, and the majority in Parliament came to the conclusion that Cromwell should be arrested. Cromwell, however, obtained word of what was intended, and left London.

Upon the same day a party of soldiers went down to Holmby, and forcibly carried off King Charles from the Parliamentary commissioners, the troops stationed at Holmby fraternizing with their comrades. The king, under the charge of these new guards, arrived at Royston on the 7th of June, and Fairfax and Cromwell met him there. He asked if they had commissioned Joyce, who was at the head of the party of men who had carried him off, to remove him. They denied that they had done so.

111

"I shall not believe you," said the king, "unless you hang him." And his majesty had good ground for his disbelief.

Cromwell returned to London and took his place in the House, and there blamed the soldiers, protesting that he would stick to the Parliament; but the same night he went away again down to the army, and there declared to them the actions and designs of Parliament. Commissioners came down on the 10th from the Commons; but the army formed up, and when the votes were read, refused to obey them. The same afternoon a letter, signed by Fairfax, Cromwell, Ireton, and ten other officers, was sent to the city, stating that they were about to advance upon London, and declaring that if the city did not take part against them "in their just desires to resist that wicked party which would embroil us and the kingdom, neither we nor our soldiers shall give you the least offense." The army marched to St. Albans, and thence demanded the impeachment of eleven members of the Commons, all leading Presbyterians. The city and Parliament were in a state of consternation. The army advanced to Uxbridge. It demanded a month's pay, and received it; but it continued to advance. On the 26th of April Parliament gave way. The eleven members retired from the House, the Commons passed a vote approving of the proceedings of the army, and commissioners were appointed.

All this time the king was treated as honorably as he had been when at Holmby House. He was always lodged at great houses in the neighborhood of the army—at the Earl of Salisbury's, at Hatfield, when the troops were at St. Albans, and at the Earl of Craven's, at Caversham, when the army moved further back. And at both of these places he was allowed to receive the visits of his friends, and to spend his time as he desired.

More critical times were now, however, at hand.

# CHAPTER XIV

## LAST ATTEMPT TO RESCUE THE KING

The king, after London had been overawed by the army, was lodged in Hampton Court. At this time the feeling throughout England was growing stronger and stronger in favor of the re-establishment of the monarchy, It was now a year since, with the fall of Oxford, the civil war had virtually concluded, and people yearned for a settled government and a return to ancient usages and manners. The great majority of that very Parliament which had withstood and conquered Charles were of one mind with the people in general; but England was no longer free to choose for itself. The army had won the victory for the Commons, and was determined to impose its will upon the nation. At this time Cromwell, Ireton, and Fairfax were disposed to an arrangement, but their authority was overshadowed by that of the preachers, who, in their harangues to the troops, denounced these generals as traitors, and then finding that they were likely to lose their influence, and to become obnoxious to both parties, henceforth threw their lot in with the army, and headed it in its struggle with the Parliament. Even yet the long misfortunes which Charles had suffered were insufficient to teach him wisdom. Had he now heartily thrown himself into the hands of the moderate majority in Parliament he might—aided by them and by the Scots, who, seeing that the Independents were ignoring all the obligations which had been undertaken by the Solemn League and government, were now almost openly hostile to the party of the army—have again mounted the throne, amid the joyful acclamations of the whole country. The army would have fought, but Charles, with England at his back, would assuredly have conquered. Unfortunately, the king could not be honest. His sole idea of policy was to set one section of his opponents against the other. He intrigued at once with the generals and with the Parliament, and had the imprudence to write continually to the queen and others, avowing that he was deceiving both. Several of these letters were intercepted, and although desirous of playing off the king against the army, the Commons felt that they could place no trust in him whatever; while the preachers and the army clamored more and more loudly that he should be brought to trial as a traitor.

Harry Furness had, after the fall of Oxford, remained quietly with his father at Furness Hall. Once or twice only had he gone up to London, returning with reports that the people there were becoming more and more desirous of the restoration of the king to his rights. The great majority were heartily sick of the rule of the preachers, with their lengthy exhortations, their sad faces, and their abhorrence of amusement of all kinds. There had been several popular tumults, in which the old cry of "God save the king," had again been raised. The apprentices were ready to join in any movement which might bring back the pleasant times of old. Cavaliers now openly showed themselves in the streets, and London was indeed ripe for an insurrection against the sovereignty which the army had established over the nation. Had the king at this time escaped from Hampton Court, and ridden into London at the head of only twenty gentlemen, and issued a proclamation appealing to the loyalty of the citizens, and promising faithfully to preserve the rights of the people, and to govern constitutionally, he would have been received with acclamation. The majority of Parliament would have declared for him, England would have received the news with delight, and the army alone would not have sufficed to turn the tide against him. Unhappily for Charles, he had no more idea now than at the commencement of the war of governing constitutionally, and instead thinking of trusting himself to the loyalty and affection of his subjects, he was meditating an escape to France. Harry received a letter from one of the king's most attached adherents, who was in waiting upon him at Hampton, begging him to repair there at once, as his majesty desired the aid of a few of those upon whom he could best rely, for an enterprise which he was about to undertake. Harry showed the letter to his father.

"You must do as you will, Harry," the colonel said. "For myself, I stick to my determination to meddle no more in the broils of this kingdom. Could I trust his Majesty, I would lay down my life for him willingly; but I cannot trust him. All the misfortunes which have befallen him, all the blood which has been poured out by loyal men in his cause, all the advice which his best councilors have given him, have been thrown away upon him. He is as lavish with his promises as ever, but all the time he is intending to break them as soon as he gets ample chance. Were he seated upon the throne again to-morrow, he would be as arbitrary as he was upon the day he ascended it. I do not say that I would not far rather see England under the tyranny of one man than under that of an army of ambitious knaves; but the latter cannot last. The king's authority, once riveted again on the necks of the people, might enslave them for generations, but England will never submit long to the yoke of military dictators. The evil is great, but it will right itself in time. But do you do as you like, Harry. You have, I hope, a long life before you, and 'twere best that you chose your own path in it. But think it over, my son. Decide nothing to-night, and in the morning let me know what you have determined."

Harry slept but little that night. When he met his father at breakfast he said:

"I have decided, father. You know that my opinions run with yours as to the folly of the king, and the wrongfulness and unwisdom of his policy. Still he is alone, surrounded by traitors to whose ambition he is an obstacle, and who clamor for his blood. I know not upon what enterprise he may now be bent, but methinks that it must be that he thinks of an escape from the hands of his jailers. If so, he must meditate a flight to France. There he will need faithful followers, who will do their best to make him feel that he is still a king who will cheer his exile and sustain his hopes. It may be that years will pass before England shakes off the iron yoke which Cromwell and his army are placing upon her neck. But, as you say, I am young and can wait. There are countries in Europe where a gentleman can take service in the army, and should aught happen to King Charles there I will enroll myself until these evil days be all passed. I would rather never see England again than live here to be ruled by King Cromwell and his canting Ironsides."

"So be it, my son," the colonel said. "I do not strive to dissuade you, for methinks had I been of your age I should have chosen the same. Should your fortunes lead you abroad, as they likely will, I shall send you a third of my income here. The rest will be ample for me. There will be little feasting or merriment at Furness Hall until the cloud which overshadows England be passed away, and you be again by my side. There is little fear of my being disturbed. Those who laid down their arms when the war ceased were assured of the possession of their property, and as I shall draw sword no more there will be no excuse for the Roundheads to lay hands on Furness Hall. And now, my boy, here are a hundred gold pieces. Use them in the king's service. When I hear that you are abroad I will write to Master Fleming to arrange with his correspondents, whether in France or Holland, as you may chance to be, to pay the money regularly into your hands. You will, I suppose, take Jacob with you?"

"Assuredly I will," Harry said. "He is attached and faithful, and although he cares not very greatly for the King's cause, I know he will follow my fortunes. He is sick to death of the post which I obtained for him after the war, with a scrivener at Oxford. I will also take William Long with me, if he will go. He is a merry fellow, and has a wise head. He and Jacob did marvelously at Edinburgh, when they cozened the preachers, and got me out of the clutches of Argyll. With two such trusty followers I could go through Europe. I will ride over to Oxford at once."

As Harry anticipated, Jacob was delighted at the prospect of abandoning his scrivener's desk.

"I don't believe," he said, when he had learned from Harry that they were going to the king at Hampton, "that aught will come of these plottings. As I told you when we were apprentices together, I love plots, but there are men with whom it is fatal to plot. Such a one, assuredly, is his gracious majesty. For a plot to be successful, all to be concerned in it must know their own minds, and be true as steel to each other. The King never knows his own mind for half an hour together, and, unfortunately, he seems unable to be true to any one. So let it be understood, Master Harry, that I go into this business partly from love of you, who have been truly a most kind friend to me, partly because I love adventure, and hate this scrivener's desk, partly because there is a chance that I may benefit by the change."

Harry bade him procure apparel as a sober retainer in a Puritan family, and join him that night at Furness Hall, as he purposed to set out at daybreak. William Long also agreed at once to follow Harry's fortunes. The old farmer, his father, offered no objection.

"It is right that my son should ride with the heir of Furness Hall," he said. "We have been Furness tenants for centuries, and have ever fought by our lords in battle. Besides, Master Harry, I doubt me whether William will ever settle down here in peace. His elder brother will have the farm after me, so it matters not greatly, but your wars and journeyings have turned his head, and he thinks of arms and steel caps more than of fat beeves or well-tilled fields."

The next morning, soon after daybreak, Harry and his followers left Furness Hall, and arrived the same night at Hampton. Here they put up at a hostelry, and Harry sent a messenger to Lord Ashburnham, who had summoned him, and was in attendance upon the king, to say that he had arrived.

An hour later Lord Ashburnham joined him. "I am glad you have come, Master Furness," he said. "The king needs faithful servants; and it's well that you have come to-day, as I have been ordered by those in power to remove from the king's person. His majesty has lost all hope of coming to an agreement with either party here. At one time it seemed that Cromwell and Ireton were like to have joined him, but a letter of the king's, in which he spoke of them somewhat discourteously, fell into their hands, and they have now given themselves wholly over to the party most furious against the king. Therefore he has resolved to fly. Do you move from hence and take up your quarters at Kingston, where no curious questions are likely to be asked you. I shall take lodgings at Ditton, and shall there await orders from the king. It may be that he will change his mind, but of this Major Legg, who attends him in his bedchamber, will notify us. Our design is to ride to the coast near Southampton and there take ship, and embark for France. It is not likely that we shall be attacked by the way, but as the king may be recognized in any town through which we may pass, it is as well to have half a dozen good swords on which we can rely."

"I have with me," Harry said, "my friend Jacob, who was lieutenant in my troop, and who can wield a sword well, and one of my old troopers, a stout and active lad. You can rely upon them as on me."

Lord Ashburnham stayed but a few minutes with Harry, and then mounted and rode to Ditton, while Harry the same afternoon journeyed on into Kingston, and there took up his lodgings. On the 11th of November, three days after their arrival, Harry received a message from Lord Ashburnham, asking him to ride over to Ditton. At his lodgings there he found Sir John Berkeley. Major Legg shortly after arrived, and told them that the king had determined, when he went into his private room for evening prayer, to slip away, and make for the river side, where they were to be in readiness for him with horses. Harry had brought his followers with him, and had left them at an inn while he visited Lord Ashburnham. William Long at once rode back to Kingston, and there purchased two good horses, with saddles, for the king and Major Legg. At seven in the evening the party mounted, William Long and Jacob each leading a spare horse. Lord Ashburnham and Sir John Berkeley joined them outside the village, and they rode together until, crossing the bridge at Hampton, they stopped on the river bank, at the point arranged, near the palace. Half an hour passed, and then footsteps were heard, and two figures approached. Not a word was spoken until they were near enough to discern their faces.

"Thank God you are here, my Lord Ashburnham," the king said. "Fortune is always so against me that I feared something might occur to detain you. Ha! Master Furness, I am glad to see so faithful a friend."

The king and Major Legg now mounted, and the little party rode off. Their road led through Windsor Forest, then of far greater extent than at present. Through this the king acted as guide. The night was wild and stormy, but the king was well acquainted with the forest, and at daybreak the party, weary and drenched, arrived at Sutton, in Hampshire. Here they found six horses, which Lord Ashburnham had on the previous day sent forward, and mounting these, they again rode on. As the sun rose their spirits revived, and the king entered into conversation with Ashburnham, Berkeley, and Harry as to his plans. The latter was surprised and disappointed to find that so hurriedly had the king finally made up his mind to fly that no ship had been prepared to take him from the coast, and that it was determined that for the time the king should go to the Isle of Wight. The governor of the Isle of Wight was Colonel Hammond, who was connected with both parties. His uncle was chaplain to the king, and he was himself married to a daughter of Hampden. It was arranged that the king and Major Legg should proceed to a house of Lord Southampton at Titchfield, and that Berkeley and Lord Ashburnham should go to the Isle of Wight to Colonel Hammond, to find if he would receive the king. Harry, with his followers, was to proceed to Southampton, and there to procure a ship, which was to be in readiness to embark the king when a message was received from him. Agents of the king had already received orders to have a ship in readiness, and should this be done, it was at once to be brought round to Titchfield.

"This seems to me," Jacob said, as, after separating from the king, they rode to Southampton, "to be but poor plotting. Here has the king been for three months at Hampton Court, and could, had he so chosen, have fixed his flight for any day at his will. A vessel might have been standing on and off the coast, ready to receive him, and he could have ridden down, and embarked immediately he reached the coast. As it is, there is no ship and no arrangement, and for aught he knows he may be a closer prisoner in the Isle of Wight than he was at Hampton, while both parties with whom he has been negotiating will be more furious than ever at finding that he has fooled them. If I could not plot better than this I would stick to a scrivener's desk all my life."

It was late in the afternoon when they rode into Southampton. They found the city in a state of excitement. A messenger had, an hour before, ridden in from London with the news of the king's escape, and with orders from Parliament that no vessel should be allowed to leave the port. Harry then rode to Portsmouth, but there also he was unable to do anything. He heard that in the afternoon the king had crossed over onto the Isle of Wight, and that he had been received by the governor with marks of respect. They, therefore, again returned to Southampton, and there took a boat for

118

Cowes. Leaving his followers there, Harry rode to Newport, and saw the king. The latter said that for the present he had altogether changed his mind about escaping to France, and that Sir John Berkeley would start at once to negotiate with the heads of the army. He begged Harry to go to London, and to send him from time to time sure news of the state of feeling of the populace.

Taking his followers with him, Harry rode to London, disguised as a country trader. He held communication with many leading citizens, as well as with apprentices and others with whom he could get into conversation in the streets and public resorts. He found that the vast majority of the people of London were longing for the overthrow of the rule of the Independents, and for the restoration of the king. The preachers were as busy as ever haranguing people in the streets, and especially at Paul's Cross. In the cathedral of St. Paul's the Independent soldiers had stabled their horses, to the great anger of many moderate people, who were shocked at the manner in which those who had first begun to fight for liberty of conscience now tyrannized over the consciences and insulted the feelings of all others. Harry and his followers mixed among the groups, and aided in inflaming the temper of the people by passing jeering remarks, and loudly questioning the statements of the preachers. These, unaccustomed to interruption, would rapidly lose temper, and they and their partisans would make a rush through the crowd to seize their interrogators. Then the apprentices would interfere, blows would be exchanged, and not unfrequently the fanatics were driven in to take refuge with the troops in St. Paul's. Harry found a small printer of Royalist opinions, and with the assistance of Jacob, strung together many doggerel verses, making a scoff of the sour-faced rulers of England, and calling upon the people not to submit to be tyrannized over by their own paid servants, the army. These verses were then set in type by the printer, and in the evening, taking different ways, they distributed them in the streets to passers-by.

Day by day the feeling in the city rose higher, as the quarrels at Westminster between the Independents, backed by the army and the Presbyterian majority, waxed higher and higher. All this time the king was negotiating with commissioners from the army, and with others sent by the Scots, one day inclining to one party, the next to the other, making promises to both, but intending to observe none, as soon as he could gain his ends.

On Sunday, the 9th of April, Harry and his friends strolled up to Moor Fields to look at the apprentices playing bowls there. Presently from the barracks of the militia hard by a party of soldiers

119

came out, and ordered them to desist, some of the soldiers seizing upon the bowls.

"Now, lads," Harry shouted, "you will not stand that, will you? The London apprentices were not wont to submit to be ridden rough-shod over by troops. Has all spirit been taken out of you by the long-winded sermons of these knaves in steeple hats?"

Some of the soldiers made a rush at Harry. His two friends closed in by him. The two first of the soldiers who arrived were knocked down. Others, however, seized the young men, but the apprentices crowded up, pelted the soldiers with stones, and, by sheer weight, overthrew those who had taken Harry and carried him off. The soldiers soon came pouring out of their barracks, but fleet-footed lads had, at the commencement of the quarrel, run down into the streets, raising the shout of "clubs," and swarms of apprentices came running up. Led by Harry and his followers, who carried heavy sticks, they charged the militia with such fury that these, in spite of their superior arms, were driven back fighting into their barracks. When the gates were shut Harry mounted on a stone and harangued the apprentices—he recalled to them the ancient rights of the city, rights which the most absolute monarchs who had sat upon the throne had not ventured to infringe, that no troops should pass through the streets or be quartered there to restrict the liberties of the citizens. "No king would have ventured so to insult the people of London; why should the crop-haired knaves at Westminster dare to do so? If you had the spirit of your fathers you would not bear it for a moment."

"We will not, we will not," shouted the crowd. "Down with the soldiers!"

At this moment a lad approached at full run to say that the cavalry were coming from St. Paul's. In their enthusiasm the apprentices prepared to resist, but Harry shouted to them:

"Not here in the fields. Scatter now and assemble in the streets. With the chains up, we can beat them there."

The apprentices gave a cheer, and, scattering, made their way from the fields just as the cavalry issued into the open space. Hurrying in all directions, the apprentices carried the news, and soon the streets swarmed with their fellows. They were quickly joined by the watermen—in those days a numerous and powerful body. These were armed with oars and boat-stretchers. The chains which were fastened at night across the ends of the streets were quickly placed in position, and all was prepared to resist the attack of the troops.

# CHAPTER XV

## A RIOT IN THE CITY

So quickly were the preparations made that by the time the cavalry came riding back from Moor Fields they found the way barred to them. The commander of the cavalry ordered his men to charge. Harry, who had now taken the command of the crowd, ordered a few of the apprentices to stand before the first line of chains, so that these would not be visible until the horses were close upon them. Behind the chains he placed a strong body of watermen with their oars, while behind these, and at the windows of the houses, were the apprentices, each armed with a quantity of stones and broken bricks. The cavalry charged down upon the defense. When they reached within a few yards of the apprentices in front, these slipped under the chain. The leading troopers halted, but were pressed by those behind them gainst the chain. Then a ram of stones and brickbats opened upon them, and the watermen struck down men and horses with their heavy oars. In vain the troopers tried with their swords to reach their opponents. In vain they fired their pistols into the mass. They were knocked down by the stones and brickbats in numbers, and at last, their commander having been struck senseless, the rest drew off, a tremendous cheer greeting their retreat, from the crowd.

"Now," Harry shouted, taking his position on a doorstep, whence he could be seen, "attend to me. The battle has only begun yet, and they will bring up their infantry now. Next time we will let them enter the street, and defend the chains at the other end—a party must hold these—do some of you fill each lane which comes down on either side, and do ten of you enter each house and take post at the upper windows, with a good store of ammunition. Do not show yourselves until the head of their column reaches the chain. Then fling open the windows and pour volleys of stones and bricks upon them. Then let those in the side streets, each headed by parties of watermen, fall upon their flanks. Never fear their musketry. They can only give fire once before you are upon them. The oars will beat down the pikes, and your clubs will do the rest. Now let the apprentices of each street form themselves into parties, each under their captain. Let all be regular and orderly, and we will show them what the Londoners can do."

With a cheer the crowd separated, and soon took post as

Harry had directed. He stationed himself at the barricade at the head of the street. A quarter of an hour later the militia were seen approaching in close column followed by the cavalry. On arriving at the end of the street the assailants removed the chain, and again advanced. The street was silent until they neared its end. The watermen had, under Harry's direction, torn up the paving stones, and formed a barricade breast high, behind which, remaining crouched, they awaited the assault.

The fight began by a volley of stones from the apprentices behind the barricade. The leading rank of the column discharged their muskets, and rushed at the barricade; the watermen sprang to oppose them. At the sound of the first shot every window in the street opened, and a rain of bricks and heavy stones poured down on all sides upon the column, while at the same time dense masses flung themselves upon its flanks, from every lane leading into it. Confused and broken by the sudden onslaught in the narrow street, the column halted, and endeavored to open a fire upon the upper windows. This, however, effected but little harm, while every brick from above told upon their crowded mass. The column was instantly in confusion, and Harry and his followers, leaping over the barricade, and followed by the watermen and apprentices behind, fell upon it with fury. In vain did the Roundheads strive to repulse the attack. Their numbers melted away as they fell, killed or senseless, from the rain of missiles from above. Already the column was rent by their assailants on the flanks, and in less than five minutes from the commencement of the assault those who remained on their legs were driven headlong out into Moor Fields.

Loud rose the triumphant cry of the defenders, "God and King Charles." Some hours elapsed before any attempt was made to renew the assault. Then toward evening fresh troops were brought up from Westminster, and the attack was renewed on two sides. Still the apprentices held their own. Attack after attack was repulsed. All night the fight continued, and when morning dawned the Royalists were still triumphant.

"How will it go, think you, Jacob?" Harry asked.

"They will beat us in the long run," Jacob said. "They have not been properly led yet. When they are, guns and swords must prevail against clubs and stones."

At eleven o'clock in the morning a heavy body of cavalry were seen approaching from Westminster. The Roundheads had brought up Cromwell's Ironsides, the victors in many a hard-fought field, against the apprentice boys of London. The Roundhead infantry advanced with their horse. As they approached the first barricade the cavalry halted, and the infantry advanced alone to within thirty yards of it. Then, just as its defenders thought they were going to charge, they halted, divided into bodies, and entered the houses on either side, and appeared at the windows. Then, as the Ironsides came down at a gallop, they opened a heavy fire on the defenders of the barricade. Harry saw at once that the tactics now adopted were irresistible, and that further attempts at defense would only lead to useless slaughter. He therefore shouted:

"Enough for to-day, lads. Every man back to his own house. We will begin again when we choose. We have given them a good lesson."

In an instant the crowd dispersed, and by the time the Ironsides had dismounted, broken the chains, and pulled down the barricade sufficiently to enable them to pass, Ludgate Hill was deserted, the apprentices were back in their masters' shops, and the watermen standing by their boats ready for a fare.

Seeing that their persons were known to so many of the citizens, and would be instantly pointed out to the troops by those siding with the army, who had, during the tumult, remained quietly in their houses, watching from the windows what was going on, Harry and his friends hurried straight to Aldersgate, where they passed out into the country beyond. Dressed in laborers' smocks, which they had, in preparation for any sudden flight, left at the house of a Royalist innkeeper, a mile or two in the fields, they walked to Kingston, crossed the river there, and made for Southampton.

The king was now closely confined in Carisbrook Castle. For the first three months of his residence in the Isle of Wight he could have escaped with ease, had he chosen, and it is probable that Cromwell and the other leaders of the army would have been glad that he should go, and thus relieve the country from the inconvenience of his presence. They had become convinced that so long as he lived quiet could not be hoped for. While still pretending to negotiate with them, he had signed a treaty with the Scots, promising to establish Presbyterianism in England, and their army was already marching south. To the Irish Papists he had promised free exercise of their religion, and these were taking up arms and massacring all opposed to them, as was the custom in that barbarous country. In Wales a formidable insurrection had broken out. Essex and Kent were up in arms, and, indeed, all through the country the Royalists were stirring. The leaders had therefore determined upon bringing the king to trial.

At Southampton Harry found Sir John Berkeley concealed in a house where he had previously instructed Harry he might be looked for. He told him that the king was now a close prisoner, and would assuredly escape if means could be provided. Leaving Sir John, Harry joined his followers, and after telling them the circumstances, they walked down to the port. Here they entered into conversation with an old sailor. Seeing that he was an honest fellow, and in no way disposed toward the fanatics, Harry told him that he and those with him were Cavaliers, who sought to cross over into France.

"There is a boat, there," the sailor said, pointing to a lugger which was lying at anchor among some fishing boats, "that will carry you. The captain, Dick Wilson, is a friend of mine, and often makes a run across to France on dark nights, and brings back smuggled goods. I know where he can be found, and will lead you to him, if it so pleases you." Upon their gladly accepting the offer he led them to a small inn by the water side, and introduced them to the captain of the Moonlight, for so the lugger was called. Upon receiving a hint from the sailor that his companions wished to speak to him in private, Wilson led the way upstairs to the chamber he occupied. Here Harry at once unfolded to him the nature of the service he required. He was to lay with his boat off the bank of the island, making to sea before daylight, and returning after dusk, and was to take his station off a gap in the cliffs, known as Black Gang Chine, where a footpath from above descended to the beach. Upon a light being shown three times at the water's edge he was to send a boat immediately ashore, and embarking those whom he might find there, sail for France. If at the end of the week none should come, he would know that his services would not be required, and might sail away whither he listed. He was to receive fifty guineas at once for the service, and if he transported those who might come down to the shore, to France, he would, on arriving there, be paid two hundred and fifty more.

"It is the king, of course, who seeks to escape," the sailor said. "Well, young gentlemen, for such I doubt not that you are, I am ready to try it. We sailors are near all for the king, and the fleet last week declared for him, and sailed for Holland. So, once on board, there will be little danger. Pay me the fifty guineas at once, and you may rely upon the Moonlight being at the point named."

Harry handed over the money, and arranged that on the third night following the lugger should beat the post appointed, and that it should at once run them across and land them at Cowes. It was now the middle of May, and Harry and his friends, who were still in the disguise of countrymen, walked across to Newport. Their first step was to examine the castle. It lay a short distance from the town, was surrounded by a high wall with towers, and could offer a strong resistance to an attacking force. At the back of the castle was a small postern gate, at which they decided that his escape must, if possible, be made. Harry had been well supplied with money by Sir John Berkeley before leaving Southampton, Sir John himself, on account of his figure being so well known at Newport, during his stay there with the king, deeming it imprudent to take any personal part in the enterprise. After an examination of the exterior of the castle Harry bought a large basket of eggs, and some chickens, and with these proceeded to the castle. There was a guard at the gate, but persons could freely enter. As Harry's wares were exceedingly cheap in price, he speedily effected a sale of them to the soldiers and servants of the officers.

"I should like," he said to the man to whom he disposed of the last of the contents of his basket, "to catch a sight of the king. I ha' never seen him."

"That's easy enough," the man said. "Just mount these stairs with me to the wall. He is walking in the garden at the back of the castle."

Harry followed the man, and presently reached a spot where he could look down into the garden. The king was pacing up and down the walk, his head bent, his hands behind his back, apparently in deep thought. An attendant, a short distance behind him, followed his steps.

"Be that the king?" Harry asked. "He don't look like a king."

"That's him," the man said, "and he's not much of a king at present."

"Where does he live now?" Harry asked.

"That is his room," the man said, pointing to a window some ten feet from the ground. After a little further conversation Harry appeared to be satisfied, and returning to the courtyard, made his way from the castle. During that day and the next they remained quiet, except that Jacob walked over to Cowes, where he purchased two very fine and sharp saws, and a short length of strong rope, with a hook. The following night they hired a cart with a fast horse, and this they placed at a spot a quarter of a mile from the castle.

Leaving the man in charge of it there, Harry and his companions made for the back of the castle. They could tell by the calls upon the walls that the sentries were watchful, but the night

125

was so dark that they had no fear whatever of being seen. Very quietly they crossed the moat, which was shallow, and with but little water in it. Then with an auger they cut four holes in a square two feet each way in the door, and, with a saw, speedily cut the piece inclosed by them out, and creeping through, entered the garden. The greater part of the lights were already extinguished, but that in the king's chamber was still burning. They made their way quietly until they stood beneath this window, and waited until the light here was also put out. Then Harry climbed on to the shoulders of his companions, which brought his face on a level with the window. He tapped at it. The king, who had been warned that his friends would attempt to open a means of escape, at once came to the window, and threw open the casement.

"Who is there?" he asked, in low tones.

"It is I, Harry Furness, your majesty. I have two trusty friends with me. We have cut a hole through the postern gate, a cart is waiting without, and a ship lies ready to receive you on the coast."

"I am ready," the king said. "Thanks, my faithful servant. But have you brought something to cut the bars?"

"The bars!" Henry exclaimed, aghast. "I did not know that there were bars!"

"There are, indeed, Master Furness," the king said, "and if you have no file the enterprise is ruined."

Harry put his hands on the stonework and pulled himself up, and felt the bars within the window.

"They are too strong for our united strength," he said, in a tone of deep disappointment. "But methinks it is possible to get between them." Putting his head between the bars he struggled though, but with great difficulty. "See, your majesty, I have got through."

"Ay, Master Furness, but you are slighter in figure than I, although you are changed indeed since first the colonel, your father, presented you to me at Oxford. However, I will try." The king tried, but in vain. He was stouter than Harry, although less broadly built, and had none of the lissomness which enabled the latter to wriggle through the bars. "It is useless," he said at last. "Providence is against me. It is the will of God that I should remain here. It may be the decree of Heaven that even yet I may sit again on the throne of my ancestors. Now go, Master Furness. It is too late to renew the attempt to-night. Should Charles Stuart ever reign again over England, he will not forget your faithful service."

Harry kissed the king's hand, and with a prayer for his welfare he again made his way through the bars and dropped from the window, by the side of his companions, the tears streaming down his cheeks with the disappointment and sorrow he felt at the failure of his enterprise. "It is all over," he said. "The king cannot force his way through the bars."

Without another word they made their way down to the postern, passed through it, and replaced the piece of wood in its position, in the faint hope that it might escape notice. Then they rejoined the driver with the cart, paid him handsomely, and told him that his services would not be required that night at least. They then returned to their lodgings in the town. The next morning early Jacob started for Cowes to buy some sharp files and aquafortis, but an hour later the news passed through Newport that an attempt had been made in the night to free the king, that a hole had been cut in the postern, and the marks of footsteps discovered under the king's window. Perceiving that it would be useless to renew the attempt now that the suspicions of the garrison were aroused, Harry and William Long, fearing that a search would be instituted, at once started for Cowes. They met Jacob close to that town, crossed in a boat to the mainland, and walked to Southampton. They hesitated whether they should join Lord Goring, who had risen in Kent, or Lord Capel and Sir Charles Lucas, who had collected a large force at Colchester. They determined upon the latter course, as the movement appeared to promise a better chance of success. Taking passage in a coaster, they sailed to the mouth of the Thames, and being landed near Tilbury, made their way to Colchester. Harry was, on his arrival, welcomed by the Royalist leaders, who were well acquainted with him. They proposed to march upon London, which would, they felt sure, declare for the king upon their approach. They had scarcely set their force in motion when they heard that Fairfax, at the head of an army, was marching against them. A debate was held among the leaders as to the best course to pursue. Some were for marching north, but the eastern counties had, from the commencement of the troubles, been wholly on the side of the Parliament. Others were for dispersing the bands, and awaiting a better opportunity for a rising. Sir Charles Lucas, however, urged that they should defend Colchester to the last.

"Here," he said, "we are doing good service to the Royal cause, and by detaining Fairfax here, we shall give time to our friends in Wales, Kent, and other parts to rise and organize. If it is seen that whenever we meet the Roundheads we disperse at once, hope and confidence will be lost."

The next day the town was invested by Fairfax, and shortly after the siege began in earnest. The Royalists fought with great bravery, and for two months every attempt of the Roundheads to storm the place was repulsed. At length, however, supplies ran short, several breaches had been made in the walls by the Roundhead artillery, and a council of war was held, at which it was decided that further resistance was useless, and would only inflict a great slaughter upon their followers, who, in the event of surrender, would for the most part be permitted to return to their homes. Harry Furness was present at the council and agreed to the decision. He said, however, that he would endeavor, with his two personal followers, to effect his escape, as, if he were taken a prisoner to London, he should be sure to be recognized there as the leader of the rising in May, in which case he doubted not that little mercy would be shown to him. The Royalist leaders agreed with him, but pointed out that his chances of escape were small, as the town was closely beleaguered. Harry, however, declared that he preferred the risk of being shot while endeavoring to escape, to the certainty of being executed if carried to London.

That night they procured some bladders, for although Jacob and Harry were able to swim, William Long could not do so, and in any case it was safer to float than to swim. The bladders were blown out and their necks securely fastened. The three adventurers were then lowered from the wall by ropes, and having fastened the bladders around them, noiselessly entered the water. A numerous flotilla of ships and boats of the Commons lay below the town; the tide was running out, however, and the night dark, and keeping hold of each other, so as not to be separated by the tide, they drifted through these unobserved. Once safely out of hearing, Jacob and Harry struck out and towed their companion to shore. While at Colchester they had been attired as Royalist officers, but they had left these garments behind them, and carried, strapped to their shoulders, above water, the countrymen's clothes in which they had entered the town. They walked as far as Brentwood, where they stopped for a few days, and learned the news of what was passing throughout the country.

Colchester surrendered on the 27th of August, the morning after they left it. Lord Capel was sent a prisoner to London to be tried for his life; but Fairfax caused Sir Charles Lucas and Sir George Lisle to be tried by court-martial, and shot. On the 10th of July the town and castle of Pembroke had surrendered to Cromwell, who immediately afterward marched north to meet the Scotch army, which six days before had entered England. The Duke of Hamilton, who commanded it, was at once joined by five thousand English Royalists under Sir Marmaduke Langdale. General Lambert, who commanded the Parliamentary troops in the north, fell back to avoid a battle until Cromwell could join him.

The Scotch army could not be called a national force. The Scotch Parliament, influenced by the Duke of Hamilton and others, had entered into an agreement with King Charles, and undertook to reinstate him on the throne. The more violent section, headed by Argyll, were bitterly hostile to the step. The Duke of Hamilton's army, therefore, consisted entirely of raw and undisciplined troops. Cromwell marched with great speed through Wales to Gloucester, and then on through Leicester and Nottingham, and joined Lambert at Barnet Castle on the 12th of August. Then he marched against the Scotch army, which, straggling widely and thinking Cromwell still at a distance, was advancing toward Manchester. On the 16th the duke with his advanced guard was at Preston, with Langdale on his left. Cromwell attacked Langdale with his whole force next morning, and the Royalists after fighting stoutly were entirely defeated. Then he fell upon the Duke of Hamilton and the force under him at Preston, and after four hours' sharp fighting in the inclosures round the place, defeated and drove them out of the town. That night the Scots determined to retreat, and at once began to scatter. General Baillie, after some hard fighting around Warrington, surrendered with his division. The duke with three thousand men went to Nantwich. The country was hostile, his own troops, wearied and dispirited, mutinied, and declared they would fight no longer; the Duke of Hamilton thereupon surrendered, the Scotch invasion of England came to an end.

# CHAPTER XVI

# THE EXECUTION OF KING CHARLES

The news of the failure of the Welsh insurrection and the Scotch invasion, while the risings in Kent and Essex were crushed out, showed Harry Furness that, for the time at least, there was no further fighting to be done. Cromwell, after the defeat of the Scotch, marched with his army to Edinburgh, where he was received with enthusiasm by Argyll and the fanatic section, who were now again restored to power, and recommenced a cruel persecution of all suspected of Royalist opinions. Now that the Scotch had been beaten, and the Royalist rising everywhere crushed out, the Parliament were seized with fear as to the course which Cromwell and his victorious army might pursue. If they had been so arrogant and haughty before, what might not be expected now. Negotiations were at once opened with the king. He was removed from Carisbrook to a good house at Newport. Commissioners came down there, and forty days were spent in prolonged argument, and the commissioners returned to London on the 28th of November with a treaty signed. It was too late. The army stationed at St. Albans sent in a remonstrance to Parliament, calling upon them to bring the king to trial, and stating that if Parliament neglected its duty the army would take the matter into its own hands. This remonstrance caused great excitement in the Commons. No steps were taken upon it however, and the Commons proceeded to discuss the treaty, and voted that the king's concessions were sufficient. On the 29th a body of soldiers went across to the Isle of Wight, surrounded the king's house, seized him and carried him to Hurst Castle. The next day Parliament voted that they would not debate the remonstrance of the army, and in reply the army at Windsor marched on the 2d of December into London. On the 5th the Commons debated all day upon the treaty.

Prynne, formerly one of the stanchest opposers of King Charles, spoke with others strongly in his favor, and it was carried by a hundred and twenty-nine to thirty-eight. The same day some of the leaders of the army met, and determined to expel from the house all those opposed to their interests. On the 7th the Trained Bands of the city were withdrawn from around the House, and Colonel Pride with his regiment of foot surrounded it. As the members arrived forty-one of them were turned back. The same process was repeated on the two following days, until over a

130

hundred members had been arrested. Thus the army performed a revolution such as no English sovereign has dared to carry out. After this it is idle to talk of the Parliament as in any way representing the English people. The representatives who supported the king had long since left it. The whole of the moderate portion of those who had opposed him, that is to say, those who had fought to support the liberties of Englishmen against encroachments by the king, and who formed the majority after the Royalists had retired, were now expelled; there remained only a small body of fanatics devoted to the interests of the army, and determined to crush out all liberties of England under its armed heel. This was the body before whom the king was ere long to undergo the mockery of a trial.

King Charles was taken to Hurst Castle on the 17th of December, and three days later carried to Windsor. On the 2d of January, 1649, the Commons voted that in making war against the Parliament the king had been guilty of treason, and should be tried by a court of a hundred and fifty commissioners. The Peers rejected the bill, and the Commons then voted that neither the assent of the Peers nor the king was necessary for a law passed by themselves.

All the encroachments of King Charles together were as nothing to this usurpation of despotic power.

In consequence of the conduct of the Peers, the number of commissioners was reduced to a hundred and thirty-five; but of these only sixty-nine assembled at the trial. Thus the court which was to try the king consisted only of those who were already pledged to destroy him. Before such a court as this there could be but one end to the trial. When, after deciding upon their sentence, the king was brought in to hear it, the chief commissioner told him that the charges were brought against him in the name of the people of England, when Lady Fairfax from the gallery cried out, "It's a lie! Not one-half of them." Had she said not one hundredth of them, she would have been within the mark.

On the 27th sentence was pronounced. On the 29th the court signed the sentence, which was to be carried out on the following day.

From the time when Harry Furness left Brentwood at the end of August until the king was brought to London, he had lived quietly at Southampton. He feared to return home, and chose this port as his residence, in order that he might, if necessary, cross into France at short notice. When the news came that the king had been brought up from Windsor, Harry and his friends at once rode to London, Every one was so absorbed in the great trial about to take place that Harry had little fear of attracting attention or of being molested should any one recognize in the young gentleman in sober attire the

131

rustic who had led the rising in the spring. To London, too, came many other Cavaliers from all parts of the country, eager to see if something might not be attempted to rescue the king. Throughout London the consternation was great at the usurpation by the remnant of the Commons of all the rights of the Three Estates, and still more, at the trial of the king. The army, however, lay in and about London, and, with Cromwell at its head, it would, the people felt, easily crush out any attempt at a rising in the city. Within a few hours of his arrival in London, Harry saw that there was no hope from any effort in this direction, and that the only possible chance of saving the king was by his arranging for his escape. His majesty, on his arrival from Windsor, had been lodged in St. James' Palace, and as this was completely surrounded by the Roundhead troops, there was no chance of effecting an invasion thence. The only possible plan appeared to be a sudden attack upon his guards on his way to execution.

Harry gathered round him a party of thirty Cavaliers, all men ready like himself to sacrifice their lives for the king. Their plan was to gather near Whitehall, where the execution was to take place, to burst through the soldiers lining the way, to cut down the guards, and carry the king to a boat in readiness behind Whitehall, This was to convey him across to Lambeth, where fleet horses were to be stationed, which would take him down to the Essex coast.

The plan was a desperate one, but it might possibly have succeeded, could the Cavaliers have gained the position which they wished. The whole of the army was, however, placed in the streets and passages leading to Whitehall, and between that place and the city the cavalry were drawn up, preventing any from coming in or going out. When they found that this was the case, the Cavaliers in despair mounted their horses, and rode into the country, with their hearts filled with grief and rage.

On the 30th, an hour after the king's execution, proclamation was made that whoever should proclaim a new king would be deemed a traitor, and a week later, the Commons, now reduced to a hundred members, formally abolished the House of Peers. A little later Lord Capel, Lord Holland, and the Duke of Hamilton were executed.

Had the king effected his escape, Harry Furness had determined to return to Abingdon and live quietly at home, believing that now the army had grasped all power, and crushed all opposition, it was probable that they would abstain from exciting further popular animosity by the persecution of those who had fought against them. The fury, however, excited in his mind by the murder of the king after the mockery of a trial, determined him to fight to the last, wherever a rising might be offered, however hopeless a success that rising might appear. He would not, however, suffer Jacob and William Long any longer to follow his fortunes, although they earnestly pleaded to do so. "I have no hope of success," he said. "I am ready to die, but I will not bring you to that strait. I have written to my father begging him, Jacob, to receive you as his friend and companion, and to do what he can, William, to assist you in whatever mode of life your wishes may hereafter lead you to adopt. But come with me you shall not."

Not without tears did Harry's faithful companions yield themselves to his will, and set out for Abingdon, while he, with eight or ten comrades as determined as himself, kept on west until they arrived at Bristol, where they took ship and crossed to Ireland. They landed at Waterford, and journeyed north until they reached the army, with which the Marquis of Ormonde was besieging Dublin. Nothing that Harry had seen of war in England prepared him in any way for the horrors which he beheld in Ireland. The great mass of the people there were at that time but a few degrees advanced above savages, and they carried on their war with a brutal cruelty and bloodshed which could now only be rivaled in the center of Africa. Between the Protestants and the English and Scotch settlers on the one hand, and the wild peasantry on the other, a war of something like extermination went on. Wholesale massacres took place, at which men, women, and children were indiscriminately butchered, the ferocity shown being as great upon one side as the other. In fact, beyond the possession of a few large towns, Ireland had no claim whatever to be considered a civilized country. As Harry and his comrades rode from Waterford they beheld everywhere ruined fields and burned houses; and on joining the army of the Marquis of Ormonde, Harry felt even more strongly than before the hopelessness of the struggle on which he was engaged. These bands of wild, half-clad kernes, armed with pike and billhook, might be brave indeed, but could do nothing against the disciplined soldiers of the Parliament. There were with Ormonde, indeed, better troops than these. Some of the companies were formed of English and Welsh Royalists. Others had been raised by the Catholic gentry of the west, and into these some sort of order and discipline had been introduced. The army, moreover, was deficient in artillery, and not more than one-third of the footmen carried firearms. Harry was, a day or two after reaching the camp of Lord Ormonde, sent off to the West to drill some of the newly-raised levies there. It was now six years since he had begun to take an active part in the war, and he was between twenty-one and twenty-two. His life of active exertion had strengthened his muscles, broadened his frame, and given a strength and vigor to his tall and powerful figure.

Foreseeing that the siege of Dublin was not likely to be successful, Harry accepted his commission to the West with pleasure. He felt already that with all his devotion to the Royalist cause he could not wish that the siege of Dublin should be successful; for he saw that the vast proportion of the besieging army were animated by no sense of loyalty, by no interest in the constitutional question at stake, but simply with a blind hatred of the Protestant population of Dublin, and that the capture of the city would probably be followed by the indiscriminate slaughter of its inhabitants.

He set out on his journey, furnished with letters from Ormonde to several influential gentlemen in Galway. The roads at first were fairly good, but accustomed to the comfortable inns in England, Harry found the resting-places along the road execrable. He was amused of an evening by the eagerness with which the people came round and asked for news from Dublin. In all parts of England the little sheets which then did service as newspapers carried news of the events which were taking place. It is true that none of the country population could read or write; but the alehouses served as centers of news. The village clerk, or, perhaps, the squire's bailiff, could read, as could probably the landlord, and thus the news spread quickly round the country. In Ireland news traveled only from mouth to mouth, often becoming strangely distorted on the way.

Harry was greatly struck by the bareness of the fields and the poverty of the country; and as he journeyed further west the country became still wilder and more lonely. It was seldom now that he met any one who could speak English, and as the road was often little more than a track, he had great difficulty in keeping his way, and regretted that he had not hired a servant knowing the country before leaving the army. He generally, however, was able to obtain a guide from village to village. The loneliness of the way, the wretchedness of the people, the absence of the brightness and comfort so characteristic of English life, made the journey an oppressive one, and Harry was glad when, five days after leaving Dublin, he approached the end of his ride. Upon this day he had taken no guide, being told that the road was clear and unmistakable as far as Galway.

He had not traveled many hours when a heavy mist set in, accompanied by a keen and driving rain, in his face. With his head bent down, Harry rode along, paying less attention than usual to his way. The mist grew thicker and thicker. The horse no longer

134

proceeded at a brisk pace, and presently came to a stop. Harry dismounted, and discovered that he had left the road, Turning his horse's head, and taking the reins over his arm, he tried to retrace his steps.

For an hour he walked along, the conviction growing every moment that he was hopelessly lost. The ground was now soft and miry and was covered with tussocks of coarse grass, between which the soil was black and oozy. The horse floundered on for some distance, but with such increasing difficulty that, upon reaching a space of comparatively solid ground, Harry decided to take him no further.

The cold rain chilled him to the bone, and after awhile he determined to try and make his way forward on foot, in hopes of finding, if not a human habitation, some walls or bushes where he could obtain shelter until the weather cleared. He fastened the reins to a small shrub, took off the saddle and laid it on the grass, spread the horse rug over the animal to protect it as far as possible, and then started on his way. He had heard of Irish bogs extending for many miles, and deep enough to engulf men and animals who might stray among them, and he felt that his position was a serious one.

He blamed himself now for not having halted immediately he perceived that he had missed the road. The only guide that he had as to the direction he should take was the wind. On his way it had been in his face, and he determined now to keep it at his back, not because that was probably the way to safety, but because he could see more easily where he was going, and he thought by continuing steadily in one direction he might at last gain firm ground. His view extended but a few yards round him, and he soon found that his plan of proceeding in a straight line was impracticable. Often quagmires of black ooze, or spaces covered with light grass, which were, he found, still more treacherous, barred his way, and he was compelled to make considerable detours to the right or left in order to pass them. Sometimes widths of sluggish water were met with. For a long time Harry continued his way, leaping lightly from tuft to tuft, where the grass grew thickest, sometimes wading knee-deep in the slush and feeling carefully every foot lest he should get to a depth whence he should be unable to extricate himself. Every now and then he shouted at the top of his voice, in hopes that he might be heard by some human being. For hours he struggled on. He was now exhausted with his efforts, and the thickening darkness told him that day was fading. From the time he had left his horse he had met with no bush of sufficient height to afford him the slightest shelter.

Just as he was thinking whether he had not better stop where he was, and sit down on the firmest tuft he could find and wait for morning, when perhaps the rainstorm might cease and enable him to see where he was, he heard, and at no very great distance, the sudden bray of a donkey. He turned at once in the direction of the sound, with renewed hopes, giving a loud shout as he did so. Again and again he raised his voice, and presently heard an answering shout. He called again, and in reply heard some shouts in Irish, probably questions, but to these he could give no answer. Shouting occasionally, he made his way toward the voice, but the bog seemed more difficult and treacherous than ever, and at last he reached a spot where further advance seemed absolutely impossible. It was now nearly dark, and Harry was about to sit down in despair, when suddenly a voice sounded close to him. He answered again, and immediately a barefooted boy sprang to his side from behind. The boy stood astonished at Harry's appearance. The latter was splashed and smeared from head to foot with black mire, for he had several times fallen. His broad hat drooped a sodden mass over his shoulders, the dripping feather adding to its forlorn appearance. His high riding boots were gone, having long since been abandoned in the tenacious ooze in which they had stuck; his ringlets fell in wisps on his shoulder.

After staring at him for a minute, the boy said something in Irish. Harry shook his head.

His guide then motioned him to follow him. For some time it seemed to Harry that he was retracing his steps. Then they turned, and by what seemed a long detour, at last reached firmer ground. A minute or two later they were walking along a path, and presently stopped before the door of a cabin, by which two men were standing. They exchanged a word or two with the boy, and then motioned to Harry to enter. A peat fire was burning on the hearth, and a woman, whose age Harry from her aspect thought must be enormous, was crouched on a low stool beside it. He threw off his riding cloak and knelt by her, and held his hands over the fire to restore the circulation. One of the men lighted a candle formed of rushes dipped in tallow. Harry paid no heed to them until he felt the warmth returning to his limbs. Then he rose to his feet and addressed them in English. They shook their heads. Perceiving how wet he was one of them drew a bottle from under the thatch, and pouring some of its contents into a wooden cup offered it to him. Harry put it to his lips. At first it seemed that he was drinking a mixture of liquid fire and smoke, and the first swallow nearly choked him. However he persevered, and soon felt the blood coursing more rapidly in his veins. Finding the impossibilty of

136

conversing, he again sat down by the fire and waited the course of events. He had observed that as he entered his young guide had, in obedience probably to the orders of one of the men, darted away into the mist.

The minutes passed slowly, and not a word was spoken in the cottage. An hour went by, and then a tramp of feet was heard, and, accompanied by the boy, eight or ten men entered. All carried pikes. Between them and the men already in the hut an eager conversation took place. Harry felt far from easy. The aspect of the men was wild in the extreme. Their hair was long and unkempt, and fell in straggling masses over their shoulders. Presently one, who appeared to be the leader, approached Harry, who had now risen to his feet, and crossed himself on the forehead and breast. Harry understood by the action that he inquired if he was a Catholic, and in reply shook his head.

An angry murmur ran through the men. Harry repressed his inclination to place his hand on his pistols, which he had on alighting from his horse taken from the holsters and placed in his belt. He felt that even with these and his sword, he should be no match for the men around him. Then he bethought of the letters of which he was a bearer. Taking them from his pocket he held them out. "Ormonde," he said, looking at the men.

No gleam of intelligence brightened their faces at the word.

Then he said "Butler," the Irish family name of the earl. Two or three of the men spoke together, and Harry thought that there was some comprehension of his meaning. Then he read aloud the addresses of the letters, and the exclamations which followed each named showed that these were familiar to the men. A lively conversation took place between them, and the leader presently approached and held out his hand.

"Thomas Blake, Killicuddery," he said. This was the address of one of the letters, and Harry at once gave it him. It was handed to the boy, with a few words of instruction. The lad at once left the hut. The men seemed to think that for the time there was nothing more to be done, laid their pikes against the wall, and assumed, Harry thought, a more friendly aspect. He reciprocated their action, by unbuckling his belt and laying aside his sword and pistols. Fresh peats were piled on the fire, another candle was lit, and the party prepared to make themselves comfortable. The bottle and wooden cup were again produced, and the owner of the hut offered some black bread to his visitor.

# CHAPTER XVII

# THE SIEGE OF DROGHEDA

Under the influence of the warm, close air of the hut, and the spirits he had taken, Harry soon felt drowsiness stealing over him, and the leader, perceiving this, pointed to a heap of dried fern lying in the corner of the hut. Harry at once threw himself on it, and in a very few minutes was sound asleep. When he awoke daylight was streaming in through the door of the hut. Its inmates were for the most part sitting as when he had last seen them, and Harry supposed that they had talked all night. The atmosphere of the hut was close and stifling, and Harry was glad to go to the door and breathe the fresh air outside.

The weather had changed, and the sun, which had just risen, was shining brightly. The hut stood at the foot of a long range of stony hills, while in front stretched, as far as the eye could see, an expanse of brown bog. A bridle path ran along at the foot of the hills. An hour later two figures were seen approaching along this. The one was a mounted horseman, the other running in front of him, at a long, easy trot, was Harry's guide of the preceding evening.

On reaching the cottage the gentleman on horseback alighted, and, advancing to Harry, said:

"Captain Furness, I am heartily sorry to hear that you have had what must have been a disagreeable adventure. The lad here who brought your letter told me that you were regarded as a prisoner, and considered to be a Protestant emissary. I am Tom Blake, and I live nearly twenty miles from here. That is the reason why I was not here sooner. I was keeping it up with some friends last night, and had just gone to bed when the messenger arrived, and my foolish servants pretended I was too drunk to be woke. However, when they did rouse me, I started at once."

"And has that boy gone forty miles on foot since last night?" Harry asked, in surprise.

"Oh, that's nothing," Mr. Blake said. "Give him half an hour's rest, and he'd keep up with us back to Killicuddery. But where is your horse, and how did you get into this mess? The boy tells me he found you in the bog."

Harry related his adventures.

"You have had a lucky escape indeed," Mr. Blake said. "There are places in that bog thirty feet deep. I would not try to cross it for a thousand pounds on a bright day, and how you managed to do so through the mist yesterday is more than I can imagine. Now, the first thing is to get your horse. I must apologize for not having brought one, but the fact is, my head was not exactly clear when I started, and I had not taken in the fact that you'd arrived on foot. My servant was more thoughtful. He had heard from the boy that an English gentleman was here, and judging that the larder was not likely to be stocked, he put a couple of bottles of claret, a cold chicken, and some bread into my wallet, so we can have breakfast while they are looking for your horse. The ride has sharpened my appetite."

Mr. Blake now addressed a few words in Irish to the men clustered round the door of the hut. One of them climbed to the top of the hill, and presently shouted down some instructions, and another at once started across the bog.

"They see your horse," Mr. Blake said, "but we shall have to wait for two or three hours. It is some four miles off, and they will have to make a long detour to bring it back."

Mr. Blake now distributed some silver among the men, and these, with the exception of the master of the house, soon afterward left. Harry heartily enjoyed his breakfast, and in cheery chat with his host the time passed pleasantly until the peasant returned with the horse and saddle. The horse was rubbed down with dry fern, and a lump of black bread given him to eat.

"What can I do for the boy?" Harry asked. "I owe him my life, for I was so thoroughly drenched and cold that I question whether I should have lived till morning out in that bog."

"The boy thinks nothing of it," Mr. Blake said. "A few hundred yards across the bog night or day is nothing to him."

Harry gave the lad a gold piece, which he looked at in wonder.

"He has never seen such a thing before," Mr. Blake laughed. "There, Mickey," he said in Irish, "that's enough to buy you a cow, and you've only got to build a cabin and take a wife to start life as a man."

The boy said something in Irish.

"I thought so," Mr. Blake laughed. "You haven't got rid of him yet. He wants to go as your servant."

Harry laughed too. The appearance of the lad in his tattered garments was in contrast indeed to the usual aspect of a gentleman's retainer.

"You'll find him useful," Mr. Blake said. "He will run errands for you and look after your horse. These lads can be faithful to death. You cannot do better than take him."

139

Mickey's joy when he was told that he might accompany the English gentleman was extreme. He handed the money he had received to his father, said a few words of adieu to him, and then started on ahead of the horses.

"He had better wait and come on later," Harry said. "He must be utterly tired now."

Mr. Blake shouted after the boy, who turned round, laughed, and shook his head, and again proceeded on his way.

"He can keep up with us," Mr. Blake said. "That horse of yours is more fagged than he is."

Harry soon found that this was the case, and it took them nearly four hours' riding before they reached Killicuddery. Here a dozen barefooted men and boys ran out at their approach, and took the horses. It was a large, straggling house, as good as that inhabited by the majority of English gentlemen, but Harry missed the well-kept lawn, the trim shrubberies, and the general air of neatness and order to which he was accustomed.

"Welcome to Killicuddery," Mr. Blake said, as he alighted. "Believe me, Captain Furness, you won't find the wild Irish, now you are fairly among them, such dreadful creatures as they have been described to you. Well, Norah," he continued, as a girl some sixteen years of age bounded down the steps to meet him, "how goes it with you this morning?"

"As well as could be expected, father, considering that you kept us awake half the night with your songs and choruses. None of the others are down yet, and it's past twelve o'clock. It's downright shameful."

"Norah, I'm surprised at you," Mr. Blake said, laughing. "What will Captain Furness think of Irish girls when he hears you speaking so disrespectfully to your father. This is my daughter Norah, Captain Furness, who is, I regret to say, a wild and troublesome girl. This, my dear, is Captain Furness, a king's officer, who has fought through all the battles of the war."

"And who has lately been engaged in a struggle with an Irish bog," the girl said, laughing, for Harry's gay dress was discolored and stained from head to foot.

Harry laughed also.

"I certainly got the worst of that encounter, Miss Norah, as indeed has been the case in most of those in which I have been engaged. I never felt much more hopeless, when I thought I should have to pass the night sitting on a tuft of grass with mud and mist all round me, except when I was once nearly baked to death in, company with Prince Rupert."

"It must have been a large oven," the girl laughed; "but come in now. I am sure you will both be ready for breakfast. But papa would keep you chattering here all day if I would let him."

Mr. Blake, Harry soon found, was a widower, and his house was presided over by his eldest daughter, Kathleen, to whom Harry was introduced on entering the house. As it was now some hours since they had eaten the food which Mr. Blake had brought, they were quite ready for another meal, at which they were soon joined by six or eight other gentlemen, who had been sleeping in the house. Breakfast over, Harry retired to his room, put on a fresh suit from his wallet, and rejoined his companions, when a sort of council of war was held. Harry learned that there was no difficulty as to men, as any number of these could be recruited among the peasantry. There was, however, an entire absence of any arms save pikes. Harry knew how good a weapon are these when used by steady and well-disciplined men. The matchlocks of those days were cumbrous arms, and it was at the point of the pike that battles were then always decided.

Mr. Blake begged Harry to make his house his headquarters during his stay in the West, and the invitation was gladly accepted. The letters of which he was the bearer were dispatched to their destinations, and a few days after his arrival the recipients called upon him, and he found himself overwhelmed with invitations and offers of hospitality. The time therefore passed very pleasantly.

A few men were found in Galway who had served in the wars. These were made sergeants of the newly raised regiment, which was five hundred strong. This was not embodied, but five central places were chosen at a distance from each other, and at these the peasants assembled for drill. Several of the sons of the squires received commissions as officers, and the work of drilling went on briskly, Harry superintending that at each center by turns. In the evenings there were generally dinner parties at the houses of one or other of the gentry, and Harry greatly enjoyed the life. So some months passed.

In July the news came that the Earl of Ormonde's force outside Dublin had been routed by the garrison, under General Jones, the governor, and shortly afterward Harry received orders to march with the regiment to join the earl, who, as the king's representative, forwarded him at the same time a commission as its colonel, and the order to command it.

It was on the 13th of August that Harry with his force joined the army of Ormonde, and the next day the news came that Cromwell had landed at Dublin, and had issued a bloodthirsty proclamation against the Irish. Harry was at once ordered to march with his regiment to Tredah, now called Drogheda, a seaport about forty miles north of Dublin. At this town Harry found in garrison twenty-five hundred English troops, under the command of Sir Arthur Ashton, an old Royalist officer, he had lost a leg in the king's service.

During the six months he had passed in the West Harry had found Mike an invaluable servant. He had, of course, furnished him with decent suits of clothes, but although willing to wear shoes in the house, nothing could persuade Mike to keep these on his feet when employed without. As a messenger he was of the greatest service, carrying Harry's missives to the various posts as quickly as they could have been taken by a horseman. During that time he had picked up a great deal of English, and his affection for his master was unbounded. He had, as a matter of course, accompanied Harry on his march east, and was ready to follow him to the end of the world if need be.

The garrison of Drogheda employed themselves busily in strengthening the town to the utmost, in readiness for the siege that Cromwell would, they doubted not, lay to it. In September Cromwell moved against the place. He was prepared to carry out the campaign in a very different spirit to that with which he had warred in England. For years Ireland had been desolated by the hordes of half-savage men, who had for that time been burning, plundering, and murdering on the pretext of fighting for or against the king. Cromwell was determined to strike so terrible a blow as would frighten Ireland into quietude. He knew that mildness would be thrown away upon this people, and he defended his course, which excited a thrill of horror in England, upon the grounds that it was the most merciful in the end. Certainly, nowhere else had Cromwell shown himself a cruel man. In England the executions in cold blood had not amounted to a dozen in all. The common men on both sides were, when taken prisoners, always allowed to depart to their homes, and even the officers were not treated with harshness. It may be assumed that his blood was fired by the tales of massacre and bloodshed which reached him when he landed. The times were stern, and the policy of conciliating rebels and murderers by weak concessions was not even dreamed of. Still, no excuses or pleas of public policy can palliate Cromwell's conduct at Drogheda and Wexford. He was a student and expounder of the Bible, but it was in the old Testament rather than the new that precedents for the massacre at Drogheda must be sought for. No doubt it had the effect at the time which Cromwell looked for, but it left an impression upon the Irish mind which the lapse of over two centuries has not obliterated. The wholesale massacres and murders perpetrated by Irishmen on Irishmen have long since been forgotten, but the terrible vengeance taken by Cromwell and his saints upon the hapless towns of Drogheda and Wexford will never be forgotten by the Irish, among whom the "curse of Cromwell" is still the deadliest malediction one man can hurl at another.

Cromwell's defenders who say that he warred mildly and mercifully in England, according to English ideas, and that he fought the Irish only as they fought each other, must be hard driven when they set up such a defense. The fact that Murrogh O'Brien, at the capture of Cashel, murdered the garrison who had laid down their arms, and three thousand of the defenseless citizens, including twenty priests who had fled to the cathedral for refuge, affords no excuse whatever for the perpetration of equal atrocities by Cromwell, and no impartial historian can deny that these massacres are a foul and hideous blot in the history of a great and, for the most part, a kind and merciful man.

Upon arriving before Drogheda on the 2d of September Cromwell at once began to throw up his batteries, and opened fire on the 10th. His artillery was abundant, and was so well served that early the same afternoon two practical breaches were made, the one in the east, in the wall of St. Mary's Churchyard, the other to the south, in the wall of the town. Sir Arthur Ashton had placed Harry in command at St. Mary's Churchyard, and seeing that the wall would soon give way under the fire of the enemy's artillery, he set his men to throw up an earthwork behind.

Seven hundred of the Roundheads advanced to the assault, but so heavy was the fire that Harry's troops poured upon them that they were forced to fall back with great slaughter. At the other breach they were also repulsed, but attacking again in great force they made their way in. Near this spot was an ancient tumulus, called the Hill Mount. The sides of this were defended by strong palisades, and here the Royalists, commanded by Sir Arthur Ashton himself, opposed a desperate resistance to the enemy. These, supported by the guns on the walls, which they turned against the Mount, made repeated attacks, but were as often repulsed. The loss, however, of the defenders was great, and seeing that fresh troops were constantly brought against them they at last lost heart and surrendered, on promise of their lives; a promise which was not kept, as all were immediately massacred.

Up to this time Harry had successfully repulsed every attack made upon the other breach, but at length the news of the

Roundheads' success at the Mount reached both assailants and defenders.

With exulting shouts the Roundheads poured over the wall. The garrison, headed by Harry and the other officers, strove hard to drive them back, but it was useless. Cromwell and Ireton were in the van of their troops, and these, accustomed to victory, hewed their way through the ranks of the besieged. Many of them lost heart, and, throwing down their arms, cried for quarter. With shouts of "No quarter!" "Hew down the Amalakites!" "Strike, and spare not!" the Roundheads cut down their now defenseless foes. Maddened at the sight, the besieged made another desperate effort at resistance, and for awhile fought so stoutly that the Roundheads could gain no ground of them.

Presently, however, a party of the enemy who had forced their way over the wall at another point took them in rear. Then the garrison fled in all directions pursued by their victorious enemy, who slaughtered every man they overtook. Mike had kept close to Harry through the whole of the struggle. He had picked up a pike from a fallen man, and had more than once, when Harry was nearly surrounded by his foes, dashed forward and rid him of one of the most pressing. Seeing, by the general slaughter which was going on, that the Roundhead soldiers must have received orders from their general to give no quarter, Harry determined to sell his life dearly, and rushed into a church where a score of the English soldiers were taking refuge. The door was closed and barricaded with chairs and benches, and from the windows the men opened fire upon the Roundheads, who were engaged in slaying all—men, women and children, without mercy. Soon, from every house around, a heavy fire was poured into the church, and several of those within fell dead under the fire. Under cover of this, the Roundheads attacked the door with axes. Many were killed by the fire of the defenders, but as the door yielded, Harry called these from their post, and with them ascended the belfry tower. Here they prepared to fight to the last.

Looking from a window, Harry beheld a sight which thrilled him with horror. Gathered round a cross, standing in an open space, were two hundred women on their knees. Even while Harry looked a body of Cromwell's saints fell upon them, hewing and cutting with their swords, and thrusting with their pikes, and did not desist while one remained alive. And these were the men who had the name of God ever on their lips! When the dreadful massacre began Harry turned shuddering from the window, and with white face and set teeth nerved himself to fight to the last. Already the door had been beaten down, and the assailants had streamed into the church. Then a rush of heavy feet was heard on the stairs. Assembled round its top stood Harry and the twelve men remaining. Each knew now that there was no hope of quarter, and fought with the desperation of men who cared only to sell their lives dearly. Fast as the Roundheads poured up the stairs, they fell, pierced by pike, or shot down by musket ball. For half an hour the efforts continued, and then the Roundheads, having lost over fifty men, fell back. Three times during the day the attack was renewed, and each time repulsed with the same terrible slaughter. Between the intervals the defenders could hear the never-ceasing sound of musket and pistol firing, as house after house, defended to the last by desperate men, was stormed; while loud, even above the firing, rose the thrilling shrieks of dying women and children.

In all the history of England, from its earliest times, there is no such black and ghastly page as that of the sack of Drogheda. Even supposing Cromwell's assertion that he wished only to terrify the Irish rebels to be true, no shadow of an excuse can be pleaded for the massacre of the women and children, or for that of the English Royalists who formed five-sixths of the garrison.

All through the night occasional shrieks and pistol shots could be heard, as the wretched people who had hidden themselves in closets and cellars were discovered and murdered. No further assault was made upon the church tower, nor was there any renewal of it next morning. As hour after hour passed on Harry concluded that, deterred by the great loss which his men had already sustained in endeavoring to capture the post, Cromwell had determined to reduce it by starvation.

Already the defenders were, from the effects of exertion and excitement, half-mad with thirst. As the day went on their sufferings became greater, but there was still no thought of surrender. The next day two of them leaped from the top of the tower and were killed by their fall. Then Harry saw that it was better to give in.

"My lads," he said, "it is better to go down and die by a bullet-shot than to suffer these agonies of thirst, with only death as the issue. We must die. Better to die in our senses as men, than mad like wild beasts with thirst. Mike, my lad, I am sorry to have brought you to this pass."

Mike put his parched lips to his master's hand.

"It is not your fault, master. My life is no differ to any."

The men agreed to Harry's proposal. There was a discussion whether they should go down and die fighting, or not; but Harry urged upon them that it was better not to do so. They were already weak with hunger and thirst, and it would be more dignified to meet

145

their fate quiet and unresistingly. They accordingly laid by their arms, and, preceded by Harry, descended the stairs.

The noise of their footsteps warned the soldiers in the church below of their coming, and these formed in a semicircle round the door to receive the expected onslaught. When they saw that the Royalists were unarmed they lowered their weapons, and an officer said: "Take these men out into the street, and shoot them there, according to the general's orders."

Calmly and with dignity Harry marched at the head of his little party into the street. They were ranged with their backs to the church, and a firing party took their places opposite to them.

The officer was about to give the order, when a divine in a high-steepled hat came up. He looked at the prisoners, and then rapidly advanced between the lines and gazed earnestly at Harry.

"Is your name Master Furness?" he asked.

"I am Colonel Furness, an officer of his majesty Charles II.," Harry said coldly. "What then?"

"I am Ebenezer Stubbs," the preacher said. "Do you not remember how seven years ago you saved my life at the risk of your own in the streets of Oxford? I promised you then that if the time should come I would do as good a turn to yourself. Captain Allgood," he said, "I do beseech you to stay this execution until I have seen the general. I am, as you know, his private chaplain, and I am assured that he will not be wroth with you for consenting to my request."

The influence of the preacher with Cromwell was well known, and the officer ordered his men to ground arms, although they muttered and grumbled to themselves at the prospect of mercy being shown to men who had killed so many of their companions. A quarter of a hour later the preacher returned with an order from the general for the prisoners to be placed in durance.

"I have obtained your life," the preacher said, "but even to my prayers the general will grant no more. You and your men are to be sent to the Bermudas."

Although Harry felt that death itself would be almost preferable to a life of slavery in the plantations, he thanked the preacher for his efforts in his behalf. A week later Harry, with the eight men who had taken with him, and twenty-seven others who been discovered in hiding-places, long after the capture of the place, were placed on board a ship bound for the Bermudas, the sole survivors of the garrison—three thousand strong—and of the inhabitants of Drogheda.

# CHAPTER XVIII

## SLAVES IN THE BERMUDAS

The Good Intent, upon which Harry Furness with thirty-five other Royalist prisoners were embarked, was a bark of two hundred tons. She carried, in addition to the prisoners, sixty soldiers, who were going out to strengthen the garrison of Barbadoes. The prisoners were crowded below, and were only allowed to come on deck in batches of five or six for an hour at a time. Four of them had died on the way, and the others were greatly reduced in strength when they landed. As soon as they reached Bermuda the prisoners were assigned as slaves to some of the planters most in favor of the Commonwealth. Four or five were allotted to each, and Harry having placed Mike next to him at the end of the line, when they were drawn up on landing, they were, together with two others of the soldiers who had defended the tower of Drogheda with him, assigned to the same master.

"He is an evil-looking scoundrel," Harry said to the Irish boy. "He looks even more sour and hypocritical than do the Puritans at home. We have had a lesson of what their idea of mercy and Christianity is when they get the upper hand. I fear we have a hard time before us, my lad."

The four prisoners were marched to the center of the island, which seemed to Harry to be, as near as he could tell, about the size of the Isle of Wight. Their new master rode in front of them, while behind rode his overseer, with pistols at his holsters, and a long whip in his hand. Upon their way they passed several negroes working in the fields, a sight which mightily astonished Mike, who had never before seen these black creatures. At that time the number of negroes in the island was comparatively small, as the slave trade was then in its infancy. It was the want of labor which made the planters so glad to obtain the services of the white prisoners from England. Many of the slaves in the island had been kidnaped as boys at the various ports in England and Scotland, the infamous traffic being especially carried on in Scotland.

When they reached the plantation the horsemen alighted in the courtyard of the residence, and the planter, whose name was Zachariah Stebbings, told the overseer to take them to the slave quarters.

"You will have," he said harshly, "to subdue your pride here, and to work honestly and hard, or the lash will become acquainted with your backs."

"Look you here, Master Stebbings, if such be your name," Harry said, "a word with you at the beginning. We are exiled to this place, and given into servitude to you through no crime but that of having fought bravely for his majesty King Charles. We are men who care not greatly for our lives, and we four, with seven others, did, as you may learn, defend the tower of Drogheda for two days against the whole army of Cromwell, and did only yield to thirst, and not to force. You may judge then, of our mettle from that fact. Now, hark you; having fallen into this strait, we are willing to conform to our condition, and to give you fair and honest work to the best of our powers; but mind you, if one finger be laid on us in anger, if so much as the end of a whip touch one of us, we have sworn that we will slay him so ventures, and you also, should you countenance it, even though afterward we be burned at the stake for doing it. That is our bargain; see you that you keep to it."

So stern and determined were Harry's words, so fierce and haughty his tone, that the planter and his overseer both turned pale and shrank back. They saw at once the manner of men with whom they had to deal, and felt that the threat would be carried out to the fullest. Muttering some inarticulate reply, the planter turned and entered the house, and the overseer, with a dogged, crestfallen look, led the way to the slave quarters. The place assigned to them was a long hut, the sides lightly constructed of woven boughs, with a thick thatch overhead. Along one side extended a long sloping bench, six feet wide. This was the bed of the slaves.

An hour afterward the other inmates of the hut entered. They consisted of four white men who had been kidnaped as boys, and two who had been apprentices, sent out, as Harry soon learned, for their share in the rising in the city, which he had headed. The negroes on the estate, some twenty in number, were confined in another hut. There were, besides, four guards, one of whom kept sentry at night over the hut, while another with a loaded firearm stood over them while they worked. The garrison of the island consisted, as Harry had learned before landing, of two hundred and fifty soldiers, besides the militia, consisting of the planters, their overseers and guards, who would number altogether about five hundred men.

The next day the work in the fields began. It consisted of hoeing the ground between the rows of young sugar canes and tobacco plants. The sun was extremely powerful, and the perspiration soon flowed in streams from the newcomers. They worked, however, steadily and well, and in a manner which gave satisfaction even to their master and his overseer. Harry had impressed upon his two men and Mike the importance of doing nothing which could afford their employer a fair opportunity for complaint. He would not, Harry felt sure, venture to touch them after the warning he had given, but he might send one or all of them back to the town, where they would be put to work as refractory slaves on the fortifications, and where their lot would be far harder than it would be on the plantation. He urged upon them above all things to have patience; sooner or later the people of England would, he felt sure, recall the young king, and then they would be restored to their country. But even before that some mode of escape, either by ship, or by raising an insurrection in concert with the white slaves scattered through the island, might present itself.

The white slaves and negroes were kept as far as possible apart during their work in all the plantations in the island. The whites were deemed dangerous, and were watched with the greatest care. The blacks were a light-hearted and merry race, not altogether discontented with their position, and the planters did their utmost to prevent the white slaves having communication with them, and stirring them up to discontent and rebellion. At the same time they were not absolutely forbidden to speak. Each slave had a small plot of ground assigned to him near the huts, and on these, after the day's work was over, they raised vegetables for their own consumption.

Mike, who, as a lad, was much less closely watched than the men, soon made friends with the negroes. He was full of fun and mischief, and became a prime favorite with them. He learned that at night, as no watch was kept over them, they would often steal away and chat with the negroes on other plantations, and that so long as there were no signs of discontent, and they did their work cheerfully, the masters placed no hindrance upon such meetings. Often at night, indeed, the sound of the negro singing and music could be heard by the prisoners, the overseers troubling themselves in no way with the proceedings of their slaves after nightfall, so long as their amusements did not interfere with their power of work next morning. Mike heard also that the treatment of the slaves, both white and black, varied greatly on different plantations, according to the nature of their masters. In some the use of the lash was almost unknown, the slaves were permitted many indulgences, and were happy and contented; while in others they were harshly and cruelly treated. Mr. Stebbings was considered one of the worst masters in the island, and, indeed, it was everywhere noticed that the masters who most conformed to the usages and talk of the Puritans at home were the most cruel taskmasters to their slaves. Many times Harry Furness' blood boiled when he saw the lash applied to the bare shoulders of the slaves, often, as it seemed to him, from pure wantonness on the part of the overseer. But the latter never once ventured to touch Harry or his three companions.

Through the negroes Mike learned that to each of the four plantations adjoining their own four white prisoners had been assigned, and among these, Harry found, on obtaining their names, were the other five soldiers who had fought with him at Drogheda.

Mike soon took to going out at night with the negroes, making his way through a small opening in the light wall of the hut. This was easily closed up on his return, and by choosing a time when the sentry was on the other side of the house, he had no difficulty in leaving or entering unseen. By means of the negroes he opened up a communication with the other soldiers, and informed them that Colonel Furness bade them hold themselves in readiness when an opportunity for escape should arise. It might be weeks or even months before this would come, but the signal would be given by a fire burning at daybreak upon a hill at no great distance from the plantation. He bade them use their discretion as to taking any white slaves with them into their confidence. At nightfall, after seeing the column of smoke, they were, as best they could, to make their way from the huts, and meet in a clump of trees near the house of Mr. Stebbings.

Harry had, indeed formed no distinct plan for escape; but he wished, should an opportunity offer, to have such a body of men at hand as might stand him in good stead.

One day, about a month after their arrival on the plantation, the overseer brutally beat an old negro who was working next to Mike. The old man resumed his work, but was so feeble that he in vain endeavored to use his hoe, and the overseer struck him to the ground with the butt end of his whip. Mike instinctively dropped his hoe and sprang to lift the old man to his feet. The infuriated overseer, enraged at this interference, brought down his whip on Mike's head and felled him by the side of the negro. In an instant Harry sprang forward, armed with his hoe; the overseer seeing him coming, retreated a step or two, drew his pistol from his belt and fired—the ball flew close to Harry's ear, and the latter, whirling his hoe round his head, brought it down with his full strength upon that of the overseer; the man fell in his tracks as if smitten with lightning. The guard ran up with his musket pointed, but Harry's two companions also advanced, armed with their hoes, and the guard, seeing that even if he shot one, he should assuredly be killed by the others, took to his heels and ran off to the house. A minute later Zachariah Stebbings with the four guards was seen running up to the spot.

"What is this?" he exclaimed furiously. "Mutiny?"

"No, Master Stebbings," Harry said calmly. "We have, as you know, worked honestly and well, but your brutal overseer has broken the agreement we made, and struck this lad to the ground without any cause. I, of course, carried out my part of the compact, though I doubt me the fellow is not killed. His hat is a thick one, and may have saved his skull. You had best leave matters alone. I and my three men are a match for you and your guards, even though they have guns, and you best know if our services are worth anything to you."

The planter hesitated. He was unwilling indeed to lose four of his best slaves, and he knew that whether he attacked them now, or whether he reported the case to the commandant of the island, he would assuredly do this. After a moment's hesitation, he said:

"The fool has brought it on himself. Do you," turning to the guards, "lift him up and carry him to the house, and let old Dinah see to his head. It is an ugly cut," he said, leaning over him, "but will do him no harm, though it will not add to his beauty."

The blow had indeed been a tremendous one, and had it alighted fairly on the top of his head, would assuredly have cleft the skull, in spite of the protection afforded by the hat. It had, however, fallen somewhat on one side, and had shorn off the scalp, ear, and part of the cheek. It was three weeks before the overseer again resumed his duty, and he cast such a deadly look at Harry as assured him that he would have his life when the occasion offered.

Two days later, when the planter happened to be in the field with the overseer, two gentlemen rode from the house, where they had been to inquire for him. The sobriety of their garments showed that they belonged to the strictest sect of the Puritans.

"I have ridden hither," one said, with a strong nasal twang, "Zachariah Stebbings, having letters of introduction to you from the governor. These will tell that I am minded to purchase an estate in the island. The governor tells me that maybe you would be disposed to sell, and that if not, I might see the methods of work and culture here, and learn from you the name of one disposed to part with his property."

At the first words of the speaker Harry Furness had started, and dropped his hoe; without, however, looking round, he picked it up and applied himself to his work.

"I should not be unwilling to sell," the planter answered, "for a fair price, but the profits are good, and are likely to be better, for I hear that large numbers of malignants, taken by the sword of the Lord Cromwell at Dundalk and Waterford in Ireland, will be sent here, and with more labor to till the fields, our profits will increase."

"I have heard," the newcomer said, "that some of the ungodly followers of the man Charles have already been sent here."

"That is so," the planter agreed. "I myself, standing well in the favor of the governor, have received four of them; that boy, the two men next to him, and that big man working there. He is a noted malignant, and was known as Colonel Furness."

"Truly he is a stalwart knave," the other remarked.

"Ay is he," the planter said; "but his evil fortune has not as yet altogether driven out the evil spirit within him. He is a man of wrath, and the other day he smote nigh to death my overseer, whose head is, as you see, still bandaged up."

"Truly he is a son of Belial," the other argued, but in a tone in which a close observer might have perceived a struggle to keep down laughter. "I warrant me, you punished him heartily for such an outbreak."

"To tell you the truth," the planter said, "the man is a good workman, and like to an ox in his strength. The three others were by his side, and also withstood me. Had I laid a complaint before the governor they would all have been shot, or put on the roads to work, and I should have lost their labor. My overseer was in the wrong, and struck one of them first, so 'twas better to say naught about the matter. And now will you walk me to the house, where I can open the letter of the governor, and talk more of the business you have in hand."

The instant the man had spoken Harry had recognized the voice of his old friend Jacob, and doubted not, though he had not ventured to look round, that he who accompanied him was William Long; and he guessed that hearing he had been sent with the other captives spared at the massacre of Drogheda to the Bermudas, they had come out to try and rescue him. So excited was he at the thought that it was with difficulty he could continue steadily at his work through the rest of the day. When at nightfall he was shut up in the hut with his companions, he told them that the Puritan they had seen was a friend of his own, a captain in his troop, and that he doubted not that deliverance was at hand. He charged Mike at once to creep forth to join the negroes, and to bid them tell one of their color who served in the house to take an opportunity to whisper to one of his master's guests—for he learned that they were biding there for the night, "Be in the grove near the house when all are asleep." The negroes willingly undertook the commission, and Mike rejoined the party in the hut. Two hours later Harry himself crept out through the hole, which they had silently and at great pains enlarged for the purpose, and made his way round to the grove. There were still lights in the house, and the negroes in their hut were talking and singing. An hour later the lights were extinguished, and soon afterward he saw a figure stealthily approaching.

"Jacob," he whispered, as the man entered the shelter of the trees, and in another moment he was clasped in the arms of his faithful friend. For some time their hearts were too full to speak, and then Harry leading his companion to the side of the wood furthest from the house, they sat down and began to talk. After the first questions as to the health of Harry's father had been answered, Jacob went on:

"We saw by the dispatch of Cromwell to Parliament that the sole survivors of the sack of Drogheda, being one officer, Colonel Furness, a noted malignant, and thirty-five soldiers, had been sent in slavery to the Bermudas. So, of course, we made up our minds to come and look after you. Through Master Fleming I obtained letters, introducing to the governor the worshipful Grace-be-to-the-Lord Hobson and Jeremiah Perkins, who desired to buy an estate in the Bermudas. So hither we came, William Long and I; and now, Harry, what do you advise to be done? I find that the ships which leave the port are searched before they leave, and that guards are placed over them while they load, to see that none conceal themselves there, and I see not, therefore, how you can well escape in that way. There seem to be no coasting craft here, or we might seize one of these and make for sea."

"No," Harry replied. "They allow none such in the port, for fear that they might be so taken. There are large rowing boats, pulled by twelve slaves, that come to take produce from the plantations farthest from the port round to ships there. But it would be madness to trust ourselves to sea in one of these. We should either die of hunger and thirst, or be picked up again by their cruisers. The only way would be to seize a ship."

"That is what William Long and I have been thinking of," Jacob said. "But there is a shrewd watch kept up, and the ships are

153

moored under the guns of the battery. We passed, on our way hither, a bark bringing a number of prisoners taken at Waterford. She is a slow sailer, and, by the calculations of our captain, will not arrive here for some days yet."

"If we could intercept her," Harry said thoughtfully, "we might, with the aid of the prisoners, overcome the guard, and then turning her head, sail for Holland."

"That might be done," Jacob assented, "if you have force enough."

"I can bring forty men," Harry answered. "There are eight here, and we have communication with those in the neighboring plantations, who are ready to join me in any enterprise. That should be enough."

"It is worth trying," Jacob said. "I will hire a rowboat, as if to bring round a cargo of sugar from this plantation to the port. I will station a man on the highest point of the hills to give me notice when a sail is in sight. He may see it thence forty miles away. The winds are light and baffling, and she will make slow progress, and may bring up outside the port that night, but assuredly will not enter until next morning. The instant I know it is in sight I will ride over here, and William Long will start with the barge from the port. When you see me come, do you send round word to the others to meet at midnight on the beach, where you will see the boat drawn up. Can you let your friends know speedily?"

"Yes," Harry replied. "My signal was to have been given at daybreak, but I will send round word of the change of hour, and that if, when they are locked up for the night, they see a fire burning on the point agreed, they are to meet on the shore at midnight. Tell William Long to haul the boat up, and let the rowers go to sleep on the shore. We will seize them noiselessly. Then we will row along the shore till off the port, and at first daybreak out to the ship if she be at anchor, or away to meet her if she be not yet come. They will think that we bear a message from the port."

After some further discussion of details the friends separated, and the next day Mike sent round by the negroes the news of the change of plans. Two days later Jacob rode up to the plantation. He had upon the first occasion told Stebbings that the sum he asked for the estate seemed to him too high, but that he would return to talk it over with him, after he had seen other properties. Immediately upon his arrival, which happened just as the slaves returned from work, Mike sent off one of the negro boys, who had already collected a pile of brushwood on the beacon hill. Half an hour later a bright flame shone out on its summit.

154

"I wonder what that means?" the planter, who was sitting at dinner in his veranda with Jacob, said angrily.

"It looks like a signal fire," Jacob remarked calmly. "I have heard that they are sometimes lit on the seacoast of England as a signal to smugglers."

"There are no smugglers here," the planter said, "nor any cause for such a signal."

He clapped his hands, and ordered the black slave who answered to tell the overseer to take two of the guards, and at once proceed to the fire, and examine its cause. After dinner was over the planter went out to the slave huts. All the white men were sitting or lying in the open air, enjoying the rest after their labor. The negroes were singing or working in their garden plots, The list was called over, and all found to be present.

"I expect," the planter said, "that it is only a silly freak of some of these black fellows to cause uneasiness. It can mean nothing, for the garrison and militia could put down any rising without difficulty and there is no hope of escape. In a week we could search every possible hiding-place in the island."

"Yes, that is an advantage which you have over the planters in Virginia, to which place I hear our Scottish brethren have sent large numbers of the malignants. There are great woods stretching no man knoweth how far inland, and inhabited by fierce tribes of Indians, among whom those who escape find refuge."

That night when all was still Harry Furness and his seven comrades crept through the opening in the hut. In the grove they were joined by Jacob. They then made their way to the seashore, where they saw lying a large shallop, drawn partly up on the beach. A man was sitting in her, while many other dark figures lay stretched on the sand near. Harry and his party moved in that direction, and found that the men from two of the other plantations had already arrived. A few minutes later the other two parties arrived. The whole body advanced noiselessly along the shore, and seized and gagged the sleepers without the least difficulty or noise. These were bound with ropes from the boat, and laid down one by one on the sand, at a distance from each other.

# CHAPTER XIX

## A SEA FIGHT

The instant the rowers were secured Harry Furness embraced his faithful follower William Long. He had learned from Jacob that the ship had appeared in sight about two in the afternoon, and that it was not thought likely by the sailors of the port that she would reach it until the breeze sprang up in the morning, although she might get within a distance of five or six miles. The whole party had, in concurrence with Harry's orders, brought with them their hoes, which were the only weapons that were attainable. It was agreed that their best course would be to row along the shore until near the lights of the port, then to row out and lay on their oars half a mile beyond the entrance, where, as it was a starlight night, they would assuredly see the ship if she had come to anchor. As soon as the first dawn commenced they were to row out and meet the ship. Wrappings of cloth were fastened round the rowlocks to prevent noise, twelve men took the oars, the boat was shoved down into the sea, and they started on their voyage. The boat rowed but slowly, and it was, Harry judged, past three o'clock when they reached the point they had fixed on off the mouth of the harbor. No ship was visible outside the port, although there was sufficient light to have seen its masts had it been there.

"We had better go another half-mile further out," he said. "Should they take it into their heads on shore, when they see us, to send a fast boat out to inquire what we are doing, it might overtake us before we could reach the ship."

An hour after they had ceased rowing a faint streak of daylight appeared in the west, and a ship could be seen about three miles seaward, while the shore was nearly that distance behind them, for they had been deceived by the darkness, and were much further out than they had thought.

"It is all the better," Harry said. "It must be some time before they think of sending a boat after us, and we shall reach the ship before it can overtake us."

As soon as it became broad daylight Harry took one of the oars himself, and all save the twelve rowers, and Jacob and William Long who sat in the stern, lay down in the bottom of the boat, where some pieces of matting, used for covering cargo, were thrown over them. There was not as yet a breath of wind, and the ship's sails hung idly against the masts. After three-quarters of an hour's hard rowing the barge approached her side. There were only a few figures on the deck.

"Are you the captain of this vessel?" Jacob asked one who seemed to him of that condition.

"Ay, ay," the sailor said. "What is the news?"

"I have come off from the island," Jacob answered, "by orders of his worshipful the governor, to warn you that there is an insurrection among the slaves of the island, and to bid you not to anchor outside, or to wait for your papers being examined, but to enter at once."

By this time the boat was alongside, and Jacob climbed on board.

"You have brought some troops with you?" he asked, "They will be wanted."

"Yes, I have eighty men whom I have brought as a reinforcement to the garrison of the island, besides a hundred and fifty prisoners from Waterford, stowed away below the hatches forward. Hullo! why, what is this? Treason!"

As he spoke Harry, followed by the rowers, swarmed on board armed with their hoes. The captain and the men round him were at once knocked down. The sentries over the fore hatchway discharged their muskets, and, with some of the crew stationed there, made aft. But Harry's party had now all joined him on deck. A rush was made, and the decks entirely cleared. A few of the soldiers who came running up through the after hatchway on hearing the tumult and noise of the fight were beaten down and hurled below on those following them, and the hatches were slipped on and secured. Then a triumphant shout of "God and the King!" was raised.

The forehatches were now lifted, and the prisoners invited to come up. They rushed on deck, delighted and bewildered, for it was the first time that they had seen the sun since they left England, having been kept below, where many had died from confinement and bad air, while all were sorely weakened and brought low. Among them were many officers, of whom several were known to Harry—although they had some difficulty in recognizing in the man, bronzed brown by his exposure to the sun and clad in a tattered shirt and breeches—their former comrade, Harry Furness. A search was at once made for arms, and ranged in the passage to the captain's cabin were found twenty muskets for the use of the crew, together with as many boarding pikes and sabers. Ammunition was not wanting. The arms were divided among Harry's band of forty men, and the twenty strongest of those they had rescued. The hoes were given to the remainder.

The captain, who had by this time recovered from the blow dealt him by Harry, was now questioned. He was told that if he would consent with his crew to navigate the vessel to Holland, he should there be allowed to go free with the ship, which it seemed was his own property; but the cargo would be sold as a fair prize, to satisfy the needs of his captors. If he refused, he would be sent with his crew on shore in the barge, and his ship and cargo would alike be lost to him. The captain had no hesitation in accepting the first of these alternatives, as he would be, although no gainer by the voyage, yet no loser either. He told Harry that for himself he had no sympathy with the rulers in London, and that he sorely pitied the prisoners he was bringing over.

The hatch was now a little lifted, and the prisoners below summoned to surrender. This they refused to do. Harry and his men then, with much labor, lowered a four-pounder carronade down the forehatch, and wheeled it to within a few feet of the bulkhead which divided that portion where the prisoners had been confined from the after part. The gun was loaded to the muzzle with grape, and discharged, tearing a hole through the bulkhead and killing and wounding many within. Then the officer in command offered to surrender.

Harry ordered them at once to hand up all their firelocks and other arms through the hatchway, which was again lifted for the purpose. When those on deck had armed themselves with those weapons, the prisoners were ordered to come up, bringing their wounded with them. As they reached the deck they were passed down into the barge, from which all the oars save four had been removed. Six of the soldiers had been killed, and the remainder having entered the barge, where they were stowed as thickly as they could pack, the head rope was dropped, and they were allowed to row away. Besides the eighty muskets of the guard, a store of firelocks, sufficient to arm all on board, was found; these having been intended for the use of the garrison. A gentle breeze had by this time sprung up from the land, and the ship's head was turned seaward.

The boat was but half a mile behind them when it was joined by an eight-oared galley, which had been seen rowing out from the harbor, whence, doubtless, it had been dispatched to inquire into the errand of the boat seen rowing off to the ship. After lying alongside the barge for a minute or two she turned her head, and made back again with all speed.

"You would have done more wisely," the captain said to Harry, "if you had retained the prisoners on board until the second boat came alongside. You could have swamped that, and sent those in it back with the others, who will not reach shore until late this afternoon, for with only four oars they will make no way until the land breeze falls."

"It would have been better—far better"—Harry agreed—"but one does not always think of things at the right time. What ships are there in port, Jacob?"

"There is the vessel I came by and two others," Jacob replied, "all about the same size as this, and mounting each as many guns. You have eight, I see, captain; the one I came out in had ten."

"They will pursue us," the captain said, "you may be sure. It is known that we are not a fast sailer, and I think, sir, you will have to fight for it."

"So be it," Harry said. "There are two hundred of us, and though they might sink the ship, they will assuredly never carry it by boarding. There is not a man here who would not rather die fighting than spend his life in slavery on that island."

The vessel had gone about six miles on her course, when from the topmast the captain announced that the galley had gained the port, now twelve miles distant. "There is a gun," he said, five minutes later. "They have taken the alarm now." He then descended to the deck, leaving a sailor in the tops. Two hours later the latter announced that the topsails of three ships coming out from the harbor were visible.

"We have nigh thirty miles' start," the captain said. "They will not be up to us till to-morrow at midday."

"Do you think it would be any use to try to lose them by altering our course in the night?" Harry asked.

"No," the captain answered. "It is but ten o'clock in the day now. They will be within ten or twelve miles by nightfall, for the wind is stronger near the land than it is here, and with their night glasses they could hardly miss us on a bright starlight night. I am ready to try if you like, for I do not wish to see the ship knocked into matchwood."

After some deliberation it was determined to hold their course, and as night came on it was found that escape would have been out of the question, for the vessels behind had overhauled the Lass of Devon faster than had been anticipated, and were little more than five miles astern. They could be plainly seen after darkness set in, with the night glasses.

"What you must do, captain, is to lay her aboard the first which comes up," Harry said; "even if they have brought all the garrison we shall be far stronger than any one of them taken singly."

During the night the pursuing vessels lessened sail and maintained a position about a mile astern of the chase, evidently intending to attack in the morning. The day spent in the open air, with plenty of the best eating and drinking which could be found in the ship, had greatly reinvigorated the released prisoners, and when at daybreak the vessels behind were seen to be closing up, all were ready for the fight. The enemy, sure that their prey could not escape them, did not fire a shot as they came up in her wake. The two immediately behind were but a cable's length asunder, and evidently meant to engage on either side. Harry ordered the greater portion of men below, leaving only sufficient on deck to fight the guns, to whose use many were well accustomed. The wind was very light, and the ships were scarcely stealing through the water.

"We had better fight them broadside to broadside," Harry said; "but keep on edging down toward the ship to leeward."

The fight began with a heavy fire of musketry from the tops, where, in all three ships, the best marksmen had been posted. Then, when they were abreast of each other, the guns opened fire. The vessels were little more than fifty yards apart. For half an hour the engagement continued without intermission. Both ships of the enemy had brought all their guns over to the sides opposed to the Royalist vessel, and fought eighteen guns to his eight. Fearing to injure each other, both aimed entirely at the hull of their opponent, while Harry's guns were pointed at the masts and rigging. The sides of the Lass of Devon were splintered and broken in all directions, while those of his assailants showed scarcely a shot mark. The fire of his men in the tops—all old soldiers—had been so heavy and deadly that they had killed most of the marksmen in the enemy's tops, and had driven the rest below. All this time the Lass of Devon was raked by the fire of the third vessel which had come up behind her, and raked her fore and aft. At the end of the half-hour the mainmast of the vessel to windward, which had been several times struck, fell with a crash.

"Now, captain, lay her aboard the ship to leeward."

They had already edged down within twenty yards of this ship, and slowly as they were moving through the water, in another three or four minutes the vessels grated together. At Harry's first order the whole of his men had swarmed on deck, pouring in such a fire of musketry that none could stand alive at the enemy's tiller to keep her head away as the Lass of Devon approached. As the vessels touched Harry leaped from the bulwark on to the deck of the enemy, followed by Jacob and his men. The Parliamentary troops had also rushed on deck, and, although inferior in numbers, for they counted but eighty men, they made a sturdy stand. Gradually, however, they were driven back, when an exclamation from Mike, who, as usual, was close to Harry, caused him to look round.

The ship behind had, the moment she perceived the Lass of Devon bearing down upon her consort, crowded on more sail, and was now ranging up on the other side of her. Bidding Jacob press the enemy hard with half his force, Harry, with the remainder, leaped back on to the deck of his own ship, just as the enemy boarded from the other side. The fight was now a desperate one. The vessel which had last arrived bore a hundred of the troops of the garrison, and the numbers were thus nearly equal. The Royalists, however, fought with a greater desperation, for they knew the fate that awaited them if conquered. Gradually they cleared the deck of the Lass of Devon of the enemy, and in turn boarded their opponent. William Long led thirty men into the tops of the Lass of Devon, and poured their fire into the crowded enemy. Every step of the deck was fiercely contested, but at last the Roundheads gave way. Some threw down their arms and called for quarter, others ran below. The Royalists, with shouts of "Remember Drogheda!" fell upon them, and many of those who had surrendered were cut down before Harry could arrest the slaughter.

A loud cheer announced the victory, and the men in the other ship, who had hitherto, although with difficulty, made front against the attacks of Jacob and his men, now lost heart and ran below. The wind had by this time entirely dropped, but battening the prisoners below, Harry set his men to thrust the ships past one another, until they were sufficiently in line for their guns to be brought to bear upon the third enemy. Crippled as she was by the loss of her mast, she immediately hauled down her colors, and the victory was complete.

The prisoners were brought on deck and disarmed. Harry found that the boats of the four ships would carry two hundred men closely packed, and but a hundred and eighty of the two hundred and fifty troops who had sailed in pursuit remained alive. These, with sufficient provisions and water to last for three days, were made to take their places in the boats, and told to row back to the island, which they should be able to regain in two days at the utmost. The crews of the captured ships were willing enough to obey the orders of their captors, for the sailors had in general but little sympathy with the doings of Parliament. Harry had lost in killed and wounded forty-two men, and the rest he divided between the four ships, giving about thirty-five men to each. He himself, with Jacob, William Long, and Mike, remained on board the Lass of Devon, officers being placed in command of the troops on board the other ships, which were ordered to sail in company with her. Twenty-four hours were spent in getting a jury-mast set in place of that which had been shot away. When this was completed the four ships hoisted their canvas and sailed together for Holland.

They met with no adventure until near the mouth of the English Channel, when one morning a fleet of eight ships was perceived. The captain of the Lass of Devon at once pronounced them to be ships of war, and their rate of sailing speedily convinced Harry that there was no chance of escape. Against such odds resistance was useless, and the other ships were signaled to lower their topsails in answer to the gun which the leading ship of the squadron fired. Anticipating a return to captivity, if not instant death, all on board watched the approaching men-of-war. Presently these, when close at hand, brought up into the wind, and a boat was lowered. It rowed rapidly to the Lass of Devon, which lay somewhat the nearest to them. Harry stood on the quarter-deck ready to surrender his sword. The boat came alongside, an officer leaped on deck and advanced toward him.

Harry could scarce believe his eyes; this gallant, in the gay dress of a cavalier officer, could be no follower of Cromwell. The officer paused and gazed in astonishment at Harry. The recognition was mutual, and the words "Furness" and "Elphinstone" broke from their lips.

"Why, Elphinstone, what squadron is that?"

"Prince Rupert's, to be sure," the officer said.

"What! did you take us for the Roundhead fleet?"

Harry made no reply, but taking off his hat, shouted to his men, "It is the Royalist fleet. Three cheers for Prince Rupert."

A cheer of joy burst from the men, caught up and re-echoed by the crews of the other ships. Harry led the officer into his cabin, and rapidly explained to him the circumstances which had taken place; ten minutes later, entering a boat, he rowed off to the flagship.

"Why! Harry Furness!" exclaimed Prince Rupert, "whither do

you spring from? I heard of you last as being sent to slave in the Bermudas, and methought, old friend, that you would stand the heat better than most, since you had served such a sharp apprenticeship with me in that oven you wot of. And now tell me how is it that you have got free, and that I find you sailing here with four ships?"

Harry related his adventure. When he had finished Prince Rupert said:

"I envy you, Furness, in that you have three faithful friends. One is as much as most men could even hope for, whereas you have three, who each seem willing to go through fire and water for you. They do remind me of the wonderful servants of whom my old nurse used to tell me as a child. They were given by a fairy to some fortunate prince, and whenever he got into sore straits were ready to do the most impossible things to free him from them. Now you must take up your quarters here until we reach Holland, whither I am on the point of sailing. We have picked up several fat prizes, which I have sent to Italy to sell, to pay the wages of my men, for his gracious majesty's exchequer is of the emptiest. But I hear that Blake is about to put to sea with the ships of the Parliament, and I care not to risk my fleet, for they will be needed to escort his majesty to Scotland ere long."

"Are the Scots then again inclined to his majesty's cause? Were I King Charles, I would not trust myself to them," Harry said. "They sold his father, and would sell him—at least Argyll and the knaves with him would do so."

"I like not these cold, calculating men of the north, myself," Prince Rupert said, "and trust them as little. Nor would my cousin venture himself again among them, if he took my advice. His majesty, however, is no more given to the taking of advice than was his father before him, unless it be of Buckingham and Wilmot, and other dissolute young lords, whose counsel and company are alike evil for him."

The same afternoon the fleet sailed for Holland, the four merchantmen accompanying it. Upon their arrival there Harry sold the three ships which he had taken, together with such cargo as was found in their holds. He sold also the cargo of the Lass of Devon, leaving the ship itself, as he had promised, to the captain, its owner, and making him and the sailors a handsome present for the way they stood by him and worked the ship during the action. The rest of the proceeds he divided between the officers and men who had sailed with him, and finding that these were ready still to share his fortunes, he formed them into a regiment for the service of the king, enlisting another hundred Royalists, whom he found there well-nigh starving, in his ranks.

It was at the end of April, 1650, that Harry reached Hamburg, and a month later came the news of the defeat and death of the Earl of Montrose. He had two months before sailed from Hamburg to the Orkneys, where he had landed with a thousand men. Crossing to the mainland he had marched down into Sunderland. There he had met a body of cavalry under Colonel Strachan, in a pass in the parish of Kincardine, now called Craigchonichan, or the Rock of Lamentation. The recruits he had raised in Orkney and the north fled at once. The Scotch and Germans he had brought with him fought bravely, but without effect, and were utterly defeated, scattering in all directions. Montrose wandered for many days in disguise, but was at last captured, and was brought to Edinburgh with every indignity. He was condemned to death by the Covenanters, and executed. So nobly did he bear himself at his death that the very indignities with which Argyll and his minions loaded him, in order to make him an object of derision to the people, failed in their object, and even those who hated him most were yet struck with pity and admiration at his noble aspect and bearing. Argyll stood at a balcony to see him pass, and Montrose foretold a similar fate for this double-dyed traitor, a prediction which was afterward fulfilled. Harry deeply regretted the loss of this gallant and chivalrous gentleman.

# CHAPTER XX

## WITH THE SCOTCH ARMY

While trying and executing Montrose for loyalty to the king, the Scots were themselves negotiating with Charles, commissioners having come over to Breda, where he was living, for the purpose. They insisted upon his swearing to be faithful to the Covenant, to his submitting himself to the advice of the Parliament and Church, and to his promising never to permit the exercise of the Catholic religion in any part of his dominions. Charles agreed to everything demanded of him, having all the time no intention whatever of keeping his promises. While he was swearing to observe everything the Scots asked of him, he was writing to Ormonde to tell him that he was to mind nothing he heard as to his agreement with the Scots, for that he would do all the Irish required. Charles, indeed, although but a young man of twenty, was as full of duplicity and faithlessness as his father, without possessing any of the virtues of that unfortunate king, and the older and wiser men among his followers were alienated by his dissolute conduct, and by the manner in which he gave himself up to the reckless counsels of men like Buckingham and Wilmot.

Harry heard with deep regret the many stories current of the evil life and ways of the young king. Had it not been for the deadly hatred which he felt to Cromwell and the Puritans for the murder of Sir Arthur Ashton, and the rest of the garrison and people of Drogheda, in cold blood, he would have retired altogether from the strife, and would have entered one of the continental armies, in which many Royalist refugees had already taken service. He determined, however, that he would join in this one expedition, and that if it failed he would take no further part in civil wars in England, but wait for the time, however distant, when, as he doubted not, the people of England would tire of the hard rule of the men of the army and conventicle, and would, with open arms, welcome the return of their sovereign.

Early in June the king sailed for Scotland, accompanied by the regiment which Harry had raised, and a few hundred other troops. He landed there on the 16th. The English Parliament at once appointed Cromwell captain-general and commander-in-chief of all the forces raised and to be raised within the commonwealth of

England. A few days later he left London, and on the 23d of June entered Scotland with sixteen thousand men. King Charles, to whom Harry had been presented by Prince Rupert as one of his father's most gallant and faithful soldiers, received him at first with great cordiality. As soon as he found, however, that this young colonel was in no way inclined to join in his dissipations, that his face was stern and set when light talk or sneers against religion were uttered by the king's companions, Charles grew cold to him, and Harry was glad to be relieved from all personal attendance upon him, and to devote himself solely to his military duties. Upon landing in Scotland, Harry, with his regiment, was encamped in the valley between Edinburgh Castle and the high hill called Arthur's Seat. A few days after his arrival he, with Jacob, who was now raised to the rank of major, and William Long, who was one of his lieutenants, entered the palace of Holyrood, where the king's court was held. Here were gathered a motley assembly. A few English Cavaliers, many loyal Scotch nobles and gentlemen, and a large number of somber men of the Covenant. Next to Charles stood a tall man, whom Harry instantly recognized. Argyll, for it was he, stared fixedly at the young colonel, who returned his look with one as cold and haughty.

"This is Colonel Furness, my lord earl," the young king said. "One of my father's bravest and most devoted followers."

"I seem to have met the gentleman before," the earl said.

"You have," Harry replied coldly. "At that time the Earl of Argyll threatened to torture me into betraying the secrets of his majesty, and would, I doubt not, have carried his threat into effect had I not escaped from his hands. The times have changed, and the Earl of Argyll now stands beside his king, but I, sir, have not forgotten the past so easily." So saying, with a deep bow to the king, Harry passed on.

"Harry," whispered Donald Leslie, a young Scotch officer who had joined the ranks of his regiment as captain at Hamburg, "hitherto I have thought you the wisest and most discreet of men. I cannot say as much now. It would have been safer to walk into a den of lions than to insult the old red fox. He was never known to forgive, and those who offend him have a short life. Beware, colonel, for henceforth you carry your life in your hand."

"My sword is as sharp as his," Harry laughed, as they issued into the open air.

"I doubt it not," Leslie said, "but it is with daggers rather than swords that Argyll fights, and with secret plottings more than either.

Edinburgh swarms with Campbells, any one of whom would think no more of running you through at his lord's command than he would of killing a rat. Mark my words, before a week is out you will be engaged in some broil or other."

Jacob and William Long heard with great disquietude the remarks of the young Scotch officer, which they knew sufficient of Argyll to be aware were perfectly true. They resolved that they would maintain a careful watch over their friend, and that night they charged Mike, who was now a tall, active young fellow of seventeen, to keep the strictest watch as he followed his master in the streets, and to have pistol and sword always in readiness.

Two days later Harry had the first evidence of the truth of Leslie's prediction. He was walking up the High Street, accompanied by Jacob, while Leslie and two or three of his officers followed a short distance behind, when three or four Scotch nobles were seen approaching. One of these, Colonel Campbell, of Arrain, a tall and powerful figure, in passing jostled roughly against Harry.

"S'death, sir!" he exclaimed. "Do you think that you are in England, that you can take up the whole of the road?"

"I'm as much entitled to the road as yourself," Harry said hotly; "you purposely jostled me."

"Well, sir, and what if I did?" Colonel Campbell replied. "If you don't like it you have your remedy," and he touched his sword significantly.

"I will meet you, sir," Harry said, "in an hour's time at the foot of the Castlehill."

The colonel nodded, and accompanied by his kinsmen strode on.

"Jacob, you and Leslie will act with me?" Harry asked.

"Willingly enough," Leslie replied. "But it is a bad business. Campbell has the name of being one of the best swordsmen in the Scottish army. Of course he has been set on to attack you."

"I have been fighting," Harry said, "for the last ten years, and was not a bad swordsman when I began. Unless I mistake, I am as powerful a man as Colonel Campbell, and I fear not him or any man."

At the time appointed Harry, accompanied by his seconds, was upon the ground, where five minutes later they were joined by Colonel Campbell, with two of his kinsmen. While the principals divested themselves of their cloaks and doublets, the seconds compared their swords. They were of entirely different fashion, Harry's being long and straight with sharp edges, while Colonel

Campbell's was a basket-hilted sword, also straight and double edged, and even larger and much heavier than Harry's; each had brought one of similar make and size to his own. Some conversation took place as to the weapons which should be used.

"I cannot fight with a plaything like that," Colonel Campbell said roughly.

"And I object equally," Harry puts in calmly, "to wield a heavier weapon than that to which I am accustomed. But I am quite content to fight with my own against that of Colonel Campbell."

The seconds at first on both sides objected to this, arguing that the weight and length of Campbell's weapon would give him an unfair advantage. Harry, however, was firm.

"A man fights better," he said, "with the sword to which he is used. Mine is of tried temper, and I have no fear of its breaking." Harry had good reason for faith in his weapon. It was a long, straight blade of Toledo steel, which he had purchased for a considerable sum from a Spanish Jew in Hamburg. Colonel Campbell put an end to the argument by roughly saying that he wanted no more talk, and that if Colonel Furness meant fighting he had better take up his ground. This had already been marked out, and Harry immediately stood on the defensive.

In a moment the swords met. Colonel Campbell at once attacked furiously, trying to beat down Harry's guard by sheer strength and the weight of his weapon. The Englishman, however, was to the full as powerful a man, and his muscles from long usage were like cords of steel. His blade met the sweeping blows of the Scotchman firmly and steadily, while his point over and over again menaced the breast of his adversary, who several times only saved himself by springing back beyond it. Harry's seconds saw from the first that the issue was not doubtful. In a contest between the edge and the point, the latter always wins if strength and skill be equal, and in this case, while in point of strength the combatants were fairly matched, Harry was more skilled in the use of his weapon, whose lightness, combined with its strength, added to his advantage. The fight lasted but five minutes. Twice Harry's sword drew blood, and at the third thrust he ran his adversary through under the shoulder. The latter dropped his sword, with a curse.

"I have spared your life, Colonel Campbell," Harry said. "It was at my mercy a dozen times, but I wished not to kill you. You forced this quarrel upon me at the bidding of another, and against you I had no animosity. Farewell, sir. I trust that ere the day of battle you will be able to use your sword again in the service of the king."

So saying, Harry resumed his doublet and cloak, and, accompanied by his seconds, returned to his camp, leaving Campbell, furious with pain and disappointment, to be conveyed home by his friends.

"So far, so good, Harry," Captain Leslie said. "The attempt will, you will find, be a more serious one. Argyll will not try fair means again. But beware how you go out at night."

The duel made a good deal of talk, and Argyll attempted to induce the king to take the matter up, and to punish Harry for his share in it. But the young king, although obliged to listen every day to the long sermons and admonitions of the Covenanters, was heartily sick of them already and answered Argyll lightly that, so far as he had heard of the circumstances, Colonel Campbell was wholly to blame. "And, indeed," added the king, "from what I have heard, the conduct of your kinsman was so wantonly insulting that men say he must have been provoked thereto by others, as the two officers appear to have been strangers until the moment when their quarrel arose."

The earl grew paler than usual, and pressed his thin lips tightly together.

"I know of no reason," he said, "why Colonel Campbell should have engaged wantonly in a quarrel with this English officer."

"No!" Charles said innocently. "And if you do not, my lord, I know of no one that does. Colonel Furness is an officer who is somewhat staid and severe for his years, and who, in sooth, stands somewhat aloof from me, and cares not for the merry jests of Buckingham; but he is a gallant soldier. He has risked his life over and over again in the cause of my sainted father, and tried his utmost to save him, both at Carisbrook and Whitehall. Any one who plots against him is no friend of mine." The young king spoke with a dignity and sternness which were not common to him, and Argyll, biting his lips, felt a deadlier enmity than ever toward the man who had brought this reproof upon his shoulders.

The following day Harry received orders from General Leslie, who commanded the royal forces, to march down toward the border, accompanied by two regiments of horse. He was to devastate the country and to fall back gradually before Cromwell's advance, the cavalry harassing him closely, but avoiding any serious conflict with the Roundhead horse. The whole party were under the command of Colonel Macleod.

"I am heartily glad to be on the move, Jacob," Harry said, on the evening before starting. "It is not pleasant to know that one is in constant danger of being attacked whenever one goes abroad. Once away from Edinburgh one may hope to be beyond the power of Argyll."

"I would not be too sure of that," Donald Leslie said. "A hound on the track of a deer is not more sure or untiring than is Argyll when he hunts down a foe. Be warned by me, and never relax a precaution so long as you are on Scottish ground. There are men who whisper that even now, when he stands by the side of the king, Argyll is in communication with Cromwell. Trust me, if he can do you an ill turn, he will."

Upon the following morning the detachment marched, with flags flying and drums beating, and the king himself rode down to see them depart. Argyll was with him, and the king, as if in bravado of the formidable earl, waved his hand to Harry, and said: "Good-by, my grave colonel. Take care of yourself, and do not spare my enemies as you spared my friend."

Harry doffed his plumed hat, and rode on at the head of his regiment. The force marched rapidly, for it was known that Cromwell was within a few days of Berwick. So fast did they travel that in three days they were near the border. Then they began the work which they had been ordered to carry out. Every head of cattle was driven up the country, and the inhabitants were ordered to load as much of their stores of grain in wagons as these would hold, and to destroy the rest. The force under Colonel Macleod saw that these orders were carried out, and when, on the 14th of July, Cromwell crossed the Tweed, he found the whole country bare of all provision for his troops. In vain his cavalry made forays to a distance from the coast. Harry's foot opposed them at every defensible point, while the cavalry hung upon their skirts. In vain the Roundheads tried to charge by them. The Scotch cavalry, in obedience to orders, avoided a contest, and day after day Cromwell's troopers had to return empty handed, losing many of their men by the fire of Harry's infantry. Thus the army of Cromwell was obliged to advance slowly upon the line of coast, drawing their supplies wholly from the fleet which accompanied it.

One evening Colonel Macleod rode up to the cottage where Harry was quartered for the night.

"I am going to beat up Oliver's camp to-night," he said. "Do you cover the retreat with your men at the ford of the river. If I can get for five minutes in his camp I will read the Roundheads a lesson, and maybe spike some of his cannon. If I could catch Cromwell himself it would be as good as a great victory."

After nightfall the force approached the enemy's camp; at the ford the infantry halted, the cavalry crossing and continuing their way to the camp, about a mile distant. An hour passed without any sound being heard. At length a sound of distant shouts, mingled with the reports of firearms, fell upon the ear.

"Macleod is among them now," Donald Leslie exclaimed. "I would I wore with him."

"You will have your turn presently," Harry replied. "A thousand horse may do a good deal of damage in a sudden attack, but they must fall back as soon as the Roundheads rally."

For five or six minutes the distant tumult continued. Then it ceased almost as suddenly as it had begun. A minute or two later there was a deep, muffled sound.

"Here come the horse," Jacob said.

The infantry had already been placed along the bank of the river on each side of the ford, leaving the way clear in the center for the passage of the cavalry. It was not long before they arrived on the opposite bank, and dashed at full speed across the river. Colonel Macleod rode at their rear.

"The Ironsides are just behind," he said to Harry. "Let your men shoot sharp and straight as they try to cross. We will charge them as they reach the bank."

A minute later, and the close files of the Roundhead cavalry could be seen approaching, the moonlight glinting on steel cap, breastpiece, and sword.

"Steady, lads!" Harry shouted. "Do not fire a shot till they enter the river. Then keep up a steady fire on the head of the column."

The Roundheads halted when they reached the river, and formed rapidly into a column, twelve abreast, for the ford was no wider. As they entered the stream a heavy musketry fire opened suddenly upon them. Men and horses went down, floating away in the river. In spite of their losses the cavalry pressed on, and though numbers fell, gained the opposite bank. Then arose the Royalist cry "King and Covenant!" and the Scottish horse swept down. The head of the column was shattered by the charge, but the Ironsides still pressed on, and breaking the center of the Scottish horse, poured across the river.

Harry had already given his orders to Jacob, who commanded the left wing of the infantry, and the regiment, drawing up on both flanks of the column of Ironsides, poured so heavy a fire upon them, while the cavalry of Macleod again charged them in front, that the

171

column was broken, and still fighting sturdily, fell back again across the river. The moment they did so a heavy fire of musketry opened from the further bank.

"Their infantry are up, Colonel Furness," Macleod said. "Draw off your men in good order. I will cover the retreat. We have done enough for to-night."

Getting his regiment together, Harry ordered them to retire at the double, keeping their formation as they went. The Roundhead cavalry again crossed the river, and several times charged the Scotch horse. Twice they succeeded in breaking through, but Harry, facing his men round, received them pike in hand, the musketeers in rear keeping up so hot a fire over the shoulders of the pikemen that the Ironsides drew rein before reaching them, and presently fell back, leaving the party to retire without further pursuit.

"I as nearly as possible caught Cromwell," Colonel Macleod said, riding up to Harry. "We got confused among the tents and ropes, or should have had him. We entered his tent, but the bird had flown. We cut down some scores of his infantry, and spiked four guns, I have not lost twenty men, and his cavalry must have lost at least a hundred from your fire, besides the damage I did at their camp."

Obtaining a stock of supplies sufficient for some days from the ships at Dunbar, Cromwell advanced to Musselburgh, within striking distance of Edinburgh. Leslie had strongly posted his army in intrenched lines extending from Edinburgh to Leith, a distance of two miles. Colonel Macleod with his detachment rejoined the army on the same day that Cromwell reached Musselburgh. Upon the day after the arrival of the English there was a sharp cavalry fight, and Cromwell would fain have tempted the Scotch army to engage beyond their lines. But Leslie was not to be drawn. He knew that if he could maintain himself in his intrenchments the English must fall back, as they had the sea behind them and on their right, Edinburgh in front of them, and a devastated country on their left. At the urgent request of Cromwell the Parliament strained every nerve to send up provisions by ships, and so enabled him to remain before Edinburgh for a month.

A few days after his arrival Harry received orders to take a hundred and fifty men of his regiment, and to post himself at Kirkglen, which blocked a road by which it was thought Cromwell might send foraging parties westward. Harry asked that a detachment of cavalry might accompany him, but the request was refused. Kirkglen stood fifteen miles south of Edinburgh, and somewhat to its west. Harry left Jacob to command the main body of the regiment, and took with him the companies of Donald Leslie and Hugh Grahame, in the latter of which William Long was lieutenant. They sallied out from the western side of the camp at daybreak.

"I like not this expedition, Colonel Furness," Donald Leslie said. "The refusal to send cavalry with us is strange. Methinks I see the finger of that crafty fox Argyll in the pie. His faithfulness to the cause is more and more doubted, though none dare wag a tongue against him, and if it be true that he is in communication with Cromwell, we shall have the Roundheads, horse and foot, down upon us."

"There is a castle there, is there not," Harry asked, "which we might occupy?"

"Assuredly there is," Leslie replied. "It is the hold of Alan Campbell, a cousin of the man you pinked. It is that which adds to my suspicion. You will see, unless I am greatly mistaken, that he will not admit us."

Such, indeed, proved to be the case. Upon their arrival at Kirkglen, Leslie went in Harry's name to demand admittance to the castle for the royal troops, but Campbell replied that he had received no orders to that effect, and that it would greatly incommode him to quarter so large a number of men there. He said, however, that he would willingly entertain Colonel Furness and his officers. Leslie brought back the message, strongly urging Harry on no account to enter the castle and put himself in the hands of the Campbells. Harry said that even had he no cause to doubt the welcome he might receive at the castle, he should in no case separate himself from his men, when he might be at any moment attacked.

"It is a rough piece of country between this and Cromwell's post," Leslie said, "and he would have difficulty in finding his way hither. There is more than one broad morass to be crossed, and without a guide he would scarce attempt it. It is for this reason that he is so unlikely to send out foraging parties in this direction. It was this reflection which caused me to wonder why we should be ordered hither."

"Mike," Harry said, "you have heard what Captain Leslie says. Do you keep watch to-night near the castle gate, and let me know whether any leave it; and in which direction they go. I will place a man behind to watch the postern. If treachery is meditated, Campbell will send news of our coming to Cromwell."

173

# CHAPTER XXI

## THE PATH ACROSS THE MORASS

Mike, when night fell, moved away toward the castle, which lay about a quarter of a mile from the village. Approaching to within fifty yards of the gate, he sat down to watch. About eleven o'clock he heard the creak of the gate, and presently was startled by seeing two horsemen ride past him. "They must have muffled their horses' feet," he said to himself. "They are up to no good. I wish there had only been one of them." Mike slipped off his shoes and started in pursuit, keeping just far enough behind the horsemen to enable him to observe the outline of their figures. For half a mile they proceeded quietly. Then they stopped, dismounted, removed the cloths from their horses' feet, and remounting rode forward at a gallop. Mike's old exercise as a runner now rendered him good service. He could already tell, by the direction which the horsemen were taking, that they were bearing to the east of Edinburgh, but he resolved to follow as far as possible in order to see exactly whither they went. The road, or rather track, lay across a moorland country. The ground was often deep and quaggy, and the horsemen several times checked their speed, and went at a slow walk, one advancing on foot along the track to guide the way. These halts allowed breathing time for Mike, who found it hard work to keep near them when going at full speed. At last, after riding for an hour, the horsemen halted at a solitary house on the moorland, Here several horses, held by troopers, were standing. Mike crept round to the back of the house, and looked in at the window. He saw two English officers sitting by a fire, while a light burned on a table. Mike at once recognized in one of them the dreaded General Cromwell, whom he had seen at Drogheda.

"What a fool I was," he muttered to himself, "to have come without my pistol. I would have shot him as he sits, and so wiped out Drogheda."

At the moment the door opened, and a trooper in Scotch uniform entered. "I have brought this letter," he said, "from Alan Campbell."

The general took the letter and opened it. "Campbell promises," he said to the other officer, "to open fire upon the detachment in the village with the guns of the castle as soon as we attack. One of the men who has brought this will remain here and guide our troops across the morass. He suggests that two hundred foot and as many horse should be here at eight to-morrow evening. All he stipulates for is that Colonel Furness, the Royalist who commands the enemy's detachment, shall be given over to him, he having, it seems, some enmity with Argyll. Furness? ah, that is the officer whom I sent to the Bermudas from Drogheda. We had advices of his having got away and captured a ship with other prisoners on board. A bold fellow, and a good officer, but all the more dangerous. Let Campbell do with him as he likes."

The other officer drew out an inkhorn and wrote, at Cromwell's dictation, his adherence to the terms offered by Alan Campbell. Cromwell signed the paper, and handed it to the messenger. Then the English general and his escort mounted and rode off. Campbell's retainers sat for half an hour drinking together. Then they came to the door. One mounted, and saying to the other, "I would rather have twenty-four hours' sleep such as you have before you, than have to ride back to Kirkglen to-night; the mist is setting in thickly," rode off into the darkness.

Mike kept close to him, until at last the man dismounted to follow the track where the morass was most dangerous. In an instant Mike sprang upon him and buried his dagger in his body. Without a cry the trooper fell. Mike felt in his doublet for Cromwell's letter. Placing this in his breast, he went a few paces from the path where he found that he sunk to his knees, the water being some inches deep over the bog. Then he returned, lifted the body of the trooper, carried it as far into the bog as he dared venture, and then dropped it. He placed his foot on the iron breastpiece, and pressed until the body sank in the soft ooze, and the water completely covered it. Then he went back to the horse, and taking the reins, followed the track until completely clear of the moorland country, where, mounting, he rode back to Kirkglen, and presented himself to Harry. The latter had, hours before, gone to bed, having posted strong guards around the village. He struck a light and listened to Mike's relation of what he had done, and ended by the production of the document with Cromwell's signature.

"Another debt to the Earl of Argyll," Harry said grimly. "However, although this proves the treachery of his kinsman, it does not convict Argyll himself, although the evidence is strong enough to hang any other man. Now, Leslie, what do you advise? Shall we send and seize the man left at the hut?"

"It is a doubtful question," Leslie answered, after a pause. "When Campbell finds that his messenger does not return before morning, he will like enough send others off to learn the reason why. If they find him gone, Campbell may suspect that his plan has failed and may send warning to Cromwell."

"At any rate," Harry continued, "we need not decide before morning. But at daybreak, Leslie, plant a party of men on the road and stop any horseman riding out. Let the sergeant in charge say only that he has my orders that none are to pass eastward. It would be a natural precaution to take, and when the news comes back to the castle, Campbell will not necessarily know that his scheme has been detected."

The next morning Leslie volunteered to go out with a couple of men and capture the guide, and arraying himself in his clothes, to take his place, and lead the Roundhead troops astray.

"Were the country other than it is," Harry said, "I would accept your offer, my brave Leslie, even though it might entail your death, for it would be difficult for you to slip away. But over such ground there is no need of this. Let the guide lead the Roundhead troops along the path. We will reconnoiter the morass to-day, and when night falls will so post our men as to open a fire on either flank of him as he comes across the track. Not more than four footmen can march abreast, according to what Mike says, and we shall surprise him, instead of he surprising us."

An hour later two horsemen rode out from the castle, but upon reaching the guard Leslie had placed were turned back. They returned to the castle, and a short time afterward a trooper rode down into the village with a note from Alan Campbell, demanding haughtily by what warrant Colonel Furness ventured to interfere with the free passage of his retainers. Harry replied that he had, as a military precaution, stationed guards on the various roads leading toward the enemy's quarter, and that they were ordered to turn back all, whomsoever they might be, who might seek to pass.

Alan Campbell returned a furious answer, that he should sally out with his garrison, and ride where he listed. Harry replied by marching fifty men up to the road leading to the castle, and by sending a message to Alan Campbell that, although he should regret to be obliged to treat him as an enemy, yet that assuredly if he strove by force to break the military rules he had laid down, he should be compelled to fire upon him. Leaving the detachment under charge of Lieutenant Long, and the main body in the village under that of Hugh Grahame, Harry, accompanied by Donald Leslie and Mike, rode off to reconnoiter the morass. They found that it was particularly bad at two points, while between these the ground was firm for a distance of twenty yards on each side of the track. Beyond the swamp was very deep for thirty or forty yards on both sides, and then it was again somewhat firmer.

Harry decided to post twenty-five men behind these quagmires. Their orders would be to remain perfectly quiet until the column, passing the first morass, should have entered the second; then, when Harry, with the main body, opened fire upon them there, they were to commence upon the flanks of the column.

Returning to the camp, Harry sent forty men with shovels, obtained in the village, to dig a trench, twelve feet wide, and as deep as they could get for the water, across the track, at the near side of the morass.

At nightfall, leaving twenty-five men under William Long in front of the castle, with orders to let none issue forth, and to shoot down any who might make the attempt, Harry marched out with the rest of his command. Crossing the ditch which had been dug, he led fifty forward, and posted them, as he had planned with Leslie; with twenty-five, he took up his own station behind the breastwork formed by the earth thrown out from the trench. The remaining fifty he bade advance as far as they safely could into the swamp on either side. Two hours later a dull sound was heard, the occasional clink of arms, and the muffled tread of many feet on the soft ground. The Roundhead infantry, two hundred strong, led the way, followed by their horse, the guide walking with the officer at the head of the column. When it approached within twenty yards of the ditch Harry gave the word, and a flash of fire streamed from the top of the earthwork. At the same moment those on either side opened fire into the flanks of the column, while the fifty men beyond poured their fire into the cavalry in the rear of the column.

For a moment all was confusion. The Roundheads had anticipated no attack, and were taken wholly by surprise. The guide had fallen at the first discharge and all were ignorant of the ground on which they found themselves. They were, however, trained to conflict. Those on the flank of the column endeavored to penetrate the morass, but they immediately sank to the middle, and had much ado to regain the solid track. The head of the column, pouring a volley into their invisible foes, leveled their pikes, and rushed to the assault. A few steps, and they fell into a deep hole, breast high with water, and on whose slippery bottom their feet could scarce find standing. In vain they struggled forward. From front and flank the fire of their enemy smote them. Those who reached the opposite side of the trench were run through with pikes as they strove to climb from it.

For ten minutes the desperate struggle continued, and then, finding the impossibility of storming such a position in the face of foes of whose strength they were ignorant, the Roundhead infantry turned, and in good order marched back, leaving half their number dead behind them. The cavalry in the rear had fared but little better. Finding the ground on either side was firm when the fire opened on their flanks, they faced both ways, and charged. But ere the horses had gone twenty strides they were struggling to their girths in the morass. Their foes kept up a steady fire, at forty yards' distance, into the struggling mass, and before they could extricate themselves and regain the pathway, many leaving their horses behind, a third of their number had fallen. Joined by the beaten infantry, they retired across the track, and made their way back toward their camp.

Leaving a strong guard at the morass to resist further attempts, Harry returned with his force to the village having inflicted a loss of a hundred and fifty upon enemy, while he himself had lost but eight men. He intrenched the position strongly, and remained there unmolested, until a week later he received orders to march back to Edinburgh. The following day he was summoned before King Charles. He found there General Leslie, the Earl of Argyll, Alan Campbell, and several of the leaders of the Covenant.

"What is this I hear of you, Colonel Furness?" the king said. "General Leslie has reported to me that you have inflicted a very heavy defeat upon a rebel force which marched to surprise you. This is good service, and for it I render you my hearty thanks. But, sir, the Earl of Argyll complains to me that you have beleaguered his kinsman, Alan Campbell, in his hold at Kirkglen, and treated him as a prisoner, suffering none to go out or in during your stay there."

"This, sire, is the warranty for my conduct," Harry said, producing the document signed by Cromwell. "This was taken by one of my men from a trooper who had borne a dispatch from Alan Campbell to the enemy. My man watched the interview between him and Cromwell himself, heard the terms of the dispatch, and saw Cromwell write and give this letter to the trooper, whom he afterward slew, and brought me the letter. The other trooper, who acted as guide to the enemy, fell in the attack."

The king took the letter and read it. "My lord," he said, "this is a matter which gravely touches your honor. This is a letter of General Cromwell's in answer to a traitorous communication of your kinsman here. He has offered to betray Colonel Furness and the troops under him to Cromwell, and has sent a guide for the English troops. He stipulates only that Colonel Furness shall be handed over to him to do as he likes with. As it was manifest to me here some time since that you and Colonel Furness are not friends, this touches you nearly."

"I know nothing of it," the earl said. "My kinsman will tell you."

"I do not need his assurances," King Charles said coldly. "He, at least, is proved to be a traitor, and methinks, my lord earl, that the preachers who are so fond of holding forth to me upon the wickedness of my ways might with advantage bestow some of their spare time in conversing with you upon the beauty and godliness of straightforwardness. General Leslie, you will arrest at once, on his leaving our presence, Colonel Alan Campbell, and will cause a court of inquiry to sift this matter to the bottom. And hark you, my lord of Argyll, see you that no more of your kinsmen practice upon the life of my faithful Colonel Furness. This is the third time that he has been in jeopardy at your hands. I am easy, my lord earl, too easy, mayhap, but let no man presume too far upon it. My power is but limited here, but remember the old saying, 'Wise men do not pull the tails of lions' whelps.' The day may come when Charles II. will be a king in power as well as in name. Beware that you presume not too far upon his endurance now." So saying, the king turned from Argyll, and bidding Harry follow him, and tell him the story of the defeat of the English troops, left the earl standing alone, the picture of rage and mortification.

"You had best beware, Master Furness," the king said. "He needs a long spoon they say, who sups with the deil. The Earl of Argyll is the real king of Scotland at present, and it is ill quarreling with him. You have got the best of it in the first three rubbers, but be sure that Argyll will play on till the cards favor him. And if you are once in his power, I would not give a baubee for your life. The proud earl treats me as a master would teach a froward pupil, but I tell you, Master Furness, and I know you are discreet and can be trusted, that as surely as the earl brought Montrose to the block, so surely shall Argyll's head roll on the scaffold, if Charles II. is ever King of England. But I fear for you, Master Furness. I can help you here not at all, and the lecture which, on your behalf, I administered to the earl—and in faith I wonder now at my own courage—will not increase his love for you. You will never be safe as long as you remain in Scotland. What do you say? Will you south and join one or other of the Royalist bodies who are in arms there?"

"Not so, your majesty. With your permission, I will play the game out to the end, although I know that my adversary holds the strongest cards. But even did I wish to leave, it would be as hazardous to do so as to stay here. So long as I am with my regiment I am in safety. I could not gain England by sea, for the Parliament ships bar the way, and did I leave my regiment and go south with only a small party, my chance of crossing the border alive would be but small. No, your majesty, I have the honor to command a king's regiment, and whether against Cromwell in the field, or against Argyll's plots and daggers, I shall do my duty to the end."

When, upon his return to the camp, Harry told his friends the purport of the interview between himself and Argyll, of Alan

Campbell being put under arrest and the earl openly reproved by the king, Donald Leslie raised his hands in despair.

"If you get through this, Furness," he said, "I shall for the rest of my life be convinced that you have a charmed existence, and that your good genius is more powerful than the evil one of Argyll. The gossips say that he is in alliance with the evil one himself, and I can well believe them. But I beg you, in all seriousness, to confine yourself to the camp. So long as you are here you are safe. But once beyond its limits your life will not be worth a straw."

Jacob added his entreaties to those of Leslie, and Harry promised that until the decisive battle was over he would keep among his men, unless compelled by duty to appear at court.

Four days afterward a soldier entered Harry's tent, and handed him a missive. It was as follows: "Upon receipt of this, Colonel Furness will proceed to Leith and will board the vessel, the Royalist, which has just arrived from Holland. There he will inspect the newly arrived recruits, who will be attached to his regiment. He will examine the store of arms brought by her, and will report on their state and condition.—David Leslie, commanding his majesty's armies."

The duty was one of mere routine. Harry showed the note to Jacob, and said, "You may as well come with me, Jacob. Your drilling is over for the day, and you can aid me looking through the stores. Mike," he said, "we shall be back to supper. We are only going down to the port." The two officers buckled on their swords, and at once started on foot for the port, which was but half a mile distant. Mike looked anxiously after his master. Since the day when danger had first threatened him he had scarce let him out of his sight, following close to his heels like a faithful dog. His present business seemed assuredly to forbode no danger. Nevertheless, the lad felt restless and anxious when he saw his master depart. A few minutes later he went to William Long's tent. "Master Long," he said, "will you see that my master's servant gets supper in readiness at the usual hour. He has gone down to the port to inspect some recruits just arrived from Holland, by order of General Leslie, and said he would return by supper. I know that it is foolish, but since the affair with Alan Campbell I am never easy when he is not near. In this case, I do not see that there can possibly be any lurking danger. Argyll could not know of his proceeding to the port, nor would he venture to attack him there where the streets swarm with our soldiers. Nevertheless, I would fain go down and assure myself that all is well."

William Long at once promised to look after the supper, and Mike hurried away after Harry and his companion. These had, however, too far a start to be overtaken, and when he reached the wharf he saw a boat rowed by two men, and having two sitters in the stern. It was already some distance from shore, and appeared to be proceeding toward a vessel which lay at anchor several hundred yards further out from the shore than the others.

"Can you tell me," he asked a sailor, "whether that ship lying there is the Royalist?"

"That is the name she goes by to-day," the sailor said, "for as I rowed past her this morning on my way from fishing, I saw the name newly painted on her stern. They have put it on her boat too, which you now see rowing toward her, and which has been lying by the pier all day, in readiness to take out any one who might wish to go off to her."

"But have they changed her name, then?" Mike asked. "What have they been doing that for?"

"She has been called the Covenant for the last two years," the sailor said. "But I suppose Johnny Campbell, her master, thought the other more suited to the times."

The name of the captain at once aroused Mike's uneasiness to the fullest.

"Tell me," he said, "good fellow, did that ship arrive this morning from Holland?"

"From Holland!" repeated the sailor. "No. She came down the coast from the north three days ago, with beasts for the army."

Mike stood for a moment thunderstruck. Then, without a word to the sailor, he turned and ran back at full speed through the town up to the camp. At a headlong pace he made his way through the camp until he stopped at the tent of General Leslie. He was about to rush in without ceremony when the sentinel stopped his way.

"Please let me pass," he panted. "I would see the general on a matter of the utmost importance."

The sentries laughed.

"You don't suppose," one of them said, "that the general is to be disturbed by every barefooted boy who wants to speak to him. If you have aught to say, you must speak first to the lieutenant of the guard."

"Every moment is of importance," Mike urged. "It is a matter of life and death. I tell you I must see the general." Then at the top of his voice he began to shout, "Sir David Leslie! Sir David Leslie!"

"Silence there, young varmint, or I will wring thy neck for thee!" exclaimed the soldier, greatly scandalized, seizing Mike and shaking him violently. But the boy continued to shout out at the top of his voice, "Sir David Leslie! Sir David Leslie!"

# CHAPTER XXII

## KIDNAPED

Unable to silence Mike's shouts, the scandalized guards began dragging him roughly from the spot, cuffing him as they went. But the door of the tent opened, and General Leslie appeared.

"What means all this unseemly uproar?" he asked.

"This malapert boy, general, wished to force his way into your tent, and when we stopped him, and told him that he must apply to the lieutenant of the guard if he had aught of importance which he wished to communicate to you, he began to shout like one possessed."

"Loose him," the general said. "Now, varlet, what mean you by this uproar?"

"Forgive me, sir," Mike pleaded, "but I come on an errand which concerns the life of my master, Colonel Furness."

"Come within," the general said briefly, for by this time a crowd had gathered round the tent. "Now," he went on, "what is it you would tell me?"

"I would ask you, sir, whether an hour since you sent an order to my master that he should forthwith go on board the ship Royalist to inspect recruits and stores of arms just arrived from Holland?"

The general looked at him in astonishment.

"I sent no such order," he said. "No ship has arrived from Holland of that or any other name. What story is this that you have got hold of?"

"My master received such an order, sir, for I heard him read it aloud, and he started at once with his major to carry out the order. Knowing, sir, how great, as you are doubtless aware, is the enmity which the Earl of Argyll bears to my master, I followed him to the port, and there learned that the ship called the Royalist had not come from Holland, but is a coaster from the north. I found, moreover, that she was but yesterday named the Royalist, and that she was before known as the Covenant, and that she is commanded by a Campbell. Then it seemed to me that some plot had been laid to kidnap my master, and I ran straight to you to ask you whether you had really ordered him to go on board this ship."

"This must be seen to at once," the general said; for having been present at the scene when Harry produced Cromwell's letter, he knew how deadly was the hatred of the earl for the young colonel.

"Without there!" he cried. A soldier entered. "Send the lieutenant of the guard here at once." The soldier disappeared, and the general sat down at his table and hastily wrote an order. "Lieutenant," he said, when the officer entered, "give this letter to Captain Farquharson, and tell him to take his twenty men, and to go on the instant down to the port. There he is to take boat and row out to the ship called the Royalist. He is to arrest the captain and crew, and if he see not there Colonel Furness, let him search the ship from top to bottom. If he find no signs of him, let him bring the captain and six of his men ashore at once."

As soon as he heard the order given Mike, saluting the general, hurried from the tent, and ran at full speed to the camp of Harry's regiment. There he related to Donald Leslie and William Long the suspicious circumstances which had occurred, and the steps which the general had ordered to be taken.

"This is bad news, indeed," Captain Leslie exclaimed; "and I fear that the colonel has fallen into the hands of Argyll's minions. If it be so Farquharson is scarce likely to find the Royalist at anchor when he arrives at the port. Come, Long, let us be stirring. I will hand over the command of the regiment to Grahame till we return. While I am speaking to him pick me out ten trusty men."

He hurried off, and in five minutes was hastening toward the port, with William Long, Mike, and ten men. Such was the speed they made that they reached the quay just at the same time with Captain Farquharson and his men.

Mike gave a cry of despair. The Royalist had disappeared. He ran up to a sailor who was still sitting on an upturned basket, smoking as he had left him before.

"Where is the Royalist?" he exclaimed.

"Halloo! young fellow, are you back again? I thought you had gone off with a bee in your bonnet, so suddenly and quickly did you run. The Royalist? ay, she hoisted her sails two minutes after her boat reached her. I was watching her closely, for I wondered whether she had aught to do with your sudden flight. Methinks that something strange has happened on board, for I saw what seemed to be a scuffle, and certainly the sun shone on the gleam of swords. Then, too, instead of heaving her anchor, she slipped the cable, and a Scotch captain must be in a hurry indeed when he does that."

"Where is she now?" Mike asked.

"Over there, full four miles away, making across the Forth for the northern point of land."

"Is she a fast ship?" Captain Leslie, who had come up, inquired.

"She has the name of being the fastest sailer in these parts."

"There is nothing here would catch her?" Donald Leslie asked. "Would a rowboat have a chance of overtaking her?"

"Not this evening," the sailor said, looking at the sky. "The wind is rising now, and it will blow a gale before morning."

"Tell me, my man," Leslie asked, "and here is a gold piece for your pains, where you think she is likely to put in?"

"That will all depend," the sailor replied, "upon what errand she is bound. I must know that before I can answer you."

Leslie looked at William Long. The latter said:

"It were best to tell this honest fellow the facts of the case. Look you, my 'man, the two king's officers who have gone on board are ill friends with the Campbells, and we doubt not that these have kidnaped and carried them off."

"The Campbells are an ill crew to deal with," the sailor said, "and I do not love them myself. If it be as you say, they might be landed either at Anstruther, near which is a hold belonging to Andrew Campbell of Glencoulie, or at St. Andrews, or at Leuchars, a little bay north of that town, whence they might take them to Kilbeg Castle, also held by a Campbell. It is a lonely place ten miles inland, and their friends would be little likely to look for them there. Besides, the Royalist might land them and sail away without any being the wiser, while at the other ports her coming would be surely noticed."

"Think you that we can obtain horses on the other side?"

"You might obtain four or five," the sailor said, "of Tony Galbraith, who keeps the inn there, and who lets horses on hire to those traveling north."

"If a storm comes on," Leslie asked, "which way is it likely to blow, and will the Royalist be like to make the bay you name?

"Ah! that is more than I can tell," the sailor replied. "Methinks 'twill blow from the west. In that case, she might be able to make her way along the shore; she might run into port for shelter; she might be blown out to sea."

"At any rate," Leslie said, "our first step is to cross. Get us a stout sailing boat. Be not sparing of promises."

The man at once went off to a group of sailors, but these at first shook their heads, and looked toward the sky. Its aspect was threatening. The wind was getting up fast, and masses of scud flew rapidly across it. Leslie went up to the group.

"Come, lads," he said, "five pounds if you put us across."

The offer was too tempting to be rejected, and the men hurried down and began to prepare a large sailing boat. Leslie and

Lieutenant Long had a hasty consultation, and agreed that, seeing the difficulty there would be in obtaining horses, it was useless to take more than ten men in all. Accordingly, as soon as the boat was in readiness, the two officers, Mike, and seven soldiers took their places in her. The sails were closely reefed, and she at once put out into the Firth. Every minute the wind rose, until, by the time they were half across, it was blowing a gale. The boat was a stout one, but the waves broke freely over her, and four of the soldiers were kept at work baling to throw out the water she took over her bows. Once or twice they thought that she would capsize, so furious were the gusts, but the boatmen were quick and skillful. The sheets were let go and the sails lowered until the force of the squall abated, and at last, after a passage which seemed rapid even to those on board, anxious as they were, she entered the little port.

Hurrying to the inn, they found that six horses were obtainable. These they hired at once. The host said that he could send to some farms, not far distant, and hire four more, but that an hour or so would elapse ere they came. Leslie and William Long had already decided that the prisoners would most probably be taken to Kilbeg Castle, as being more secluded than the others. They now agreed that they themselves with Mike and three soldiers should start at once, to intercept them if possible between the sea and the castle. When the other horses arrived two of the soldiers were to ride with all speed to Anstruther, and two to St. Andrews, and were there to keep sharp watch to see if the Royalist arrived there, and landed aught in the way either of men or goods.

The point to which they were bound lay fully forty miles away. They determined to ride as far as the horses would carry them, and then, if able to obtain no more, to walk forward. Night was already setting in, and a driving rain flew before the gale.

"We shall never be able to keep the road," Leslie said, "Landlord, have you one here who could serve as guide? He must be quick-footed and sure. Our business is urgent, and we are ready to pay well."

A guide was speedily found, a lad on a shaggy pony, who had the day before come down from the north with cattle. While the horses were being prepared the party had taken a hasty supper, and Leslie had seen that each of the soldiers had a tankard of hot spiced wine. So quickly had the arrangements been made that in half an hour after their arrival at the port the party started from the inn. The ride was indeed a rough one. The country was heavy and wild. The rain drenched them to the skin in spite of their thick cloaks, and the wind blew at times with such violence that the horses were fain

185

to stop and stand huddled together facing it to keep their feet. Hour after hour they rode, never getting beyond a walk, so rough was the road; often obliged to pause altogether from the force of the gale. Twice they stopped at inns at quiet villages, knocked up the sleeping hosts, and obtained hot wine for themselves and hot gruel for their horses. Their pace grew slower as the animals became thoroughly knocked up, and at last could not be urged beyond a walk.

At the next village they stopped, and as they found that there was no possibility of obtaining fresh horses, they determined to push forward on foot. It was now four o'clock in the morning, and they had ridden over forty miles. Another guide was obtained, and they set forward. Although they had hurried to the utmost, it was ten o'clock in the morning before they came down upon a valley with a narrow stream which their guide told them fell into the sea, near Leuchars. They were, he said, now within two miles of the castle, the track from which to the sea ran down the valley. The wind was still blowing a gale, but the clouds had broken, and at times the sun streamed out brightly.

"Thank Heaven we are here at last," Donald Leslie said, "for a harder night I have never spent. I think we must be in time."

"I think so," William Long said. "Supposing the Royalist made the bay safely, she would have been there by midnight, but the sea would have been so high that I doubt if they would have launched a boat till morning. It was light by five, but they might wait for the gale to abate a little, and after landing they have eight miles to come. Of course, they might have passed here an hour ago, but a incline to think that they would not land till later, as with this wind blowing off shore, it would be no easy matter to row a boat in its teeth."

The guide saying that there was a cottage a mile further up the valley, he was sent there with instructions to ask whether any one had been seen to pass that morning. After being half an hour absent he returned, saying that there was only an old woman at the hut, and that she had told him she was sure no one had passed there since daybreak. They now followed the stream down the valley until they came to a small wood. Here they lay down to rest, one being placed upon the lookout. Two hours later the sentry awoke them with the news that a party of men were coming up the valley. All were at once upon the alert.

"Thank Heaven," Leslie said, "we have struck the right place. There seem to be ten or twelve of them, of whom two, no doubt, are the prisoners. We shall have no difficulty in overcoming them by a sudden surprise. Capture or kill every man if possible, or we shall have hot work in getting back to Edinburgh."

When the party came nearer it could be seen that it consisted of eight armed men, in the center of whom the two Royalist officers were walking. Their arms were bound to their sides. Leslie arranged that he with Mike and one of the soldiers would at once spring to their aid, as likely enough, directly the attack began, the captors might endeavor to slay their prisoners, to prevent them from being rescued. Mike was instructed to strike no blow, but to devote himself at once to cutting their cords, and placing weapons in their hands.

The surprise was complete. The sailors forming the majority of the party, with two trusty retainers of the earl, who had special charge of the affair, were proceeding carelessly along, having no thought of interruption. So far their plans had succeeded perfectly. The moment the two officers had reached the quay they were addressed by the men sent on shore with the Royalist's boat. Unsuspicious of danger they took their place in it, and therefore missed the opportunity, which they would have had if they had entered any of the other boats, of learning the true character of the Royalist. They had been attacked the instant they gained the deck of the vessel. Harry, who was first, had been knocked down before he had time to put his hand to his sword. Jacob had fought valiantly for a short time, but he too had been knocked senseless by a blow with a capstan bar. They had then been roughly tumbled below, where no further attention had been paid to them. The Royalist had been blown many miles out to sea, and did not make her anchorage until ten o'clock in the morning. Then the hatches were removed, and the prisoners brought on deck.

The inlet was a small one, and contained, only a little fishing village; the prisoners saw the Royalist sail off again, directly they had been placed in the boat. They had from the first moment when they regained consciousness entertained no doubts whatever into whose hands they had fallen, and they felt their position to be desperate. The plan, indeed, had been skillfully laid, and had it not been for Harry reading the order aloud in Mike's presence, there would have been no clew to their disappearance. During the night the young men were too overpowered with the violence of the storm, and the closeness of the atmosphere in the hold, in which they had been thrown, to converse. But as the motion moderated in the morning they had talked over their chances, and pronounced them to be small indeed. Harry, indeed, remembered that Mike had been present when he asked Jacob to accompany him on board ship, but he thought that no uneasiness would be felt until late that night, as it might well be thought that their duties had detained them, and that they had supped on board. The storm might further account for their non-appearance till morning. Then they imagined that inquiry would be made, and that it would be found that the Royalist had sailed. Their captors would then have a start of twenty-four hours, and in such troubled times it was scarce likely that anything would be done. Nor indeed did they see how they could be followed, as the destination of the ship would be entirely unknown. The very fact that they had not been thrown overboard when fairly out at sea was in itself a proof that their captors entertained no fear of pursuit; had they done so, they would have dispatched them at once. The captives felt sure that it was intended to land them, in order that Argyll himself might have the pleasure of taunting them before putting them to death. Against Jacob, indeed, he could have no personal feeling, and it was by accident only that he was a sharer in Harry's fate. But as a witness of what had taken place, his life would assuredly be taken, as well as that of his companion. As they walked along they gathered from the talk of their guards the distance which they had to go, and the place of their destination. They had never heard of Kilbeg Castle, but as they had no enemies save Argyll, they knew that it must belong to one of his clan. They spoke but little on the way. Harry was wondering how the news of his disappearance would be received in the camp, and thinking of the dismay which it would occasion in the minds of Mike and William Long, when suddenly he heard a shout, and on the instant a fierce fight was raging around him.

Although taken completely by surprise, the sailors fought steadily. But two were cut down before they could draw a sword, and the others, outmatched, were driven backward. The leader of the party shouted again and again, "Kill the prisoners," but he and each of his men were too hotly engaged with the adversaries who pressed them, to do more than defend their own lives. In a minute the fray was rendered still more unequal by Harry and Jacob joining in it, and in less than three minutes from its commencement seven of the guards lay dead or dying upon the ground. The other, an active young fellow, had taken to flight early in the fight, and was already beyond reach.

The contest over, there was a delighted greeting between the rescued prisoners and their friends.

"Come," Leslie said, "we have not a moment to lose. That

fellow who has escaped will take the news to Kilbeg, and we shall be having its garrison at our heels. He has but three miles to run, and they will beat to horse in a few minutes after he gets there. We must strike across the hills, and had best make a great circuit by Stirling. If we avoid the roads and towns they may not pick up our track."

Their guide fortunately knew the country well, and leaving the path by which they had traveled, the party started on their return. All day they tramped across the moorlands, avoiding all villages and scattered farmhouses. They had, they knew, three-quarters of an hour's start, and as their pursuers would be alike ignorant whence they came or whither they were going, the chances of their hitting the right route were small.

Making a circuit round Kinross and Alloa, where the Campbells might have ridden in pursuit, and sleeping in a wood, they arrived next day at Stirling. Here was great excitement, for Cromwell's army, marching south of Edinburgh, had approached the town. They remained, however, a few hours only, collecting what previsions they could, and then falling back again to their former camp at Musselburgh. The following day Harry and his party marched to Edinburgh. That night Harry reported to Sir David Leslie what had befallen him and the next morning he accompanied the general to Holyrood, and laid a complaint before the king.

His majesty was most indignant at the attempt which had been made upon his follower, but he said to General Leslie, "I doubt not, Sir David, that your thoughts and mine go toward the same person. But we have no evidence that he had an absolute hand in it, although the fact that this ship was commanded by a Campbell, and that the hold of Kilbeg belongs to one of his kinsmen, point to his complicity in the affair. Still, that is no proof. Already the earl is no friend of mine. When the day comes I will have a bitter reckoning with him, but in the present state of my fortunes, methinks that 'twere best in this, as in other matters, to hold my tongue for the time. I cannot afford to make him an open enemy now."

General Leslie agreed with the king. Cromwell's army was in a sore strait, and would, they hoped, be shortly driven either to surrender or to fight under disadvantageous circumstances. But the open defection of Argyll at the present moment, followed as it would be by that of the whole fanatical party, would entirely alter the position of affairs, and Harry begged his majesty to take no more notice of the matter, and so returned to the camp.

# CHAPTER XXIII

# THE BATTLE OF WORCESTER

The next morning the Scotch army moved after that of Cromwell, which had fallen back to Dunbar, and took post on the Doon hill facing him there. Cromwell's army occupied a peninsula, having on their face a brook running along a deep, narrow little valley. The Scotch position on the hill was an exceedingly strong one, and had they remained there Cromwell's army must have been driven to surrender. Cromwell himself wrote on that night, "The enemy hath blocked up our way at the pass at Copperspath, through which we cannot pass without almost a miracle. He lieth so upon the hills that we knoweth not how to come that way without much difficulty, and our lying here daily consumeth our men, who fall sick beyond imagination."

The Scotch had, in fact, the game in their hands, had they but waited on the ground they had taken up. The English had, however, an ally in their camp. The Earl of Argyll strongly urged that an attack should be made upon the English, and he was supported by the preachers and fanatics, who exclaimed that the Lord had delivered their enemies into their hands. General Leslie, however, stood firm. The preachers scattered in the camp and exhorted the soldiers to go down and smite the enemy. So great an enthusiasm did they excite by their promises of victory that in the afternoon the soldiers, without orders from their general, moved down the hill toward the enemy. The more regular body of the troops stood firm, but Leslie, seeing that the preachers had got the mastery, and that his orders were no longer obeyed, ordered these also to move forward, in hopes that the enthusiasm which had been excited would yet suffice to win the victory.

Cromwell saw the fatal mistake which had been committed, and in the night moved round his troops to his left, and these at daybreak fell upon the Scottish right. The night had been wet, and the Scottish army were unprovided with tents. Many of their matchlocks had been rendered useless. At daybreak on the morning of the 3d of September the English, led by General Lambert, fell upon them. The Scotch for a time stood their ground firmly; but the irregular troops, who had by their folly led the army into this plight, gave way before the English pikemen. The preachers, who were in vast numbers, set the example of flight. Many of the regiments of infantry fought most fiercely, but the battle was already lost. The

Scotch cavalry were broken by the charge of the Ironsides, and in less than an hour from the commencement of the fighting the rout was complete. Three thousand Scotch were killed, and ten thousand taken prisoners.

Harry's regiment was but slightly engaged. It had been one of the last to march down the hill on the evening before, and Harry and Jacob foresaw the disaster which would happen. "If I were the king," Harry said, "I would order every one of these preachers out of camp, and would hang those who disobeyed. Then I would march the army on to the hill again. If they wait there the English must attack us with grievous disadvantage, or such as cannot get on board their ships must surrender. Charles would really be king then, and could disregard the wrath of the men of the conventicles. Cromwell will attack us to-morrow, and will defeat us; his trained troops are more than a match for these Scotchmen, who think more of their preachers than of their officers, and whose discipline is of the slackest."

"I agree with you entirely," Jacob said. "But in the present mood of the army, I believe that half of them would march away if the general dismissed the preachers."

The next day, when the fight began, Harry moved forward his regiment to the support of the Scottish right, but before he came fairly into the fray this had already given away, and Harry, seeing that the day was lost, halted his men, and fell back in good order. Again and again the Ironsides charged them. The leveled pikes and heavy musketry fire each time beat them off, and they marched from the field almost the only body which kept its formation. Five thousand of the country people among the prisoners Cromwell allowed to depart to their homes. The remainder he sent to Newcastle, where great numbers of them were starved to death by the cruelty of the governor, Sir Arthur Hazelrig. The remainder were sent as slaves to New England.

Leslie, with the wreck of his army, fell back to Stirling, while Charles, with the Scotch authorities, went to Perth. Here the young king, exasperated beyond endurance at the tyranny of Argyll and the fanatics, escaped from them, and with two or three friends rode fifty miles north. He was overtaken and brought back to Perth, but the anger of the army was so hot at his treatment that the fanatics were henceforth obliged to put a curb upon themselves, and a strong king's party, as opposed to that of the Covenant, henceforth guided his counsels.

The winter passed quietly. The English troops were unable to stand the inclemency of the climate, and contented themselves with capturing Edinburgh Castle, and other strongholds south of the

Forth. Cromwell was compelled by ill health to return for some months to England. Leslie's army was strongly intrenched round Stirling. In June Cromwell again took the field, and moved against Perth, which he captured on the 31st of July. Charles, who had joined his army at Stirling, broke up his camp and marched toward England, the road being open to him owing to Cromwell and his army being further north at Perth.

During the time which had elapsed since the battle of Dunbar no events had happened in Harry's life. Remaining quietly in camp, where the troops, who had been disgusted by the conduct of the fanatics at Dunbar, were now ill disposed toward Argyll and his party, he had little fear of the machinations of the earl, who was with the king at Perth.

Argyll refused to join in the southern march, and the army with which Leslie entered England numbered only eleven thousand men. As soon as he crossed the border, Charles was proclaimed king, and proclamations were issued calling on all loyal subjects to join him.

The people were, however, weary of civil war. The Royalists had already suffered so heavily that they held back now, and the hatred excited, alike by the devastations of the Scotch army on its former visit to England, and by the treachery with which they had then sold the king, deterred men from joining them. A few hundred, indeed, came to his standard; but upon the other hand, Lambert and Harrison, with a strong force, were marching against him, and Cromwell, having left six thousand men in Scotland, under Monk, was pressing hotly behind with the victors of Dunbar. On the 22d of August Charles reached Worcester. On the 28th Cromwell was close to the town with thirty thousand men.

"This is the end of it all, Jacob," Harry said that night. "They outnumber us by three to one, and even if equal, they would assuredly beat us, for the Scotch are dispirited at finding themselves so far from home, in a hostile country. Things look desperate. If all is lost to-morrow, do you and William Long and Mike keep close to me. Get a horse for Mike to-night. You and Long are already mounted. If all is lost we must try and make our way to the seacoast, and take boat for France or Holland. But first of all we must see to the safety of the king. It is clear that at present England is not ready to return to the former state of things. We must hope that some day she will weary of the Roundhead rule, and if the king can reach the Continent he must remain there till England calls him. At present she only wants peace. It is just nine years now since King Charles' father set up his standard at Nottingham. Nine years of wars and troubles! No wonder men are aweary of it. It is all very well for us,

192

Jacob, who have no wives, neither families nor occupations, and are without property to lose, but I wonder not that men who have these things are chary of risking them in a cause which seems destined to failure."

Upon the 3d of September, 1651, the anniversary of the battle of Dunbar, Cromwell advanced to the attack. Harry's regiment was placed among some hedges around the city, and upon them the brunt of the fight first fell. In spite of the immense numbers brought against them they defended themselves with desperate bravery. Some of the Scottish troops came up, and for a time Cromwell's footmen could make but little way. At other parts, however, the resistance was more feeble, and the Scotch fell rapidly into confusion. Contesting every foot of the way, Harry's regiment was driven back into the town, where a terrible confusion reigned. Still keeping his men together, he marched to the marketplace. Here he found the king with a considerable body of horse. The greater part, however, of the horse had fled through the town without drawing rein, while the foot were throwing away their arms and flying in all directions.

"If all my troops had fought like your regiment, Colonel Furness, we should have won the day," the king said. "As it is now, it is a hopeless rout. It is useless for your brave fellows to throw away their lives further. They will only be cut down vainly, seeing that the rest of my army are disbanded. Thank them from me for their services, and bid them seek their homes as best they may and wait for better times. They are English, and will meet with better treatment from the country people than will the Scotch. Then do you join me. I am going to head my horsemen here in a charge against the Roundhead cavalry, and so give more time for the army to get away."

Harry rode up to his troops, now reduced to half their former strength. Leslie and Grahame had both been killed, and William Long was sorely wounded. He gave the men the message from the king, and the brave fellows gave a cheer for King Charles, the last he was to hear for ten years. Then they marched away in orderly array, with their arms, intending to beat off all who might attack them before nightfall, and then to break up and scatter, each for himself. William Long had friends near Gloucester, and as his wound would prevent him from traveling rapidly with Harry, he took farewell of him, and rode away with the regiment. Harry, with Jacob and Mike, rejoined the king, and they rode toward the gate by which the Roundhead troops were already entering the town. The horsemen, however, had but little stomach for the fight, and as the king advanced, in twos and threes they turned their horses' heads and rode off.

Harry was riding close to the king, and looking round said at length, "It is useless, your majesty. There are not a dozen men with us."

The king looked round and checked his horse. Besides his personal friends, Buckingham, Wilmot, and one or two other nobles, scarce a man remained. The king shrugged his shoulders. "Well, gentlemen, as we cannot fight, we must needs run." Then the party turned their horses and galloped out on the other side of Worcester. The country was covered with fugitives. They soon came upon a considerable body of horse, who at once attached themselves to the party. "These, gentlemen," the king said, "would not fight when I wanted them to, and now that I would fain be alone, they follow me."

At last, when darkness came on, the king, with his personal friends and some sixty others, slipped away down a by-road, and after riding for some hours came to a house called the White Ladies. Here for a few hours they rested. Then a council was held. They had news that on a heath near were some three thousand Scotch cavalry. The king's friends urged him to join these and endeavor to make his way back into Scotland, but Charles had already had more than enough of that country, and he was sure that Argyll and his party would not hesitate to deliver him up to the Parliament, as they had done his father before him. He therefore determined to disguise himself, and endeavor to escape on foot, taking with him only a guide. The rest of the party agreed to join the Scotch horse, and endeavor to reach the border. After a consultation with Jacob, Harry determined to follow the example of the king, and to try and make his way in disguise to a seaport. He did not believe that the Scotch cavalry would be able to regain their country, nor even if they did would his position be improved were he with them. With the destruction of the Royalist army, Argyll would again become supreme, and Harry doubted not that he would satisfy his old grudge against him. He was right in his anticipations. The Scots were a day or two later routed by the English horse, and comparatively few of them ever regained their country. Out of the eleven thousand men who fought at Worcester, seven thousand were taken prisoners, including the greater part of the Scottish contingent. The English, attracting less hostility and attention from the country people, for the most part reached their homes in safety.

As soon as the king had ridden off, Harry with Jacob and Mike, started in another direction. Stopping at a farmhouse, they purchased from the master three suits of clothes. Harry's was one of the farmer's own, the man being nearly his own size. For Jacob, who was much shorter, a dress, cloak and bonnet of the farmer's wife was procured, and for Mike the clothes of one of the farmer's sons. One of the horses was left here, and a pillion obtained for the other. Putting on these disguises, Harry mounted his horse, with Jacob seated behind him on a pillion, while Mike rode by his side. They started amid the good wishes of the farmer and his family, who were favorable to the Royalist cause. Harry had cut off his ringlets, and looked the character of a young farmer of twenty-four or twenty-five years old well enough, while Jacob had the appearance of a suitable wife for him. Mike was to pass as his brother.

In the course of the first day's journey they met several parties of Roundhead horse, who plied them with questions as to whether they had seen any parties of fugitives. Making a detour, they rode toward Gloucester, not intending to enter that town, where there was a Parliamentary garrison, but to cross the river higher up. They stopped for the night at a wayside inn, where they heard much talk concerning the battle, and learned that all the fords were guarded to prevent fugitives crossing into Wales, and that none might pass who could not give a good account of themselves. They heard, too, that on the evening before a proclamation had been made at Gloucester and other towns offering a reward of a thousand pounds for the capture of Charles, and threatening all with the penalties of treason who should venture to aid or shelter him; a systematic watch was being set on all the roads.

They determined to ride again next morning toward Worcester, and to remain in that neighborhood for some days, judging that less inquiry would be made there than elsewhere. This they did, but journeyed very slowly, and slept a mile or two from Worcester.

Before reaching their halting-place they took off a shoe from Mike's horse, and with a nail wounded the frog of the foot, so that the animal walked lame. Under this pretense they stopped three days, feigning great annoyance at the delay. They found now that orders had been issued that none should journey on the roads save those who had passes, and these had to be shown before entering any of the large towns. They therefore resolved to leave their horses, and to proceed on foot, as they could then travel by byways and across the country. There was some debate as to the best guise in which to travel, but it was presently determined to go as Egyptians, as the gypsies were then called. Harry walked into Worcester, and there, at the shop of a dealer in old clothes, procured such garments as were needed, and at an apothecary's purchased some dyes for staining the skin.

The next day, telling the landlord that they should leave the lame horse with him until their return, they started as before, Mike walking instead of riding. They presently left the main road, and finding a convenient place in a wood, changed their attire. Harry and Mike were dressed in ragged clothes, with bright handkerchiefs round their necks, and others round their heads. Jacob still retained his attire as a woman, with a tattered shawl round his shoulders, and a red handkerchief over his head. All darkened their faces and hands. They took the saddle from the horse, and placed the bundles, containing the clothes they had taken off, on his back. Mike took the bridle, Harry and Jacob walked beside, and so they continued for some miles along the lonely roads, until they came to a farmhouse. Here they stopped. The farmer came out, and roughly demanded what they wanted. Harry replied that he wanted to sell their horse, and would take a small sum for it.

"I doubt me," the farmer said, looking at it, "that that horse was not honestly come by. It suits not your condition. It may well be," he said, "the horse of some officer who was slain at Worcester, and which you have found roaming in the country."

"It matters not," Harry said, "where I got it; it is mine now, and may be yours if you like it, cheap. As you say, its looks agree not with mine, and I desire not to be asked questions. If you will give me that donkey I see there, and three pounds, you shall have him."

The offer was a tempting one, but the farmer beat them down a pound before he agreed to it. Then shifting their bundles to the donkey, they continued their way. At the next village they purchased a cooking-pot and some old stuff for a tent. Cutting some sticks, they encamped that night on some wild land hard by, having purchased provisions for their supper. Very slowly they traveled south, attracting no attention as they passed. They avoided all large towns, and purchased such things as they needed at villages, always camping out on commons and waste places. They could hear no news of the king at any of their halting-places. That he had not been taken was certain; also, that he had not reached France, or the news of his coming there would have been known. It was generally supposed that he was in hiding somewhere in the south, hoping to find an opportunity to take ship to France. Everywhere they heard of the active search which was being made for him, and how the houses of all suspected to be favorable to him were being searched.

Traveling only a few miles a day, and frequently halting for two or three days together, the party crossed the Thames above Reading, and journeyed west into Wiltshire. So they went on until they reached the port of Charmouth, near Lime Regis. Here, as in all the seaport towns, were many soldiers of the Parliament. They did not enter the town, but encamped a short distance outside, Harry alone going in to gather the news. He found that numerous rumors concerning the king were afloat. It was asserted that he had been seen near Bristol, and failing to embark there, was supposed to be making his way east along the coast, in hopes of finding a ship. The troops were loud in their expressions of confidence that in a few days, if not in a few hours, he would be in their hands, and that he would be brought to the scaffold, as his father had been.

Uneasy at the news, Harry wandered about the town, and at nightfall entered a small public house near the port. Calling for some liquor, he sat down, and listened to the talk of the sailors. Presently these left, and soon after they did so three other men entered. One was dressed as a farmer, the other two as serving-men. Harry thought that he noticed a glance of recognition pass between the farmer and the landlord, and as the latter placed some liquor and a candle on the table before the newcomers, Harry recognized in the farmer Colonel Wyndham, a Royalist with whom he was well acquainted. He now looked more closely at the two serving-men, and recognized in them the king and Lord Wilmot.

He sauntered across the room as if to get a light for his pipe, and said, in low tones:

"Colonel Wyndham, I am Harry Furness. Is there any way I can serve his majesty?"

"Ah! Colonel Furness, I am glad to see you," the king said heartily; "though if you are hunted as shrewdly as I am, your state is a perilous one."

"The landlord is to be trusted," Colonel Wyndham said. "We had best call him in. He said nothing before you, deeming you a stranger."

The landlord was called in, and told Harry was a friend, whereupon he barred the door and closed the shutters, as if for the night. Then turning to Colonel Wyndham, whom alone he knew, he said:

"I am sorry to say that my news is bad, sir. An hour since I went round to the man who had engaged to take you across to St. Malo, but his wife has got an inkling of his intentions. She has locked him into his room, and swears that if he attempts to come forth she will give the alarm to the Parliament troops; for that she will not have herself and her children sacrificed by meddlings of his in the affairs of state."

# CHAPTER XXIV

## ACROSS THE SEA

The announcement of the innkeeper struck consternation into the party.

"This is bad news indeed," Colonel Wyndham said; "what does your majesty advise now?"

"I know not, my good Wyndham," King Charles replied. "Methinks 'twere better that I should give myself up at once. Fate seems against us, and I'm only bringing danger on all my friends."

"Your friends are ready to risk the danger," Colonel Wyndham said; "and I doubt not that we shall finally place your majesty in safety. I think we had best try Bridport. Unfortunately, the Roundheads are so sure of your being on the coast that it is well-nigh impossible to procure a ship, so strict is the search of all who leave port. If we could but put them off your scent, and lead them to believe that you have given it up in despair here, and are trying again to reach Scotland, it might throw them off their guard, and make it more easy for us to find a ship."

"I might do that," Harry said. "I have with me my comrade Jacob, who is about the king's height and stature. I will travel north again, and will in some way excite suspicion that he is the king. The news that your majesty has been seen traveling there will throw them off your track here."

"But you may be caught yourself," the king said. "The Earl of Derby and other officers have been executed. There would be small chance for you were you to fall into their hands."

"I trust that I shall escape, sire. My friend Jacob is as cunning as a fox, and will, I warrant me, throw dust in their eyes. And how has it fared with your majesty since I left you at White Ladies?"

"Faith," Charles replied, laughing, "I have been like a rat with the dogs after him. The next night after leaving you I was in danger from a rascally miller, who raised an alarm because we refused to stay at his bidding. Then we made for Moseley, where I hoped to cross the Severn. The Roundheads had set a guard there, and Richard Penderell went to the house of Mr. Woolfe, a loyal gentleman, and asked him for shelter for an officer from Worcester. Mr. Woolfe said he would risk his neck for none save the king himself. Then Richard told him who I was, and brought me in. Mr. Woolfe hid me in the barn and gave me provisions. The neighborhood was dangerous, for the search was hot thereabout, and I determined to double back again to White Ladies, that I might hear what had become of Wilmot. Richard Penderell guided me to Boscabell, a farmhouse kept by his brother William. Here I found Major Careless in hiding. The search was hot, and we thought of hiding in a wood near, but William advised that as this might be searched we should take refuge in an oak lying apart in the middle of the plain."

"This had been lopped three or four years before and had grown again very thick and bushy, so that it could not be seen through. So, early in the morning, Careless and I, taking provisions for the day, climbed up it and hid there, and it was well we did so, for in the day the Roundheads came and searched the wood from end to end, as also the house. But they did not think of the tree. The next two days I lay at Boscabell, and learned on the second day that Wilmot was hiding at the house of Mr. Whitgrave, a Catholic gentleman at Moseley, where he begged me to join him. That night I rode thither. The six Penderells, for there were that number of brothers, rode with me as a bodyguard. I was well received by Mr. Whitgrave, who furnished me with fresh linen, to my great comfort, for that which I had on was coarse, and galled my flesh grievously, and my feet were so sore I could scarce walk. But the Roundheads were all about, and the search hot, and it was determined that I should leave. This time I was dressed as a decent serving man, and Colonel Lane's daughter agreed to go with me. I was to pass as her serving man, taking her to Bristol. A cousin rode with us in company. Colonel Lane procured us a pass, and we met with no adventure for three days. A smith who shod my horse, which had cast a shoe, did say that that rogue Charles Stuart had not been taken yet, and that he thought he ought to be hanged. I thought so too, so we had no argument. At Bristol we could find no ship in which I could embark, and after some time I went with Miss Lane and her cousin to my good friend Colonel Wyndham, at Trent House. After much trouble he had engaged a ship to take me hence, and now this rascal refuses to go, or rather his wife refuses for him. And now, my friend, we will at once make for Bridport, since Colonel Wyndham hopes to find a ship there. I trust we may meet ere long in France. None of my friends have served me and my father more faithfully than you. It would seem but a mockery now to take knighthood at the hands of Charles Stuart, but it will not harm thee."

Taking a sword from Colonel Wyndham, the king dubbed Harry knight. Then giving his hand to the landlord to kiss, Charles, accompanied by his two companions, left the inn.

A few minutes later Harry started and joined his friends.

Jacob agreed at once to the proposal to throw the Roundheads off King Charles' track. The next day they started north, and traveled through Wiltshire up into Gloucestershire, still keeping their disguises as gypsies. There they left their donkey with a peasant, telling him they would return in a fortnight's time and claim it. In a wood near they again changed their disguise, hid their gypsy dresses, and started north on foot. In the evening they stopped at Fairford, and took up their abode at a small inn, where they asked for a private room. They soon ascertained that the landlord was a follower of the Parliament. Going toward the room into which they were shown, Jacob stumbled, and swore in a man's voice, which caused the servant maid who was conducting them to start and look suspiciously at him. Supper was brought, but Harry noticed that the landlord, who himself brought it in, glanced several times at Jacob. They were eating their supper when they heard his footstep again coming along the passage. Harry dropped on one knee, and was in the act of handing the jug in that attitude to Jacob, when the landlord entered. Harry rose hastily, as if in confusion, and the landlord, setting down on the table a dish which he had brought, again retired.

"Throw up the window, Jacob, and listen," Harry said. "We must not be caught like rats in a trap."

The window opened into a garden, and Jacob, listening, could hear footsteps as of men running in the streets.

"That is enough, then," Harry said. "The alarm is given. Now let us be off." They leaped from the window, and they were soon making their way across the country. They had not been gone a hundred yards before they heard a great shouting, and knew that their departure had been discovered. They had not walked far that day and now pressed forward north. They had filled their pockets with the remains of their supper, and after walking all night, left the road, and climbing into a haystack at a short distance, ate their breakfast and were soon fast asleep.

It was late in the afternoon before they awoke. Then they walked on until, after darkness fell, they entered a small village. Here they went into a shop to buy bread. The woman looked at them earnestly.

"I do not know whether it concerns you," she said, "but I will warn you that this morning a mounted man from Fairford came by warning all to seize a tall countryman with a young fellow and a woman with him, for that she was no other than King Charles."

"Thanks, my good woman," Jacob said. "Thanks for your warning. I do not say that I am he you name, but whether or no, the king shall hear some day of your good-will."

200

Traveling on again, they made thirty miles that night, and again slept in a wood. The next evening, when they entered a village to buy food, the man in the shop, after looking at them, suddenly seized Jacob, and shouted loudly for help. Harry stretched him on the ground with a heavy blow of the stout cudgel he carried. The man's shouts, however, had called up some of his neighbors, and these ran up as they issued from the shop, and tried to seize them. The friends, however, struck out lustily with their sticks, Jacob carrying one concealed beneath his dress. In two or three minutes they had fought their way clear, and ran at full speed through the village, pursued by a shouting crowd of rustics.

"Now," Harry said, "we can return for our gypsy dresses, and then make for the east coast. We have put the king's enemies off the scent. I trust that when we may get across the water we may hear that he is in safety."

They made a long detour, traveling only at night, Harry entering alone after dusk the villages where it was necessary to buy food. When they regained the wood where they had left their disguises they dressed themselves again as gypsies, called for the donkey, and then journeyed across England by easy stages to Colchester, where they succeeded in taking passage in a lugger bound for Hamburg. They arrived there in safety, and found to their great joy the news had arrived that the king had landed in France.

He had, they afterward found, failed to obtain a ship at Bridport, where when he arrived he here found a large number of soldiers about to cross to Jersey. He returned to Trent House, and a ship at Southampton was then engaged. But this was afterward taken up for the carriage of troops. A week later a ship lying at Shoreham was hired to carry a nobleman and his servant to France, and King Charles, with his friends, made his way thither in safety. The captain of the ship at once recognized the king, but remained true to his promise, and landed him at Fécamp in Normandy.

Six weeks had elapsed since the battle of Worcester, and during that time the king's hiding-places had been known to no less than forty-five persons, all of whom proved faithful to the trust, and it was owing to their prudence and caution as well as to their loyalty that the king escaped, in spite of the reward offered and the hot search kept up everywhere for him.

Harry had now to settle upon his plans for the future. There was no hope whatever of an early restoration. He had no thought of hanging about the king whose ways and dissolute associates revolted him. It was open to him to take service, as so many of his companions had done, in one or other of the Continental armies, but Harry had had more than enough of fighting. He determined then to cross the ocean to the plantations of Virginia, where many loyal gentlemen had established themselves. The moneys which Colonel Furness had during the last four years regularly sent across to a banker at the Hague, for his use, were lying untouched, and these constituted a sum amply sufficient for establishing himself there. Before starting, however, he determined that if possible he would take a wife with him. In all his wanderings he had never seen any one he liked so much as his old playmate, Lucy Rippinghall. It was nearly four years since he had seen her, and she must now be twenty-one. Herbert, he knew by his father's letters, had left the army at the end of the first civil war, and was carrying on his father's business, the wool-stapler having been killed at Marston Moor. Harry wrote to the colonel, telling him of his intention to go to Virginia and settle there until either Cromwell's death, and the dying out of old animosities, or the restoration of the king permitted him to return to England, and also that he was writing to ask Lucy Rippinghall to accompany him as his wife. He told his father that he was well aware that he would not have regarded such a match as suitable had he been living at home with him at Furness Hall, but that any inequality of birth would matter no whit in the plantations of Virginia, and that such a match would greatly promote his happiness there. By the same mail he wrote to Herbert Rippinghall.

"My DEAR HERBERT: The bonds of affection which held us together when boys are in no way slackened in their hold upon me, and you showed, when we last met, that you loved me in no way less than of old. I purpose sailing to Virginia with such store of money as would purchase a plantation there, and there I mean to settle down until such times as these divisions in England may be all passed. But I would fain not go alone. As a boy I loved your sister Lucy, and I have seen none to take the place of her image in my heart. She is, I know, still unmarried, but I know not whether she has any regard for me. I do beseech you to sound her, and if she be willing to give her to me. I hear that you are well married, and can therefore the better spare her. If she be willing to take me, I will be a good husband to her, and trust some day or other to bring her back to be lady of Furness Hall. Although I know that she will care little for such things, I may say that she would be Lady Lucy, since the king has been pleased to make me Sir Harry Furness. Should the dear girl be willing, will you, since I cannot come to you, bring her hither to me. I have written to my father, and have told him what I purpose to do. Trusting that this will find you as well disposed toward me as ever, I remain, your affectionate friend, HARRY FURNESS."

This letter, together with that to his father, Harry gave to Mike. The post in those days was extremely irregular, and none confided letters of importance to it which could possibly be sent by hand. Such a communication as that to Herbert Rippinghall was not one which Harry cared to trust to the post. Mike had never been at Abingdon, and would therefore be unknown there. Nor, indeed, unless they were taken prisoners in battle or in the first hot pursuit, were any of lower degree meddled with after their return to their homes. There was therefore no fear whatever of molestation. At this time Jacob was far from well. The fatigues which he had undergone since the king broke up his camp at Stirling had been immense. Prolonged marches, great anxiety, sleeping on wet ground, being frequently soaked to the skin by heavy rains, all these things had told upon him, and now that the necessity for exertion was over, a sort of low fever seized him, and he was forced to take to his bed. The leech whom Harry called in told him that Jacob needed rest and care more than medicine. He gave him, however, cooling drinks, and said that when the fever passed he would need strengthening food and medicine.

Hamburg was at that time the resort of many desperate men from England. After Worcester, as after the crushing out of the first civil war, those too deeply committed to return to their homes sought refuge here. But though all professed to be Cavaliers, who were suffering only from their loyalty to the crown, a great many of them were men who had no just claim to so honorable a position. There were many who took advantage of the times in England to satisfy private enmities or to gratify evil passions. Although the courts of law sat during the whole of the civil war, and the judges made their circuits, there was necessarily far more crime than in ordinary times. Thus many of those who betook themselves to Hamburg and other seaports on the continent had made England too hot for them by crimes of violence and dishonesty.

The evening after Mike sailed Harry, who had been sitting during the afternoon chatting by Jacob's bedside, went out to take the air. He strolled along the wharves, near which were the drinking-houses, whence came sounds of singing, dancing, and revelry, mingled occasionally with shouts and the clash of steel, as quarrels arose among the sailors and others frequenting them. Never having seen one of these places, Harry strolled into one which appeared of a somewhat better class than the rest. At one end was a sort of raised platform, upon which were two men, with fiddles, who, from time to time, played lively airs, to which those at the tables kept time by stamping their feet. Sometimes men or women came on to the platform and sang. The occupants of the body of the hall were mostly sailors, but among whom were a considerable number of men, who seemed by their garb to be broken-down soldiers and adventurers.

Harry took his seat by the door, called for a glass of wine and drank it, and, having soon seen enough of the nature of the entertainment, was about to leave, when his attention was attracted by a young girl who took her place on the platform. She was evidently a gypsy, for at this time these people were the minstrels of Europe. It would have been considered shameful for any other woman to sing publicly. Two or three of these women had already sung, and Harry had been disgusted with their hard voices and bold looks. But he saw that the one who now took her place on the platform was of a different nature. She advanced nervously, and as if quite strange to such a scene, and touched her guitar with trembling fingers. Then she began to sing a Spanish romance in a sweet, pure voice. There was a good deal of applause when it finished, for even the rough sailors could appreciate the softness and beauty of the melody. Then a half-drunken man shouted, "Give us something lively. Sing 'May the Devil fly off with Old Noll.'"

The proposal was received with a shout of approval by many, but some of the sailors cried out, "No, no. No politics. We won't hear Cromwell insulted."

This only led to louder and more angry shouts on the part of the others, and in all parts of the room men rose to their feet, gesticulating and shouting. The girl, who evidently did not understand a word that was said, stood looking with affright at the tumult which had so suddenly risen. In a minute swords were drawn. The foreign sailors, in ignorance of the cause of dispute, drew their knives, and stood by the side of those from the English ships, while the foreign soldiers seemed ready to make common cause with the English who had commenced the disturbance. Two or three of the latter leaped upon the platform to insist upon their wishes being carried out. The girl, with a little scream, retreated into a corner. Harry, indignant at the conduct to his countrymen, had drawn his sword, and made his way quietly toward the end of the hall, and he now sprang upon the platform.

"Stand back," he shouted angrily. "I'll spit the first man who advances a step."

"And who are you, sir, who ventures to thrust yourself into a quarrel, and to interfere with English gentlemen?"

"English gentlemen," Harry said bitterly. "God help England if you are specimens of her gentlemen."

"S'death!" exclaimed one. "Run the scoundrel through, Ralph."

In a moment Harry slashed open the cheek of one, and ran the other through the arm. By this time the fray had become general in the hall. Benches were broken up, swords and knives were used freely. Just as the matter began to grow serious there was a cry of "The watch!" and a strong armed guard entered the hall.

There was an instant cessation of hostilities, and then both parties uniting, rushed upon the watch, and by sheer weight bore them back out of the place. Harry looked round, and saw that the girl had fled by a door at the back of the platform. Seeing that a fight was going on round the door, and desiring to escape from the broil, he went out by the door she had taken, followed a passage for some distance, went down a dimly-lighted stair, and issued through a door into the air. He found himself in a foul and narrow lane. It was entirely unlighted, and Harry made his way with difficulty along, stumbling into holes in the pavement, and over heaps of rubbish of all kinds.

"I have got into a nice quarter of the town," he muttered to himself. "I have heard there are places in Hamburg, the resort of thieves and scoundrels of the worst kind, and where even the watch dare not penetrate, Methinks that this must be one them."

He groped his way along till he came to the end of the lane. Here a dim light was burning. Three or four other lanes, in appearance as forbidding as that up which he had come, met at this spot. Several men were standing about. Harry paused for a moment, wondering whether he had better take the first turning at random, or invite attention by asking his way. He determined that the former was the least dangerous alternative, and turned down the lane to his right. He had not gone ten steps when a woman came up to him from behind.

"Are you not the gentleman who drew a sword to save me from insult?" she asked in French.

Harry understood enough of the language to make out what she said.

"Yes," he said, "if you are the singer."

"Good heavens! sir, what misfortune has brought you here? I recognized your face in the light. Your life, sir, is in the greatest danger. There are men here who would murder you for the sake of a gold piece, and that jewel which fastens your plume must have caught their eyes. Follow me, sir, quickly."

# CHAPTER XXV

# A PLOT OVERHEARD

As the gypsy ended her warning she sprang forward, saying, "Follow me, for your life, sir." Harry did not hesitate. He heard several footsteps coming down the lane, and drawing his sword he followed his guide at a run. As he did so there was a shout among the men behind him and these set off in hot pursuit. Harry kept close to the girl, who turned down another lane even more narrow than that they were leaving. A few paces further she stopped, opened a door and entered. Harry followed her in and she closed the door behind her.

"Hush!" she whispered. "There are men here as bad as those without. Take off your shoes."

Harry did as directed. He was in pitch darkness. Taking him by the hand, the girl led him forward for some distance.

"There is a staircase here," she whispered.

Still holding his hand, she began to mount the stairs. As they passed each landing Harry heard the voices of men in the rooms on either side. At last they arrived at the top of the house. Here she opened a door, and led Harry into a room.

"Are you here, mother?" she asked.

There was no answer. The girl uttered an exclamation of thankfulness; then, after groping about, she found a tinder-box, and struck a light.

"You are safe here for the present. This is my room, where I live with my mother. At least," she sighed, "she calls herself my mother, and is the only one I have known."

"Is it possible," Harry asked in surprise, "that one like yourself can live in such an abode as this?"

"I am safe here," she answered. "There are five men of my tribe in the next room, and fierce and brutal as are the men of these courts, none of them would care to quarrel with the gypsies. But now I have got you here, how am I to get you away?"

"If the gypsies are so feared, I might go out with them," Harry said.

"Alas!" the girl answered, "they are as had as the others. And even if they were disposed to aid you for the kindness you have shown me, I doubt if they could do so. Assuredly they would not run the risk of thwarting the cutthroats here for the sake of saving you."

"Could you go and tell the watch?" Harry asked.

"The watch never comes here," the girl replied, shaking her head. "Were they to venture up these lanes it would be like entering a hive of bees. This is an Alsatia—a safe refuge for assassins and robbers."

"I have got myself into a nice mess," Harry said. "It seems to me I had better sally out and take my chance."

"Look," the girl said, going to the window and opening it.

Peering out, Harry saw below a number of men with swords and knives drawn. One or two had torches, and they were examining every doorway and court. Outside the window ran a parapet.

"They will search like hounds," the girl continued. "They must know that you have not gone far. If they come here you must take to the parapet, and go some distance along. Now, I must try and find some disguise for you."

At this moment the door opened, and an old woman entered. She uttered an exclamation of astonishment at seeing Harry, and turning angrily to the girl, spoke to her in the gypsy dialect. For two or three minutes the conversation continued in that language; then the old woman turned to Harry, and said in English:

"My daughter tells me that you have got into a broil on her behalf. There are few gentlemen who draw sword for a gypsy. I will do my best to aid you, but it will be difficult to get a gallant like yourself out of this place."

Her eye fell covetously upon the jewel in Harry's hat. He noticed the glance.

"Thanks, dame," he said; "I will gladly repay your services. Will you accept this token?" And removing the jewel from the hat, he offered it to her.

The girl uttered an angry exclamation as the old woman seized it, and after examining it by the candle light, placed it in a small iron coffer. Harry felt he had done wisely, for the old woman's face bore a much warmer expression of good-will than had before characterized it.

"You cannot leave now," she said. "I heard as I came along that a well-dressed gallant had been seen in the lanes, and every one's mouth is on water. They said that they thought he had some woman with him, but I did not dream it was Zita. You cannot leave to-night; to-morrow I will get you some clothes of my son's, and in these you should be able to escape without detection."

Very slowly the hours passed. The women at times talked

207

together in Romaic, while Harry, who had possession of the only chair in the room, several times nodded off to sleep. In the morning there was a movement heard in the next room, and the old woman went in there.

"Surely that woman cannot be your mother?" Harry said to the girl.

"She is not," she answered. "I believe that I was stolen as a child; indeed, they have owned as much. But what can I do? I am one of them. What can a gypsy do? We are good for nothing but to sing and to steal."

"If I get free from this scrape," Harry said, "you may be sure that shall not be ungrateful, and if you long to leave this life, I can secure you a quiet home in England with my father."

The girl clasped her hands in delight.

"Oh, that would be too good!" she exclaimed. "Too good; but I fear it can never be."

She put her fingers to her lips, as the door again opened. The old woman entered, carrying some clothes.

"Here," she said; "they have gone out; put these on, Zita and I will go out and see if the coast is clear."

Harry, smiling to himself at the singularity of his having twice to disguise himself as a gypsy, rapidly changed his clothes. Presently the old woman returned.

"Quick," she exclaimed; "I hear that the news of the riot in the drinking-house has got about this morning, and it is known that an Englishman, something like the one seen in the lanes, took Zita's part, and there are suspicions that it was she who acted as his guide. They have been roughly questioning us. I told her to go on to avoid suspicion, while I ran back. You cannot stir out now, and I heard a talk of searching our rooms. Come, then, we may find a room unoccupied below; you must take refuge there for the present."

Harry still retained his sword, incongruous as it was with his attire, but he had determined to hide it under his clothes, so that, if detected, he might be able at least to sell his life. Taking it in his hand, he followed the old woman downstairs. She listened at each door, and continued downward until she reached the first floor.

"I can hear no one here," she said, listening at a door. "Go up a few steps; I will knock. If any one is there I can make some excuse."

She knocked, but there was no answer. Then she drew from her pocket a piece of bent wire, and inserted it in the keyhole.

"We gypsies can enter where we will," she said, beckoning

Harry to enter as the door opened. "Wait quiet here till I come for you. The road will be clear then." So saying, she closed the door behind him, and again shot the bolt.

Harry felt extremely uncomfortable. Should the owner of the room return, he would be taken for a thief, although, as he thought, looking round the room, there was little enough to steal. It was a large room, with several truckle beds standing against the walls. In the center was a table, upon which were some mugs, horns, and empty bottles, with some dirty cards scattered about. The place smelled strongly of tobacco, and benches lying on the ground showed that the party of the night before had ended in a broil, further evidence to which was given by stains of blood on one of the beds, and by a rag saturated with blood, which lay beside it. At one side of the room was a door, giving communication into the next apartment. Scarcely had Harry entered when he heard voices there, and was surprised to find that the speakers were English.

"I tell you I'm sick of this," one of the speakers said. "I might be as well hanged at home as starved here."

"You might enlist," another voice said, in sneering tones. "Gallant soldiers are welcome in the Low Countries."

"You'd best keep your sneering tongue between your lips," the other said angrily. "If I don't care for fighting in the field, I can use a knife at a pinch, as you know full well. You will carry your gibes too far with me some day. No," he went on more calmly, after a pause, "I shall go back to England next week, after Marmaduke Harris and his gang have finished Oliver. The country will be turned so topsy-turvy that there will be no nice inquiry into bygones, and at any rate I can keep out of London."

"Yes, it will be wise to do that," the other said, since that little affair when the mercer and his wife in Cheap were found with their throats cut, and you—"

"Fire and furies! John Marlow, do you want three inches of steel in your ribs?"

"By no means!" the other answered. "You have become marvelously straightlaced all at once. As you know, I have been concerned in as many affairs as you have. Aha! I have had a merry time of it!"

"And may again," the other said. "Noll once dead, there will be good times for us again. It is a pity that you and I were too well known to have a hand in the job. Dost think there is any chance of a failure?"

"None," the other replied. "It is in good hands. Black Harry has bribed a cook wench, who will open the back door. They say he was to return to London this week, and if so Sunday is fixed for the affair. Five days yet, and say another week for the news to get here. In a fortnight we will be on our way to England. There, I am thirsty, and we left the bottle in the next room. We had a late night of it with the boys there."

During this conversation, to which Harry listened breathlessly, he had heard the tramp of feet going upstairs, and just as they finished speaking these had descended again. A moment later the door between the two rooms opened, and a man in the faded finery of a Royalist gentleman entered.

"Fires and furies!" he exclaimed. "Whom have we here? Marlow, here is an eavesdropper or a thief. We will slit his weasand. Aha!" he said, gazing fixedly at Harry, "you are Colonel Furness. I know you. You had me flogged the day before Worcester, for helping myself to an old woman's purse. It is my turn now."

Joined by his fellow ruffian he fell upon Harry, but they were no match for the Royalist colonel. After a few rapid thrusts and parries he ran his first assailant through the body and cut down the man called Marlow, with a sweeping blow which nearly cleft his head asunder.

Scarcely was the conflict ended when the door opened, and the old gypsy entered. She started at seeing the bodies of the two ruffians.

"I have been attacked," Harry said briefly, "and have defended myself."

"It is no business of mine," the old woman remarked. "When I have guided you out I will come back again. It's strange if there's not something worth picking up. Now, pull your hat well over your eyes and follow me."

Closing and locking the door again, she led the way downstairs.

"Do not walk so straight and stiff," she said. "Slouch your shoulders, and stoop your head. Now."

Harry sallied out into the lane, keeping by the side of his guide, with his head bent forward, and his eyes on the ground, walking, as far as he could, with a listless gait. The old woman continued to chatter to him in Romaic. There were many people about in the lane, but none paid any heed to them. Harry did not look up, but turned with his guide down several lanes, until they at length emerged on the quays. Saying she would call next day at his hotel for the reward he had promised her, she left him, and Harry, with his head full of the plot against Cromwell's life, crossed at once to the vessels by the quay.

"Is any ship sailing for the Thames to-day?" he asked.

"Yes," the sailor said. "The Mary Anne is just hoisting her anchor now, out there in midstream. You will be but just in time, for the anchor's under her foot."

Harry sprang into a boat and told the waterman to row to the ship. The latter stared in astonishment at the authoritative manner in which this gypsy addressed him, but Harry thrust his hand into his pocket, and showed him some silver.

"Quick, man," he said, "for she is moving. You will have double fare to put me on board."

The man pulled vigorously, and they were soon alongside the brig.

"Halloo! what now?" the captain said, looking over the side.

"I want a passage to England, and will pay you your own price."

"You haven't been killing any one, have you?" the captain asked. "I don't want to have trouble when I come back here, for carrying off malefactors."

"No, indeed," Harry said, as he lightly leaped on the deck. "I am Sir Harry Furness, though I may not look it, and am bound to England on urgent business. It is all right, my good fellow, and here is earnest money for my passage," and he placed two pieces of gold in the captain's hand.

"That will do," the captain said. "I will take you."

Harry went to the side.

"Here, my man, is your money, and a crown piece beside. Go to the Hotel des Etoiles and ask for the English officer who is there lying sick. Tell him Colonel Furness has been forced to leave for England at a moment's notice, but will be back by the first ship."

The man nodded, and rowed back to shore as the Mary Anne, with her sails hoisted, ran down the river.

Never did a voyage appear longer to an anxious passenger than did that of the Mary Anne to England. The winds were light and baffling, and at times the Mary Anne scarce moved through the water. Harry had no love for Cromwell. Upon the contrary, he regarded him as the deadliest enemy of the king, and moreover personally hated him for the cruel massacre of Drogheda. In battle he would have gladly slain him, but he was determined to save him from assassination. He felt the man to be a great Englishman, and knew that it was greatly due to his counsels that so little English

211

blood had been shed upon the scaffold. Most of all, he thought that his assassination would injure the royal cause. The time was not yet ripe for a restoration. England had shown but lately that there existed no enthusiasm for the royal cause. At Cromwell's death the chief power would fall into the hands of fanatics more dangerous and more violent than he. His murder would be used as a weapon for a wholesale persecution of the Royalists throughout the land, and would create such a prejudice against them that the inevitable reaction in favor of royalty would be retarded for years. Full of these thoughts, Harry fretted and fumed over the slow progress of the Mary Anne. Late on Saturday night she entered the mouth of the Thames, and anchored until the tide turned. Before daybreak she was on her way, and bore up on the tide as far as Gravesend, when she had again to anchor. Harry obtained a boat and was rowed to shore. In his present appearance, he did not like to go to one of the principal inns for a horse, but entering a small one on the outskirts of the place, asked the landlord if he could procure him a horse.

"I am not what I seem," he said, in answer to his host's look of surprise. "But I have urgent need to get to London this evening. I will pay well for the horse, and will leave this ring with you as a guarantee for his safe return."

"I have not a horse myself," the landlord said, with more respect than he had at first shown; "but I might get one from my neighbor Harry Fletcher, the butcher. Are you willing to pay a guinea for his use? Fletcher will drive you himself."

Harry agreed to the sum, and a quarter of an hour later the man, with a light horse and cart, came to the door.

"You are a strange-looking carle," he said, "to be riding on a Sunday in haste; I scarce like being seen with thee."

"I have landed but an hour ago," Harry said, "and can buy no clothes to-day; but if you or mine host here, who is nearer my size, have a decent suit which you can sell me, I will pay you double the sum it cost."

The landlord at once agreed to the terms, and five minutes later Harry, clad in the sober garb of a decent tradesman, mounted the cart. The horse was not a fast one, and the roads were bad. It was nigh six o'clock before they reached London. Paying Fletcher the sum agreed upon, Harry walked rapidly westward. Cromwell was abiding in a house in Pall Mall. Upon Harry arriving there he was asked his business.

"The general is ill," the servant said, "and can see no one."

"I must see him," Harry urged. "It is a matter of the extremest importance."

"See him you cannot," the man repeated, "and it were waste of words to talk further on the matter. Dost think that, even were he well, the general, with all the affairs of the Commonwealth on his shoulders, has time to see every gossiping citizen who would have speech with him?"

Harry slipped a gold piece into the man's hand.

"It is useless," the man said. "The general is, as I truly told thee, ill."

Harry stood in despair, "Could you gain me speech with the general's wife?"

"Ay," the man said. "I might do that. What name shall say?"

"She would not know my name. Merely say that one wishes to speak to her on a matter nearly touching the safety of the general."

"Hadst thou said that at once," the man grumbled, "I might have admitted you before. There are many rumors of plots on the part of the malignants against the life of the general. I will take your message to Madam Cromwell, and she can deal with it as she will."

The man was absent for a few minutes. Then he returned with an officer.

"Can you tell me," the latter asked, "what you have to reveal?"

"No," Harry replied, "I must speak with the general himself."

"Beware," the officer said sternly, "that you trifle not. The general is sick, and has many things on his mind; 'twill be ill for you if you disturb him without cause."

"The cause is sufficient," Harry said. "I would see him in person."

Without a word the officer turned and led the way to a room upstairs, where Cromwell was sitting at a table, His wife was near him. A Bible lay open before him. Cromwell looked steadily at Harry.

"I hear that you have a matter of importance to tell me, young man, and one touching my safety. I know that there are many who thirst for my blood. But I am in the hands of the Lord, who has so far watched over His servant. If there be truth in what you have to tell you will be rewarded."

"I seek for no reward," Harry said. "I have gained knowledge of a plot against your life. Do you wish that I should speak in the presence of this officer?"

"Assuredly," the general said.

"Briefly, then, I have arrived from Hamburg but now to give you warning of a matter which came to my ears. I overheard, how it matters not, a conversation between two rascals who gave

213

themselves out as Royalists, but who were indeed rather escaped criminals, to the effect that men had gone over thence to England with the intention of killing you. The plot was to come off to-night, Whether there be any change in the arrangements or no I cannot say, but the matter was, as they said, fixed for to-night. One of the women servants has been bribed to open the back entrance and to admit them there, More than this I know not."

"You speak, sir, as one beyond your station," Cromwell said; "and methinks I know both your face and figure, which are not easily forgotten when once seen."

"It matters not who I am," Harry replied, "so that the news I bring be true. I am no friend of yours, but a servant of King Charles. Though I would withstand you to the death in the field, I would not that a life like yours should be cut short by assassination; or that the royal cause should be sullied by such a deed, the dishonor of which, though planned and carried out by a small band of desperate partisans, would yet, in the eyes of the world, fall upon all who followed King Charles."

"You are bold, sir," Cromwell said. "But I wonder not, for I know you now. We have met, so far as I know, but once before. That was after Drogheda, where you defended the church, and where I spared your life at the intercession of my chaplain. I heard of you afterward as having, by a desperate enterprise, escaped, and afterward captured a ship with prisoners; and as having inflicted heavy loss and damage upon the soldiers of Parliament. You fought at Dunbar and Worcester, and, if I mistake not, incurred the enmity of the Earl of Argyll."

"I am Sir Harry Furness," Harry said calmly; "his majesty having been pleased to bestow upon me the honor of knighthood. Nor are you mistaken touching the other matters, since you yourself agreed at the lonely house on the moor to hand me over to Colonel Campbell, as his price for betraying the post I commanded. That matter, as you may remember, turned out otherwise than had been expected. I am not ashamed of my name, nor have I any fear of its being known to you. I have come over to do you service, and fear not harm at your hands when on such business."

"Why then did you not tell me at once?" Cromwell asked.

"Simply because I seek no favor at your hands. I would not that you should think that Harry Furness sought to reconcile himself with the Commons, by giving notice of a plot against your life. I am intending to start for Virginia and settle there, and would not stoop to sue for amnesty, though I should never see Furness Hall or England again."

Harry spoke in a tone of haughty frankness, which carried conviction with it.

"I doubt you not," Cromwell said. "You have been a bitter foe to the Commons, Colonel Furness, but it is not of men like you that we need be afraid. You meet us fairly in the field, and fight us loyally and honorably. It is the tricksters, the double-dealers, and the traitors, the men who profess to be on our side but who burrow in the dark against us, who trouble our peace. In this matter I am greatly beholden to you. Now that you have given us warning of the plot, it will be met if attempted. But should these men's hearts fail them, or for any other cause the attempt be laid aside, I shall be none the less indebted to you. I trust, Colonel Furness, that you will not go to the plantations. England needs honest men here. There is a great work yet to be done before happiness and quiet are restored; and we need all wise and good men in the counsels of the state. Be assured that you are free to return and dwell with the Cavalier, your father, at your pleasure. He drew aside from the strife when he saw that the cause he fought for was hopeless, and none have interfered with him. Charles will, methinks, fight no more in England. His cause is lost, and wise men will adapt themselves to the circumstances. Let me know where you lodge to-night. You will hear further from me to-morrow."

# CHAPTER XXVI

## REST AT LAST

Harry slept at an inn in Westminster, and the next morning on going down to his breakfast, he found people much excited, a rumor having gone about that an attack had been made upon Cromwell's house during the night, and that several had been killed, but no harm done to the general. An hour afterward a messenger brought word that General Cromwell wished to see Colonel Furness. After his breakfast Harry had at once gone out and purchased clothes suitable to a country gentleman; in these he proceeded to the general, and was at once shown up to his room.

"Your news was trustworthy, Colonel Furness, and Oliver Cromwell owes his life to you. Soon after midnight one of the serving wenches opened the back door, and eight men entered. Had no watch been set, they would doubtless have reached my room unobserved, by the staircase which leads from that part of the house. As it was, I had a guard in waiting, and when the men were fairly inside they fell upon them. The soldiers were too quick with them, being hot at the plot which was intended against my life, and all were killed, together with the wench who admitted them, who was stabbed by one of the men at the first alarm, thinking doubtless she had betrayed them. I hear that none of them have the air of gentlemen, but are clearly broken men and vagabonds. The haste of my soldiers has prevented me from getting any clew as to those who set them on, but I am sure that no English gentleman, even although devoted to the cause of Charles Stuart, would so plot against my life. And now, sir, I thank you heartily for the great service you have rendered me. My life is, I think, precious to England, where I hope to do some good work before I die. I say only in return that henceforth you may come and go as you list; and I hope yet that you will sit by me in Parliament, and aid me to set things in England in order. Do not take this, sir, as in any way a recompense for saving my life. The war is over; a few of those who had troubled, and would always trouble the peace of England, have been executed. Against the rest we bear no malice. They are free to return to their homes and occupations as they list, and so long as they obey the laws, and abstain from fresh troubles and plots, none will molest them. But, sir, in order that no molestation or vexation may occur to you, here is a free pass, signed by General Fairfax and two of the commissioners, saying that you are at liberty to go or

216

come and to stay where you please, without hindrance or molestation from any."

Harry took the document, bowed, and withdrew.

"It is a thousand pities," he said to himself, "that his majesty the king has not somewhat of this man's quality. This is a strong man, and a true. He may have his faults—ay, he has them—he is ambitions, he is far more fanatical for his religion than was Charles I. for his. He is far more absolute, far more domineering than was King Charles. Were he made king to-morrow, as I hear he is like enough to be, he would trample upon the Parliament and despise its will infinitely more than any English king would ever have dared to do. But for all that he is a great man, honest, sincere, and, above all, to be trusted. Who can say that for the Stuarts?"

Upon the day of his arrival Harry had written to Jacob telling him the cause of his sudden departure, and promising to return by the first ship, He hesitated now whether he should sail at once, or go down to see his father, but he determined that it would be best, at any rate in the first place, to return to Hamburg and look after his companion, and then to come over to see his father, before carrying out his intention of proceeding to Virginia. A ship would, he found, be sailing in three days, and he wrote to his father telling him that he had been in London for a day or two, but was forced by the illness of Jacob to return at once; but that upon his friend's recovery he would come back to Abingdon for a short time before leaving. He arrived at Hamburg without adventure. On reaching the hotel he was informed that Jacob was delirious, and that his life was despaired of. The rascally boatman could not have given the message with which he had been charged, since Jacob, upon the day after he was first missed, had risen from his bed, and insisted on going in search of him. He had, after many inquiries, learned that one answering to his description had taken part in a fray in a drinking-house—interfering to protect a Bohemian singer from insult. Beyond this nothing could be heard of him. He had not been seen in the fray in the street, when several of the rioters had been captured and carried off by the watch, and some supposed that he might have left the place at the back, in which case it was feared that he might have been fallen upon and assassinated by the ruffians in the low quarter lying behind the drinking hall. Jacob had worked himself into a state of high fever by his anxiety, and upon returning to the hotel had become so violent that they were forced to restrain him. He had been bled and blistered, but had remained for a fortnight in a state of violent fever and delirium. This had now somewhat abated, but he was in such a weak state that the doctors feared the worst.

The return of Harry did more for him than all the doctors of Hamburg. He seemed at once to recognize his voice, and the pressure of his hand soothed and calmed him. He presently fell into a deep sleep, in which he lay for twelve hours, and on opening his eyes at once recognized his friend. His recovery now was rapid, and in a week he was able to sit up.

One morning the servant told Harry that a gentleman wished to speak to him, and a moment after his father entered. With a cry of delight father and son flew into each other's arms. It was four years since they had met, and both were altered much. The colonel had aged greatly, while Harry had grown into a broad and powerful man.

"My dear father, this is an unexpected pleasure indeed," Harry said, when the first burst of delight was over. "Did you not get my letter from London, saying that I hoped shortly to be with you?"

"From London!" the colonel exclaimed, astonished. "No, indeed; I have received no letter save that which your boy brought me. We started a week later for Southampton, where we were detained nigh ten days for a ship."

"And who is the we, father?" Harry asked anxiously.

"Ah," the old man said, "now you are in a hurry to know. Who should it be but Master Rippinghall and a certain young lady?"

"Oh, father, has Lucy really come?"

"Assuredly she has," Colonel Furness said, "and is now waiting in a private room below with her brother, for Sir Harry. I have not congratulated you yet, my boy, on your new dignity."

"And you really consent to my marriage, sir?"

"I don't see that I could help it," the colonel said, "since you had set your mind on it, especially as when I came to inquire I found the young lady was willing to go to Virginia. But we must talk of that anon. Yes, Harry, you have my full consent. The young lady is not quite of the rank of life I should have chosen for you; but ranks and classes are all topsy-turvy in England at present, and when we are ruled over by a brewer, it would be nice indeed to refuse to take a wool-stapler's sister for wife. But seriously, Harry, I am well contented. I knew little of the young lady except by common report, which spoke of her as the sweetest and kindest damsel in Abingdon. But now I have seen her, I wonder not at your choice. During the fortnight we have been together I have watched her closely, and I find in her a rare combination of gentleness and firmness. You have won her heart, Harry, though how she can have kept thee in mind all this time is more than I can tell. Her brother tells me that he placed no pressure upon her either for or against, though he desired much for your sake, and from the love he bore you, that she should accept of your suit. Now you had better go down, and learn from her own lips how it stands with her."

It need not to describe the meeting between Harry and his old friends. Herbert was warm and cordial as of old. Lucy was but little changed since Harry had seen her four years before, save that she was more fair and womanly.

"Your letter gave me," Herbert said, "a mixed feeling of pleasure and pain. I knew that my little sister has always looked upon you as a hero of romance, and though I knew not that as a woman her heart still turned to you, yet she refused so sharply and shrewishly all the suitors who came to her, that I suspected that her thoughts of you were more than a mere child's fancy. When your letter came I laid no pressure upon her, just as in other cases I have held aloof, and indeed have gained some ill-will at the hands of old friends because I would not, as her brother, and the head of the family, lay stress upon her. I read your letter to her, and she at first said she was ready to obey my wishes in the matter, and to go with you to Virginia if I bade her. I said that in such a matter it was her will and not mine which I wished to consult, and thus pressed into a corner, she owned that she would gladly go with you."

"Harry," the girl said, "for my tongue is not as yet used to your new title, under other circumstances I should have needed to be wooed and won like other girls. But seeing how strangely you are placed, and that you were about to start across the sea, to be absent perhaps for many years, I felt that it would not be worthy either of me or you were I to affect a maiden coyness and so to throw difficulties in your way. I feel the honor of the offer you have made me. That you should for so many years have been absent and seen the grand ladies of the court, and have yet thought of your little playfellow, shows that your heart is as true and good as I of old thought it to be, and I need feel no shame in acknowledging that I have ever thought of you with affection."

For the next few days there was much argument over the project of going to Virginia. Herbert, when he heard what had happened in London, joined his entreaties to those of Sir Henry, asserting that he had only consented to Lucy's going to so outlandish a place in the belief that there was no help for it, and that he did not think it fair for Harry to take her to such a life when he could stay comfortably at home. Sir Henry did not say much, but Harry could see how ardently he longed for him to remain. As for Lucy, she stood neutral, saying that assuredly she did not wish to go to Virginia, but that, upon the other hand, she should feel that her consent had been obtained under false pretenses, and that she had been defrauded of the enjoyment of a proper and regular courtship, did it prove that Harry might have come home and sought her hand in regular form. Harry's reluctance to remain arose principally from the fact that he had gained permission to do so by an act of personal service which he had done the king's great enemy. Had he been included in a general amnesty he would gladly have accepted it. However, his resolution gave way under the arguments of Herbert, who urged upon him that he had no right, on a mere point of punctilio, to leave his father in his old age, and to take Lucy from her country and friends to a life of hardship in the plantations of Virginia. At last he yielded. Then a difficulty arose with Lucy, who would fain have returned to Abingdon with her brother, and urged she should there have time given her to be married in regular fashion. This Harry would by no means consent to, and as both Sir Henry and Herbert saw no occasion for the delay, they were married a fortnight later at the Protestant church at Hamburg, Jacob, who was by this time perfectly restored to health, acting as his best man.

One of the first steps which Harry took after his return to Hamburg was to inquire about the gypsy maid who had done him such service. She was still singing at the drinking-house. Harry went down there in the daytime and gave one of the drawers a crown to tell her quietly that the Englishman she knew would fain see her, and would wait for her at a spot he named on the walk by the river bank, between ten and twelve the next day. Here, accompanied by Lucy, who, having heard of the service which the girl had rendered him, fully entered into his anxiety to befriend her, he awaited her the next day. She came punctual to the appointment, but in great fear that the old gypsy would discover her absence. Upon Harry telling her that Lucy, who was about to become his wife, would willingly take her to England and receive her as a companion until such time as some opportunity for furthering her way in life might appear, Zita accepted the proposal with tears of joy. She abhorred the life she was forced to lead, and it was only after many beatings and much ill-usage from the gypsies that she consented to it, and it made her life the harder, inasmuch as she knew that she had not been born to such a fate, but had been stolen as a child.

"What could have been their motive in carrying you away?" Lucy asked.

"I believe," the girl said, "from what they have told me, that I was taken in revenge. My father had charged one of the gypsies with theft, and the man having been hung, the others, to avenge themselves, carried me off."

"But why did you not, when you grew old enough, tell your story to the magistrates, and appeal to them for assistance?"

"Alas!" the girl said, "what proofs have I for my tale?

Moreover, even were I believed, and taken from the gypsies, what was there for me to do, save to beg in the streets for charity?"

They now arranged with her the manner of her flight. She was afraid to meet them again lest her footsteps should be traced, for she was sure that the gypsies would carry her away to some other town if they had the least suspicion that she had made friends with any capable of taking her part, as the whole party lived in idleness upon the money she gained by singing. It was arranged, therefore, that the night before they were to depart Harry should appear in the singing hall, and should take his place near the door. She should let him know that she perceived him by passing her hand twice across her forehead. When the performance was over she should, instead of leaving as usual by the back way, slip down the steps, and mingle with those leaving the hall. Outside the door she would find Harry, who would take her to the hotel, where dresses would be provided for her. There she should stop the night, and go on board ship with them in the morning.

These arrangements were all carried out, and four days after the wedding of Harry and Lucy the party, with Zita, sailed for England. Had the tenantry on the Furness estate known of the home-coming of their young master and his bride, they would have given him a grand reception; but Harry and his father both agreed that this had better not be, for that it was as well to call no public attention to his return, even though he had received Cromwell's permission.

After all his adventures, Sir Harry Furness dwelt quietly and happily with his father. In the following years the English fleet fought many hard battles with the Dutch, and the Parliament, in order to obtain money, confiscated the property of most of those Cavaliers who had now returned under the Act of Amnesty. Steps were taken against Sir Henry Furness, but as he had taken no part in the troubles after the close of the first civil war, Cromwell, on receiving an application from him, peremptorily quashed the proceedings.

On April 20, 1653, Cromwell went down to the House with a body of troops, and expelled the Parliament, who were in the act of passing a bill for their own dissolution, and a new representation. He thus proved himself as tyrannous and despotic as any sovereign could have been. A new Parliament was summoned, but instead of its members being elected in accordance with the customs of England, they were selected and nominated by Cromwell himself. The history of England contains no instance of such a defiance of the constitutional rights of the people. But although he had grasped power arbitrarily and by force, Cromwell used it well and wisely, and many wise laws and great social reforms were passed by the Parliament under his orders. Still the fanatical party were in the majority in this body, and as Cromwell saw that these persons would push matters further than he wished, he made an arrangement with the minority, who resigned their seats, thereby leaving an insufficient number in the House to transact business. Cromwell accepted their resignation, and the Parliament then ceased to exist.

Four days later, on the 16th of December, Cromwell assumed the state and title of Lord Protector of the Commonwealth. For the next five years he governed England wisely and well. The Parliament was assembled, but as its proceedings were not in accordance with his wishes, he dissolved it, and for the most part governed England by his own absolute will. That it was a strong will and a wise cannot be questioned, but that a rising, which originally began because the king would not yield to the absolute will of Parliament, should have ended in a despotism, in which the chief of the king's opponents should have ruled altogether without Parliaments, is strange indeed. It is singular to find that those who make most talk about the liberties of Englishmen should regard as their hero and champion the man who trod all the constitutional rights of Englishmen under foot. But if a despot, Cromwell was a wise and firm one, and his rule was greatly for the good of the country. Above all, he brought the name of England into the highest honor abroad, and made it respected throughout Europe. Would that among all Englishmen of the present day there existed the same feeling of patriotism, the same desire for the honor and credit of their country, as dwelt in the breast of Oliver Cromwell.

On August 30, 1658, Cromwell died, and his son Richard succeeded him. The Parliament and the army soon fell out, and the army, coming down in force, dissolved Parliament, and Richard Cromwell ceased at once to have any power. The army called together forty-two of the old members of the Long Parliament, of extreme republican views, but these had no sooner met than they broke into divisions, and England was wholly without a government. So matters went on for some time, until General Monk, with the army of the north, came up to London. He had for weeks been in communication with the king. For a time he was uncertain of the course he should take, but after awhile he found that the feeling of London was wholly averse to the Parliament, and so resolved to take the lead in a restoration. A Parliament was summoned, and upon the day after its assembling Monk presented to them a document from King Charles, promising to observe the constitution, granting full liberty of conscience, and an amnesty for past offenses. Parliament at once declared in favor of the ancient laws of the kingdom, the government to be by King, Lords and Commons; and on May 8, 1660, Charles II. was proclaimed king, and on the 30th entered London in triumph.

Sir Harry Furness sat in the Parliament which recalled the king, and in many subsequent ones. His father came to London to see the royal entry, and both were most kindly received by the king, who expressed a warm hope that he should often see them at court. This, however, was not to be. The court of King Charles offered no attractions to pure-minded and honorable men. Sir Henry came no more to London, but lived quietly and happily to the end of a long life at Furness Hall, rejoicing much over the happiness of his son, and in the society of his daughter-in-law and her children. Herbert Rippinghall sat in Parliament for Abingdon. Except when obliged by his duties as a member to be in London, Sir Harry Furness lived quietly at Furness Hall, taking much interest in country matters. Twenty-eight years later James II fled from England, and William of Orange mounted the throne. At this time Sir Harry Furness was sixty-one, and he lived many years to see the freedom and rights for which Englishmen had so hotly struggled and fought now enjoyed by them in all their fullness.

A few words as to the other personages of this story. Jacob, three years after Harry's return to England, married the Spanish girl Zita, and settled down in a pretty house called the Dower House, on the Furness property, which, together with a large farm attached to it, Sir Henry Furness settled upon him, as a token of his affection and gratitude to him for the faithful services he had rendered to his son.

William Long was made bailiff of the estate, and Mike remained the attached and faithful body-servant of Sir Harry, until he, ten years later, married the daughter and heiress of a tradesman in Abingdon, and became a leading citizen of that town.

Although Harry was not of a revengeful disposition, he rejoiced exceedingly when he heard, two or three months after the king's restoration, of the execution of that doubly-dyed traitor, the Earl of Argyll.

THE END

www.ingramcontent.com/pod-product-compliance
Lightning Source LLC
Chambersburg PA
CBHW022045240626
47154CB00007B/2565